A Song of Silence

Inspired by a Heartbreaking True Story

Steve N Lee

Blue Zoo
England

Copyright © Steve N. Lee 2024

While inspired by real events and real historical characters, this is a work of fiction and of the author's imagination. Other than those in the public domain, names, characters, places, incidents, businesses, and organizations are used fictitiously. Any resemblance to real persons, living or dead, business establishments, events, or locales is entirely coincidental.

All rights reserved. No part of this work may be reproduced, stored in a retrieval system, or transmitted in any form or by any means – electronic, mechanical, photocopying, recording or otherwise – without the prior permission of the publishers.

Published by Blue Zoo, Yorkshire, England.

For those they took
whose names we'll never know
because no one was left to remember them.

1

Poland, Fall 1939.

The red-haired boy's bottom lip quivered and tears welled in his big brown eyes. Gripping Borys's arm with both hands as they stood at the front of the classroom, the boy gazed up at Mirek like a puppy who'd been caught stealing food from the table and was expecting to be kicked.

Mirek softened his deep voice. "Hello, Jacek. I'm Mirek Kozlowski, the director of this orphanage. You can call me 'Mr. Kozlowski,' 'Mr. Director,' 'sir,' or..." He gestured behind him to the rows of school desks squashed together so that thirty-one children could fit into a room meant for twenty.

In unison, the children said, "Papa Mirek."

He wrote *Papa Mirek* on the blackboard in white chalk — new arrivals had become such a regular occurrence, he and his children had established quite the welcome routine. He smiled at Jacek.

Sunlight streamed through the windows, particles of dust dancing in its embrace to the song of a blackbird drifting in from the courtyard's apple tree.

The boy pulled partway behind Borys, his fingers clawing into the stocky man's black overcoat. He peeked out, chin trembling.

"Don't be afraid, you're safe here. And as you can see"— Mirek swept a hand toward the children —"there are lots of new friends waiting to meet you."

Faces smiled from behind the cramped desks, and eyes sparkled with life.

Jacek pressed tighter against Borys.

Borys planted his palm in the boy's back and shoved, but Mirek held up his hand. "Give him a second."

The boy's knuckles whitened on Borys's coat.

Mirek wasn't surprised, considering what the child had suffered. He crouched so he wasn't a big thirty-seven-year-old man towering over a tiny six-year-old boy but a person on the same eye level.

Jacek released the coat, but instead of shuffling forward, he shot under the table with the globe sitting on it next to the wall. Curling into a ball, he pulled as far as he could into the corner formed with a bookcase.

Borys shrugged, stroking his bushy brown beard.

"I'll give him some time," said Mirek. "Let him see for himself it's safe here." He pointed at a boy in a blue sweater sitting in the front row. "Piotr, fetch the treat Baba Hanka has prepared, please."

"Yes, Papa Mirek." The boy darted for the door.

"And, Piotr?"

He turned.

"No licking it, please."

The boy's shoulders slumped. "Yes, Papa Mirek." He left.

Mirek slung his arm around Borys's broad shoulders. "A word."

They ambled out and Mirek closed the door. Children's paintings plastered the corridor. Joyous. Vibrant. Flamboyant. Everything the world used to be until the Nazis had done the unthinkable only weeks earlier.

Fortunately, his sleepy little backwater had thus far escaped occupation, and with Britain and France having already declared war on Germany, maybe the conflict would be over before he and his children were dragged into the nightmare.

Borys clicked his tongue. "The kid's been skittish all the time we've had him, but I never thought he'd react so badly."

"It's not surprising." Mirek gestured to himself. "Blond hair, blue eyes, square jaw… I probably look just like the Nazi who shot his mother in front of him."

Borys pursed his lips. "Makes sense."

"You're sure he's not Jewish? Maybe he speaks Yiddish, not Polish."

"Believe me, he understands when he wants to."

"Okay." Mirek nodded. "Now listen, you can bring me all the children you like, but you have to bring me food as well. I can't help them if I can't feed them."

"We're supplying what we can, but you know what it's like. And things are only getting worse."

"Eighty-eight children, Borys. Sorry, eighty-nine now. What am I supposed to give them? Grass and a smile?"

Borys blew out his cheeks. "Look, no promises, because we're getting pulled every which way, but if I can find something, it's yours."

"Well, it better be something big, and it better be something regular."

"The kid's new papers should arrive tomorrow. Maybe I'll have something then."

"See that you do." Mirek held out his hand. They shook, then Borys strolled away as Piotr dashed back with a hunk of cake on a white plate.

"Thank you." Mirek took the cake as he opened the classroom door.

While Piotr retook his seat, Mirek crouched beside the table with the globe.

Jacek crunched into a tighter ball.

Mirek slid the plate over the wooden floor toward the boy. He smiled, then stood and addressed the class. "Okay, where were we? Agata, was it your turn to read?"

With an expression of angelic innocence, a seven-year-old girl with curly brown hair shook her head. She shoved a book from in front of her onto the desk of the big-nosed boy beside her.

"Agata? Are you sure?" asked Mirek.

"But I read something yesterday."

"And you'll be reading something every day for the next seventy years or more, but only if you practice now."

"I won't need to read *every* day."

"No? So how will you choose something on a restaurant menu, or understand letters from friends, or learn of a sale at a clothing store?"

Agata gazed into space, twiddling her hair. Finally, she said, "How often are these clothing sales?"

7

"Every few months. But if you don't practice your reading, you'll never know when they are."

She shrugged. "I don't have any money anyway."

"Do you think you'll have money if you get a great job because you've read every book in my library to know everything about everything?"

Her eyes widening at the prospect, she snatched the book, cleared her throat, and—

The classroom door burst open. A boy in his early teens rushed in, sweat beading on his brow beneath a floppy brown cap.

"Papa Mirek, Papa Mirek."

"Now, what have we agreed about entering a room, Pawel? Especially when I'm teaching?"

"But—"

"No buts. What's the rule?"

Panting, Pawel exited and shut the door. He knocked.

Mirek purposefully waited a moment. "Remember, children, manners cost nothing, but sometimes, they can get you more than money ever could." Finally, he said, "Come."

Pawel flung the door open and scurried in. "Sorry to disturb you, Papa Mirek, but—"

Mirek held up his hand to stop the boy, then tapped his head.

"Huh?" Pawel looked up. "Oh... sorry." He whipped off his cap. "Sorry to disturb you, Papa Mirek, but..." He glanced at the class, all eyes anxiously drilling into him, then looked back at Mirek. "They're here."

2

Mirek burst out of the orphanage's black front door and across the courtyard, feet pounding into the cobbles. The apple tree rustled in the breeze, swathed in greens, reds, and golds, the odd late-ripening fruit clinging to its branches. With food prices soaring since the invasion, Mirek had mandated that only Hanka could pick this precious treasure, she being best able to judge its ripeness. He darted to the wooden gate in the courtyard wall.

Pawel had to be wrong. Surely Borys would have known if *they* were so close. There had been false alarms before. This had to be another. Had to be.

His heart hammering, he ripped open the gate and dashed onto the sidewalk just as chubby Filip Goldblatt stepped out of his tailor's store in the row of gray stucco buildings opposite.

The roar of engines yanked Mirek's gaze to the town square at the end of the street on his right. A street down which friends and neighbors raced as if the world was aflame.

German soldiers on motorcycles growled into the square, followed by officers lounging in the back of a gray open-topped car. The squat vehicle pulled out of sight, and a truck rumbled past with rows of troops sitting in the back. Then another. And another.

"Oh Lord, help us," said Mirek.

They really were here.

Across the street, Filip clasped his face, the flap of hair combed over his bald spot flailing in the wind.

Their eyes met. For an instant, time froze, heavy with possibility. In the moment a tossed coin was spinning, the outcome was both heads and tails, both good and bad. But that moment was only fleeting. Inescapably, the coin would land and the outcome would be sealed.

Mirek dragged his hands through his hair. Had their fate just been set? Or was the coin still spinning so that they had time, had choices, had a future as yet unwritten?

A brown horse whinnied, shattering the moment, as it heaved a hay cart along the cobbled street so hard that the driver jolted up and down.

Mirek hurtled back into his courtyard.

Children were already streaming out of the building, wide-eyed with a mixture of fear and curiosity.

"Inside, please. Everyone inside." Holding his arms wide, he shooed them back. But those still pushing to get out blocked the entrance.

Mirek stabbed at the doorway. "Inside. Now!"

Everyone retreated inside, and Mirek locked the door.

Pawel gulped. "What are we going to do, Papa Mirek?"

"We follow the plan, Pawel. Find Baba Hanka and ask her to do a head count, please? And tell her no one leaves the house without my permission."

"Yes, Papa Mirek." He scooted away.

Children milled about, desperate for answers.

"Back to the classroom, please." Mirek guided them down the corridor. He'd planned for this. Planned in meticulous detail. While he'd prayed the day he'd have to execute that plan would never come, deep down, he'd always known it would.

A bald man with glasses opened the door to the second classroom. "Please tell me it's not true."

"Sorry, Henryk, but they're here."

The blood drained from the man's face.

"You know what needs doing," said Mirek. "Go through the list with your students, then get off home to your family."

He nodded and ducked back inside.

Mirek returned to his classroom.

"Take—" His voice broke, so he cleared his throat. "Take your seats, please. Quickly as you can."

The pupils shuffled to their chairs.

Muttering and anxious glances flew around. Two girls were already in tears, but comforting them would have to wait.

At the front of the class, Mirek forced the best smile he could. "We've talked about this every day so we'd be ready, haven't we? That means there's no need to worry, no need to rush, and no need to be frightened."

No need to be frightened? No, they shouldn't be frightened; they should be absolutely terrified.

"Everyone knows what to do because we've practiced, so let's get to it. If we do that, everything is going to be just fine."

He didn't like lying to his children, but the truth would only make things worse. Especially since everyone knew Warsaw had been under siege for weeks. Not to mention the wild rumors circulating about the horrors perpetrated elsewhere.

Mirek scanned the faces looking to him for reassurance. Like some of the others, Agata stared, her face scrunched up as if she could burst into tears with only the gentlest of nudges. Yet despite her young age, she clenched her jaw, battling to hold it all in.

Mirek beckoned. "Agata, Kuba."

She and a skinny boy with a hooked nose scuttled over. Mirek pointed at a wooden chest in the corner. He didn't so much need help, but giving the pupils tasks would distract them from the implications of the Nazis' arrival.

"You know what goes in there. Try not to miss anything." To be safe, he'd double-check everything later.

"Beata, Ola. Can you help them, please?"

The four children packed the chest with books from a small bookshelf and resources from a table.

"You three." Mirek pointed to particular children, then at the wall nearest them. "Wall hangings, please."

The children climbed onto their desks, first removing a map of Poland, then a Polish flag.

Mirek assigned everyone a job. Working together, they packed away everything the Nazis could deem prejudicial to their great plan for a thousand-year Reich.

Once it was all clear, they Germanized the room, Mirek taking care of the two most important elements himself. He hung a Nazi flag along the wall where the Polish one had been, ensuring it was level, unwrinkled, and spotless. Finally, he placed a photograph in a polished wood frame on his desk, turning it to face his children. With his usual sour-faced grimace, Adolf Hitler glared at the class.

Mirek swallowed hard, fighting the urge to vomit at the transformation he'd instigated. But he had to protect his children at any cost. Had to.

He clapped three times. "Good job, everyone. Now, all of you away to your rooms, and make sure they're just as we've practiced. I'll be inspecting them later, so no cutting corners, please."

The children scurried out, chattered along the hallway, then pounded their way up the staircase.

The rest of the house had to be similarly cleared, not least his study and bedroom. If only he knew how much time they had. Mirek held his head. Maybe he was panicking over nothing. Maybe the Germans were merely passing through and wouldn't stay. Was there any chance he'd be so lucky? There was only one way to find out.

Heart hammering, Mirek strode toward the front door. His hand trembled as he reached for the handle, so he clutched it to his chest and glanced around. He had to be strong in front of the children, so they couldn't see even the tiniest of weaknesses or doubt. It was the only way they'd get through this.

With no one around, he yanked open the door. The worst sound imaginable greeted him.

3

Gunshots.

And screaming.

So much screaming.

All from the direction of the town square.

Who was shooting? Why? The Resistance was active here, as it was in every Polish village, town, and city, but surely the few local members weren't crazy enough to fight such a large German contingent.

Mirek's breath coming in pants, he cracked open the courtyard gate and peeked out.

Private cars and vehicles tore away from the square. A fat woman with a brown shawl scrambled toward him, dragging two small boys wearing shorts. Wanda Pazdan was the local busybody, so it wasn't good if she was running instead of rubbernecking.

"Hide, Mirek!" She scurried by. "They're shooting everyone."

Everyone? What did she mean, *everyone*? This was a quiet backwater town. Why would the Germans shoot *anyone*, let alone everyone? Wanda had to be spicing things up in her own inimitable way. Like an occupying force would indiscriminately blast the residents. That was how the outrageous rumors had started about the atrocities the Germans were committing elsewhere. So irresponsible.

Mirek had no choice — he had to witness this for himself.

Having locked the house door so no one could follow him, he crept onto the sidewalk.

Townsfolk poured down both sides of the road, so Mirek hugged the wall of stucco buildings and shuffled toward the square, passing the blue apartment building, the apothecary, more apartments, the hardware store...

He clutched his mouth. Down the opposite sidewalk, a hunched older man in a black overcoat supported a younger man whose left arm dangled lifelessly at his side, blood dripping from it. Ludomir and Patryk Sajdak – father and son. Mirek and Ludomir had tried to teach Patryk how to hunt when he was a teenager and it had been a disaster. The boy had shot a rabbit, then thrown up without even seeing the body. Patryk had refused ever to go again. No way was he a Resistance fighter.

Oh...

But he was a Jew.

And the synagogue was in the square.

Still, the rumors couldn't be true. That was the great thing about rumors – an educated person knew to take whatever they heard and reduce it by half or on occasion, even ignore it completely. In life, a person could only be certain of three things: taxes, death, and rumors being mere flights of fantasy.

More rifles blasted in the square.

What the devil was happening?

Mirek peered ahead. His orphanage's road opened onto the north west corner of the square, so no matter how close he crept, the last building obscured his view.

A cloud of brown smoke billowed across the end of the road.

Mirek gulped. He looked back to his property, to safety. He longed to run to it, bolt his gate, and never open it again until news came that the war had ended. But he had to protect his children, and to do that, he needed the one thing he didn't have: information.

He trudged on, each step feeling like he was dragging a great chain.

Shouting, gunfire, vehicle engines... engulfed by a chaotic cacophony, Mirek struggled to make sense of the unfolding events.

Finally reaching the last building, the Flower of Poland guesthouse and restaurant, Mirek plastered himself to the wall. His breaths came hard and labored, as if he'd been sprinting. From inside, a crouched woman stared over the windowsill, eyes wide, terror carving lines into her face. A tear-streaked girl cowered next to her.

What had they seen that they were frozen in such fear?

No, he definitely couldn't run. He needed to judge for himself exactly how bad things were. No choice.

Pressing his back against the wall so hard it would scrape threads from his jacket, he shuffled to the corner that met the square.

This was it. Just one quick glimpse and then run home. Easy.

He screwed his eyes shut. He'd parted ways with God during the Great War after witnessing the horrors He allowed to exist, but in that moment, how Mirek ached to say a prayer, even if it went unheard.

Panting, he clutched his chest.

Just a glimpse. Then run.

Okay, on three.

One. He braced to lunge around the corner.

Two. He heaved a massive breath to give him strength.

Three. He tensed to move but froze like a stone gargoyle.

He shook his head. No, he couldn't do this. Who would look after his children if something happened to him?

He beat his elbow into the wall. But how could he protect them if he didn't know what he was protecting them from?

Mirek lurched around the corner onto the edge of the square.

His jaw dropped.

Eyes widened.

And an icy fist crushed his heart.

Bodies littered the square, twisted, broken, bloody. In the center, the bronze statue of Nicolaus Copernicus, Poland's most celebrated astronomer, lay on its side on the ground. Beside it, a bonfire of ancient books and religious icons from the nearby synagogue blazed.

German soldiers prowled everywhere, guns threatening.

A woman in a blue dress ran to the burning pile and snatched a menorah. Clutching the gold seven-branched candelabrum with one hand, she reached for a leather-bound book, but flames licked at her fingers, so she whipped her hand away.

A soldier kicked her in the side. She smashed into the cobbles, the menorah skidding across the stone. He raised his rifle butt to cave in her skull, so she flung her arms up to protect herself.

Mirek ached to run and help but... he didn't move. Just stared. Eyes like saucers. Trembling hand clutching his gaping mouth.

Two young Polish men raced over. One flung himself at the soldier, and they both crashed to the ground. The other grabbed the woman and heaved her up. The three townsfolk ran for their lives.

A hail of bullets sliced through them. They crumpled like rag dolls discarded by a bored child.

Mirek's gaze followed a trail of candies strewn across the ground near the bodies. They led to a bench, behind which Ula Stern cowered. The young woman usually sat on the curb selling single candies from a tray in her lap to people who couldn't afford a full packet but wanted a treat. Trembling, eyes closed, palms together, Ula appeared to be praying.

Gunfire erupted from the Great Synagogue, and four soldiers ran out. Turning back for an instant, one trained his rifle on the entrance while the other three hurled in grenades. The four of them then darted away.

Thunder exploded inside the synagogue. The building's six arched windows and the magnificent rose window blew out, glass shards stabbing the air. An enormous fireball burst through the roof, and tiles and wooden beams hurtled skyward only to crash down a moment later, crunching into the building, the sidewalk, the road... the stench of burning gasoline hung thick.

Wrapped in flames, a figure staggered out of the building's burning debris.

Frozen, Mirek gave the barest shake of his head. Eyes teary, he mouthed, "No."

A soldier raised his rifle to shoot, but his comrade pushed the barrel down. They walked away, smiling. Behind them, the figure flailed its arms in some macabre dance with death, then crunched face-first into the ground.

Mirek gazed on, his throat burning with rising bile. He ached not to watch anymore, but he couldn't look away. He would never have believed such atrocities could happen — anywhere — let alone in his quiet little town. Each horror was worse than the last. And each utterly mesmerizing because, despite how unbelievable, it was happening before his eyes.

Rounds blasted the wall behind him, shocking him from his stupor. He ducked, shielding his head, and ran around the corner onto his road. He bolted, mind reeling. Before he knew it, he'd reached his gate. He dove through and slammed it shut.

Slumping against the wood, he slid the top and bottom bolts over, then fell onto all fours and vomited.

Protect his children? How could he protect his children from *that?*

4

Back inside the building, Mirek dashed toward his classroom, pocketing the key to the locked front door. Not to keep the Germans out — like an old oak door could do that — but to keep the children in.

Tomorrow, if things had calmed outside, he'd find Borys. If the Resistance could bring him children, they had to be able to move them to other places too. Safer places. But how many could they move at once?

Pulling up, he shook his head. Why torture himself with unanswerable questions? The best plan to protect them — right now — was to give the Germans no possible excuse for punishing anyone under his roof.

Mirek rubbed his brow. It didn't seem like the Nazis needed much of an excuse to hurt anyone, so he had to check and double-check everything. Reaching the classroom, he froze, staring through the small window in the door.

Inside, a strange thirtyish woman browsed one of the few remaining books — a picture book that taught the basics of reading. Her long reddish-brown hair hung over the left side of her face while a flowing blue dress, gathered at the waist, highlighted a slender figure. Who the devil was she? And more to the point, what was she doing in *his* house?

He set his jaw. He couldn't do anything about invaders of his town, but he sure could about invaders of his home.

However, reaching for the doorknob, he stopped. Frowned.

Standing sideways to him, the woman moved her lips as if she were silently reading. But her lips moved slowly, so incredibly slowly, like she was stumbling over the words. He drew a breath to calm his misplaced anger. The threat was outside. Not inside. He opened the door.

The woman jumped. Half turning, she hid the book behind her back. And instead of pushing the hair away from her face, she brushed it forward to hide her even more.

"May I help you?" asked Mirek.

"Sorry." She revealed the book. "I just liked the picture on the front."

"I know the author. I could get you a signed copy, if you like."

"Thank you, but I don't have children." She placed the book on the table. "Hanka sent me with a message for Mr. Kozlowski."

"Hanka did?"

"I'm her new housekeeping assistant. She said Mr. Kozlowski had gone out. Do you know if he's back yet?"

"He is." Mirek opened his arms and arched his eyebrows.

"You? Oh, I'm so sorry. For some reason, I thought Mirek Kozlowski was an old bald man."

He snorted. "I've been called many things, but never old and bald."

"I'm not making a very good first impression, am I? I'll get out of your way and leave you to your work." Her hair still obscuring her face, she strode for the door, dragging her left leg as if she'd hurt her knee.

Mirek said, "Hanka won't be impressed if you go back without delivering your message."

"Oh my stars." She slapped her forehead. "I'm sorry. The Germans arriving has completely thrown me."

"That's understandable."

"Hanka says she believes everyone is accounted for, but she's going to recount to double-check."

"Thank goodness for that."

Barely glancing in his direction, the woman shot him the briefest of smiles. "Yes."

"And you are?"

"Sorry." She snickered. "I seem to be saying 'sorry' every other word, don't I?" She held out her right hand. "Anna-Maria Kisiell. Call me Ania."

He grasped her hand. "Kisiel? Like the pudding?"

"Uh-huh, but with two *L*'s." They shook hands.

"Pleased to meet you, Ania." Mirek dipped his head slightly, curious to see around her drooping hair, but she brushed the strands farther across her face. She was obviously conscious about her looks, so he wouldn't push it. "If Hanka doesn't need you right now, I could use a hand here."

"You're the boss."

"Don't let Hanka hear you say that or you'll be sacked on the spot."

She laughed. "What do you need help with?"

"Finding anything to which the Germans might object."

"Such as?" She scanned the room.

"Anything that celebrates Poland. Anything that criticizes Germany. Anything that could teach children about Polish history or geography. Books by Polish authors..." He threw his hands up. "Just grab anything that's even remotely suspect."

Limping to the table, she picked up the picture book again. "Are things like this okay?"

He sighed. "An hour ago, I'd have said yes, but now..." He shrugged.

"So how do you get signed copies?"

He pointed to his name printed on the cover in large red letters. She said, "You know him?"

"I *am* him."

"Ohhh." She almost looked him in the face, then turned away and flicked through the book. Each page featured a bright watercolor painting of a rabbit accompanied by a few words. "I thought Mirek Kozlowski wrote long, serious books about the struggles of life."

He tapped the book. "If you were a rabbit and you lost your tail, you'd think life was a serious struggle, wouldn't you?"

She chuckled. "I guess so."

"*The Rabbit Who Lost His Tail* was my first success. If it hadn't been for that, I wouldn't have written anything else, so I could never have funded any of this." He gestured to the building.

"Wow." She caressed the book's cover, then squinted at him. "But I heard bookstores were being closed."

"Uh-huh. Libraries too."

"So how are you going to continue paying for everything?"

"Why do you think the only staff here are me, Hanka, and now you?"

She gestured to the hallway. "Wasn't there a man in the other classroom earlier?"

"Henryk. He's only volunteering until they rebuild his school."

"Why, what happened?"

"An air raid targeted the ball bearing factory, but a few stray bombs hit the schools next door and fire ripped through them. Luckily, it was a Sunday, so no children were injured. Until that raid, the teaching here was solely to help those struggling academically, but now, it's all the children have."

She patted the book on the table. "The 'maybe' pile."

He wasn't sure yet, but he suspected Ania had a reading problem. And the last thing he wanted was to embarrass her. "If I check the books, can you wander around the room and see if anything hits you as being somehow objectionable?"

"But I don't know what to look for."

"That might actually be an advantage, because heaven knows the criteria are so broad, anything could be a problem."

"Okay." She wandered away, gazing about the room, then rooted through a wooden box. She held up a soccer ball. "Things like this?"

Someone had painted a white and a red band on the ball, which looked innocent enough but actually represented the Polish flag.

"Exactly like that. Good find." He returned to perusing the bookcase.

She peered into the box again. "Was that shooting I heard earlier?"

"Unfortunately, yes." He didn't want to describe what he'd seen. Especially to someone he'd only just met. For all he knew, she could be the world's worst gossip so an exaggerated version of what he described would be flying around the house within minutes. A house filled with terrified children.

She said, "And was that thunder or an explosion?"

"An explosion."

"Oh my. I hope no one was hurt."

The image of the flailing person ablaze seared his thoughts. He cringed. "If you don't mind, can we focus on the job? I don't want problems later because we were distracted."

"Of course. Sorry, Mr. Kozlowski."

"Mirek."

She nodded.

They continued in silence.

Twenty minutes later, a small chubby woman with graying hair tied in a bun stood in the doorway, her hands on her hips. "If I'd known it was going to be such a big job, I'd have sent some of the older boys to help you."

Ania clutched her mouth. "Sorry, I was—"

"It was my fault, Hanka." Mirek stood from bending to a low cupboard at the back of the classroom. "My apologies, I should've sent word I'd conscripted your staff."

"You do know it's dinnertime and our eighty-nine hungry mouths aren't going to feed themselves?"

Mirek looked at Ania and gestured to the door. "Thanks for your help, Ania, but Hanka needs you more than I do."

"I could come back afterward," said Ania.

"No one's expecting you at home?"

She shook her head. "I only moved here a couple of months ago."

"Well, if your idea of a fun evening is hiding children's books so they don't offend Hitler, you're very welcome."

She chuckled. "Okay." She wandered over to Hanka.

Hanka squinted at Mirek. "You aren't eating with everyone tonight?"

"I was going to eat later after making sure at least this floor will pass a Nazi inspection."

"With the noises coming from the square, don't you think it will be reassuring for the children if you're with them as usual?"

Hanka was right. As she was with infuriating regularity.

He added a geography book to the pile of things to be removed as he ambled to the door. "So what culinary delights do we have in store tonight? A brace of pheasants? Or a rack of lamb perhaps?"

Hanka raised an eyebrow. "Beef goulash and a slice of bread."

"Goulash *and* a slice of bread?" Mirek patted his stomach. "Please, Hanka, I'm going to have to let these pants out again if you keep spoiling us like this."

She slapped his arm. "Watch this one, Ania. He's the biggest child here. And the naughtiest."

"Don't believe a word, Ania." He gestured to the door.

Hanka said, "Aren't you forgetting something?"

Mirek scanned the classroom, then questioned Hanka with a look.

"Oh, for heaven's sake." She bustled past. Groaning, she bent and peered under the table on which the globe had earlier sat before being added to the chest.

She smiled, her voice soothing. "Jacek, come on out, dear."

"He's still under there?" asked Mirek. There was nothing under the table that had needed checking, but how had they not noticed a boy huddled in the shadows?

"Come on, dear." Hanka offered her hand. "I've got some lovely warm goulash waiting for you."

Whether it was the promise of food or a soothing female voice, Jacek took her hand and shuffled out. Hanka led him toward the door.

"I don't know how you keep track of eighty-nine children when you can't keep track of one." She shook her head at Mirek. "Thank heaven Piotr told me where the poor kid was or he'd have been under there all night."

Outside the dining room, children of varying ages milled while others crammed the entrance and staircase. A group of girls sat at the foot of the stairs, each puffy-eyed. Everywhere, tiny faces lined with worry and hands fidgeted with anxiety.

Mirek had wanted to delay discussing the day's distressing events, hoping that while his household might suspect danger was looming, they wouldn't appreciate just how close it was. Unfortunately, from the snippets of conversation he caught, it seemed that while none of the children had been outside, enough of them had looked through the upstairs windows to witness the terror on the streets. That left him with little choice.

Hanka unlocked the dining room door, and the children filtered in. She passed Jacek's hand to a black-haired boy who'd only been with them two weeks since suffering a similar situation. "Tomek, this is Jacek. Let him eat with you, then take him up to your room. I've laid out carpet and blankets for him."

"Yes, Baba Hanka."

While Hanka and Ania walked through and into the kitchen, Mirek strolled to the six-foot-wide hatch in the dividing wall where two huge brass saucepans sat steaming. He took a plate from the pile of mismatched dishes and held it out. Hanka tipped a ladle of goulash onto it and handed him a piece of dry crusty bread while Ania served Agata from the second pan.

"Thank you." Mirek strolled past three rows of long wooden tables and took a seat halfway along the last row.

Agata sat beside him. "Bon appétit, Papa Mirek."

"Bon appétit, Agata." He winked. "Smells good, doesn't it? Baba Hanka has done us proud again, hasn't she?"

Agata agreed, dipping her bread into such insipid gravy it looked more like water with a few lumps of potato and a lonely morsel of meat.

Instead of tucking into his food while it was still hot, Mirek watched all the children find seats, giving a reassuring nod to anyone who caught his eye. His calmness, not to mention the warm meal, dissipated the tension that had existed earlier. Laughter and childhood banter once more returned.

Mirek swallowed hard. Maintaining a positive demeanor was torture when he was about to break so many little hearts with the news he had to impart. Especially when little eyes kept gazing his way as if expecting an imminent announcement.

He poured a glass of water from a jug and sipped.

Finally, two boys at the end of his table stood, holding empty plates to return to the hatch.

Mirek cleared his throat. "When you've finished eating, please stay in your seat because I have some important news."

The laughter and banter fizzled out, and the number of stares heading his way skyrocketed. They were only children, but they weren't stupid. Rumors spread like chickenpox in such a close-knit environment. They knew something was coming, something very bad, but had no idea exactly what.

If Mirek withheld too much information now, their imaginations would go into overdrive, so he'd cause more harm than good. His only option was to tell them the truth. Or at least some of it. He just had to ensure they grasped the severity of the situation without necessarily grasping the horrific danger that lay only a few hundred yards away. Danger that could kick down their door at any second.

Many of the highlights of his life had occurred in this room, not least in the news he shared with his children. Laughter and tears, hopes and dreams, successes and surprises... so many wonderful occasions. Who would ever have dreamed he'd have to stand here and say what he was about to say?

A hollow in the pit of his stomach that no amount of food could ever fill gnawed at him, but he stood. Everyone in the room drilled their gaze into him.

"I—" His voice croaked, so he cleared his throat. "I have a few announcements. Firstly, there's going to be a room inspection in the morning, so double-check that you've followed the checklist on the back of your bedroom door properly. No excuses, please." He ran a hand through his hair and rubbed the back of his neck. "Secondly, over the, uh, the next few days, some new rules will be coming that will help to keep you safe. I can't stress enough how important it is that you follow these." He blew out his cheeks. "Which, uh, brings me to my last point."

Everyone waited. Staring.

Mirek sipped his water.

And the stares drilled into him deeper and deeper.

He gulped. He couldn't delay this any longer. "I'm guessing you've all heard the rumor that the Germans have arrived. I'm afraid it's true. I've seen them myself. Right in the middle of our beloved town. I don't know what happened to explain why they did what they did, but there was some shooting, some people were, eh, injured, and at least one building caught fire — the synagogue."

Tens of children gasped in unison at that one word.

"It isn't all bad news, though. Yes, the Germans are here. But so are we." He gazed around the faces mesmerized by his every word. "We still have our home, we still have food, and more importantly"— he held his palms out toward them —"we still have each other. And look at how brave you're all being. Each and every one of you. I tell you, I'm so proud of you all right now."

He clapped, smiling at a selection of the gazes that caught his. From the kitchen, Baba Hanka clapped, and Ania joined in. Beside him, Agata clapped, then someone else, and someone else. Within seconds, the whole room was standing, clapping, and cheering.

Tears welled in Mirek's eyes, the warm glow of pride blossoming in his heart. So the Germans were here. So what? He and his children were going to get through this. Every single one of them. When his children could be so brave, what could the Germans ever do to them?

5

As the children filtered out of the dining room, Mirek finally picked up his spoon. Pools of congealed fat lay on the surface of his gravy. He scooped up a piece of potato and discovered a slight peppery edge and a fruity aftertaste; Hanka had worked her usual magic with herbs and spices to turn what could have been nothing but a watery soup into a dish that actually tasted like a meal. He was lucky to have her. Someone so resourceful and loyal. It was a pity his food was stone cold because he'd wanted to acknowledge everybody who glanced his way.

Beside him, Agata licked her plate until it looked as clean as if it had been washed.

Ania appeared. She placed a plate of steaming goulash before him. "I saw you weren't eating, so kept a little on a low light."

"That's very kind. Thank you."

She turned to leave.

"Won't you join me?"

"I was going to eat with Hanka."

"She won't be eating for a while. She likes to supervise the cleaning up."

Ania gazed through the hatch. Hanka was sitting on a stool, a cigarette dangling from her mouth. Out of sight, children talked and clattered dishes.

"Okay." Ania toddled away.

The smell wafting from the hot food made his mouth water, but he held off digging in to wait for his dinner guest.

Agata continued licking her plate. Had it always been plain white or had it once had a pattern on it?

Ania returned with her meal and sat across the table.

Picking up her spoon, she acknowledged his waiting with a nod.

"Bon appétit," said Agata as she left.

Ania frowned. "Huh?"

Mirek said, "It's French for 'enjoy your meal.'"

"Oh." She called after the girl, "Thank you." She wrinkled her nose to Mirek. "I don't speak French."

"I only know the odd phrase. It's the one place I'd love to visit, so I'm drawn to the language."

She gave a little nod as she ate.

He dipped his bread into the goulash and then chomped into it.

Flicking her gaze up, she said, "It was nice what you said to the children. Very reassuring."

He shrugged. "I try, but sometimes, finding the words is difficult."

"You found them tonight."

"I didn't say too much? Or too little? It's hard judging how much to share so they're aware of the danger but don't live in terror every waking moment."

"I think you got it just right."

He ate another spoonful.

She gestured to the building. "Would you mind if I asked why you do all this?"

"Run an orphanage?"

"Uh-huh. Shouldn't a successful author be living the high life in Switzerland or America? Anywhere but here, now, with everything that's going on."

He tilted his head. "My wife."

Ania's eyebrows rose. "I thought it was just you and Hanka. I didn't know you were married. When will I be meeting her?"

"She died."

"I'm sorry."

He waved his hand, though pain still twisted his heart. "It was a long, long time ago."

Ania ripped her bread in half. Burn scars smothered her left hand. Was that why she combed her hair to cover part of her face — she'd been in a fire?

If they were going to work together, and more importantly considering the day's events, trust each other, maybe sharing would be a wise move.

He pursed his lips. Did he really want to do this? "It was our wedding day."

"Hmmm?"

"The day she died. It was our wedding day."

Ania gasped.

"We'd been in love for... well, forever, but the month before our wedding, she developed a fever and a rash. It didn't seem like much to start with, but it was typhus. Right up to the last moment, I thought she was going to pull through." Gazing into space, he gritted his teeth. "Such a fighter." He looked back at Ania. "It was supposed to be our wedding day, so I had the priest come to the house and marry us, then I held her in my arms until she slipped away."

Ania clutched her mouth, tears in her eyes.

Mirek scooped up more goulash. "But like I said, it was a long, long time ago."

Ania reached across the table and cupped his free hand. He liked that she didn't feel she had to say anything, didn't try to make him feel better with some pathetic platitude.

He said, "The hardest part was having to scrub myself clean and burn all her clothes immediately afterward. Scrubbing every last bit of her from my life, as if she'd never existed, just so I wouldn't get infected."

Ania squeezed his hand. "When my father died, Mama said, 'It isn't only the love we've lost that makes it hurt so much, it's the love we'll never get to give.'"

Mirek swallowed hard. That was so right — it wasn't only that he'd lost his soulmate, it was that he had to suppress his love as if it had never existed, instead of being able to shower it upon her.

"Your, eh..." He rubbed his face, a pain in his heart like he'd been shot in the chest. "Your mother sounds very wise."

She squeezed his hand once more, then released it.

"Anyway, to answer your question, this"— he waved his spoon toward the walls —"is for her. She was an orphan, so she knew

29

what a hard life that was, and she'd always dreamed of doing something to help others in that situation. So, when I came into some money…" He opened his palms. "What else was I going to do with it?"

"She'd be very proud."

"I hope so. What about you?"

"Me? I've never—"

A little girl with blond ringlets shuffled into the dining room, hands rubbing her eyes as she bawled.

"Excuse me." Mirek dashed over and knelt before her. "What's wrong, princess?"

"Marius—" Sniffle. "M-Marius said"— snort —"the G-Germans will"— whimper —"will take me away, if i-if I don't"— her voice rose higher with every word —"give him my bedtime cookie."

"Awww, come here, princess."

She fell into his arms, and he hugged her. Because of food shortages, the cookies were little more than whole-wheat flour, salt, baking soda, and water with a spoonful of vinegar, but the children adored their bedtime treat.

Mirek said, "Marius is a mean stinker, isn't he?"

She nodded, blubbering against his shoulder.

"Don't you worry, princess, I'll never let the Germans take you away. If they come here, we'll frighten them off with Marius's stinky feet because everyone knows he has the stinkiest feet in Poland, don't they?"

She pinched her nose, a smile escaping. "They stink worse than boiled cabbage."

"So you go back upstairs and you tell Marius that Papa Mirek says, as a punishment, he has to share his bedtime cookie with you or he won't get another until next week. Okay?"

Beaming, she dashed out. "I'm getting the stinker's cookie!"

"Only half," called Mirek.

She ran down the hallway. "I'm getting half the stinker's cookie!"

Hanka smirked through the hatch, still sitting on her stool. "Someone's on a roll tonight."

Mirek squinted. "Huh?"

"With the ladies." Hanka raised an eyebrow and tipped her head toward Ania. "There's nothing a woman finds more attractive than a man who's good with children."

He rolled his eyes. "Like I have time for that."

"Who says you'll have the choice?"

"So I get no say?"

"Do you know how many years I was with my beloved Jaroslaw, rest his soul?"

Mirek knew exactly. "Forty-three years."

"Forty-three years," she said as if he hadn't answered. "And do you know the secret to how we stayed together for so long with barely a cross word?"

"His premature deafness?"

Hanka scowled.

He gestured with an open hand. "Sorry. Go on."

She took her pack of cigarettes from her pocket. "That's okay. If you don't want the benefit of my experience…" She stuck a cigarette in her mouth.

"No, please, enlighten me, oh Oracle of the East — what is the secret to unending matrimonial bliss?"

Lighting the cigarette, Hanka drew on it, then blew a cloud of smoke. It was one of those cheap Soviet things again that smelled like burning tires.

He wafted the smoke away.

Hanka leaned closer and whispered, "Always let the man believe he's the one making the important decisions."

Mirek snorted. While her point about decisions possibly had merit, her notion concerning Ania was outright crazy. He glanced at the four children gathered around two sinks behind her, washing and drying dishes. "Don't you have some souls to torment?"

Hanka shrugged. "I can't help seeing what I see."

"Well, there's nothing to see here. If there was, I'm darn sure I would have noticed."

"You would?"

"Not much gets past me because I'm a student of human psychology. How do you think I create complex characters in my books or manage to keep this place going?"

"I often wonder." Hanka flicked ash into a cup overflowing with cigarette butts. "So, if nothing gets past you, where's the new boy?"

"Jacek? Probably with Tomek, settling into his room."

She arched an eyebrow again.

"I don't know what you're getting at."

Hanka jabbed her cigarette toward his table.

He glanced back. There was nothing to see but Ania exactly where he'd left her. He stared blankly at Hanka.

"Lower," said Hanka.

He frowned. What the devil did that mean?

He looked back again, then bent sideways to see under the tables. The red-haired boy was huddled near to their seats. "Well, I'll…" He snorted.

Hanka said, "Seems like someone's looking for a surrogate mama and tata. But you'll already be aware of that because nothing gets past you." She winked.

With a sigh, he rubbed his hands together. "Okay, it's been enlightening, as always, Hanka, but I have a child to accommodate and a house to Germanize."

"Don't panic." She slid off her stool. "I've got Jacek."

"Thank you. That will be a big help."

She pointed her cigarette at Ania. "But don't say I didn't warn you."

"Warn me?" He sniggered. He had eighty-nine children to look after, a three-story house to maintain, and an occupying army to placate. Like this was a time for romance, even if he wanted it.

6

Mirek ushered Ania into his study.

"Wow." She gazed at a six-foot-wide floor-to-ceiling bookcase without an inch of space in it — the dominant feature of the room.

She sniggered. "Why do you have so many books? If you live to be a hundred, you'll never read them all."

"I already have. Some twice."

She spluttered a laugh. "Never."

He nodded.

She squinted at him as if judging whether he was trying to fool her. "You've read *all* those." She pointed at the bookcase, as if clarification was needed.

"Uh-huh. And the heartbreaking thing is that now, I have to get rid of eighty percent of them."

"Why?"

He snorted. "Exactly."

"What?" She scratched her head.

Her question hadn't been rhetorical? "Because the Germans believe books can incite people to think for themselves, or to question authority, or even to rise up. Throughout history, all dictators have one thing in common — they all fear a scholar more than they fear a soldier because you can kill a man, but you can't kill an idea."

She smirked. "So reading all these must make you the most dangerous man in Poland."

He laughed. "I'm going to have to keep my mouth shut, aren't I? Or they'll be shipping me off to a labor camp."

"Don't worry, I'll mail you your bedtime cookie."

They laughed again.

Mirek clapped his hands once. "Okay, shall we get started?"

She glanced at his brown leather armchair — his reading chair — its arms scuffed from decades of use, then his battered desk at which he'd written each of his books. Finally, she gazed at the painting of the Eiffel Tower at sunset hanging over the fireplace — the one location he was determined to visit before he died.

Ania said, "What would you like me to do?"

"How about I identify the problem books and pass them to you to pack in the chest?" He pointed to the chest he'd brought in earlier.

"Okay."

Mirek removed *Autumn*, the first book in Wladyslaw Reymont's *The Peasants* quartet. The series being an exploration of the cultural and spiritual heart of Poland, if ever there was a Polish author's work the Germans would relish throwing on a pyre, this was it. Especially as the series had gained critical acclaim, winning Reymont the Nobel Prize in Literature.

He held up the book. "Whatever you do, don't let me open a single one of these. And under no circumstances let me sit in that armchair with one."

"Got it." She snatched the book and tossed it into the chest.

He stared, mouth agape. Had she never loved a book? Never wanted to hug and cherish it? Never ached for it to never end?

"What?" she said innocently.

"Nothing." His radio behind his desk caught his eye. "Oh my word, I better not forget that." He placed it in the chest.

Some of his happiest memories were of the times his household had huddled under blankets in the dining room on cold winter nights, listening to music. Or had lain on those same blankets in the garden on summer nights, marveling at the stars to music. And every day, the radio regaled them with news, filling their tiny lives with the entire world.

"You have to get rid of that?" asked Ania.

"Nowadays, it's dangerous to own one because you can be imprisoned for listening to a foreign station — and how can you prove you haven't done that?"

They continued chatting as they worked.

He passed her the next book. "So, you know my story. Can I ask what brought you to our quiet little town?"

"Me? I don't have a story."

"Everyone's got a story."

"Not me. I've never been anywhere or done anything."

"Everyone's done *something*."

Ania shook her head. "Until I moved here, I'd never been more than twenty miles from home."

Moving farther from home than she'd ever traveled would have been a giant step. "So what prompted such a big move?"

Crouched, she squashed books tight into the corner of the chest. "It will sound stupid when you've done so much."

"It's not stupid if it's important to you."

"My mother died. She was all I had, so I decided to make a fresh start and see something of the world." She rolled her eyes. "And I made it all of fifty miles."

"You can't go on a long journey without going the first fifty miles."

She laughed. "That's kind of my plan now — this year fifty miles, next year five hundred."

He nodded. "Five hundred east or five hundred west?"

"That kind of depends on the Germans."

"And the Soviets. And the Allies. And just about everyone except you and me."

She froze. "Do you really think it will go on that long?"

He shrugged.

Her brow knitted and she nodded to the bookcase. "But having read all these books, you must be the smartest man in town, so if you don't know..."

"The war started weeks ago and yet not one single German ever appeared, so, foolishly, I thought we might see out the war pretty much unscathed, *if* the British and the French mobilized quickly enough. But then today came." He gazed away and winced as the flailing, blazing figure haunted his thoughts.

She touched his arm. "What is it?"

He shook his head. Even the Nazis could never perpetrate anything so nightmarish again, so there was no reason to torment anyone else with such a horrific image.

Ania stood. "You saw something you didn't tell us about at dinner, didn't you?"

He met her gaze and barely nodded. "I couldn't tell them. Not my children. I couldn't let them see what I'd seen."

"It was that bad?"

He nodded again.

"Do you want to tell me?"

No one deserved to have to picture such a sight. "I can't."

She returned to packing. "So let's pray you never see anything like that again."

Pray? That was what the people in the synagogue were doing. If his household was going to get through this war, they were going to have to rely on a heck of a lot more than prayer.

He handed her another couple of books, then another two, the sudden silence prickling in his mind like ants crawling over his skin. Germanizing the house was going to take hours. No way could they do it in a silence like this one.

Mirek said, "Why two *L*'s?"

She squinted at him. "Excuse me?"

"Your name — Kisiell. Why two *L*'s? It's usually only one."

"Mama and Tata had four boys in a row and then I came along. Tata was so happy to finally have a little girl that he went out to celebrate and got completely pickled — falling-down, singing-in-the-street pickled. The next morning, when he went to register my birth, he was still pie-eyed, so he spelled our own family name wrong — two *L*'s instead of one."

Mirek laughed. H patted her shoulder. "You see, you do have a story!"

Ania smiled up at him. And her hair fell from her face. The skin from her left temple to her jaw was twisted, pocked, and mottled, as if it had been melted.

She gasped and jerked away, frantically brushing her hair back in place. "Sorry."

"Sorry? Ania, you've nothing to apologize for. It's not your fault if you've been burned."

"That's easy for you to say. You should see how people recoil."

"Am I recoiling?"

She shuffled away and stood with her back to him. "No. But you're not normal."

"Thank you." There was nothing like being called abnormal to make one feel warm inside.

She half turned. "I didn't mean that in a bad way. You know things. You have a good heart. You aren't like the people out there." She jabbed outside. "Pointing, sniggering, staring, cringing..."

He reached toward her but pulled back. Touching a woman he barely knew would be highly inappropriate. Even if it was well intentioned.

He said, "And it's obvious to me — even as someone certified abnormal — that you have a good heart too. You'll always be welcome in this house, Anna-Maria Kisiell with two *L*'s."

Her voice faltered. "Thank you."

"Now, are you going to help with these books, or has Hanka employed the biggest shirker in town?"

She snickered and dawdled back to the chest.

For a few minutes, they worked in silence. But this was a healthy silence, a comfortable silence, a silence born out of mutual respect and blossoming friendship.

Without looking at him, she said, "If I'm to continue working here, can you promise me one thing, please?"

"If it's within my power to do it, yes."

"Ask me to do anything except help with your teaching."

"Okay, I promise."

"Thank you."

Without looking at her, so she wouldn't feel he was staring even if he wasn't, he said, "Can I ask when you were burned? You don't have to tell me if you don't want to."

"I was seven."

He winced. He didn't need to know anything else. From what she'd said already, he could imagine the nightmare her life had become. Especially her school life. Children could be so inquisitive, caring, and surprising, yet they could also be unbelievably cruel, vindictive, and intolerant.

But she hadn't finished. "I don't remember much about it, except holding my arm up and seeing it not just on fire but bits of it falling off. And the smell – like burning pork." She hung her head. "Mama said I'd always been the happiest little girl she'd ever met, but everything changed that day. Everything."

"I can't imagine what you must have gone through."

"And that was only the beginning. By the time I went back to school, I was so far behind, I had to go into another class. There, no one knew the old me, only this new one – the monster. They made my life hell."

He placed the book he was holding back on the shelf. Keeping hold of it felt like taunting her. "You know, if there's any part of your schooling that you'd like to catch up on, I'd be more than happy to help."

"Catch up on?" She sniggered, holding up a copy of *Pan Tadeusz* by Adam Mickiewicz, a man often referred to as the Polish Shakespeare. "I can't even read this cover, let alone the words inside."

She tossed the book in the chest.

Mirek had been the teacher's pet in almost every class he'd been in. Almost. When it came to physical education, until a growth spurt in his teens, he'd been as athletic as a two-legged cow. A fact other children had taken great joy in pointing out as often as they could.

He crouched beside her. She turned her face away. He wasn't sure if it was to hide tears or hide her scars.

"From tomorrow, for thirty minutes after dinner every day, we're going to study," he said. "We'll start simple, but I promise you, this time next year, when you're five hundred miles away, there won't be a book anywhere you can't read."

She turned to him. Fully. Tears dribbling over her scars. "You'd do that? *For me?*"

"For you, Anna-Maria Kisiell with two *L*'s."

She smiled. For the first time, he saw her face properly, saw her eyes sparkling. Such dazzling hazel eyes.

Last year, he and Hanka had thrown a surprise birthday party for Agata, and Lech, his farmer friend, had brought a baby goat for her to pet. He could still picture the pure joy on Agata's face. And now, here was that expression again.

A warm glow welled up from his stomach. He enjoyed nothing better than helping the forsaken, but here was one lost soul who was special, one who deserved a second chance, even if it was coming somewhat late in life. He was going to see she got it. Nothing was going to stand in his way.

They returned to work, and after clearing his study, they moved into the second classroom. Finally, he brought a couple of armfuls of things from his bedroom, and with six chests filled, including the one from his classroom, the job was done. However, with midnight approaching and heaven only knew how many Germans prowling the streets, there was no way he was letting Ania walk home, even under his escort.

A few minutes later, he stood in Hanka's bedroom doorway, an oil lamp in one hand, a lumpy pillow and two worn blankets in the other. His dim light revealed little in the darkened room, other than a mound under heaped blankets in the bed and Ania patiently waiting to one side.

Handing Ania the bedding, he shrugged. "With so many children now, I'm afraid this is all I could find."

Ania took them. "They'll be fine, don't worry. Thank you. Good night."

"Good night. And thank you again for all your help. You turned a frustrating and tediously long job into—"

The mound in bed said, "The lady said *good night* already. Some of us have to be up at 5:00 a.m., you know."

Smiling, he mouthed, "Thank you."

Ania mouthed back, "You're welcome."

Turning to leave, he said loudly, "Good night, Hanka. Sweet dreams."

Ania stifled a giggle.

"Dear Lord," said Hanka, "I got a better night's sleep during the last air raid."

Mirek chuckled to himself as he descended the bare wooden staircase, until the fourth step creaked loudly, making him cringe. The stairs had become much louder since they'd taken up the carpeting, but with too few mattresses coupled with too few zlotys, folded carpet was providing makeshift mattresses for many children.

On the middle floor, he paused and scanned the darkened hallway. No light bled from underneath any of the doors and all was silent. Good, everyone was asleep.

He crept along the hallway to a door in the middle: his bedroom. As he reached for the doorknob, he glanced back to the stairs. Ania was going to make a valuable addition to the house. Maybe a valuable friend, too. He snorted at the remark Hanka had made about women and relationships.

"Batty, Hanka. Just plain batty."

But then an image flashed into his mind. An image the night's pleasant conversation had managed to hold at bay: the flailing, blazing figure.

He cringed. At least things could only get better tomorrow.

7

Mirek gazed at the sunlight filtering through the trees of the small park adjoining the orphanage's back garden as birds sang in the branches. The world was bathed in a beautiful golden glow of stillness and peace. It was as if the incident in the square had never happened. At least for some.

Could the Germans have moved on? Their sleepy little town was nowhere near the front lines, and it had few resources or industries that could help the war effort. Maybe his household might yet ride out the war relatively untouched. Someone had to. After all, the Germans couldn't wipe every single Polish person from existence. So, yes, maybe their town had seen the worst of it. Maybe yesterday, the war had come and gone, so for them, it was now all over.

Behind him, something heavy crashed against something solid. He turned.

Clattering through the orphanage's back door, four of the older teenage boys, two front and two rear, heaved a chest suspended on ropes threaded through its handles. The chest banged into the wall again.

"Shhh!" Mirek checked his watch: 6:21 a.m.

This was taking too long. Some neighbors would be awake now and preparing for their day. Any one of them could look out at any moment and question what was happening.

He scanned the windows of the nearby buildings. His neighbors were good people, but even good people could let things accidentally slip, so the fewer who knew about his secret cache, the better.

All appeared quiet.

The four boys trudged toward a group shoveling dirt from a massive pile into a twenty-foot-long hole to bury the five chests already inside. They lowered the last chest in, then grabbed spades to help cover it.

Nearby, Mirek poured gasoline into a metal drum filled with his least valuable and least loved books. He tossed in a lit match, and it burst into flames.

After a few minutes, he fished out four of the blazing books with metal tongs and set them on the ground. He let these burn to charred stumps and then doused them with water. The remains would be buried in the cinders in the drum for any German search team to stumble upon as undeniable evidence he'd burned his entire collection, with the majority having been reduced to ash.

Once Britain and France attacked from the west, the Germans would have no option but to pull out of Poland to reinforce their lines. With the Nazis gone, the Poles could drive the Soviets out of eastern Poland. By the spring, life would undoubtedly be back to normal, and he'd be able to unearth all his treasure chests.

He patted one of the large wooden raised beds he'd had constructed. "Use what's left over to fill these, boys, please." He pointed to the hole. "But be sure to stamp that down and then top it up, so it doesn't sink."

Panting, sweat beading on their brows, the boys finished the burial and moved on to the raised bed.

Mirek transplanted kale, gooseberry, and turnip seedlings from pots into the filled hole. How many would survive, he had no idea, but with food prices spiraling, they had to try whatever they could.

The work done, he said, "Good job, boys. Now get yourselves to the dining room, where Baba Hanka will have an extra-big breakfast waiting for you as a thank-you."

The boys eagerly dashed inside.

Mirek scanned the neighboring windows again. No one looked out. Excellent. He went in, too.

Children gathered in the hallway, playing and gabbling while the clatter of silverware and dishes came from the dining room. Holding the banister rail, Ania hobbled down the stairs. She smiled on seeing him.

He tipped his head. "Morning. Sleep well?"

"Surprisingly well, thank you. Have you been busy already?"

"Just finishing off what we started yesterday."

She reached the bottom. "I'd offer to help, but I have to be at the mayor's by eight."

"The mayor's?"

"I help his wife in the morning. But I'll be back here for midday."

"Good. I look forward to seeing you. And having our first lesson."

She frowned. "You still want to do that?"

"Why wouldn't I?"

"I thought you were just saying it to be nice."

"I was saying it because I meant it. Thirty minutes after dinner — I'm all yours."

She beamed.

I'm all yours. That might've been a bad choice of phrase, considering Hanka's ridiculous notion. Ania was helpful and pleasant company, but the last thing he wanted was to give her the wrong impression.

He gestured to the dining room. "Breakfast?"

She nodded.

In the dining room, Hanka raised an eyebrow at Mirek as she ladled porridge.

Sternly, he said, "Thank you, Hanka."

With an unusually cheery tone, she said, "You're welcome, Mirek."

He and Ania sat.

Mirek asked, "So what do you do for the mayor's wife?"

"Cleaning, washing, ironing... anything she needs." She leaned closer and whispered, "They have a phonograph. Sometimes, if the mayor is out and I finish early, we drink tea and listen to American jazz records."

"Really?"

"Duke Ellington, Glenn Miller, and my favorite, Louis Armstrong. Do you know him?"

"No."

"Oh, he's wonderful. When he sings, it's like cookies crumbled into melted chocolate."

Cookies crumbled into melted chocolate. For someone who couldn't read, she had a remarkable poetry to her. "I'll have to seek him out."

She ate a spoonful of porridge. "So, you know the story of my name, how about yours? Why Papa Mirek, not Tata Mirek?"

Mirek chuckled. "A boy called Michal Dubanowski came here years ago. He'd been raised in a single room and had to sleep in a closet, so when he saw the size of this place, he was flabbergasted. He said only a duke or a prince could ever live somewhere so grand, so for fun, he'd sometimes adopt a posh accent and call me Papa. And it just caught on."

"That's sweet."

Mirek finished his bowl. "I'm sorry, but I'm going to have to run. I have room inspections, food deliveries, teaching…"

She waved. "Of course."

"Listen, it's as quiet as usual outside, but I'd still take the back streets to be safe."

"Okay."

He stood. "So my study, after dinner?"

She pursed her lips as if undecided but then nodded.

Learning to read, especially as an adult, wasn't just hard and frustrating but a major commitment. He hoped she'd turn up, but if she didn't, she didn't. He left.

Mirek spent the next few hours inspecting the middle- and top-floor rooms, collecting the items the children had left out and checking hiding places for anything they were trying to conceal. When he'd finished, he had three heavy sackfuls. In the back garden, he tipped it all into two more chests for the boys to bury.

"Mirek?"

He turned.

Hanka stood in the doorway. "We've had no food delivery today."

"Nothing?" They should've had something from both the baker and the grocer.

Hanka shook her head.

It was midmorning, and so far, no screams or gunfire had come from the square. Maybe the Germans really had left and it was safe again. Either way, he was going to have to venture out. Food was scarce enough because of the war, and what was available was getting more expensive by the day. But his children needed food. That gave Mirek only one option.

8

Mirek peeked through the courtyard gate. The street seemed just as safe as it had from the upstairs windows. He opened the gate fully and stepped out.

Private vehicles rumbled along, pedestrians bustled about, and stores offered their wares. It looked like just any other day.

He prowled toward the square, a prickle on the back of his neck getting stronger and stronger the closer he got.

Someone said hello. The word registered, but not the person who said it. Mirek flicked a wave in their general direction. Why was life going on as if it were just an ordinary day? Even if people hadn't witnessed the horrors themselves, word must have spread, and the destruction would be blatantly evident.

Across the road, Wanda Pazdan, the local gossip, was shopping as usual, her two youngest children in tow. And there was Ludomir Sajdak. Only yesterday, he'd been lurching down the street with his blood-drenched son, yet there he was waltzing into the hardware store.

Was Mirek missing something? He stopped and gazed around.

Wanda and her two kids staggered away, weighed down with so many groceries they swayed as if they were drunk. Why were they buying so much stuff?

Ludomir reappeared, carrying planks of wood, a bag of nails, and a new hammer. What was he building?

A woman with a black hat scurried past, a large woven basket overflowing with groceries in each hand.

Why were these people on spending sprees?

He shuffled farther. As he neared The Flower of Poland guesthouse, his heart raced. This was where the nightmare had started yesterday. Yet today, there was no screaming, no gunshots, no smoke.

Balling his fists, he edged toward the end of the road and emerged into the square.

The Germans had gone. As had the bodies. The toppled statue lay amid the rubble of its plinth, and handfuls of flowers lay scattered across the ground in memory of the fallen. In the corner of the square, wisps of smoke curled from the smoldering, blackened remains of the synagogue, its roof caved in and two walls partially collapsed. Some people rooted through the smoking debris, others gazed on in a daze, while a few wailed uncontrollably.

Yet the town hall, with its great granite columns guarding its entrance, still stood proud. At the far end, the railway station remained unscarred, the stone lion atop its portico gazing down benevolently upon the square. The Catholic church, the restaurants with their outdoor tables, the most expensive apartment building in town... unscratched. Other than that one smoldering corner, everything else appeared untouched.

And not a sign of the Germans. Had they left?

He hadn't expected this. The crushing darkness within Mirek lifted and he felt lighter. He marched farther into the square. The town had paid a truly horrendous price, but the Germans had gone. Maybe yesterday was as close to the war as they were ever going to get. Thank the Lord.

Then he saw it.

He squinted, focusing his one good eye on the street leading away from the square to his right.

"What the...?"

He marched toward it, quickening his pace as curiosity ate at him.

He shook his head. No, this was a joke. Had to be.

Approaching the bakery, he gawked at a chalkboard sign with enormous white letters saying *NO BREAD*.

It wasn't even midday. How had the bakery run out of bread?

But that wasn't the most worrying sight. A line of people hugged the buildings on the other sidewalk and disappeared around the corner onto the next street.

Again, Mirek shook his head. "You've got to be kidding."

A gnawing ache in his gut, he crossed and turned the corner. "No, no, no."

The line of people disappeared into the grocery store.

He ran past the line to the store. The crates at the front that usually overflowed with potatoes and cabbages and carrots and turnips... all empty.

Two young men emerged from the store, each carrying a box piled high with produce. Mirek blocked their way. "Why are you emptying the stores? Other people need food too, you know."

One barged him out of the way. "Beat it, pal. Do you think you're the only one with mouths to feed?"

A man with a bushy mustache, the next in line to enter the store, glared at Mirek. "Back of the line, Jack. Or you and me are going to have a problem."

Mirek backed away. If he tried to push in, this mob might lynch him.

However, instead of leaving, he rapped on the window. Inside, a bald man in a white apron rolled his eyes but gestured for Mirek to wait. The man finished serving a customer, then squeezed outside.

Mirek said, "What's going on, Julek? Where was my delivery?"

Julek pointed at the line. "See all these people? Do you know what they're doing? Every single one of them is *paying with money*. Not credit. Money, Mirek. Come back when you've got some." He turned away.

Mirek grabbed his arm. "You know I'm always good for it."

"You are, if you're alive. But after yesterday, I have to put my family first." He marched away.

"So how am I supposed to feed my children?"

Julek ignored him.

In the doorway, a woman with three wicker baskets smirked. "You shouldn't have kids if you can't feed them. It's called being a responsible parent."

Mirek glared at her and stomped away.

What was he going to do? He trudged to the square, where a bearded figure caught his eye.

Waving, he shouted, "Borys!"

Borys ambled over.

Mirek said, "People are clearing out all the food stores. What am I supposed to do?"

Borys frowned. "I thought you had food delivered."

"I do."

"So what's the emergency?"

"There's so much demand, it's cash only."

"So pay with cash."

Mirek slapped his forehead. "Why didn't I think of that?" He glared at the man. "The Germans are closing bookstores everywhere they go, so my publisher isn't going to be paying me anything anytime soon. And they've shut down the newspaper I write for."

"So use your savings."

Mirek grimaced.

"A line of credit?"

"What do you think we've been living on?"

Borys clicked his tongue. "That's a tough one."

"Do you think? Please tell me you've got something for me. Yesterday, you said you would."

"I just dropped it off with Hanka."

"Oh, thank God." Mirek grabbed Borys's hand and shook it. "Thank you, Borys."

"It's not a lot, but..."

"It doesn't matter. Until this madness settles down, just bring us anything."

Borys grimaced. "Settles down? Mirek, this is only just getting started. Did you hear what happened yesterday?"

Mirek looked at the spot where the burning figure had fallen. "Hear it? I saw it. But"— he rubbed his face —"how could they do that? That's not war. That's senseless butchery."

"With Hitler in command, did you really think an occupying force would stick to humanitarian conventions? I've seen *Mein Kampf* on your bookshelf. You have read it, haven't you?"

Yes, he'd read Hitler's book. And it had terrified him. Not the book — that was a diabolical piece of junk, being little more than the immature ramblings of a deluded loser. Hitler dreamed of righting wrongs that had never existed and turning the entire world upside down to create a new world order, all because he believed the world treated him unfairly. So, no, the actual book wasn't the issue. What was terrifying was how it had become such a huge bestseller because so many Germans bought into its poisonous philosophy.

Mirek pointed at the remains of the synagogue. "Would decent Germans really condone that?"

"A lot of them, probably not. But if you were a decent person in Germany right now, would you stand up and say something? For years, they've been shipping thousands of their own citizens to labor camps as enemies of the state, so this"— he nodded to the ruins —"is nothing to them."

Mirek swallowed hard.

Borys slung his arm around Mirek's shoulders. "Why do you think we need as much help as we can get?"

Mirek shrugged him off. "After what happened yesterday?" He snorted. "Do you really think I'm going to put my children in danger?"

Borys gestured to the synagogue. "Were they doing anything illegal? Or were they just peacefully trying to get on with their lives?"

His friend had a point. None of the people who'd died yesterday were attacking the Germans, and most were probably doing nothing to support the Resistance. Yet they were still dead.

"Borys, if it were just me, you know I'd be standing at your side, but it isn't. Every single person in my house is family. And anything I do impacts them. So ideology and patriotism be damned — my family comes first. Or do you really expect me to risk having some Nazi toss a grenade into our dining room while we're all eating?"

Borys held up his hands in surrender.

Mirek said, "Anyway, where did the Germans disappear to?"

"They're camped outside town, near the forest."

"So they'll be back?"

Borys raised an eyebrow.

Stupid question. Mirek clutched his brow. What carnage would they wreak next time? And how could he ensure his children didn't get caught up in it?

9

As Mirek and Borys meandered through the square, a woman in a black headscarf dashed by, cradling her baby. Then a man bolted past, potatoes and carrots dropping from his basket and scattering over the cobbles. He ran on as if he didn't care.

Mirek glanced back. He gasped.

Germans!

Borys grabbed him, and they dove behind a tree trunk — the nearest cover available — as a truck pulled into the middle of the square. Pedestrians scattered like ripples from a pebble dropped in water.

Six soldiers leapt from the cargo area, then trained their rifles on twelve filthy men dressed in rags as they clambered from the vehicle and unloaded ladders and painting equipment. A soldier split the men into groups of four, each under the guard of two soldiers, then pointed to the Polish flag waving atop the town hall and in two other spots around the square. The three groups headed off, one toward the town hall, one the church, and one the orphanage's road.

Nearby, a hunched old woman pulling a wooden cart of groceries hobbled to get out of the Nazis' way but couldn't move quickly enough. She apologized in Polish.

A soldier who looked little older than some of the Mirek's teenagers kicked her cart over. He shouted in German, "No Polish in public!"

She apologized again, adding that she didn't speak German.

The soldier shoved her so hard, she crashed to the ground.

Mirek stepped forward, but Borys jerked him back.

"What the hell, Borys? She needs help."

"It's not worth it."

A man in a blue suit dashed to the woman and helped her up. In German, he said, "She is German-speaking not."

The soldier clubbed the man with his rifle, sending him smashing into the cobbles. "Don't disrespect the beautiful German language by butchering it, you scum."

Mirek's jaw dropped in horror. He stared at the woman wailing; the man clutching his face, blood oozing between his fingers; the Nazi waltzing away, joking with his comrade.

What was happening to his beloved town? To Poland? He'd heard the stories that Poles were suffering inexplicable violence in some cities but had ignored them, believing them the result of rumormongers each adding a little more flavor to make their tale more interesting than the last version. But he was wrong. It was all true.

How? The Germans were people just like the Polish. How could they treat innocent civilians with such obscene brutality? The German people might want war. But this? This wasn't war. This was something else. Something the civilized world had never seen.

Borys grabbed Mirek's arm and dragged him toward his home.

"Why are they doing this, Borys? It's—" He shook his head. "It's just plain evil."

"Now you know why I keep asking for your help. Why it's so vital more people support us."

Mirek's eyes popped wider and he pointed back at the square. "You think I'm going to do something to bring *that* into my house?"

"*That* is nothing. Believe me."

"So what's the Resistance going to do about it?"

Borys shot him a sideways glance.

Mirek said, "Someone's got to do something."

"That's what I've been telling you."

Mirek stopped dead and grabbed the man's arm. "Hey, don't lay this at my door."

Borys ripped his arm free. "We can't do it alone. We don't have the manpower and we don't have the firepower."

"So you're telling me we have to live with *that*." Again, he stabbed at the square.

"I'm saying, if good people do nothing, *that* is going to be everyday life." He shoved Mirek toward the house. "Now, can we get the hell off the street?"

Mirek stumbled on. Even if the French and British won every battle, it could take months — God forbid, years — for Poland to be free again. If the Resistance couldn't help him, his sleepy little town was going to become hell on earth.

They ran down and in through Mirek's gate. Mirek slumped against the wall, panting.

He said, "You know I'd help more if I could, don't you? But if I were caught doing anything or hiding something, monsters like that wouldn't kill me, they'd make me watch while they killed my children."

Borys sighed. "Mirek, it isn't that I don't understand — I feel for you and the position you're in. Honestly, I do. But there'll come a day when you approach us for help, and what do you think is going to happen? If you won't help us now, when we and your countrymen need you most, why would we ever put our lives on the line to help you?"

Mirek hoped such a day would never come. But what if it did?

10

As Mirek ate his evening meal in silence, a question clawed at him. Children chattered all around him, some trying to engage him in conversation; however, all he could muster was a smile or the most cursory of answers. His children were his world, but could he live with himself if he did nothing after seeing what he'd seen?

He pawed soggy cabbage with his fork.

If his children were safe, yes, he could live with himself.

Except, how long would it be before the horrors outside forced their way inside? If he did nothing, he'd be to blame for the nightmare getting in.

Slinging down his fork, he stared into space.

He had no choice — he had to help the Resistance. It was the only logical solution. He rubbed his head. But was it logical? Or was it a purely emotional response to the atrocities he'd witnessed?

If only he could retire to his study and lose himself in a book. Calm his mind so he could think clearly. Not that he had any right to complain. After seeing that flailing, blazing figure, he never had the right to complain about anything ever again.

So what could he do to take his mind off this dire situation in order to look at it later with fresh eyes?

He tramped away, leaving his dirty plate on the pile near the hatch.

In his study, he slumped in his armchair. Other than times with his wife, the most contented moments of his life had been sitting in his chair. Totaling all those hours would likely add up to years. Happy, happy years. Would he ever see the likes again? Ever appreciate the poetry of life once more?

Cookies crumbled into melted chocolate. He smiled and checked his watch. She'd likely be finished in the kitchen soon, yet he'd been so busy that he'd thought nothing about her lesson. He'd promised to teach her, though. He would not break that promise.

After a quick visit to his classroom, he returned with a chair and three children's books covering a range of reading levels. He placed the chair beside his desk, took a cushion from his armchair to make the seat more comfortable, then flicked through the books he'd selected to decide which might be most appropriate to start.

His thirty-minute lesson planned, he leaned back behind his desk and looked at the door, waiting.

After a few minutes, he checked his watch again. Anytime now. He sat upright, straightened his tie, and pulled his vest down so it no longer bunched up.

He snorted. What was he doing? This wasn't a date! All he was doing was teaching a new employee a new skill. A skill that, ultimately, would benefit him and his pupils. He clicked his tongue. This was all Hanka's doing — putting those crazy ideas in his head. As if he didn't have enough to worry about.

He slouched in his chair and closed his eyes. Recently, the days were fraught with such stress that he never seemed to have a second to stop and do nothing.

The tension in his shoulders melted away and he sighed deeply. Never would he have thought a moment of quiet solitude could be such a joy. He relaxed, bathing in stillness.

But then he checked his watch again. Where was she? Had she changed her mind about coming?

He stared at his desk, a wave of disappointment washing over him as a sinking feeling filled his stomach.

Someone knocked on his door.

He sat up, eyes wide and alert. "Come."

As the doorknob turned and the door eased open, he realized he was smiling. What the devil was wrong with him?

Pawel entered. "Sorry to disturb you, Papa Mirek, but Baba Hanka asks if you can see her before she retires tonight, please."

"Tell her I'll be along shortly. Thank you, Pawel."

"Yes, Papa Mirek." He left, closing the door.

Checking his watch yet again, Mirek sighed. She wasn't coming. Probably for the best because he wasn't comfortable with these weird feelings and ridiculous thoughts. Hanka had a lot to answer for. Their relationship was so close they could joke about almost anything, but enough was enough. This ended now.

He stood, snatching the reading books, and rolled his eyes. Good grief, he'd only met the woman yesterday — she wasn't even a friend — so why was this bothering him so?

Well, at least he could put Hanka straight. Let her know just how wrong she'd been. So very, very wrong. Romance? Dear Lord, as if he didn't have enough on his plate. Oh yes, correcting Hanka was going to be a real pleasure. Like they said, every cloud...

Mirek trudged for the door. Still, it was strange that she hadn't come. Last night, they'd seemed to have some sort of connection.

He snorted. Yes, because he was the expert, not having been near a woman for sixteen years. How was he supposed to know how the devil they worked?

He ripped open the door but stopped short. "Oh..."

Ania stood in the hallway, straightening her blue dress. "I'm sorry I'm late. If you're too busy, I can—"

"No, come in. Please."

She nodded a thank-you.

Ushering her in, he realized he was smiling again. More worryingly, he didn't want to stop.

He pulled out the chair for her. "Please."

As she sat, he eased it in for her.

"Thank you," she said.

He retook his seat behind his desk.

Ania picked at her fingernails. "I almost didn't come."

"But you did. That's what matters."

"You'll go easy on me, won't you? Because it's more years than I can remember since I did anything like this."

He picked up the books. "Don't worry, reading is like riding a bicycle — you'll be surprised how quickly it will all come flooding back."

"I can't ride a bicycle."

"A horse, then."

She grimaced. "I wish. That's something I've always dreamed of doing."

"Well, regardless, I'm sure you'll be thrilled with how much you remember." He laid the three books side by side. "The easiest way to start is to establish your current reading level. When you last learned, do you remember if it was from books with lots of pictures and only a few words, or books with longer sections of text?"

Looking down, she heaved a breath, then mumbled, "Pictures."

"Hey, that's nothing to be ashamed of. We all started that way."

She flicked her gaze up to him.

"Honestly, if I hadn't started reading from picture books, I'd never have read all those." He pointed to his bookcase, now bare but for one and a half shelves of books. "You know what I mean."

"Okay."

"Do you remember this one?" He slid a copy of *Story Primer for Children* toward her, its colorful cover of two birds and flowers now battered from all the little hands that had turned the pages over the years.

She pursed her lips and picked it up. Flicking through it, she said, "I remember Falski's book. It's for little kids." She set it down.

"Okay, so how about this one?" He slid over the book he'd caught her looking at when they'd first met.

"The book by the bald old man?"

He sniggered. "Yes, that one."

She picked it up and exhaled loudly.

Mirek said, "When you're ready, start reading to me and we'll see how you go."

"Read out loud?"

"Well, I have to hear to know how you're doing."

She looked to the heavens. "Oh my stars."

He rested a hand on hers. "It's okay. I've been through this process hundreds of times."

"You promise you won't laugh?"

"I promise."

Under her breath, as she opened the book, she said, "Oh boy, oh boy, oh boy."

Straightening her back and clearing her throat, she stared at the first page. Her hands trembled.

"Take your time," said Mirek. "There's no rush."

"Oh boy." She drew a huge breath, then spoke slowly and purposefully. "Rabbit woke up one s-sunny mor-mor-morn-ing, morning"— she panted —"and f-foun-found his tail m-missing."

She slung the book on the desk. "No. This is ridiculous." She pushed out of the chair.

"That was really good, Ania. In fact, if you haven't read a book for over twenty years, it was absolutely amazing!"

"You're just saying that." She closed her eyes for a second. "Dear God, what am I doing? I've never been so embarrassed."

She scurried for the door.

"Wait." He opened the bottom drawer of his desk and rooted inside.

"What's the point? I'm a cleaner — that's what I know, that's what I'm good at. Just let me clean."

"I thought you might feel like that, so I saved this from the chests." He put another picture book on the desk.

She wagged a finger at him. "I've tried once, I'm not trying again."

"It's not you who's going to try."

She frowned. "What?"

He held the book up. It had a cartoonish picture of a gigantic metal tower on the front and a man in a beret. "This is French. Pick a page."

"Why?"

"Humor me."

She sighed, tramped back, and snatched the book. Flicking through, she stopped at a random page, then handed it back. "Happy now?"

He laid the book on the desk so she could see a picture of a black cat curled up asleep under a kitchen table and the accompanying text. Running his index finger under the words, he read aloud slowly, "*Le chat n-noir est sou-sous la table dans la*"— he huffed —"*dans la cui-*"— he scratched his head —"*cuisine. Dans la cuisine.*"

He blew out a breath, then raised an eyebrow. "See?"

"You did that on purpose."

"No." He gestured to her seat. "I did that because learning to read is always a struggle. I can't read French, but I want to learn, so I'm going to keep trying."

She stared at him, then at the chair, then at him again. Finally, she slumped back down.

"Thank you." He slid her book to her.

Slowly, she paged through to where she'd left off.

Ania read for the next half hour, Mirek helping her, especially with pronunciation where an accent changed a letter's sound.

After the agreed thirty minutes, Mirek ended the lesson, not wanting to push her too far on the first day. He then escorted her out of the house.

On the sidewalk, Ania said, "You're sure these lessons won't take too much of your time?"

"Of course not." He stepped toward the square.

She caught his arm. "You don't need to walk me home."

"But I need to know you're safe."

"I'll be fine. I'll use the back streets again. And you need to help Hanka with the children."

She was right. He'd missed the bedtime routine yesterday because of all the Germanization. It wasn't fair to dump that on Hanka again. Not when her workday started before dawn.

He said, "Okay. See you tomorrow."

"Bye." She strode up the street.

He ached to chase after her and escort her home. Instead, he went inside.

As he climbed the stairs with his oil lamp, Hanka's voice boomed from the far end of the middle floor. "If this light is on again when I come back, no one is getting breakfast tomorrow. Understand?"

Squabbling, lost teddy bears, stomachaches, last-minute trips to the toilet... what was supposed to be a fifteen-minute job to settle everyone could easily take an hour or two. Such nights were so draining after a long day.

As he reached the top floor, a little girl wailed from within the first bedroom. He sighed. So it was going to be one of *those* nights. But maybe not. Maybe, after this one girl, everything else would go like a dream.

He knocked, then entered. Bathed in the yellowy glow of his lamp, two little girls lay in roughly constructed bunk beds on the left, and another two lay in ones on the right. Between them, on a mattress on the floor, two more little girls lay top to tail, one completely covered by a blue blanket, the other, Kasia, curled up in only her white nightgown.

Mirek checked the bed roster on the back of the door, which listed Kasia and Marta as sleeping on the floor tonight.

Mirek crouched. "Marta, what's going on? Why have you pulled the blanket off Kasia?"

The chubby-faced girl hogging the blanket peeked from under it. But it wasn't Marta. Rena said, "Marta took my bed, so it's only fair I have all the blanket."

Mirek rubbed his brow. Oh boy, it really was going to be one of those nights.

"Marta?" He watched the four girls in the beds. "Marta?"

The girl in the bottom-right bed pulled the blanket up to hide her face.

"Marta, you know the rules — everyone gets a turn in a bed, but they also get a turn on the floor. It's the only way to be fair."

The girl shuffled farther down into the bed.

Mirek said, "I can see you, Marta. I know you're not asleep."

Marta bolted upright and flung her arm toward Kasia. "She farts in her sleep. I can't share a bed with her."

Kasia slapped her mattress. "That wasn't me, it was Karol!"

Another girl joined the fray. "No, it wasn't."

Kasia said, "Anyway, you snore, Marta. Like a horse with a cough. Everyone says so."

"I do *not* snore!" Marta threw her pillow at Kasia. "Take that back."

Everyone started shouting.

"Okay, okay, okay," said Mirek. "Quiet, please."

They settled down.

He said, "Hands up who likes snoring."

No one put their hand up.

"Hands up who likes farting."

Again, no one responded.

"Okay, so we're all agreed no one likes snoring and no one likes farting. Now, hands up if you don't like tonight's sleeping arrangements, so you want to sleep with Baba Hanka?"

Marta scrambled out of bed and dove onto the floor mattress while Rena scooted into the bunk.

Mirek smiled. "Now, if I have to come here again tonight, the troublemaker will be spending not just tonight but all week sleeping in Baba Hanka's room. Understood?"

With varying degrees of horror-tinged obedience, they all said, "Yes, Papa Mirek."

He left. With space such an issue, he'd have to study his options for having the second classroom turned into a dormitory. Mattresses on the floor were short-term fixes, but bunk beds comfortably fit almost twice as many children in the same area. However, because of the state of his finances, renovations would involve bartering, and anything worth bartering might be better reserved for food. Unless he could give Borys a big enough reason to bump him up the list to get extra help from the Resistance.

11

As Mirek strode out of the dining room after breakfast, Hanka beckoned him over through the hatch, then handed him a list.

He scanned it: eight sacks of potatoes, four sacks of cabbages, three sacks of turnips, four dozen loaves, three dozen plucked chickens...

Mirek said, "So this will last, what, a month, maybe two, if we push it?"

"Yes. Assuming the older children eat the younger ones."

He squinted at her.

She folded her arms. "Ten days. If cannibalism is out of the question."

His eyebrows raised. "Ten? That's all?"

"We're feeding nearly one hundred people. Three times a day."

"Oh boy." He rubbed his chin. He'd known it was bad, but there was bad and then there was *brutal*.

He studied the list. "You can't stretch it any further?"

"I can. But the children won't just be peckish, they'll be ravenous. And we all know what that means."

Arguments, tears, tantrums, belligerence, fights, and cheekiness. Nothing caused more problems than a hungry child.

Mirek said, "I'll reach out to some of our benefactors. Hopefully there are some who haven't been hit so badly by the invasion."

"How about your publisher?"

"There'll be some royalties to come at the end of the year, but after that..." Mirek shook his head.

"No foreign sales? Aren't German bookstores still open?"

Mirek frowned. The Germans were closing libraries and bookstores here, but what were they doing back home? Some of his work had German language editions. Plus, he had titles translated into French and Italian too. If they were still on sale, then there was a glimmer of hope for the future, assuming such international trade continued through the occupation.

He nodded. "I'll make some inquiries. That's a nice little nest egg for next year. Good thinking, Hanka."

Hands on her hips, she said. "Next year?"

Mirek shrugged. "Those are the terms of my contract."

"So renegotiate. Tell them you'll accept a ten percent cut if they pay you now."

He rubbed his chin. "That's not a bad idea."

Hanka waddled away. "Like I said, always leave the important stuff to the women."

Mirek smirked. What would he do without her?

He followed her into the kitchen and rested against the wooden table in the middle of the room while she set to preparing lunch.

He said, "I'm going to see Julek. See how little I can get away with paying for him to restart our deliveries. Can you keep an eye on everyone and make sure the door stays locked, please? We don't want anyone on the streets until we know exactly what's going on."

"Of course. There's nothing I like more than being rushed off my feet and then being given extra duties."

"Then it's a good thing you do it all for love."

Hanka sniggered. "Well, it certainly isn't for the money."

He kissed her on the cheek. "Thank you."

"Away with you." She slapped him with a wooden spoon but couldn't stifle a smile.

In the courtyard, his hand trembled as he reached for the gate. When his hectic schedule had allowed, he'd enjoyed sitting in the square to watch the world drift by, exchange pleasantries with the neighbors, and revel in the fine architecture. Their little town would never be a Krakow or a Warsaw, but that didn't mean it was devoid of charm. Now? Now he wanted to vomit just at the thought of leaving the house.

Unfortunately, they needed food.

The gate creaked open, and the world flooded into his sanctuary. Amazingly, it seemed little different. People and vehicles scuttled by with a little more urgency than usual, but not as if the world was ending. He strained to hear gunfire or screams.

Nothing.

Maybe Borys was wrong. Maybe the Germans had done everything they needed to do here and had moved on. After all, why would they linger in a backwater like this?

Across the street, Filip Goldblatt's tailor's store was open as usual. Mirek wandered over. Inside, mannequins showed Filip's menswear creations, and shelves were crammed with bolts of different fabrics in a variety of colors. Behind the counter, Filip marked cloth with a fine line of chalk.

"Mirek? Don't tell me you're finally updating your wardrobe."

"If only I had the money, Filip." He felt the heavy weave of a navy suit on display. He nodded. Very nice, but sadly, an inexcusable luxury when their food supply was so low. He held out a few zlotys. "Could I use your phone, please?"

"Yours not working?"

"Not since I stopped paying the bill."

"Things are tight for all of us, my friend. But your money's no good here." Filip beckoned. "Come through."

Mirek shoved the money at him. "I insist."

"You do, do you? And how many Jewish children could that feed?" He shook his head, staring at Mirek over his glasses. "Do you know what Rabbi Grodzinski would say if he learned I was talking food from the mouths of orphans?"

"That's very kind, Filip. Thank you."

He guided Mirek into a tiny office with a tiny desk and three shelves piled with papers, catalogs, and fashion magazines. Another door led to the Goldblatt's lower-floor living accommodation. On the left-hand corner of the desk sat a black phone.

"I'll give you some privacy." Filip toddled back into the store.

Mirek dialed the operator.

On the other end of the line, a woman said, "Hello, how may I help you?"

"I'd like to place a long-distance call to Warsaw, please." He read the number from his publisher's letterhead. "Number 33266."

"Connecting you now, sir."

Mirek waited. And waited. He frowned. It didn't usually take so long. "Hello? Is there a problem?"

"I'm sorry, sir, but that number no longer appears to be in service."

"What? It must be. They're one of the longest-established publishers in the country. Please try again."

"I've tried three times, sir. Are you sure you're trying the correct number?"

"Yes."

"Then I'm sorry, but there's nothing more I can do."

"Okay. Thank you." He hung up.

He groaned. That wasn't good. Unlike here, Warsaw had suffered unrelenting bombardment for weeks. Was his connection problem due to a simple downed telegraph pole? Or had the Nazis razed the capital to the ground?

He dropped his head into his hands. If he couldn't boost his finances, how would he sustain his orphanage? But maybe it was a temporary issue. Perhaps in a day or two, he'd have more success, so it was best not to let disillusionment get the better of him.

Thanking Filip, Mirek left for the square. As he reached the pharmacy, Ludomir exited.

"Ludomir, how's Patryk?"

"Oh, what a world we live in, Mirek. What a world. My poor boy — he can barely move his arm and lost so much blood that he hasn't the strength to stand. But, praise the Lord, the doctor says he should recover."

Mirek patted him on the shoulder. "That's good news. I'm pleased for you all."

"I'll tell him you asked after him."

"If there's anything I can do, Ludomir, you know where I am."

"Bless you, Mirek."

They parted, Mirek continuing on.

But as he turned the corner into the square, he clutched his chest. A chill ran through his veins as if someone had drained his blood and replaced it with ice water. Townsfolk went about their lives without being gunned down, two boys in shorts tussled over a toy car only to be scolded by their mother, and, barring the synagogue, all the buildings stood tall and proud in the autumn sunshine. Even Ula Stern was in her usual spot — sitting on the curb outside the barbershop, selling single candies from a tray in her lap.

All perfectly normal. Except...

Mirek gawked at the town hall, a sign above the entrance now proclaiming it the *Rathaus*. Its Polish flag had disappeared too, replaced by a black swastika inside a white circle on a blood-red background. And its great stone columns that gave it such a majestic air now taunted him with a gigantic red swastika banner hanging down each one.

He stared at a number of German vehicles parked outside. "Oh, good grief."

The Nazis weren't just here — they'd put their headquarters slap-bang in the middle of his beloved town.

He turned in a circle, scanning the square. Everything else seemed fi—

"What the...?"

He marched over to a lamppost and stared at the sign giving the square's name as *Adolf Hitler Square*. Even the hotel on the corner had changed. Part of the sign along the front had been cut down to remove "of Poland," leaving the name as simply "the Flower."

Shaking his head, Mirek turned to leave only for another horror to catch his eye.

"No, no, no. Please, no." He stared at a wall-mounted sign on the road to his home. *Reich Street*.

It was like the Germans were trying to erase everything that made Poland *Poland*. His countrymen weren't supposed to speak Polish in public; they couldn't enjoy Polish newspapers, literature, or radio; they couldn't celebrate Polish achievements through monuments or place names. This wasn't war. No, this was something else. This was cultural extermination.

Why the devil were the Germans doing this? There had to be some long-term goal. But what was it? And what were they going to do next?

Drained by his national identity vanishing before him, Mirek trudged toward the grocery store. But the hairs on the back of his neck prickled — he had the distinct feeling he was being watched.

Again, he scanned the area. No one showed even the slightest interest in him. Weird. He tramped to the street leading off the square.

A chestnut horse clomped by hauling a cart. A man and woman sat in the front, a small child in each of their laps, and the back was piled with cases, bags, boxes, furniture, paintings, a hat stand, chairs... a precarious heap that looked like it would topple with only the tiniest gust of wind.

The whole of Poland was occupied, so where this family thought they were going to find safety, God alone knew. And though only God could see they found it, Mirek doubted He would pick out their prayers to honor while forsaking the tens of millions of others. There was nowhere to run.

As he slouched down the sidewalk, activity outside the bakery dragged him from his dark thoughts. Markus Kaminski cursed as he frantically scrubbed at the wall, where someone had daubed in white paint *For our freedom and yours!*, a slogan used by Polish freedom fighters for over a century.

Mirek did not want to be around when the Germans spotted that. He crossed the street.

At the grocery store, a line snaked along the sidewalk again.

Mirek marched to the front and shouted inside, "Julek!"

A beefy customer shoved him. "Back of the line, pal."

Mirek staggered backward, just catching himself at the curb as a black van honked.

Julek glared through the window. Mirek waved banknotes — his emergency fund. The man's expression immediately lightened. He beckoned Mirek.

Beefy Guy barred his way. "What did I just tell you?"

"Let him in," said Julek, "or you'll be explaining to your wife why you've gone home empty-handed."

Sneering, Beefy Guy stepped aside.

Mirek squeezed inside. "At least someone's doing well from the occupation."

Julek heaved a breath. "I tell you, so many eager customers might seem the perfect situation, but I've already had to break up two fights, and now I'm having to impose rations so I don't disappoint my regulars." He whispered, "And on top of that, some Nazi scum took a third of my stock away in a truck without paying one single grosz."

"So maybe I can brighten your day. How much do I owe?"

Julek flicked through a blue journal beside the register, then wrote something on a scrap of paper and handed it to Mirek.

Mirek nodded, appreciating his discretion. The sum was smaller than he'd imagined. Excellent. And as he was one of Julek's biggest customers, he hoped there was a deal to be struck.

"I can't pay all of it today, but how much would I need to clear to have my deliveries reinstated?"

Clutching each of the apron straps over his chest, Julek peered down his nose at Mirek. "Half."

Mirek counted it out. "It's a pleasure to do business with you, Julek."

"Likewise, Mirek. Expect my boy bright and early."

As he exited the store, he caught a glimpse of a boy ducking around the corner. Mirek had more important things to concern him, so he ignored it.

On his way home, he took a wide berth around the town hall and ambled down to the blackened remains of the synagogue. Amid the rubble, a group of thirty or forty men and boys dug through the debris, searching. Were there bodies still to be found? Maybe even survivors?

In the dark days they were facing, the community had to come together. Mirek opened his mouth to offer his help and that of his bigger boys.

"Run!" shouted a male voice behind him.

Mirek spun.

A teenage boy hared down the road. "For God's sake, run!"

67

12

The teenager flew past as Mirek scanned the area. A woman pushed a stroller toward the jewelry store, men chatted outside the bank, a small boy pulled behind a tree trunk, and a couple walked hand in hand toward a café's outside seating. Everything seemed normal, so what was the teenager so horrified o—

Wait. Mirek squinted at the town hall with his one good eye. His stomach roiled.

Two soldiers raised their rifles at three men sauntering by.

Mirek backed away, fixed on the developing scene, heart racing.

But the soldiers didn't shoot. Instead, they gestured with their rifles for the men to move toward their vehicles, where other soldiers ordered a group of seven men into the back of one of their trucks.

The Germans' position had cut off Mirek's usual route home, so he glanced across at Brudno Street in the south east corner of the square. Clear.

All around the square, more and more women, children, and men scurried away from the town hall area.

In the destroyed synagogue, the men continued shifting the debris, the noise drowning the sounds from the street.

Mirek shouted at the searchers, "Hey!"

No one looked.

"Hey!"

Still no response.

Beside the German trucks, one German spoke to another, pointing to the synagogue.

"Hey!" Mirek hurled a stone at three men carrying a charred beam. It hit one on the arm.

He glowered. "What the...?"

Mirek waved. "Something's wrong. Get away. They're coming!"

"We've got dead here. Show some respect, you gentile idiot."

Marching toward the synagogue, a soldier pointed at Mirek and then the searchers, shouting in German. "You there, come here!"

"Hide!" Mirek backed away.

The soldier marched closer. And raised his rifle.

If Mirek didn't do something, he'd be hauled into one of the trucks. Where would they take him? Would he ever see his children again?

The soldier aimed directly at Mirek.

Mirek gulped. He did the only thing he could — he froze, hands up.

The searchers still hadn't seen the soldier, who shouted again. "You! Here, now!"

A searcher with a black beard looked at the soldier, then shrugged at his portly friend. They continued digging.

Didn't they understand German?

The soldier swung his rifle toward them. "You Polish pigs, come here!"

Eyes as wide as saucers, Mirek stared. What should he do? If he ran, the soldier might shoot him in the back. But if he didn't, he might be taken away and never see his home again.

Trembling, he took a teetering step backward. Nothing happened. His legs shaking, he took another. Then another.

Still the soldier didn't shoot him, being far more concerned with those ignoring his commands.

Mirek took one last step, then...

He spun. Arms and legs pumping faster than he ever thought possible, he bolted. Feet hammering into the cobbles, he flew toward Brudno Street. He prayed no one was chasing him, but all he could hear was his blood pounding in his ears.

He ran and ran. Terrified to glance back. Picturing a soldier just inches behind him, hand outstretched to grab him.

Mirek pushed himself harder, hurtling across the square. Finally, at the start of Brudno Street, he grabbed the corner of the building wall and flung himself around to be flat against it. He panted, lungs burning, yet no matter how wide his mouth gaped, he couldn't suck in enough air.

At the far end of Brudno Street, the road was still narrowed to one lane, the rest blocked by great piles of rubble from the bombing of the ball bearing factory. A single remaining blackened wall stood, windows staring out like dead eyes. Beside that, two schools lay as charred as the synagogue.

Mirek peeked around the wall. Four German soldiers guided the entire group of searchers toward their trucks. What new nightmare was this?

All around the square, soldiers rounded up men and herded them to their trucks while other townsfolk fled.

And to think Mirek had intended to bring his children to help search the synagogue.

His legs wobbly, he braced to push away from the wall and race down Brudno Street but clutched his mouth. "No. Dear Lord, no."

A small boy cowered behind a trash can, clinging to it as if it might somehow save him. A small boy with red hair. Jacek.

That explained the creepy feeling that he was being watched earlier — he was being. Jacek must have somehow sneaked out to follow his surrogate father.

Mirek beckoned.

Wide-eyed, the boy stared but didn't budge.

Mirek waved again, mouthing, "Come here."

Still, the boy remained frozen.

Jacek was much younger than any of the boys from the abducted search party, but would that matter?

Mirek tensed to sprint to the trash can and grab the boy. He gulped a big breath, then surged forward.

A gunshot blasted.

Mirek skidded to a stop, then dove back to the safety of the wall.

Panting, he peeked again. Farther up the square, five soldiers shouted at a group of people dashing into the bank. One fired into the air. The group stopped dead.

Mirek whispered, "Jacek."

Nothing.

Louder. "Jacek."

Jacek shook his head, staring with wide, terrified eyes.

Nearby, three soldiers marched toward a café.

Mirek called louder, "Jacek, come here!"

One of the three glanced around, so Mirek ducked. He clutched his mouth, praying German boots wouldn't stomping toward him.

Grimacing with the effort of doing something that every atom of his being screamed not to, he peeped around the corner again.

The soldiers strode into the café, shouting in German.

No other soldiers were in this area — this was his last chance.

Mirek darted to the trash can, grabbed Jacek, then spun to dart away. But Jacek gripped the can's metal rim and jerked Mirek back.

One of the soldiers emerged from the café, six residents behind him and his comrades bringing up the rear.

Ducking behind the can, Mirek held his breath. Clutched Jacek. Prayed they wouldn't be seen.

But they couldn't stay here. They had to get away. Cold sweat clinging to his back, Mirek peeped out.

One of the rear two soldiers said, "I'll check down here."

Mirek cringed. This was it. This was when his life disappeared. His heart pounded like it was about to explode.

His comrade said, "Let's see how many more we need first."

Mirek dared to breathe and peeped again. The soldiers were marching the detained group away. This was his only chance to escape. But he had to run now.

Mirek swallowed hard to fight the urge to vomit, then ripped Jacek free from the trash can. Holding the boy in his arms, he raced to Brudno Street and out of sight of the square.

Opposite the hospital, he dashed into a small park and along the main tree-lined avenue. A gray-haired couple sitting on a bench stared and muttered to themselves as he panted past, sweat dripping.

He circled the stone fountain, dry since the bombings had disrupted the street's water supply, then cut through rhododendron bushes at the far side. Finally, he lowered Jacek over a brick wall and, with all the elegance of a sack of turnips falling from a truck, he tumbled into the back garden of his house.

Mirek lay on his back on the damp ground, gasping.

Five teenage boys broke off from kicking a soccer ball and stared.

Feliks, a black-haired boy, said, "Papa Mirek, with skills like that, you should've competed in the vault in the Berlin Olympics."

Everyone laughed, including some girls tending to the seedlings.

Mirek clambered up. "Get inside. Now!"

The laughing immediately stopped.

The boy said, "Sorry, Papa Mirek. I only—"

"Now!" Mirek stabbed his hand at the door.

Everyone scurried inside. Mirek followed.

He locked the door, his hand trembling as he removed the key. He stared at it, then gripped it with his other. Turning, he found everyone staring at him with wide-eyed anxiousness.

"In your rooms, please."

A girl with straight brown hair said, "But, Papa Mirek, we haven't—"

"Whoever isn't in their room in the next thirty seconds gets no dinner." He gestured to the other children nearby. "You was well."

He grabbed the black-haired boy's arm. "Feliks, see Jacek gets to his room, please. He's sharing with Tomek."

Feliks nodded and snatched Jacek's hand.

The children stampeded upstairs, tens of pounding feet shaking the house.

"All right, all right, who's making all this ungodly noise?" Hanka marched out of the dining room. Her mouth gaped. "Mirek? What's happened?"

Mopping his face with a white cotton handkerchief, Mirek pointed to his study. "I need to see you."

Ania poked her head out too. "Is everything okay?"

Mirek beckoned. "You as well, please, Ania."

Ania dodged back inside for a moment, then they all went into the study.

Mirek wasn't sure what he'd just witnessed, but whatever it was, it terrified him. Innocent people rounded up at gunpoint? What could it all mean? And more to the point, how could he avoid it happening to those he loved?

13

Mirek doddered toward his desk, his legs wobbly. He caught a glimpse of himself in his round oak-framed mirror and froze at the ashen face staring back at him. Resting a hand on his desk, he steadied himself for a moment, then sat.

Hanka squeezed his shoulder. "For God's sake, Mirek, what's happened?"

He shook his head. "I honestly don't know."

Ania offered a glass of water that she must have grabbed when she'd ducked out of sight.

He reached for it, but his hand trembled.

"Let me." Ania lifted it to his lips, and he sipped.

"Thank you."

Hanka said, "Mirek, please. What have you seen?"

He gestured for them to sit, so they did, faces drawn with worry.

"The Nazis. They..." He wasn't sure what he'd witnessed to describe it. "They're rounding people up at gunpoint. There were men searching the ruins of the synagogue for bodies, and soldiers just... just herded them like stray dogs."

"And what did they do with them?" The lines deepened in Hanka's face.

"Forced them onto trucks."

"To take where?"

He shook his head again. "They were coming for me, so I ran."

Ania clutched her mouth.

Hanka said, "So they were taking just anyone?"

Were they? Mirek relived the scene again, wincing at the horror. "Men. A few boys. Most of them Jews."

"Oh, no." Ania teared up. "The rumors... I..."

Mirek leaned closer. "You've heard something about this?"

"The mayor's wife. She said they've been rounding up people in other towns. Those who came back said they were forced to work in appalling conditions, like slaves."

Hanka held Ania's hand. "Those who came back? You mean some didn't?"

Ania nodded.

"What are we going to do, Mirek?" asked Hanka. "What if they come for the children?"

"There's only one thing we can do." Mirek marched for the door. "Please call everyone into the dining room immediately."

A few minutes later, with everyone in attendance, some of them crying, some whispering, all anxious, Mirek banged his glass on the table in his usual place. Quiet descended.

"I'm afraid I have some bad news. Reasons for why the doors are locked, and must remain locked. A few minutes ago, Feliks made a joke about the Berlin Olympic Games, which some of you will remember because we listened to it on the radio in this very room. And boy, how we cheered when our fabulous athletes won those six medals to show the world what amazing people we Poles are. I can still picture Pawel dancing on the table for each one."

Everybody laughed.

Mirek sighed. Young children shouldn't need to know about the horrors adults could inflict on their world.

"What you probably didn't know is that the games almost never took place because Germany wanted to stop Jewish people and black people from participating. That only changed when many countries refused to go under those conditions. The problem is that Germany is ruled by a man called Adolf Hitler, and this man is—"

Mirek pursed his lips, wondering how much he could say without terrifying the younger ones.

"He's a positively horrible man. And you know I never say such things lightly." He held in his arms wide. "You see, under this roof everyone is equal. We live together, we play together, we work together. Adolf Hitler doesn't like that. He wants to build walls between people, in some cases literally." He pointed at pairs of children sitting together. "If Hitler had his way, Pawel, you couldn't play with Piotr. Marta, you couldn't sleep in the same room as Karol. Agata, you couldn't even talk to Kuba."

Across the room, Agata clutched Kuba and hugged him.

Mirek continued, "Hitler doesn't want people to be equal. So he's filling the world with hatred and pain and violence. But worse, he's taking people away from their friends and family. Sometimes taking them away forever."

Many of the children held each other, tears streaming. He hated having to frighten them, but better they were frightened and safe than carefree and snatched.

"I understand that this is very scary," said Mirek, "but you know that I am always honest with you, so to protect you from this nasty man, there are things I must say. And the most important one is this"— he smiled —"I will always be here for you."

Some of the sniffling stopped.

Mirek said, "We will get through this. All of us. And to do that, I'll be introducing some new rules. But for now, the number one rule is that no one can leave the house except with written permission from me. Is that understood?"

Here and there, children nodded.

But a nod wasn't good enough. Not considering the severity of the situation.

"I said, *no one* can leave the house without written permission from me. *Is that understood?*"

Many children said, "Yes, Papa Mirek."

Mirek scanned the frightened faces. He couldn't leave them to focus solely on the nightmare outside. "Okay, as you all know, whenever there is bad news, there is always good news. And today, the good news is"— he paused to let them bask in the warmth of anticipation after the horrors he subjected them to —"all lessons and chores for today are canceled."

The children cheered.

"So what are you waiting for?" He waved them away. "Go have fun. But remember, inside only."

As the children filtered out, chatting amongst themselves, Hanka and Ania ambled over.

Ania said, "That seemed to go well."

"We're going to have our hands full keeping them all in," said Hanka.

Mirek said, "If they appreciate the dangers so know they're being protected, not punished, they'll be fine." He rubbed his face. "But there's another problem."

"As if we don't have enough. What now?" said Hanka.

"Jacek."

"What's Jacek got to do with anything?" asked Hanka.

"He followed me into town. And as if that isn't dangerous enough, when the soldiers were rounding people up, he froze behind a trash can and refused to move when I called him."

"Oh, dear Lord." Hanka cupped her face.

Mirek held the back of his neck. "If he sneaks out, being abducted is a real danger, but that's only part of the problem. A major issue is what he might witness. Borys said his mother was shot in front of them, so he's obviously traumatized already. We don't want him seeing the Germans abusing innocent people when we've told him he's safe here."

Ania said, "A week after I lost my father and brothers, I found a stray cat, and from that day on, I took it everywhere with me. Literally everywhere. I think I'd have jumped off the railway bridge if it hadn't been for that cat."

Hanka nodded. "Yes, I think he's adopted you, Mirek, whether you like it or not."

"But why? He wouldn't come near me when he first arrived."

Hanka scratched her head. "What did you two talk about that day?"

Mirek shrugged. "The devil if I know."

"Well, whatever it was," said Hanka, "it obviously sparked something in him enough to latch onto you."

"Great." Mirek groaned. "So how do we wean him off?"

"I know I'm only a cleaner and have never dealt with children before," said Ania, "but why not simply talk to him?"

14

Mirek ascended the stairs to the middle floor, which accommodated all the boys. If Jacek really was traumatized, this situation had to be handled sensitively. Instead of requesting Jacek come to Mirek's study like a naughty boy being summoned to the headmaster's office, Mirek was going to him.

Mirek had seen goslings trailing after Lech, his farmer friend, having adopted him as a surrogate parent, even though he was the wrong species. Small creatures did that. The error couldn't be explained to them, but he hoped it could be to Jacek.

Three boys roughhoused on the mattress on the floor of Jacek's bedroom, with others shouting encouragement from the bunks on either side. Jacek was slumped on a lower bunk, staring at the floor.

Mirek made a point of ignoring the red-haired boy, wanting to give the impression that his visit didn't concern him. He laughed as a fat boy, Zygmunt, sat on two skinny ones. "If I were you two, I'd say uncle as quickly as I could."

Zygmunt bounced up and down, making his two opponents groan.

The squashed boys shouted, "Uncle! Uncle!"

Zygmunt rolled off.

"Boys," said Mirek, "could I have a word in private with our latest arrival, please?" He purposefully didn't use Jacek's name, but Jacek immediately looked at Mirek.

Excellent. Definitive proof the boy wasn't deaf and understood Polish.

Once they were alone, Mirek crouched to Jacek's level.

This time, the boy didn't pull away. But his eyes oozed such sadness, Mirek could have wept.

"I'm sorry for what happened to your mama." Mirek cupped the boy's hand. "Now you're living with us, I promise to do everything I can to keep you safe. On top of that, you'll have friends, food, and warmth. Everything you need. I hope that, even after the horrible things that have happened, one day you'll be happy again. I'm going to do everything I can to make that possible."

Jacek just stared with the saddest eyes Mirek had ever seen.

Mirek said, "Unfortunately, for me to look after everyone here, I have to set rules. Some are easy to follow, whereas others are harder. But the only reason these rules exist is to keep you safe. Do you understand?"

Jacek lowered his gaze.

"Jacek, it's important you understand. Do you?"

The boy nodded once.

"So I can rely on you to follow the rules?"

The boy looked up. But he didn't say anything and didn't nod.

Mirek sighed. The boy had interacted to a degree and, as far as Mirek could tell, had understood the instructions. To push him further could undo the good Mirek had just done – the tentative connection he'd established. Instead, he'd leave it for now and monitor the boy over the coming days.

Mirek left.

The following morning, lessons and chores resumed. As, thankfully, did food deliveries. With no good reason to go outside, for the next few weeks, Mirek, Hanka, and his children didn't leave the house.

One evening, Mirek and Ania exited the study after her reading lesson. While he locked the door, she placed a hand on his arm.

"I can't tell you how much I appreciate you doing this for me."

"You're a valuable member of my staff, so you're more than welcome."

She smiled. "Thank you."

"Tell Hanka I'll be along in a moment. I have to collect something from the classroom."

"Okay." Ania strolled away.

Walking past, a dark-haired teenage girl smirked at him.

"Something to say, Lena?"

"You know she likes you, don't you?"

Mirek groaned. "What's Baba Hanka been saying?"

"Baba Hanka? Nothing. She doesn't have to. I've got eyes."

"Yes, well, you and those eyes better find something else to look at. Understood?"

Her smirk faded. "Yes, Papa Mirek."

A few minutes later, he joined Ania and Hanka in the deserted dining room. Every evening, Ania provided news from the "outside world," though no one seemed to know exactly what was happening. Even the Germans – they changed the laws governing what Poles and Jews were allowed to do almost daily. Confusion abounded.

Sitting at the table, Hanka snorted. "Well, it sounds like collaborating to me."

Mirek said, "Doing what you must do to live is *not* collaborating, Hanka, it's surviving."

"So if I end up"– she made quotation marks in the air with her fingers –"*surviving*, you have my permission to shoot me."

Mirek looked at Ania. "So how does this Jewish Council choose who to send to work for the Germans?"

"I don't know."

Hanka sipped a glass of water. "Apart from finding slave labor for the Germans, does this council do anything worthwhile?"

Ania shrugged.

"But it's only Jews?" asked Mirek.

"Yes."

"And the people they take are either working in the quarry or laying railroad track?"

"As far as I know."

"Why?" Mirek scratched his head. "Where does the track go?"

Hanka said, "Julek's delivery boy said it goes toward the forest."

Mirek frowned. "Why the devil would the Germans waste time building a railway track to a forest?"

Ania said, "Maybe it's just a way to punish the Jews. Like you said, it's slave labor, so does it need to actually achieve anything?"

Maybe it didn't. Stories of anti-Semitism-fueled persecution were coming from all corners of Poland. Whatever the Germans had in mind, it wasn't easy to fathom. But did that matter? Every day, the Jewish Council selected up to one hundred men and boys over the age of fourteen. To date, most of them had come home safe. Exhausted, hungry, and often beaten, but safe.

It was a small price to pay if it was going to see their town safely through the war. After all, if the residents were following the new rules, no matter how ridiculous or arbitrary they seemed, why would the Nazis further disturb the status quo?

Hanka pointed at the clock above the hatch. "It's nearly eleven. We've been going around in circles for hours trying to second-guess the Germans. I think that's enough for one day, don't you?"

"You're right." Mirek rose to leave. "Let's call it a day."

Ania didn't move. "There's one more thing."

He sank, Ania's tone suggesting it was not good news coming.

"They're sacking the mayor," said Ania. "In fact, they're sacking all the town officials and replacing them with German administrators."

"Oh good grief, no," said Hanka.

"What about our funding?" asked Mirek. The orphanage received a small amount from the community coffers. His eyes widened. "And your job? You won't have to move away, will you?" Ania was already a valuable member of his extended family.

"Markus says if it comes to it, I can help in the bakery to cover my rent."

Mirek said, "But—"

Hammering on the front door made everyone jump.

15

Mirek glared at the front door. Again, someone pounded the other side, the door shaking under the force. It was way too late for any sort of social call or delivery, so what nightmare were they about to be dragged into?

Hanka and Ania peeked from the dining room doorway, huddled together.

The stairs creaked behind him. Mirek jumped, then spun.

Three children crept down, and more gathered in the gloom higher up.

He stabbed a finger upstairs and whispered, "Bed. Now."

Swallowing hard, he reached for the key in his breast pocket. With nearly one hundred people in the house, it was impossible to pretend there was no one home. He had no choice but to answer.

The key trembled in his hand. "Who is it?"

"Ludomir Sajdak. Let me in, quick."

Ludomir? At this time?

Fumbling the key, Mirek unlocked the door. Ludomir had been a good friend over the years, but what if he'd been selected by the Jewish Council and was looking for somewhere to hide? If he failed to show up for work and the Germans found him here...

Mirek pulled the door open, ready to sympathize with Ludomir but to make it clear that some forms of help were beyond him.

Ludomir barged in, carrying a heavy body-shaped mass wrapped in a canvas over his shoulder. "I thought you were never going to answer."

"Ludomir, I'm sorry but—"

The man slung the canvas mass off. It thudded into the floor. "For you."

Mirek squinted at it, then at Ludomir. Whatever it was, it was dead.

Mirek crouched, loosened the ties, then lifted one edge of the canvas. Bloody flesh stared up at him.

Ludomir smiled. "It's only half, but I hope it helps."

Mirek pulled the canvas away to reveal a side of wild boar.

"It's a little big for a midnight snack," Mirek offered his hand, "but I'm sure we'll find some use for it. Thank you."

Ludomir shook Mirek's hand. "Many in the Jewish community appreciate what you're doing for our lost children, but life is, shall we say, somewhat trying at the moment, so showing that appreciation isn't always easy."

"Come on through." Mirek beckoned toward the dining room. "Hanka, the vodka and some glasses, please."

Ludomir chuckled. "It is the Sabbath, but if the good Lord hadn't intended for us to drink vodka, He'd never have created Poland."

Mirek carried the boar into the kitchen and then they all sat in the dining room, Hanka bringing a tantalus containing three decanters. Mirek selected the correct key from his key ring, unlocked the wooden block across the bottom of the wooden, caddy-like contraption, and removed the middle decanter.

Glancing at Ludomir, he said, "Can't be too careful with so many children around."

He poured four drinks and passed them around.

They toasted. "Cheers."

"We've just been talking about the Jewish Council," said Mirek. "Do you know anything about it? Like who's on it and what have you?"

"Rabbi Grodzinski, Rosenbaum, Mayor Silberman, Wojcik... there's twelve in all." Ludomir rubbed his face. "I can't say that I agree with the whole thing, but the alternative..." He winced. "At least this way the community retains some control."

"It's collaborating," said Hanka. "Plain and simple."

"That's as may be, Hanka," said Ludomir, "but this way we get to choose who goes to work — the fit, the healthy, the young. That has to be better than the Germans snatching whoever they feel like off the street, Jew or non-Jew."

"I suppose that's one way of looking at it," said Hanka.

Ludomir toyed with his glass. "The Council says they're going to be able to help the community, but I'm not seeing it so far."

Mirek said, "Is it true the workers are building a railway line?"

Ludomir nodded. "A spur from the mainline."

"To where?"

"They're building something near the forest."

Mirek leaned closer. "What?"

Ludomir sipped his drink, then held the glass up and admired it. "Mmm. Smooth."

Mirek said, "Only the best after the gift you brought us. Now, this thing in the forest, what are the Germans building?"

"I don't know."

Mirek scratched his head. "I thought you said Jews from our town were building it?"

"No. They're only building the rail line."

Mirek leaned back. "So no one's seen this thing?"

"Oh, I've seen it all right." Ludomir took another swig. "Ohhh, that's nice."

"So...?"

"As far as I can tell, it's some sort of camp."

"Like an army barracks?"

"Maybe. It was hard to tell. I stumbled upon it while hunting, but I didn't want to get too close for obvious reasons." He pointed at Mirek. "Not far from our hide. Though it might be wise to relocate that now."

"I don't understand," said Ania. "If the townsfolk are only building the railway line, who's building the camp? The Germans?"

All eyes turned to Ludomir.

He laughed. "The Germans? Like the Germans are going to dirty their hands when they've got a free labor force."

Ania said, "So who's doing it?"

"I don't know."

Mirek rubbed his brow. While he appreciated Ludomir's generosity in bringing them food he could've kept for his own family, trying to get information from him was as painful as walking in ill-fitting wooden clogs.

Ludomir enjoyed another drink. "They're bringing them in by train."

Mirek's eyebrows raised. "Excuse me?"

"The people building the camp. The Nazis are shipping them in by train. Our people working on the line have seen them. They ship them in packed in cattle wagons, so whoever they are, you can bet they're not German." Ludomir finished his drink. "That's all I know."

So who were these people? And what the devil were they building in the middle of nowhere?

16

Winter 1940.

The Jewish Council continued supplying a daily workforce, which appeared to appease the invaders because while the workers suffered beatings and hellish conditions, Mirek didn't hear of anyone being abducted from the streets.

Unfortunately, though the peace in the town was good news, the bad news was that the peace in the house had long since fractured. Almost one hundred people crammed into such a small space was bound to lead to conflict, so each day of self-imposed imprisonment brought more tension.

Mirek pulled two boys apart in the dining room, one with a busted lip, the other a bloody nose. All around, children gawked at the spectacle.

The boys squirmed to break free.

"Stop it. Now!" Mirek tightened his grip. "If you think being locked in the house is restricting, imagine what it would be like being locked in your room."

The boys calmed.

Hanka stormed over. "You again, Bruno? Your lip's still swollen from yesterday. And you, Tomek? You've never thrown a punch before in your life. What's caused this now?"

Tomek said, "He stole my spoon."

"I did not." Bruno swiped at Tomek again, but Mirek held him at bay. "It's my spoon. I've been using it all week."

Hanka folded her arms. "A spoon? You two are best friends, but you're making each other bleed over a spoon?"

She shook her head at Mirek.

Mirek sighed. This wasn't working. Something had to change. But there was only one thing he could do. One. And if it went wrong, the consequences would haunt him forever.

The boys having cooled off, Mirek released them. "Okay, shake hands and then you're both helping Hanka with whatever chores she sees fit."

Begrudgingly, they shook hands, then tramped to the kitchen. Hanka stood, hands on her hips. "This isn't working, Mirek."

"I know."

"So you know what has to be done."

"But—" He hung his head. If anything happened to just one child, he'd never forgive himself.

"We can't coddle them forever." She pointed at the floor. "Here, right now, we are the ones making them prisoners, not the Germans."

Mirek nodded.

She said, "So?"

He rubbed his face. "It's time to open the door."

She patted his arm. "You know it's the only way. Free people need to feel that they're free. They need a reason to carry on."

Hanka was right. Locking the children in the house made them physically safe, but mentally, it was crippling them. There hadn't been a killing all month, so maybe now was the time to risk letting them remember what life was all about — living it.

At the foot of the stairs, Mirek banged the dinner gong, an instrument rarely used these days because everyone was always so hungry that, approaching mealtimes, they all hung around the area. Within seconds, everyone had squeezed into the dining room again.

With all eyes on him, Mirek opened his mouth to speak but shut it again. Could he really do this? He looked to Hanka. She nodded.

There was a time for long speeches, and then there was a time when just a handful of words could deliver the most wondrous of messages. What did this moment call for?

Mirek gazed at the expectant faces. He turned away and strolled out of the dining room. Whispers and puzzlement engulfed the house.

He poked his head back in. "The sun's out."

Silence descended and bewildered gazes shot around the room.

Mirek wiggled the front door key. "Anyone coming?"

He laughed as tens of children scrambled to be the first outside. Mirek opened the door.

The apple tree's branches drooped under inches of snow, and a deep carpet of glistening white hid the ground. Within seconds, hurtling snowballs, gleeful shrieks, and the wondrous sound of children's laughter filled the air.

"Stay this side of town, please. The square is off-limits." As more children pushed out, he repeated, "Stay this side of town, please. Anyone caught beyond the hardware store will be confined to the house for a week."

Children streamed out of the courtyard, grinning, laughing, joking, simply being children.

Mirek smiled at the joy. At how something as simple as leaving the house could make one feel so rejuvenated, so empowered, so free.

As the last few children trickled out, Hanka approached. "You had to do it."

He grimaced. "But what if something bad happens?"

"Then something bad happens while everyone is happy instead of while they're miserable. Isn't that better?"

Looking at it that way, yes, it was better. Much better.

Hanka said, "So what are you going to do with your free afternoon?"

His jaw dropped. Of course. If all the children had gone, there was no one to teach. He smirked, picturing his armchair in his study, a book, and a house completely devoid of interruptions and noise. Heaven.

Ania squeezed through the children playing near the courtyard gate. Face aglow with the contagious happiness, she sauntered over. "What's all this?"

Mirek shrugged. "Time off for good behavior."

She laughed. "Wouldn't you just know it, I missed the big event."

Standing in the doorway, Mirek rubbed his chin. A book was one way to go, but maybe there was another option.

Ania gestured to the hallway. "So are you going to let me in?"

"Uh..." He bit his lip. "Actually, no."

Ania frowned. "What's going on?"

He grinned. "Do you like surprises?"

17

Mirek and Ania stepped into a street bustling with more children than Mirek had seen in it for what felt like years. Across the road, Pawel laughed with two children outside the tailor's store.

"Give me a second, please," said Mirek.

Ania said, "Of course."

He strolled over and gave Pawel instructions and five zlotys, plus a few extra grosz to treat himself for running this errand. He then rejoined Ania.

Gesturing in the opposite direction to the square, he said, "This way."

Fifteen minutes later, Mirek held aside the dangling branches of a weeping willow. Beside it, a fast-flowing river glistened in the winter's sharp sunshine. Snow tumbled onto the path.

"So are we going anywhere in particular?" Ania strolled past.

"Do we have to be?"

"No."

"Because we can go back, shut ourselves in my stuffy study, and stick our faces in another dusty book if you'd prefer."

She arched an eyebrow.

He pointed back. "Really. It's no trouble."

She smirked. "So if I hadn't turned up at that very moment, can you swear, hand on heart, that being shut in that *stuffy study with another dusty book* isn't exactly what you were dreaming about with all the children gone?"

Straight-faced, he said, "It never crossed my mind."

She shot him a sideways glance. "If that's your poker face, you'd better pray you're never interrogated."

He frowned. Was he such a bad liar? He'd always believed he could tell a convincing white lie or spin a credible story if the occasion demanded it. However, most of the time, that was when interacting with children. Maybe he needed to brush up on adult psychology.

A bird with shimmering blue plumage darted across the river. Mirek pointed. "Kingfisher."

She smiled, following his gaze.

He said, "In many parts of the country, they fly south for the winter because the rivers freeze, but this one's too fast-flowing, so they usually stay."

"I can see why it stayed. It's lovely here. Thanks for bringing me."

"I didn't."

Her brow wrinkled. "Excuse me?"

"*Here.*" He pointed downward. "I didn't bring you *here.*"

"So where did you bring me?"

He pointed away across a field. "There."

Pawel and a chubby man in muddy coveralls stood at the far side of the field near a barn. Between them stood a brown mare, her coat gleaming in the sun.

Ania clutched her mouth. "That's not..."

"For you? Who else would it be for?"

She stared at the horse.

"But..." She laughed. "I've never..." She laughed again.

Mirek guided her toward a stile in the stone wall. "You said it was something you'd always dreamed of doing, so..."

She took his hand when he offered it and negotiated the stile. "But I've never even sat on a horse."

"And you'd never read a book through, until you did."

He climbed over behind her.

"But what if I fall off?"

"And what if you don't and you have a wonderful time?"

She grabbed a handful of her flowing black skirt. "But look at what I'm wearing."

Mirek pointed at Lech. "No problem. I'm sure Lech's wife has something you can borrow."

"You've got an answer for everything, haven't you? You're really going to make me do this."

"What a monster." He winked.

They ambled across the meadow, the ankle-deep snow crunching underfoot. As they neared the barn, Ania brushed her hair down over the left side of her face.

"Pawel, you get off now. Thanks for your help."

The boy scooted away.

"Afternoon, Lech." Mirek offered his hand and they shook. "This is Ania."

"Mirek, Ania." Lech patted his horse. "Here she is, saddled and ready when you are."

"I'm sorry, Lech, but this lunatic"— Ania elbowed Mirek —"never told me what we were doing, so I didn't come prepared. I can't possibly ride like this, can I?"

"Don't worry, there's something in the barn of my Danuta's that should fit."

Mirek smiled. "I told you — there's no getting out of this."

Biting her bottom lip, Ania trudged into the barn. She glanced around, then disappeared behind hay bales. Meanwhile, Lech adjusted the stirrups for Ania's height.

A few minutes later, she shuffled out wearing baggy blue pants. Again, she combed her hair to hide her face.

Ania stared at the horse and gulped. Her voice faltered. "It's so big. It won't bite if I do something wrong, will it?"

Lech stroked the horse's mane. "Never you mind, Ania. Felka here's as gentle as a lamb and twice as forgiving."

He handed the reins to Mirek. "I'll let you take it from here." He toddled away.

Mirek reached for Ania, standing on the left-hand side of the horse, the reins in one hand. "Come meet Felka."

Hunched, Ania tottered nearer and, her hand shaking, reached for his.

He guided her closer, then stroked the horse's neck. "You try."

She reached out as if wary of touching something that could be scorching hot. Finally, her hand lightly brushed the brown hide.

The horse merely stood, minding its own business.

Ania smiled, running her hand down the horse's neck. "It's so smooth."

"She. Felka's female."

"Hello, Felka." Ania petted her. "I hope you're going to be gentle with me."

"Don't worry, as long as you follow the one golden rule, everything will be fine."

She looked at him expectantly. "And that is?"

"If you fall off, don't land on your head."

"Oh, really?"

"See? Simple, isn't it?"

She shot him a sideways glance and stroked Felka again. "Can't we just do this for a while, then go home? Hanka will be panicking without me there to help."

Before leaving, Mirek had had a quick chat with Hanka, reminding her that what he was contemplating was actually her idea, thus giving her no grounds to object.

Mirek patted the saddle. "Come on."

Ania drew a huge breath, then plodded closer. "Oh my stars, oh my stars…"

He pointed to the saddle's horn. "Hold this with the left hand."

She did.

"Now put your left foot in here." He gestured to the left stirrup.

She did.

"Now, pull yourself up and throw your right leg over to sit in the saddle."

Her eyes widened with fear. "Seriously?"

"Seriously." He nodded. "It might sound complicated, but once you push off the ground, it will feel a perfectly natural movement."

She stared at the saddle, panting.

He said, "Take your time."

Her whole body tensed as if she was going to mount, but she didn't move. Instead, she relaxed again.

He said, "Whenever you're ready."

Quietly, as if talking to herself, she said, "This time. This time."

She took a huge gulp, heaved on the horn while pushing down into the stirrup, and left the ground. Her right leg swung over the horse's back, and she plonked into the saddle.

With a look of utter astonishment, she said, "I did it! I did it!"

Mirek raised his hand as if to slap the horse's rump, pointing with his other hand at the five-foot-high hedge down the left-hand side of the field. "About five paces from the hedge, dig your heels into the horse's sides and she'll fly over."

"What?" Ania's eyes almost popped out of her head.

Mirek laughed.

She slapped his shoulder. "Don't do that."

"Yes. Sorry." Mirek held the lead rope and gave the reins to Ania. "Don't pull on these, just get used to holding them. Okay?"

"Okay."

"Ready?"

Fear and joy lining her face, Ania nodded.

Standing at Felka's left shoulder, Mirek gently pulled the horse forward. "Walk, girl. Walk."

Felka set off. Ania gasped, her knuckles white on the saddle horn. "Don't leave me."

"I won't."

"Really. Please don't."

They slowly walked out into the field. When Mirek next turned, Ania was smiling. They continued on — slowly — toward the bottom of the field.

Every time Mirek checked on Ania, she was beaming. Her hair flew in the light breeze, revealing her scars, but never once did she try to cover them.

At the bottom, they turned and walked back up.

When they reached the barn, Mirek said, "Are you okay?"

"Wonderful."

"You feel safe?"

"Uh-huh."

"So you want to ride more?"

Grinning, she nodded.

They walked in a circle and then a figure eight.

Approaching the bottom of the field, Ania said, "We've got a spy."

"What?"

"A spy. Near the stile." She pointed at the wall on the riverbank. "He's just ducked out of sight."

A spy? Why would anyone be spying on them?

Mirek led the horse to the wall and peered through the stile. A little boy huddled behind the wall.

"Jacek!"

Jacek bolted back along the path.

So much for their talk having resolved the issue. Maybe he'd let Hanka try in the hope that the boy responded better to women.

Mirek led Felka in another figure eight.

Next, he instructed Ania on using the reins to turn Felka. They then completed more figure eights, Ania using the reins and he only guiding the horse if Ania seemed to struggle.

Finally, they stopped near the barn. He stroked Felka. "Well?"

"I could do this all day, but if that's it..."

"That wasn't the question."

"So what was?"

He nodded over his shoulder. "The field's there. And you're holding the reins."

Her eyes widened with anxiety. "By myself?"

"Uh-huh."

She puffed out her cheeks. "But you have to walk alongside."

"I will."

"You can't go anywhere."

"I won't."

"Promise."

"I promise. I'll stay with you the whole time."

"Okay."

He gestured to the field. "Ready when you are."

"Walk, Felka." She gave the horse a pat and they set off, Mirek walking alongside.

Ania beamed all the more. "Mirek, look. I'm riding a horse. I'M RIDING A HORSE!"

Over the years, he'd shared more than one thousand birthday celebrations, and yet, at that moment, it was as if he was witnessing pure joy for the very first time.

In another world, another time, maybe he and Ania would have a shot at a relationship. Possibly even a life together. But here, now? Was it just a fantasy or, despite the nightmare engulfing them, was there a chance they might share happiness?

18

That night, the evening meal was late, Hanka having had to prepare much of it without Ania's help. However, with everyone having been liberated from their prison, no one cared. The house glowed with laughter and warmth.

As everyone ate, Mirek listened to the conversations around him — who'd done what, who'd met who, what they intended to do tomorrow... Things almost felt "normal," as if the occupation had ceased to exist. And after his magical afternoon with Ania, he too couldn't help but wonder what joys the morning might bring. Maybe living under the Nazis wouldn't be that bad after all.

Once the children left, and skipping Ania's lesson because it was already late, he, Hanka, and Ania met for their nightly chat. However, while Mirek and Hanka talked, Ania picked at a hangnail. Then stared at the table top. All in silence.

After how elated Ania had been that afternoon, why was she now so subdued? Had Mirek overstepped his bounds in forcing her to do something she'd been afraid of? Or worse, had he coerced an employee into spending time with her employer as if they were friends?

Whatever it was, something was wrong. He'd believed they'd had a wonderful time — together — but that was obviously not the case. Still, he wasn't going to push the issue by opening his big mouth.

Hanka nodded. "Okay, I'll see if I can get through to him. We can't have him following you, even if it is safer right now." She looked at Ania. "Are you okay, Ania? You've barely said a word."

Mirek cringed. The last thing he wanted was this being dragged up.

"I..." Ania looked at Mirek with sadness in her eyes. "I didn't want to say anything earlier because it's been such a special day, but..."

So maybe it wasn't anything he'd done. "But what?"

"The mayor's wife told me something. Something horrible."

Hanka slumped. "Not more bad news, please."

Ania hung her head. "Sorry. Forget I said anything."

"No, I'm sorry." Hanka patted Ania's hand. "It's not your fault. What is it?"

"In some towns, the Germans are creating ghettos. They're evicting whole areas and cramming thousands of Jews into just a few city blocks."

Hanka wrinkled her nose. "No. That's just another one of those ridiculous rumors."

"It's true, Hanka. It's happened in Otwock, Radomsko, Plock... lots of places."

"Thousands?" Mirek frowned. "But how do they all fit?"

"They're packing four or five families into an apartment meant for one. In some places, there're ten or twelve people sleeping in each room."

"Those poor souls." Mirek rubbed his brow. "And we thought we were overcrowded."

Hanka gasped. "Does that mean they're going to do it here?"

"They haven't done it in Warsaw yet, so..." Ania shrugged.

"How about Krakow? Poznan? Wroclaw?" asked Mirek.

Ania winced. "I don't think so."

If it hadn't been done in the big cities, maybe those mentioned were isolated cases caused by localized issues. That meant it probably wasn't something that would be rolled out across the country. Mirek had to hope so. Cramming so many people together was inhumane. It was as if the Germans didn't see Jews as people but as another species, an inferior species. Hitler's anti-Semitism was one thing, but for an entire nation to adopt his philosophy and persecute a minority... what had the world come to that good people would sit by and let such atrocities happen?

Hanka clutched her mouth. "If it happened here, would they take all our Jewish children away?"

Mirek held her hand. "Don't torment yourself. Ania says it hasn't happened in Warsaw, so we're probably safe."

"*Probably*? But what if we're not?" Tears formed in Hanka's eyes.

A pain swelled in Mirek's chest. He longed to tell her it would *never* happen here because he'd protect them if the Germans tried anything so outrageous, but he couldn't — she'd know that was impossible because the husbands, brothers, fathers, and grandfathers in Radomsko would have told their families exactly the same thing.

Hanka wiped her eyes. "Mirek, we have to leave."

"Leave? Leave where?"

"Here."

"*Here?* You mean leave our home?"

"It's our only choice. We can't risk the Germans taking our children. We have to protect them."

"Hanka..." Mirek cupped his face. Could she be right?

Finally, he said, "Where would we go? Between them, the Germans and Soviets control every single border. Plus, how the devil could we even smuggle nearly a hundred people to another town, let alone another country?"

"Borys can help. He can get us all false papers."

"Papers saying what? That we're a particularly large family? It's impossible to move so many people in one go."

A tear trickled down her cheek. "But we can't just sit and do nothing."

"So where would we run to? Even if we knew of a town that's managing better than ours, there's no guarantee that would last. We might get there only for things to be ten times worse within a week."

Ania said, "Maybe it's a case of better the devil you know, Hanka."

"Exactly," said Mirek. "It sounds like we have it better than many places, so let's not do anything rash and ruin that."

Hanka slapped the table. "We can't do nothing."

Mirek held his hands up. "Okay. Then tell me where we'll all be safe and I'll have every child down here with a packed bag within the hour."

Hanka stared. Her lips moved, but no words came out. There were none.

19

"Mirek?" shouted Hanka, waddling from the kitchen as he was leaving the dining room.

"Yes?"

"Will you be seeing Lech today?"

"I wasn't intending to. Why?"

She waved a piece of paper. "There's been a new ordinance."

"Oh no."

The worst of the winter months had passed largely without incident. Thanks to the labor provided by the Jewish Council, the Germans seemed content to maintain the status quo, forsaking the brutality they'd exhibited earlier. The town escaped a ghetto being established, which was a huge relief for the entire community, but the Nazis did impose other restrictions. Most aimed at the Jews, but not all.

Hanka gestured around the corner outside the dining room so they could talk away from the children enjoying breakfast.

Mirek said, "Don't tell me it's the rations again."

"They've cut the meat again — nine ounces for the Aryans and two for the Jews."

Mirek shrugged. "Could be worse."

"Worse? That's per week, Mirek. *Per week*."

"Oh, dear Lord." This time last year, nine ounces had represented one large steak at the Flower of Poland. Now that was to last a week?

In isolation, many of the restrictions were manageable, though not all. Some were inconvenient, some insulting, some cruel, some criminal, some punitive. But because they were imposed gradually over months, people generally accepted them and got on with their lives as best they could. However, when taken as a whole, the restrictions made normal living impossible, with life being absolute hell for some.

Hanka said, "Even sharing everything equally, everyone's going to go hungry. *Everyone.*"

Mirek did a double take at a boy coming down the stairs in a coat.

"Excuse me, Hanka." He dashed over. "Pawel?"

"Yes, Papa Mirek?"

Mirek pointed to the boy's sleeve. "Where's your armband?" In public, every Jew over ten years old had to wear an armband with a Star of David.

Pawel rolled his eyes. "Sorry." He tramped back toward the stairs.

"Don't be sorry, be careful." Mirek returned to Hanka. "Where's Feliks? Isn't he supposed to be on star duty?"

"Sorry, my fault. He's running an errand."

"Hanka, someone has to be on the front door checking armbands."

"I'm sorry, leave it with me. Now, what are we going to do—"

"Hanka, *now.*" Mirek held his brow. "We need someone on the door *now*. Just because the Germans haven't yet shot anyone for not wearing a star doesn't mean they won't."

Under German law, the Nazis were entitled to execute anyone on the spot, and Mirek didn't want the first victim to be one of his children.

"You're right." She toddled into the dining room. "Lena, if you've finished eating, can you do star duty until Feliks gets back, please?"

The teenage girl said, "Okay, Baba Hanka."

Hanka rejoined Mirek while Lena sauntered into the foyer.

Hanka waved her paper. "Black market prices are outrageous. Do you think Lech might help?"

"I can ask. Borys is bringing another two children today and swore he'd bring food as well, but I'll twist his arm for more."

"More children? Including you, me, and Ania, that's 101 mouths to feed. Mirek, we can't go on like this."

"I know, but—"

A deafening voice blasted from outside. Distorted and in German. *"Achtung! Achtung!"* An announcement followed, but with the thickness of the house walls and the distortion, it was difficult to comprehend.

Mirek's jaw dropped. "What the...?"

Mirek and Hanka dashed into the street. A black car with a megaphone mounted on its roof drove by. An announcement came in German and then in Polish.

"Attention! Attention! All citizens must report to Adolf Hitler Square at noon today."

Wide-eyed, Hanka looked at him. Her chin trembled.

Was this it? Was this when their household was ripped apart?

***

At 11:30 a.m., Mirek tramped through slush to lead his household to the square, with Hanka at the rear encouraging the stragglers. He didn't want to go early but feared the consequences of being unable to squeeze into the square as instructed.

Already, hordes of people gathered, with more streaming in. The last time he could recall such a gathering was after the Great War. Poland hadn't existed for 123 years because of conflicts, occupations, and annexations. Then, on November 11, 1918, Poland had reclaimed its independence. And boy, had the Poles celebrated.

Today, however, there was no drinking, no singing, no jubilation. Today, darkness drenched every single face, and an unnerving quietness hung over the square. Mirek would have thought it impossible that so many people could be so quiet.

Soldiers lined the stone steps to the town hall entrance, and the narrow lawned grounds directly in front had been cordoned off, with machine-gun-toting soldiers stationed every few feet. Two cars sat within the grounds – the one with the megaphone and another partially shrouded under a tarpaulin.

Mirek followed the crowd as soldiers and Blue Police guided everyone into the square to keep the access routes clear.

People already packed the outermost edges of the square, the farthest point from the Nazi HQ they could be, leaving the middle empty. Mirek led his group into the space, thanking heaven they'd set off early so they wouldn't be crammed right in front of the HQ. He watched the latecomers squash in front of him, creating a buffer of hundreds of people between his group and those machine guns.

As the church bells chimed midday, everyone stared at the town hall's heavy black doors. Waiting.

The doors didn't open. The soldiers didn't move.

Silence lingered like that of a graveyard at midnight, and the hair on the back of Mirek's neck prickled.

In other towns, residents had been evicted and crammed into ghettos. Was that what was about to happen?

A hand clutched his, causing him to jump. He looked down – Agata. Another small hand joined it, while another held his coat, and another. All around, children clutched him for reassurance. If only he could give them some.

Still the doors stood motionless.

What were the Germans doing? Why force them to be here and then torture them like this?

Finally, the right-hand door creaked open.

In a long black leather coat, a German officer strutted down the steps with an aide. Halfway down, he stopped. The aide gestured, and a soldier handed the officer a microphone, its cable leading to the car with the megaphone.

From his higher vantage point, he scanned the crowd. He leaned to his aide, holding the microphone away so it wouldn't catch what was said.

The aide nodded. He dashed down the steps, gave instructions to one of the soldiers, then shouted at the crowd. "Children to the front. Children to the front."

A woman near Mirek wrapped her long coat around a small girl to hide her. Mirek had so many children that they'd be visible from all directions. Especially when the people in front of him parted to let him through, knowing it meant they could move farther away.

Agata cried. "I don't like it. I want to go home."

Sweating, Mirek said, "We'll, eh, go soon, princess. We just have to, eh, go a little closer first."

His legs stiff, as if they didn't want to move, he shuffled forward and guided his household to the front, childless adults only too eager to exchange places.

All the hands clinging to Mirek clung even tighter as he stood barely six feet from a soldier with a jagged scar across his left cheek and a machine gun aimed directly at Mirek. That gun's black muzzle could fill his world with so much blood and pain.

Some of his children whimpered, some trembled, others wept silently.

Mirek hated seeing his children petrified, but he was partly thankful – they were so upset they'd never see how he was shaking.

With hundreds of families and children squashed to the front, the aide returned to his commander's side.

Now closer, Mirek could see the officer clearly – tall, muscular build, square-jawed, blond. Everything an Aryan was supposed to be.

The officer spoke. "I am SS-Hauptsturmführer Kruger."

He waited, as if his name was supposed to mean something.

"You" – he paused – "are ungrateful scum." His voice boomed around the square from the speaker. "I'm sure you've heard about the ghettos in other towns, the evictions, the harsh restrictions. Far, far worse than those I have imposed here. And how do you repay this kindness?"

He waited as if expecting a reply.

Throughout the crowd, whispered voices translated the German for others.

With a tip of his head, Kruger signaled his aide, who whipped the tarpaulin off the covered car.

Down the side of the black vehicle, in large white letters, was daubed *For our freedom and yours!*

Mirek gulped. If this Kruger was so upset he'd called a town meeting over one tiny bit of graffiti, there was no telling what he would judge appropriate retribution.

"But I don't blame you," said Kruger. "No, I blame myself. Foolishly, I treated you with a velvet glove when what is obviously needed is an iron gauntlet. But let me assure you that I learn from my mistakes, so will not be making that one again." He descended a couple more steps. "Now, which one of you believes themselves an artist?"

Mirek pulled the children nearest him closer. This was not going to end well, and he didn't want his family being dragged into it. He tried to back away, but with so many people packed in behind him, he couldn't budge an inch.

Kruger said, "Come now, make yourself known. Surely if you're so proud to be Polish, you'll relish an opportunity to prove it in front of your whole community."

Anxious glances flashed around thousands of faces.

The animal part of Mirek's brain screamed at him to run. Run and never, never stop. But even if he could fight his way through so many people, he could never abandon his children.

Kruger pointed at a boy in blue. "Was it you?"

The boy shook his head vigorously.

Kruger prowled farther and pointed at a girl with pigtails. "You?"

Her face screwed up and she cried.

Kruger rolled his eyes. He prowled on, stopping directly in front of Mirek. He stared into Mirek's face.

The world stopped.

Mirek didn't know what to do. Which would be more of an insult: holding the man's gaze or looking away?

His stomach turned to stone, but his legs turned to jelly. He swallowed hard, praying the Nazi would move along and pick on someone else before his weakness got everyone in his household blasted by machine-gun fire.

Finally, Kruger looked away.

But only as far as Agata. He put his black-gloved hand under her chin and raised her tear-stained face. "Was it you?"

Mirek pulled her to him. Tight. So tight. "No."

The Nazi glowered at him. This time, Mirek didn't want to vomit. No, this time, he yearned to smash his fist into this monster and see German blood splash the cobbles. But Mirek did nothing. Assaulting a German officer was a guaranteed death sentence. And not only for him — they'd punish everyone he cared about.

The German smirked and sauntered away.

Mirek gasped a giant breath. His legs wobbled so much, if it wasn't for all the children packed around him, he'd have crumpled. He gripped the hands of those holding his, both trying to reassure them and to regain some sort of composure.

Kruger grabbed a black-haired boy, ripping him from his mother's grasp. She screamed but stifled the outcry under Kruger's glare. She stood a shaking wreck.

He dragged the boy to his car and threw him to the ground. "Lick it off."

Eyes wide, mouth agape, he stared at the German, then at his mother.

Tears streaming her face, she nodded. "Lick it, Aleksander. Lick it, baby."

Whimpering, the boy licked the painted letters but, unsurprisingly, had little effect on removing them.

Kruger clicked his tongue. "Pathetic." He whipped out his pistol and shot the boy in the back, blood splattering the car door.

His mother screeched. A man beside her struggled to quiet her, probably worrying that if she was too distraught, the gun would be turned on her.

Kruger looked into the crowd. "I ask again, who is the artist?"

En masse, the crowd drew back, like a gigantic animal realizing danger loomed.

The Nazi scanned the crowd as if seriously believing the perpetrator would own up. No one did.

He grabbed a small girl clutched in her father's arms. When the father didn't release her, Kruger pistol-whipped him. The man fell against the people behind him.

The girl screamed as Kruger dragged her toward the car. He flung her down. She stared up at him, blubbering, saliva stringing from her mouth.

He raised his pistol.

"It was me!" a young male voice shouted.

All heads turned to look for the owner of the voice.

Seven or eight rows from the front, a teenager with a big nose and the first signs of stubble thrust his hand up. "Me!"

A chubby man next to him fought to push the boy's hand down, but the boy resisted. Beside him, a dark-haired woman wailed and two girls screamed.

Kruger stabbed a finger at the boy. "Come here."

Under the glare of a psychotic German with an itchy trigger finger, the crowd magically found space to part, giving the boy room to walk to the front.

The boy stood before Kruger, as recklessly defiant as only youth can be.

Kruger looked the boy up and down as if impressed he'd taken responsibility. He pointed into the crowd. "Is that man your father?"

The boy nodded.

"Your mother? Two sisters?"

Another nod.

"Your family must be very proud to have a son who shows such courage and integrity."

The boy frowned, obviously confused.

"But this?" Kruger pointed at the vandalized vehicle. "For you to do this, your father must have done a truly shameful job of raising you." He offered the boy his pistol. "Shoot him."

The boy flinched at the gun being so close.

"Shoot him. Show him how disappointed you are that he's failed you so."

The boy staggered backward, wide-eyed.

Kruger gestured to his soldiers. "If he doesn't shoot the father, shoot the whole family."

The soldiers aimed their machine guns into the crowd. Bystanders screamed and fought to push away from the family.

Again, Kruger offered the pistol.

His hand trembling, the boy reached for it but pulled back and stared at his parents.

Kruger gestured to his soldiers. "On my command—"

The boy grabbed the pistol. He pointed it at his father, his face twisted with the unimaginable pain of facing such a dilemma.

The father nodded.

But the boy shook his head.

His father shoved his wife and two wailing daughters farther away, then moved closer. "It's okay, Radek. Do it, son."

Kruger leaned closer. "Listen to your father, Radek. This might be the only piece of sound advice he's ever given you."

Radek squealed. And pulled the trigger. The shot slammed his father in the chest and the man sank to the cobbles. Radek's legs gave out, and he slumped against the car, a blubbering heap.

Kruger snatched his pistol. Looking at two of his men, he said, "Take him to the camp. He can learn a trade under the guidance of a responsible adult."

Soldiers hauled Radek away.

Raising his pistol, Kruger blasted the mother and two sisters.

The crowd gasped en masse.

Kruger waltzed up the steps with his microphone, his back to the crowd, showing he believed the thousands of people were absolutely no threat. "I hope we've now established the ground rules so there won't be a need for any further town meetings."

He glanced over his shoulder, his gaze passing over Mirek before he continued on his way. He handed the microphone to his aide, said something in private, then disappeared inside.

Mirek stared. Dazed by such unspeakable evil.

Something prodded him in the back. He turned, his mind whirling as if he'd woken from a dream.

"Mirek, for God's sake, let's get out of here," said Hanka.

"Of course." He herded his children away.

A voice came from behind. "Mirek Kozlowski?"

He glanced back. And almost collapsed from shock. A German soldier glared at him, machine gun raised.

20

Silent, Mirek stared at the floor in the doorway at the back of the mayor's office in the town hall. His breath faltered as panicked thoughts flooded his mind.

Silhouetted against the windows, Kruger gazed down at the people clearing the square.

"Look at them scurry. Thousands of them. So many they could have easily overpowered us today and taken back their town, but instead…" He sniggered. "Cowards. The lot of them." He turned to one of the four military personnel present. "And that's why the Reich will triumph."

He saw the soldier standing with Mirek.

The soldier saluted. "Herr Hauptsturmführer, Mirek Kozlowski, as requested."

Kruger dismissed the soldier and beckoned Mirek.

Mirek shuffled in. The room had changed since last he'd seen it. Discolored rectangles on the walls showed where pictures of the town's notable residents and famous Polish scenes had been removed, and the bookcases were as bare as his. A giant swastika flag hung on the far wall.

Kruger said, "So you're the man with the big house full of other people's children."

Bowing his head, Mirek swallowed hard, his mouth as dry as if he'd gargled with sand. "I run the orphanage, yes."

"It's a privilege to meet you, Herr Kozlowski." Kruger saluted, clicking his heels together. "SS-Hauptsturmführer Hans Josef Kruger, at your service."

Mirek's jaw dropped. What was happening? Was this more of the Nazi's psychological torture?

Mirek acknowledged him with a gentle nod.

Kruger said, "A house should be filled with the love and laughter of a family. Have you never yearned to take a wife? To have your own children?"

"I have my own children. Ninety-eight of them."

Kruger laughed. "Waifs, strays, and vagabonds. You can't possibly love them as you would your own flesh and blood."

Why was Kruger being almost cordial? Did he want something? What could the director of an orphanage in a sleepy little town have that could be of interest to a sadistic SS officer?

Mirek frowned. He might get a bullet in the head, but chances were that was going to happen anyway, so there was nothing to lose in pushing to discover Kruger's intentions. "Tell me, do you always take such an interest in the residents of the places you occupy?"

"Only the important ones."

"Important? I have a run-down orphanage in a dead-end town."

Kruger drew his pistol.

Mirek gritted his teeth. Tensed. Saw the faces of all the children he wished he'd said goodbye to.

"Such modesty? With *your* body of work?" Kruger snorted. "Your writing hasn't gone unnoticed by the Party. Nor my daughter — she adored your *Rabbit Who Lost His Tail*."

Mirek's knees almost buckled. This monster knew of him?

Kruger opened a drawer in the mayor's massive teak desk, removed a handful of rounds, then pulled the magazine out of his pistol's grip and reloaded it. Smiling, he holstered the weapon. "You never know when you might need a full magazine."

He sat at the desk, leaned back in the leather chair, and put his feet up.

"In a world in turmoil, men of vision can seize opportunities that most would never even recognize and thus forge their own destiny. Assuming they're smart enough to see the forest for the trees regarding the world order, of course." He squinted at Mirek. "Can you see the forest for the trees, Herr Kozlowski?"

Was this Nazi asking him to collaborate? Why would Kruger think he'd ever do that? "I... know nothing about botany."

Kruger belly-laughed. He pointed at Mirek. "What wonderful wordplay. Even if the subtext is misguided."

Subtext? What the devil was going on here?

"Drink?" Kruger gestured to a number of decanters on a table.

A drink? Could this get any weirder? "No. Thank you."

Kruger nodded to his aide. As the man scampered over to pour one, Kruger said, "You're German, yes?"

"I have German heritage but, no, I'm Polish."

"Your paternal roots are...?"

The aide handed Kruger a glass of dark liquid.

"German. From Heidelberg."

"Ah, excellent. One of my brothers is an Oberarbeitsleiter for the Party in Heidelberg."

Was Mirek supposed to be impressed by that?

Kruger smiled. "Small world, isn't it?"

Way, way too small. Mirek wanted to be a thousand miles away already.

"And your maternal side?" asked Kruger.

"My mother was born in Poland, but her family is from Munich. My parents met when my father moved here for work."

"So all good *blood and soil* stock."

Mirek nodded. As far back as he knew, he had no Jewish ancestry. Not that it would have bothered him if he had.

Kruger looked at his aide. "And he says he's not German." He sauntered over to Mirek. "Look at you, you're almost as German as I am."

There was a similarity. Both fair-haired, both square-jawed, both tall... both far more Nordic than Slavic. Typically Aryan, according to the criteria set forth by the Nazis.

Kruger said, "Why are you still here? Why haven't you joined the Reich to support the Fatherland?"

Mirek snorted. "Joined the Reich?"

"You have signed up for the Volksliste? Having authored your books in German yourself, you'd be looked upon most favorably."

Yes, he was fluent in German. And, yes, his ancestry was Germanic. But to register as Volksdeutsche? To officially be an ethnic German and help the Nazis further their plan for a new world order?

"I..." There was no answer that would make a resounding *No* at all palatable.

Kruger rubbed his chin. "Now that worries me."

Being noncommittal would only get Mirek so far, then it could land him in trouble. "I couldn't join any army. Polish or German. I'm blind in one eye."

Kruger leaned closer and stared into Mirek's eyes. His breath smelled of smoked bacon. Mirek's mouth watered at the memory of the taste, and he hated himself for it. How could he be envious, even subconsciously, of such a monster?

The German shook his head. "I see no difference."

Mirek pointed to his left eye. "I fell out of a tree when I was ten. Apart from getting flashes of light, everything seemed fine. Then my vision darkened and my peripheral vision deteriorated. The doctors couldn't do anything, and pretty soon, I just couldn't see. It's been like that ever since."

"You couldn't serve the Fatherland as a cook? Someone has to feed the troops, and you don't need two eyes for that."

"Are you saying you're conscripting me?"

Kruger waved his hand and strolled away. "No, no, no. For a man of your talents, there are far greater contributions you can make than peeling potatoes."

Mirek's knees almost gave again. What did this sadist have planned?

But Kruger turned back. He pointed to Mirek's right eye, the good one. "Cover that eye."

Mirek put his hand over it. He waited. Being blind in a room full of Nazis, he breathed harder as sweat ran down his spine. He had no idea what was going on, but he guessed Kruger was pretending to poke his left eye to see if he flinched. To be safe, Mirek strained not to blink.

"Okay," said Kruger.

Mirek uncovered his eye. The tip of a dagger rested dangerously close to his left eyeball. He jerked his head back.

"Good." Kruger strutted away. "So you'll consider my suggestion?"

"Your suggestion?"

He turned. "The Volksliste. Or wouldn't your household benefit from a privileged status and special benefits like an increased food allowance?"

"I... eh... yes, I'll give it serious consideration."

"Good. Good. Then I look forward to us chatting again soon." He waved him away. A soldier standing nearby opened the door for him to leave.

Mirek gulped. "Chat about...?"

Kruger snorted. "Do men of intellect need to predetermine a topic about which to converse?"

Mirek spread his lips into as near a smile as he could fake. He nodded a goodbye and headed for the door, as shell-shocked as if he'd been on the front lines during an artillery barrage. Chat again soon? That was beyond doubt the most terrifying thing he'd ever heard. What did this Nazi want of him?

21

At his desk in his study, Mirek poured another vodka from his tantalus, the liquid splashing from the glass in his still shaking hands.

Ania said, sitting beside the desk, "Chat soon? What's that supposed to mean?"

"Exactly," said Mirek.

Hanka folded her arms in his reading chair. "Well, the Volksliste is obviously out of the question. Unless you want to be spat at on the street. Or worse."

"I don't think it would come to that."

Hanka wagged a finger. "If people see you as collaborating, it will. You could kiss goodbye to food donations, cheap repairs by tradesmen... everything. All the goodwill we've built up over the years would go out the window."

"But what if I don't have any choice?" asked Mirek.

"Is that what he said?" asked Ania.

"No. He was"— Mirek grimaced, struggling for the words —"unnervingly gracious."

Hanka frowned. "Gracious? The man who shot a young boy and a family in cold blood?"

Mirek threw his hands up. "It makes no sense."

Someone knocked on his door, and a girl's voice said, "Papa Mirek, can you—"

"Come back later, please," called Hanka. "We're busy."

Mirek sipped his vodka.

"I told you we should've left months ago," said Hanka.

"And gone where? For all his brutality, Kruger is right — the restrictions here aren't as harsh as in many places."

"So you still want to stay?" Hanka threw her arms up. "After what happened today?"

"No, of course I don't. But where can we go? Seriously. Where?"

Hanka said, "I think you should ask Borys."

Mirek flashed a glare at Hanka.

Ania laughed. "I'm not stupid, you know."

"Excuse me?" said Mirek.

"I know Borys is Resistance."

Mirek sipped his vodka, undecided whether to confirm she was right or snigger at such an outrageous claim.

Hanka touched Ania's arm. "It would be best if you forgot that."

"Really?" Ania glanced at Mirek.

He nodded.

But maybe Hanka was right. And wrong. Talking to Borys was probably the best idea, but not for the reason she was imagining.

After an hour's rest and three glasses of vodka, Mirek's nerves settled. He wrote a note, which Pawel delivered to Borys's residence, asking for a quote for the construction of four bunk beds.

Three days later, having received a note back, Mirek went to meet Borys. He splashed through puddles, the sidewalk slick after heavy rainfall, only for his right foot to suddenly feel cold and wet. Resting against the hardware store wall, he looked at the sole — worn through. Great. Like he had money to waste on new shoes, or even a cobbler. He tramped on, his right shoe squelching with each step.

In the square, Mirek clutched his mouth. He stared at the four streetlights nearest the town hall.

He shuffled closer. "Oh, may God forgive us..."

A body hung from each lamppost. A man, a woman, and two young girls — the graffiti artist's family. Ania had mentioned this abomination, saying it was meant as a warning of the consequences of disobedience, but that hadn't prepared him for the horror of seeing it.

He stumbled over.

Her eyes half-open, one of the girls gazed down at him, her skin discolored, the scent of rotting flesh heavy in the air. Strangely, she looked at peace, as if all the struggles of life had been lifted from her tiny shoulders. What kind of a world had they created where the only peace someone so innocent could find was when dangling from a rope? This had to end. But how?

He scanned the ground. A few crushed crocus petals lay strewn about. Probably stamped into the ground by a German boot. Other than that, there wasn't a flower or token of remembrance anywhere — people were obviously terrified of acknowledging the family, fearful it would give the Nazis an excuse to string them up too.

Wiping away a tear, Mirek trudged across the square to the white stone church.

A horse lumbered past pulling a cart piled with possessions, a man, woman, and small boy riding on the bench. Another family with dreams of a brighter future elsewhere. Another family destined for disappointment and heartache.

Mirek shook his head. People everywhere went about their business, some wearing white armbands, some not. How strange it was that, after all that had happened, life was continuing. But then, what else could it do?

Borys arrived, and they ambled along the wide store-lined sidewalk.

Rolling a cigarette, Borys said, "How's the food situation?"

Mirek said, "I'll put it this way, whatever you've got, we want it, no matter how old, moldy, or stale."

"And the children?"

"Good. Considering."

Mirek glanced around, half expecting to see a red-haired boy ducking into a doorway. "Still a few problems with Jacek, but it's nothing compared to what other people are struggling with." He gazed at the four bodies.

Borys sighed. "Some message, huh? Did you witness the performance?" He lit his cigarette.

"That's partly what I want to talk about."

Borys winced. "There's nothing we could've done. By the time—"

"No, that's not it." He leaned closer. "Where does the Resistance stand on the Volksliste?"

Borys blew out his cheeks. "That's a tough one. Some say it's collaborating, others that staying alive through any means necessary is a form of resistance. Why? You haven't registered, have you?"

He shook his head.

"But you're thinking of doing so?"

Mirek gestured toward the town hall. "I was summoned. Because of my German heritage, Kruger wants me to play the nice little Aryan and support the Fatherland."

Borys sucked through his teeth. "Oh boy."

"Hanka wants us all to run."

Borys sniggered. "All of you? And go where?"

"We hoped you might know. You've brought us children from all over, so you've obviously got the contacts. Could any of them help?"

"You mean help to smuggle a hundred people in one go?"

"Would that be possible?"

"What do you think?" He dragged on his cigarette, then flicked ash onto the ground.

Mirek's stomach clenched. He'd thought it was a long shot but had hoped he was wrong.

Borys scratched his beard. "You know, if one person does another a favor, they'll probably be done a favor in return."

Mirek slumped. "This again?"

The man held up his hands defensively. "I'm just saying."

Mirek leaned right in to Borys's ear. "I do enough for the Resistance, taking in every single child you bring me. If I'm caught with weapons, or codebooks, or anything, it won't just be me they string up like that"— he gestured to the dead family —"it'll be all my children too. Is that what you want?"

"Then don't get caught."

Mirek gritted his teeth and glared.

Borys said, "Look, all I'm saying is, here and now, you're low-priority. But you show how useful you can be to us and we'll take better care of you. It's that simple."

"Maybe I should speak to someone in charge."

Borys blew a cloud of smoke. "You know it doesn't work like that. The fewer contacts we all have, the fewer we can give up if we're caught. That protects you just as much as it protects us."

"So what are you telling me? That we're screwed?"

"I'm telling you to find a way to be more valuable."

"Like what? Infiltrate the town hall? Broadcast Polish propaganda messages? Spy on the camp in the forest?"

"For example."

"Seriously?" Mirek snorted. He was a writer, not a secret agent.

Borys held his hands up again. "Hey, don't shoot the messenger."

"So who gets what resources isn't your decision?"

"No. But"— Borys sighed —"I can't say I disagree with the current allocation." He put his arm around Mirek to guide him toward the street home. "Listen, I'll report how much you're struggling and emphasize everything you've done for us. See if we can reassess your situation. Okay?"

"Thank you." It wasn't the best outcome, but he had to take whatever he could get. But maybe he had one card yet to play to prove his value. "Ludomir Sajdak said the Nazis have built a spur from the mainline so trains can go right into that camp."

Borys nodded. "That's how they're shipping in the supplies and workers."

"So the rumors are true — it's an army barracks?"

"Not with watchtowers and a double fence, it isn't." He crushed the cigarette butt under his foot.

Mirek raised his eyebrows. "You've seen it?"

"From Krolik Hill."

"So it's a prisoner of war camp?"

Borys grimaced. "I don't know, but I don't like it. Something about it just… just feels wrong." He tipped his head toward the hanging bodies. "I can't help feeling they might have had a lucky escape."

If Mirek helped the Resistance, one day, it could be him up there with heaven only knew how many of his children. But as if he could do anything anyway with his limited skills.

Wait…

An idea clawed from the back of his mind. He was a writer, not a secret agent. A writer.

He rubbed his jaw. That might just work.

22

Having left Borys, Mirek ambled home. Kruger had been right — times like these called for men of vision to seize unusual opportunities. Wild ideas flew through Mirek's mind. Maybe he could help the Resistance, and in so doing help his household.

Across the street, Filip Goldblatt staggered out of his tailor's store, cradling a tatty brown suitcase. A German soldier shoved him in the back, making him stumble. Three other soldiers waited outside.

Zuzanna Goldblatt stood nearby, bundled up in a fur coat, and beside her, their teenage son and three daughters clutched bags. And each sported an armband.

Filip handed his keys to a soldier, who locked the store, marked something on a clipboard, then pointed to another building along the street.

The soldiers marched away.

Dazed, the Goldblatt family floundered as if they'd each been kicked in the head by a mule.

Mirek dashed over. Farther along the street, one of the soldiers hammered on another door with the butt of his rifle.

"What's going on, Filip?" asked Mirek.

The man stared wide-eyed. "They-they've taken my store."

"What do you mean, they've taken your store?" Mirek frowned. "Why would the Germans want a tailor's store?"

"They want it for a German family. Where are we supposed to go?"

Mirek didn't hesitate. "Come with me. All of you."

He guided them into his house.

In classroom #2, he said, "I'm sorry, the bedrooms are already overcrowded, but you can stay here until you find somewhere."

Filip grabbed Mirek's hand and shook it vigorously. "You're a good man, Mirek. God bless you."

Zuzanna, his wife, collapsed in a heap on the floor and burst into tears. Her children flung themselves at her. They huddled into a big bawling mass.

"I'll give you some privacy." Mirek left.

Just when he thought life was at its most brutal, the Germans did something to prove him wrong by making things even worse. What would they think of next?

A group of children played in the hallway.

Mirek said, "Agata, please tell Baba Hanka that the Goldblatts will be staying in classroom #2 for a few days and to take them some tea."

She scampered away.

Ania strolled through the front door, and Mirek smiled. Even in the darkest days, there was always a glimmer of light. But she didn't smile back.

"I hope you don't mind, Mirek, but..." She pushed the door wide.

A man with graying temples and a tailored blue suit stood outside. With him were an equally well-dressed woman, a gray-haired elderly couple, a woman in her late teens, and a man in his early twenties arm in arm with a woman holding a crying baby. Everyone except the baby had a suitcase. And an armband.

The well-dressed man nodded. "Mr. Kozlowski."

"Mayor Silberman."

The man grimaced. "Just plain old *Mister* Silberman now."

Ania said, "The Germans evicted them. I said it would probably be okay if they stayed in your spare classroom for a while."

Ten minutes later, Mirek stood atop a stepladder, hammering a nail into the middle of classroom #2's wall. Once in, Ania passed him the end of a piece of string. He took up the slack and tied it around the nail. They then pegged sheets onto it, dividing the room — the Goldblatts on one side, the mayor and his extended family on the other. All the while, the mayor's family carried in furniture from a cart outside: mattresses, bedding, dressers, mirrors, paintings, chairs... they gave a few items to the Goldblatts as a gesture of goodwill.

While the families arranged their furniture, Ania whispered, "I'm so sorry, Mirek. I had no idea the Goldblatts were here."

"Don't worry. I wouldn't have seen them on the street."

Within an hour, they'd created two cramped — but reasonably comfortable — living spaces.

Zuzanna Goldblatt hugged Monika, the mayor's wife. "Thank you so much. I had visions of sleeping on a bench in Brudno Park, so this—"

Thunderous hammering came from the hallway.

"What the...?" Mirek darted out, Ania following.

Hammering came from the front door.

He yanked it open. "What the hell—"

He gasped. Four German soldiers glared at him.

His heart pounding, he said, "My apologies for keeping you waiting. How may I help you?"

A soldier with a weaselly face said, "Is this where the ex-mayor is?"

"Yes, I'll fetch—" Mirek moved, but the soldier grabbed his arm.

"He's got twenty-four hours to return the furniture." Weasel strutted away.

"What? It's his furniture." The words had been an automatic response, but Mirek cringed instantly.

The soldier froze in midstep, then turned, scowling as though Mirek had suggested his mother had slept with a donkey.

Mirek gulped.

The soldier stalked back, his comrades adjusting their grips on their weapons.

Mirek ached to slam the door shut and run. But he had nowhere to run to. He held up his hands. "I'm so, so sorry. I'll tell the Silbermans immediately."

Weasel glowered. He slammed his rifle butt into Mirek's stomach.

Clutching his gut, Mirek crumpled to the floor.

Children screamed and darted upstairs. Two ran for the dining room, shouting, "Baba Hanka, Baba Hanka!"

The soldier reared over him. "Do you expect Hauptsturmführer Kruger to sleep on the floor?" He spat on Mirek. "Polish filth." He stormed out.

Ania crouched by Mirek's side, tears in her eyes. "It's all my fault for bringing them here. I'm so sorry."

Pain sliced through Mirek as if he'd been stomped on by a horse. His hand trembling, he reached for hers and grasped it. He groaned when he tried to speak. "It's not your fault."

Hanka rushed over. "Mirek! Oh my word, Mirek."

Taking an arm each, Ania and Hanka helped Mirek clamber up, but he flinched when he straightened.

"Come and sit down." Hanka gestured to the dining room.

They helped him in, and he collapsed onto the nearest chair.

Ania dashed for a glass of water and held it to his lips.

He sipped. "Thank you, but I'm okay now. And I have things to do."

He pushed up to leave but sucked through his teeth as pain twisted in his gut.

Hanka pressed on his shoulder. "You'll sit there until you're right, is what you'll do."

He shot Hanka a sideways look. "This is important, Hanka."

"And your health isn't?"

"Not compared to this." He staggered for the door. "Can you see that the furniture is sent back?"

Hanka nodded.

Ania said, "Can I help?"

"Not with this, thank you."

Enough was enough. The time had come to fight back. Fight mean, and fight dirty.

119

23

For the next three days, Mirek shut himself in his study, only venturing out to hunt for research materials and to help two further evicted families move into the only remaining space that wasn't indispensable — classroom #1.

Cross-legged on his study floor, he stared at the open books, magazines, and newspapers fanned before him, all in German. Sheets of paper lay scattered, scrawled with partially realized ideas that had ultimately led nowhere. The concept was sound, but he just couldn't find the correct way in which to execute his plan.

He flung his pen at the wall and cursed. Why couldn't he do this? This was what he did, this was his life, so why, when he needed it more than ever before, had his creativity deserted him? He'd always dismissed writers who claimed they couldn't write because they were "blocked" — an excuse for the lazy, the inept, the pretenders — and yet, no matter what he tried, the words simply refused to flow.

Someone knocked on his door. He ignored it. They knocked again.

Without looking up, he called, "Busy."

However, the person eased open the door.

Mirek glared at it. He yelled, "Busy!"

Ania peeped in. "I'm really sorry, but this can't wait any longer."

He sighed but beckoned her.

She gazed at the littered floor. "It's Hanka's birthday soon. I wondered if we could give her the day off."

"Whatever you think, Ania." Only half listening, Mirek scanned a newspaper article that claimed that Jews often carried infectious diseases due to hygiene issues. The article advised decent people to keep their distance.

"With the horrible year we're all having, I thought maybe we could throw her a party as well." She crouched beside him.

Mirek rubbed his brow. "A party? Seriously?"

"I know there's no money for gifts or food, but we could play games and sing songs. And it wouldn't just be for Hanka — a party would cheer up everyone."

Mirek squinted at her, thoughts swirling around his mind.

She stood and headed for the door. "I'm sorry. I shouldn't have disturbed you."

He grabbed a piece of paper and scribbled.

Ania turned the doorknob. "I won't bother you again."

"Wait!"

She glanced back, eyes sullen.

He offered a few crumpled banknotes from his pocket. "Raspberry schnapps. She's never been that fond of vodka."

Beaming, Ania grabbed the money. "Thank you."

"No, *thank you*."

As she left, he scribbled the essence of the idea before he lost his train of thought, then gave Feliks a note to deliver to Borys. By the time Borys was available, everything would be finished. He grinned.

The next morning, Mirek revised and revised a number of texts, constantly comparing them to German propaganda newspaper articles and materials to ensure the tone, style, and sentence construction were perfect.

Someone again knocked on his door.

"Busy."

Hanka opened the door. "I'm sorry, Mirek, there's someone in the courtyard insisting on speaking with you. A Jewish family."

Mirek rolled his eyes. "We've got no more room."

"I've told them."

"So...?"

"So... just come and listen."

Heaving a breath, he trudged out.

A young couple with a toddler gazed at him, each with puffy red eyes. He'd seen such looks so often recently, but he had *no* space.

A man with bushy eyebrows whipped off his cap. "Mr. Koz—"

Mirek held up his hand. "Sorry, but we have no more space."

The man pointed at the street. "But they're loading some of the evicted onto trucks, and no one knows where they're taking them."

"Maybe it's to accommodations elsewhere." He shoved the door to close it.

The man held the door open. "Please. I beg you. They took my parents a week ago, and we haven't heard a word from them."

Mirek frowned. "So where did they say they were taking them?"

"They didn't. All these people just get loaded onto trucks and"— his eyes welled with tears —"no one hears from them again." He pointed to his child. "Please, Mr. Kozlowski, Jakub's only four. He doesn't deserve this."

Mirek cupped his face. He had no room, yet if this young family turned up in a ditch, riddled with bullet holes, could he ever again look his children in the eye?

He swung the door open. With beaming smiles while they drowned him in gratitude, they rushed in.

"Where are you putting them?" asked Hanka.

"Where else? My study."

"No."

"It's the only space left that we can do without."

Hanka shook her head. "*We* can do without it, but *you* can't. And if you fall apart, so does all of this." She gestured to the house. "You *need* your space, Mirek, so you are *not* giving up your study."

"Hanka, it's the only choice."

She grabbed his arm. "And what about that"— she made quotation marks in the air —"*chat* that monster Kruger wants to have? What if he comes here to have it and you have to use the dining room because there's nowhere else? And what happens when he doesn't like the way one of our children looks at him?"

Mirek gulped. That *chat* could destroy his world. Hanka was right. A private space wasn't a luxury but a necessity.

"Okay, so I'll squeeze them into classroom #1." Mirek showed the family to the classroom and explained that the room would have to be further divided, then returned to his study.

Two days later, Borys leaned back in Mirek's armchair, chuckling at a typed piece of paper. Settling down, he said, "And you can translate this into German?"

"Already have." Mirek slid a second sheet across to him. "If your printer can match the typesetting"— he pointed to a German propaganda leaflet —"this could be a winner."

"A winner? This is genius." Borys studied the German version, pointing at the bottom. "And the information line is a genuine phone number?"

Mirek nodded. "The Nazi Party headquarters in Heidelberg."

Borys chortled. "Genius. A two-day public holiday to celebrate the Führer's birthday."

Mirek said, "The twentieth of April last year was declared a national holiday to celebrate Hitler's fiftieth birthday, so if you send this leaflet to a few thousand carefully selected businesses two or three days before the twentieth, a lot will just accept it, thinking Hitler is trying to outdo last year's celebrations. Those who question whether it's true or not won't have time to verify it because the headquarters will be bombarded with too many calls to handle."

"Any reason you chose Heidelberg?"

"Kruger's brother works in the Nazi Party office there."

Borys laughed and slapped his thigh. He pointed to a rectangular block at the bottom of the Polish version again. "And a voucher for three free beers as a gift from the Nazi Party." He laughed again. "Oh boy, I wouldn't want to be staffing the phones in Heidelberg HQ that week. Or tending bar anywhere."

"Obviously, a lot of people are going to realize it's fake, especially if the Nazis manage to put out a last-minute radio broadcast to deny it, but..." Mirek shrugged.

"But a lot won't. Factories will close, there'll be riots in bars that refuse the vouchers, and hospital admissions will soar." Borys waved the paper in the air. "Absolute genius."

"I'm pleased you like it."

"And you can create more things like this?"

"I have some ideas, yes."

Borys offered his hand. "Then it looks like you've just proven your value to the Resistance, and then some."

Mirek grinned. Excellent. So the fight back had begun, and stronger relationships had been formed. Maybe for him and his household, the war had just turned.

24

Spring 1940.

Mirek stood before the portable blackboard at the front of the dining room, the children using the tables as desks. Continuing the children's education was vital, not just for them but for the world they would rebuild once this war ended, so he'd scheduled each ability level to receive at least one lesson per day in the only remaining space.

He pointed at the board. "And this accent on an S—"

"Sorry to interrupt." Hanka tramped in from the hall.

"Excuse me, class." He turned his back and whispered, "Is there a problem?"

Hanka whispered back, "Another three cases of diarrhea."

"Oh good grief. Maybe if we—"

"No, no, no. There's only one solution, and you know what it is."

He did — more food.

With so many extra mouths, and many of them Jewish, food had surpassed space as the major issue. The Aryan ration was small, but the Jewish ration was downright evil. Borys had supplied false papers for the few Jewish children who could pass for Aryan, but even when all the rations were combined, everyone was permanently hungry. Fatigue, depression, diarrhea, mood swings, cognitive issues... illness plagued the house.

Mirek canceled the day's classes, then trudged around classrooms #1 and #2. He held his cap before Monika, the mayor's wife.

"Again?" She scowled. "You expect us to contribute *again?*"

"I'm asking everyone, not just you."

"But we're regularly giving more than everyone else. What are the Steins giving this time? Buttons?" She snorted.

"You're right – the Steins have nothing compared to you. But they're good people." He held up a silver pocket watch. "This is the only keepsake Bozydar has of his father's, yet it's in the cap because he knows the only way we'll get through this is together. Of course, if you don't like the accommodations here, you're free to move on."

She huffed, snatched off her gold earrings, and dropped them onto the assortment of jewelry in the cap.

Mirek raised an eyebrow at her.

"Fine." She dropped in the matching necklace.

"Thank you."

She winced a smile.

Between the contributions from benefactors and the Jewish Council, plus a minuscule allowance from the town's German administration, his household was surviving. But there was a huge difference between merely existing and truly living. Somehow, he had to address that imbalance.

Near the church in the square, Mirek emptied his booty onto the rosewood counter of the watchmaker's store, the town's two jewelry stores having been seized and their stocks confiscated, both having belonged to Jewish families.

Display cases with wristwatches and pocket watches stood at either end of the counter, while behind it, clocks ticked.

A man with a face so lined he looked as old as time squinted through an eyeglass at the workings in the back of Bozydar's watch. "It's a nicely crafted little timepiece. Bavarian. Turn-of-the-century. Seventeen jewels. Mmmm."

He placed it beside the other pieces, then peeled banknotes from a bundle and placed them on the counter. Stony-faced, he looked at Mirek.

"For the watch?" asked Mirek.

"For everything."

"You're joking." He poked Monika's jewelry. "This alone has to be worth more than that."

"Nine-karat Soviet scrap."

Mirek cupped his face. It was no good taking people in if doing so meant they starved.

The watchmaker pursed his lips, studying Mirek. "I've heard about what you're doing." He laid five more bills on the counter. "Sometimes there's more to life than making a profit."

Mirek grabbed the man's hand and shook it. "Thank you."

He left.

As he strolled across the square, uneasiness clawed at Mirek as sharply as the spring air. Was someone spying on him? He turned again, but again, there was nothing. Were the Germans following him? Or someone else?

After splitting half the money between Julek, the grocer, and Markus, the baker, he kept the rest for Hanka, whose nephew was now trading in black market goods, meaning she got a sizable discount.

On his way home, Mirek caught a glimpse of movement near a tree. Casually, he sat on one of the black wooden benches dotting the square. He closed his eyes for a moment and bathed in the solitude. How wonderful it was to be away from everyone and everything. Even if only for a few minutes. And even if, strictly speaking, it wasn't in solitude.

Over his shoulder, he said, "I know you're there, so you may as well come and sit down."

No reply.

"Behind the tree, over my right shoulder." He patted the bench beside him.

A red-haired boy ambled over and sat without saying a word or even looking at him.

Mirek said, "I thought we'd talked about this, Jacek."

To be accurate, at different times, he'd talked, Hanka had talked, and Ania had talked. Jacek? The boy hadn't said a word.

"The streets are very dangerous since the Germans arrived. I can't protect you if I don't always know you're there. Do you understand?"

The boy looked at him, then looked away.

"I'll take that as a yes." Mirek stood and held out his hand to the boy. The boy took it, and they ambled across the square hand in hand.

***

The following Thursday was Hanka's birthday. She'd insisted that the only gifts she wanted were not to have to set foot in the kitchen all day and, instead of having to get up at 5:00 a.m., to lie in until at least 8:00.

At 8:20, Agata ran into the dining room, munching on a piece of charred toast and beaming. "She's coming. She's coming."

From the deserted hallway came the sound of someone clomping down the stairs.

Hanka called from the foyer, "Hello? Where is everyone?"

Standing in the doorway, Mirek strained to hear.

Hanka sniffed loudly. "Something's burning."

Mirek dashed out, soot smeared on his hands and face. "Oh, thank goodness. Quick, Hanka, we've had a small accident."

"I knew it was too good to be true." She shook her head. "Please don't tell me you've burned down my kitchen."

Following Mirek, she marched into the dining room. And froze.

Homemade garlands of newspaper hung across the ceiling, and vases of daffodils dotted the room. Standing in the midst of it all, the children, Mirek, Ania, and the evictees sang the birthday song:

One hundred years, one hundred years, may you live!

One hundred years, one hundred years, may you live!

Once again, once again, may you live!

May you live!

But who?

Everyone shouted, "Baba Hanka!" They all clapped and cheered.

"Oh my days," said Hanka, eyes wide, staring at the joy-filled faces.

Grinning, Agata presented Hanka with a huge piece of folded cardstock, the front and back of which were adorned with tens of tiny drawings while the inside was plastered with signatures.

"We all signed it." Agata pointed to a picture of an old woman holding a little girl's hand on the front. "That one's mine."

Tears welling, Hanka kissed Agata. "Thank you, dear, it's the loveliest card I've ever seen." She looked up. "Thank you, all of you."

She mouthed a thank-you to Mirek.

He shook his head and pointed at Ania.

Hanka opened her arms, so Ania scurried over and hugged her.

After a four-count, the mayor's son beat a drum, Pawel strummed a guitar, and Filip Goldblatt played a fiddle, filling the room with vibrant music. Standing before them, swaying in time to the rhythm, Lena sang with the most angelic voice.

We won't forsake the land from whence we came,
We won't let our speech be buried.
We are the Polish nation, the Polish people,
From the royal line of Piast.
We won't let the enemy oppress us.

Hanka wept at "The Oath," the song her husband had often sung. Mirek hugged her.

With sweeps of her hands, Lena encouraged the crowd to join in. Originally a poem from 1908 that protested Germany's oppression of Poland, "The Oath" had become one of their most cherished songs of independence, so the room echoed with over one hundred voices of defiance.

Mirek gazed at Lena. Despite being only fourteen years old, she oozed such confidence, such maturity. When the war was over, she would easily be able to pursue a career in music. And even at her young age, it was obvious she was going to be a real heartbreaker when it came to looks. Yes, the world would be her proverbial oyster.

As the song ended, everybody clapped and cheered. Lena bowed, then retired, and the band played traditional folk music.

Mirek offered his hand to Hanka. "May I have the first dance with the birthday girl?"

"Birthday *girl*." She playfully slapped him. "Have you unlocked your tantalus already!"

She took his hand and they danced. Children joined in and joy embraced the room.

Hanka had two dances and then, huffing and puffing, wiped her brow. She pointed at Ania dancing with Agata and Kuba. "There's someone in need of a bigger partner."

Mirek shook his head. "Maybe later."

Hanka grabbed his hand and marched him over as she would a naughty child. She took Ania's hand and put it into his. "It's my birthday, so give me this one gift."

Mirek shrugged to Ania. "I suppose it would be rude to disappoint the birthday girl."

"I suppose so," said Ania.

They danced. Music and laughter enveloped them, but everything else faded next to being so close to Ania. He'd sat beside her teaching her for months, they'd occasionally walked into town together, and they'd had that magical day on the horse. But they'd never been close simply for the sake of being close.

A warmth blossomed from Mirek's gut to fill his whole body with a golden glow he hadn't felt for over a decade. A feeling he'd believed he'd never again feel.

Ania gazed into his eyes. He held her tighter, and they whirled around, the music flowing over them, through them, with them. For a few brief moments, it was as if they were alone, as if the world and its problems no longer existed. There was only a man, a woman, and a moment.

But then the moment was gone.

Agata tugged on his arm. "Can you dance with me, Papa Mirek?"

He ached to scream "No, leave me alone!" but the girl pleaded with such soulful blue eyes. And then Ania smiled at him and nodded. He said, "Of course, princess."

Forsaking Ania, he swept Agata up, and twirled around with her, the little girl giggling and giggling.

The fun went on into the afternoon when they ate the lunch that the lady evictees had cooked, after which Mirek presented Hanka with her bottle of raspberry schnapps and the biggest candy bar anyone had ever seen.

He said, "Promise me you'll enjoy it yourself and not just break it into tiny bits to share."

Hanka said, "I promise I'll enjoy half of it myself, but the rest will wait until we next have some flour, then it will make chocolate-chip cookies for everyone."

After dining, they bobbed for apples, played drop the handkerchief, and with their impromptu band facing the wall, enjoyed a frenetic game of musical chairs, which remarkably, Hanka won, thanks mainly to Ania surreptitiously signaling the band. Mateusz Dudek, the local historian, even popped in with his camera, and the entire household squashed together for a group photograph.

Dancing resumed. Mirek gazed across the room at Ania chatting with Zuzanna.

Lena plonked down in the seat next to him. "She'll say yes."

"Excuse me?"

Lena arched an eyebrow. "Do I look stupid?"

So the game was up, was it? "You really think she'll say yes?"

"She did earlier, didn't she?"

"She didn't have any choice because Hanka shoved us together."

Lena rested her hand on his arm. "Trust me. If you don't get a yes, I'll wash the evening dishes for a month."

"Oh boy." His heart pounding, he shuffled toward Ania, his legs wobbly.

What had it come to that he was taking relationship advice from a fourteen-year-old?

But it was only a dance. Just a dance. With someone he saw every day. Nothing special. Nothing to get so worked up about. But the closer he got, the drier his mouth became. Conversely, his palms felt more and more clammy. So much so, Ania would undoubtedly recoil in disgust at their touch. But he had to try.

Ania caught his eye.

Oh Lord. Now she knew he was coming. What if Ania said no in front of all these people?

Maybe it was best not to try.

No. They'd had a "moment" earlier. She must've felt it too. He had to take advantage of that, to try to build on it while the memory was still fresh for both of them.

And then he was almost there. She looked up expectantly.

Feliks swooped in. "Miss Ania, may I have a dance, please?"

She looked at Mirek.

He opened his mouth, but no words came out. Instead, he smirked and nodded once.

Ania danced with the teenager, twirling around and laughing like a young girl.

Mirek took her seat. Zuzanna babbled on about heaven only knew what, so he nodded when he felt it appropriate, but he couldn't take his eyes off Ania. She'd come here to help Hanka, an embarrassed, self-conscious loner constantly trying to hide, both literally and figuratively. How she'd blossomed.

A romance? No, he couldn't risk it. An outright rejection wouldn't just be crushing, it would impact on their working relationship. Maybe so much that she'd leave. That would be a disaster for everyone, not least the children, who loved her, and Hanka, who relied on her.

But what if it wasn't a rejection? What if she felt the same?

Felt the same for how long? They might start out believing they were a prefect match, but so did most couples before the problems and doubts started. Was a few weeks, months, even years of happiness worth the loss that would ultimately come when they broke up and she moved on because she couldn't bear to be near him?

He had two choices: forever love or no love. There was no guarantee of the first, so the safer option was the latter — the only one for a man in his position.

He smiled as Marta and Karol squeezed in between Ania and Feliks, grabbing Ania's hands. The four of them danced together, each grinning and swaying as if it was the best day of their lives. And not once did Ania brush her hair across her face.

Yes, dancing with her would've been a joy, but seeing her so relaxed, so beloved, so at ease... That was wonderful, too.

He settled back in his seat. It was better this way. Better for everyone. Not least Ania.

The war? The war had done horrendous things to hundreds of thousands of people, and yet it had reawakened in him feelings he had thought long since dead. It had also introduced a lonely woman to a family she'd never thought she'd have. What wonders might it bring tomorrow for those who could see beyond its horrors?

25

The following week, as warming sunlight shafted through the window, Mirek stared at the larder's whitewashed walls, now all too visible behind the empty rows of shelves. Some sacks of potatoes, cabbages, and turnips, a few loaves of bread, plucked chickens and cured trout hanging from hooks, a dozen jars of home-pickled goods, and a few other bits and pieces. The place had never been so bare.

"Five days," said Hanka, "then we'll be all out."

"Can't you stretch it?" asked Mirek.

"That is stretching it."

"How about the garden?"

"That's including what we've grown. Have you heard from Borys?"

Mirek rubbed his chin. "He says he'll try, but the whole town's starving. Fortunately, there's an idea I've been toying with."

He visited his study just long enough to take the book he needed and to unlock the bottom-left drawer of his desk, from which he retrieved his secret weapon, which he hid in his pocket.

On returning to the dining room, Mirek announced that everyone should remain seated after eating because he had an announcement. He then partook of a dismal breakfast of watery porridge, after which he thumbed through the book while waiting for everyone else to finish.

Once everyone had eaten, Mirek stood. "Thank you all for waiting. I'm sure you'll be pleased you did because I have some wonderful news for you today — classes are canceled."

The children cheered.

"And the best part is that, instead of lessons, we're having a day of grand adventures, during which three of you will each win one of these." Mirek held up his secret weapon — three small chocolate bars.

Children gasped and chattered excitedly.

Mirek said, "Now, who wants to volunteer for a grand adventure?"

Hands shot into the air and voices cried, "Me! Me! Me!"

Mirek smiled. "Wonderful. So here's how it's going to work — everyone under the age of eleven move to the left side of the room, and everyone else move to the right."

The children shifted around.

Mirek pointed at the younger group. "If you volunteer for Team One, you'll be going down by the river with Miss Ania to forage for these plants." Holding his book aloft, he flipped through to show Polish botany described in text and watercolor plates. "Baba Hanka will then make them into meals so delicious, you'll wonder why we don't eat them all the time."

"Ewww." Kuba stuck his tongue out.

Hanka arched an eyebrow. "Are you suggesting I'm a bad cook, young Master Kuba?"

His eyes widened, and he shook his head vigorously.

Mirek looked to the older children. "Team Two volunteers will be coming to the outskirts of the forest with me, where we'll cut down a small tree, chop it into logs, then go door to door exchanging firewood for food."

He scanned the two groups. "Now, here's the most important part — how someone wins the chocolate." He held the bars aloft again.

"That's easy. You'll all label whatever you bring home, then at the end of the day, Baba Hanka will judge which three children found the best things, and they'll get a bar all to themselves." He clapped once. "So, hands up, who's ready for a grand adventure?"

Two-thirds of the children grinned, thrusting their hands up as high as they could, but the others stared at him with either sullenness or disinterest.

"Excellent. Thank you, everyone. Team One, if you'll get your coats and meet Miss Ania outside. Team Two, please make your way into the garden for us to choose our tools."

The children filtered out.

Finally, Mirek looked at everyone who hadn't volunteered, then turned to Hanka. "Wonderful! Looks like you've got an eager bunch of volunteers for cow pie duty."

The remaining children gasped in horror, then all sorts of shouts came in a garbled mass. "I want Team One." "Me too." "I can't, I've hurt my arm."

Mirek wagged a finger. "You know the rules. Everyone pulls their weight. You had the chance to volunteer but chose not to. However, Baba Hanka will be more than happy to address any complaints."

Hanka glowered across the room, arms folded.

Mirek said, "So, anyone not happy about the arrangements?"

Silence.

"Good." He handed the book to Ania, its illustrations showing plants such as dandelion, stinging nettle, chickweed, sorrel, and daisy. "Any fruiting plants will have been picked clean, but you've a good chance of finding some of the ones I've marked. Okay?"

She nodded. "What's cow pie duty?"

"Dung cakes."

She frowned.

He said, "For fuel?"

Her frown deepened.

Mirek grinned and used his hands demonstratively. "You collect cow pies, add a little water and some straw, then get your hands in to mix it up nice and stodgy and form it into cakes. Once those are dry, you can burn them for cooking, heating, or whatever."

She laughed. "No."

"Seriously. They've been doing it in India and Africa for centuries."

"But you're sending a team to cut wood. Why not just cut more trees?"

Mirek smirked. "You can't send a five-year-old out with an ax, but you can with a bucket."

With that, their day of grand adventures began.

***

In the larder, Pawel scrawled his name on a scrap of paper and placed it before three potatoes and half a cabbage sitting on a shelf.

"Thank you, Pawel," said Mirek, standing in the doorway to ensure no one cheated by labeling someone else's food, three-quarters of the larder's shelves once again filled.

Hanka weighed a wedge of cheese in her hand that Feliks had procured in exchange for firewood, nodding with a satisfied *Mmm*. She made a note on her paper, grading Feliks's trade. Next, she inspected the freshness of Pawel's contribution.

The stench of cow dung wafted into the room.

Mirek ducked out and into the hall. The back door was open onto the garden, where the cow pie gatherers were processing the household's new supplementary fuel source.

Mirek shouted, "Keep the door shut to keep the smell out, please."

Someone closed the door. He returned to the larder.

Hanka said, "I hope your dung cakes aren't as pungent when they're burning or they'll stink us out of the house."

"With things as bad as they are, we have to try whatever we can."

"On the bright side, I suppose the stench might spoil people's appetite, so two birds, one stone." Hanka shot him a wry glance and returned to her grading.

On the left-hand shelving sat Team One's finds — piles of wild vegetation that Mirek could imagine the average cow turning its nose up at. His book said everything was edible, but looking at this "indoor compost heap," he found that hard to believe. Hanka could work wonders in the kitchen, but that was with proper food. How the devil was she going to turn this leafy mass into something a human being could stomach?

An odd assortment of food sat on the right, all traded by Team Two in exchange for firewood. While everything here was guaranteed edible, it posed yet another headache for Hanka — the amounts were so small for a household of his size that instead of her being able to cook giant saucepans full of one dish, she'd have to create lots of tiny dishes.

Hanka finished assessing what each child had brought home and handed him a list. "Your three winners."

"Thank you." Mirek scanned the names and smirked, then nodded to the larder shelves. "A pretty good haul, huh? Think you can work your magic with it?"

She jabbed at a variety of items. "Soup, pickle, no idea, dry, goulash, no idea, no idea, soup, tea… we won't starve, but mealtimes won't be the highlight of the day anymore."

"Forget about the taste. Just keep us going long enough to get through the war. That's all I ask."

Hanka nodded. "That I can do."

26

Mirek dipped his spoon into a bowl of stinging nettle goulash and chuckled at Agata grimacing beside him in the dining room. The grand adventure had been such a success, they'd had two more.

Agata shoveled in another spoonful of goulash, shuddered, then shoveled in another one, only to shudder again. She managed two more spoonfuls, then grabbed what remained of the chocolate bar she'd won on the very first adventure, stuck out her tongue, and rubbed the chocolate onto it with a satisfied *ahhh*.

Putting the chocolate down, she guzzled more goulash but winced with each mouthful.

Feliks and Zygmunt had won the other bars, both of which had disappeared within seconds. Agata, on the other hand, had been licking hers only on "special occasions" or "in emergencies," intent on making it last as long as possible. Now, the bar was just a deformed, sticky blob.

Hanka scurried over, face ashen and hands shaking. "Mirek, Mirek. Oh my days, Mirek."

Hanka never got flustered. Never. His stomach knotted. "What is it?"

"Oh my. It's—" She pointed toward the hallway. "Oh my days. The German."

"The Germans are here?"

"No. Just one."

"One? Which one?" Why would one German come here? And why would only one cause such a reaction from the strongest person he'd ever known?

"Kruger."

Mirek dropped his spoon as the blood drained from his face. "Here?"

"I didn't know what to do. I asked him to wait in your study."

Mirek stared into space. So many questions whirled around his mind that he couldn't think straight. Kruger had said they'd meet again to "chat." At the time, it had terrified Mirek, but that was weeks and weeks ago, so he'd decided it was merely more of the monster's psychological torture.

Mirek gulped. What on earth could an SS officer want from him?

Hanka shook his shoulder. "Mirek, do something!"

He clambered up and, feeling like his shoes were glued to the floor, trudged for the hall. His heart hammered harder with every step.

From the doorway, he called back, "Put the heating on. The last thing we want is for him to be cranky because he's cold."

Outside his study, Mirek tried to swallow, but his mouth was too dry. His hand hovered over the doorknob. What should he do? More to the point, what *could* he do?

Finally, he gripped the handle, turned it slowly, and eased open the door. He peeked in. Would this be the moment he died?

Standing before the bookcase, Kruger turned. And smiled. "As I suspected, you're a lover of fine literature like myself." Wedging his swagger stick under his arm, he selected *Mein Kampf*, volume two. "Such an inspiration, isn't it?"

Mirek staggered in. Ania had said he was a bad liar. He prayed she was wrong.

He cleared his throat, hoping there was a voice there to come out. "Yes, I've often turned to it for guidance, Herr Hauptsturmführer."

He hated the immature ramblings of the deluded loser.

Mirek pointed to the next book along. "But I prefer volume one and the insight into the Führer's victories over his earlier setbacks."

Like the chapter on how Hitler had thrown a tantrum when he was rejected by Vienna's Academy of Fine Arts and confronted the rector to demand an explanation, even though the explanation was simple: Hitler was a lousy artist!

"Interesting." Kruger ensured no one was behind Mirek and scrunched up his face. "To be honest, I never finished it. I found it a little dry and a little clichéd, though there's no denying its passion." He shrugged. "But I'm pleased you found it enlightening. I knew we'd have a lot in common." He waved his stick at the bookcase. "But where is the Mickiewicz, Zeromski, Konopnicka? I don't even see your beloved Wladyslaw Reymont."

"All forbidden texts." Mirek winced. "Burned, as they should be."

"So not in a box in your attic?"

Mirek gestured to the door. "I have nothing to hide. Please go wherever you so wish."

Kruger dismissed the idea with a wave. "A trivial matter between men who, but for an unfortunate geographical twist of fate, could easily be the best of friends."

Friends? Was that the root of this mysterious behavior?

Book lovers came in many forms. Most put an author on a pedestal so high that they could never reach them. However, having read the author's work, a minority believed they knew them so intimately that they'd instantly be friends should they ever meet.

Mirek gestured to the armchair. "Sit, Herr Hauptsturmführer, please."

A gleam in his eye, Kruger pointed to the swivel chair behind Mirek's desk. "Would it be too forward if I..."

As if Mirek could say no. "Be my guest."

With childlike wonder, Kruger sat in the chair. He lovingly caressed the leather-covered wooden arms, then ran a hand over the desk as one of devotion might over a religious icon. "And this is where you wrote all your books?"

"Yes."

"*The Rabbit Who Lost His Tail?*"

"Yes."

"*The Road to Darkness?*"

"Yes."

"*A Fury Beyond the Sky?*"

"All of them, yes."

Kruger once more admired the desk.

Mirek said, "I doubt someone of your stature has time for social calls, so is there something I might help you with?"

Kruger gestured to Mirek's armchair. "Please."

Mirek sank into it.

Gazing around the room while twisting in the chair, Kruger said, "How many children do you have here?"

"Ninety-eight."

"Why so many from such a small town?"

"The war, disease, poverty... all manner of reasons."

"And how many are of Germanic decent?"

"I don't know, sorry."

Kruger stopped swiveling. "Could I see your records?"

"I don't keep records."

"But you're a writer."

"Of fiction. My word, I'd go insane if I had to keep books like some accountant."

Kruger squinted at Mirek for a moment, then waved his hand. "A fair point. So can you at least tell me how many are Jews?"

"Sorry. Not off the top of my head."

"Guess."

"But I wouldn't want to mislead you."

"Humor me. I'll forgive you if you're wrong."

Mirek tried to swallow again, but it was like trying to eat sawdust. "I guess... maybe... eh... around thirty-six are Jewish."

"And do you allow this thirty-six to practice their vile faith?"

Mirek said, "Ours is a secular establishment. Religion has caused more misery over the centuries than everything else combined, so you won't find me stoking its fires."

As if satisfied, Kruger nodded. He turned the copy of *Mein Kampf* around and around on the desk. "I don't believe you've registered for the Volksliste yet. Or am I wrong?"

"I've considered it, as I said I would."

Kruger stared at him while taking a cigarette from a silver case. "*Considering* and *doing* are two vastly different processes." He lit the cigarette. "You are aware that someone actively supporting the Reich would receive certain benefits and privileges not afforded to others? For example, the director of an orphanage might find he still has a house full of children to care for."

Kruger exhaled, a cloud of smoke veiling his face, but not his threat.

Mirek gulped.

Drawing on the cigarette, Kruger said, "This doesn't interest you?"

"By, eh, active support you mean, eh, collaboration." Mirek gripped the arms of his chair, knuckles white.

Kruger frowned. "It's only collaboration if you don't believe the Reich's cause just. Or were you being less than sincere when you mentioned your admiration for the Führer's work?" He patted *Mein Kampf.*

Mirek felt a bead of sweat dribble from his temple down his cheek. He prayed Kruger wouldn't notice it. "I'm Polish by birth. I wouldn't want to betray my countrymen."

"Betray?" Kruger pointed with his cigarette. "How is saving lives a betrayal? By setting an example, thereby encouraging others to register as Volksdeutsche, you'll be guaranteeing their safety and that of future generations. You want to help children, so help the Reich. You'll help more children than you ever dreamed possible."

Kruger made it sound so simple. It was easy to see how people were lured into the Nazi Party and its abhorrent philosophy — baby steps.

"Are you saying it will be impossible for me to maintain this orphanage if I don't register?"

The Nazi opened his palms. "Who is to say what the future might bring?"

"So I either betray my country or sacrifice the ninety-eight souls in my care?"

"Of course not."

Mirek raised his eyebrows. "No?"

So he had a choice? Maybe Kruger was more reasonable than Mirek had thought.

"Ninety-eight? We're not monsters." Kruger snickered. "Only thirty-six are Jews."

They couldn't take his children. Dear Lord, he couldn't let them take his children. But how could he save them without betraying everything he believed in and everything he taught them to believe in? Maybe by steering the conversation back to where it had started, back to what Kruger seemed to have a bewildering fascination with.

Mirek said, "Maybe you're right. Maybe the Volksliste is the best solution."

Kruger nodded impassively.

Mirek continued, "Maybe I could write a series of children's books that extol the virtues of the Führer's goals, so future generations will more readily build the world he envisions."

Could he really brainwash tens of thousands of children just to save his?

Dragging on his cigarette, Kruger stared into space. "I like that."

A wave of relief washed over Mirek.

"But"— Kruger jabbed his cigarette —"can you write such a series, books capable of moving hearts and minds, if your own heart isn't truly in it?"

"I haven't said my heart isn't in it. I'm sorry if I gave you that impression."

Kruger stroked the desk again. "I've dragged a pen across a blank sheet of paper, so I appreciate the struggle of breathing life into prose that can move a reader."

"You write? How wonderful."

Kruger waved his hand and spoke with feigned modesty, obviously besotted with his own work and bursting to talk about it. "Oh, it's nothing. A minor pastime. The foolish ramblings of a dream-filled amateur."

"I'm sure you're being too modest," said Mirek. "You'll have to let me read something. Maybe offer a few notes."

He snickered. "I couldn't possibly."

"It would be my pleasure. The least I can do for a fellow writer."

Staring, Kruger stroked his chin.

Had Mirek just found the key? Was this what was going to save everything he loved?

"I insist," said Mirek. "You're clearly passionate about literature, so refusing to nurture your talent would be doing a great disservice to the writing community." Mirek bit his tongue, praying he hadn't gone overboard.

Kruger toyed with his cigarette, probably considering whether Mirek's offer was genuine or a cheap manipulative trick.

Mirek's gaze fell to the pistol at the Nazi's hip. In the square, Kruger had used it with such terrifying nonchalance that a bullet would probably slam into the Mirek's forehead before he even registered the gun had been drawn.

Kruger blew smoke. "Well, I can't say I hadn't dreamed of the perfect outcome of this meeting, but…" His gaze drilled into Mirek as if judging him in that very second. He slammed his hand onto the desk. "I'll have the manuscript sent to you."

"You have a finished manuscript?"

"Many. Only the other day, I finished my most ambitious work to date. This one is… " He winced. "No. Modesty forbids. Especially in such illustrious company. I won't say another word about it but let you judge it with a clear mind and a clear heart."

That was some coincidence – Kruger just happened to call on a published writer immediately after finishing a cherished project.

"Excellent," said Mirek. "I look forward to reading it."

And to seeing inside that twisted, barbaric mind to understand how best to manipulate it.

Kruger stood, smiling. "You see, I knew we'd hit it off. There was just something about you. I knew it. Instantly."

So this was nothing more than a social call? Mirek smiled back, relief flooding his tense muscles, the conversation having reached an obvious conclusion. Kruger would be gone in a matter of seconds, so it seemed any crisis had been averted. Thank the Lord.

Mirek said, "Yes, I sensed a connection, too." And a way to save everything he cared about.

Kruger gestured to the hallway. "This has been very pleasant, but let's get to the real reason I'm here."

27

Mirek opened the study door. In the hallway, children ducked into doorways, around corners, and into the staircase's shadows. He ushered Kruger toward the front door, hoping the visit might yet be concluded.

Kruger covered his nose and mouth with a handkerchief. "What is that ungodly stench?"

"Stench? Oh, dung cakes." Mirek had grown so used to the "earthy" aroma that he barely noticed it.

"You eat dung?"

Mirek laughed. "Heavens no. We burn it. As fuel."

"What's wrong with coal or wood?"

"Coal costs money and tree-felling takes effort. Dung?" Mirek shrugged. "Any fool can wander about a field with a bucket."

"Only a fool would want to!"

"It's been used for centuries all over the world. If it was good enough for the pharaohs..." Mirek opened the door. "Some fresh air, Herr Hauptsturmführer?"

Outside, Kruger sucked in sweet spring air and exhaled with a satisfied *Ahhh*.

Mirek strode toward the courtyard gate. "It's been a pleasure, Herr Hauptsturmführer. Be sure to send me your manuscript so I—"

Kruger wasn't walking with him but was standing before the apple tree, studying its delicate new leaves that dared to brave the world. Without looking, he stabbed his stick at the gate. "Instruct my men to join us."

More Nazis were coming into his home? Mirek's gut twisted but, having no option, he did as instructed.

Three soldiers waltzed into the courtyard.

Kruger said, "I hope you won't let this mar what has been a very pleasant visit, but"— he rolled his eyes —"while bureaucracy is tiresome, it's a necessary evil."

A nerve in Mirek's cheek twitched. He hoped it was only a sensation apparent to him and not a physical manifestation that the Nazis would perceive as weakness or fear. He forced a smile. "How might I help, Herr Hauptsturmführer?"

"Your children are home?"

"We've just had lunch, so most of them should be."

Kruger gestured to the courtyard. "Have them line up."

His mind a whirl, Mirek struggled for a reason to refuse or an explanation for why that was impossible. He dithered.

Kruger frowned. "Is there a problem?"

"I..." If he stalled, maybe he'd think of an excuse — or someone inside would hear and everyone would escape through the back.

He slumped. Escape to where? The only thing stalling would achieve would be to irritate this sadist. Did he really want to risk that?

"I'll fetch them immediately."

His breaths coming in sharp pants, Mirek trudged into the house and repeatedly banged the gong. He shouted, "Everyone into the courtyard, please. As quickly as you can."

Exchanging anxious glances and hushed comments, the children crept out.

Hanka appeared, her face lined. "What's going on?"

He pointed outside. "Have them all line up, please."

"Why?"

"Now's not the time, Hanka. Just do it, please."

Hanka lined the children up in rows. Some held hands, some fixed their gaze to the ground, a few glared defiantly at the Germans.

Kruger walked before them, eyeing each of them individually.

Mirek said, "Can I ask what this is about, please?"

The Nazi didn't even look at him. "No."

"They're all good children who respect German authority. They don't steal, don't daub graffiti, don't—"

Kruger held his palm up for silence, then continued his inspection until he'd studied each person. He then walked back along and flicked his stick at a little blonde girl. "That one."

A soldier yanked her out of the line. She screeched.

Mirek's jaw dropped. He lurched to intervene but caught himself.

The soldier bundled her over to the gate, where she sobbed. She reached for Mirek. "Papa Mirek!"

The words sliced through him like a saber. But he didn't move. He *couldn't* move.

Kruger indicated a tall boy with a square jaw. Another soldier hauled him away and shoved him next to the girl. They grabbed each other, clinging on as if their lives depended on it. Mirek prayed it didn't.

A pale-skinned girl was taken next, then a blue-eyed boy with fair hair, another with a narrow, straight nose...

Mirek studied the expanding group imprisoned by the gate. They all had a particular appearance — tall and lean with long faces, prominent chins, fair skin. Oh no...

He looked to the street. The canvas top of a truck towered over the wall. Mirek clutched his mouth. They were taking his children!

Eleven children selected, Kruger nodded. "That will do for now."

For now? No, this had to stop. Mirek strode toward the children clinging to each other in tears.

He held his palms up submissively. "Please, there's no need for this. There must be some arrangement we can come to. The Volksliste. I'll register this afternoon."

"Good." Kruger waved the soldiers away. "Take them."

The eleven children were herded away, some sobbing, some wailing, some begging for "Papa Mirek."

Mirek's heart twisted as if he'd been stabbed in the chest. "Please. This is their home."

"And soon they'll each have a new home with respectable German parents. Now they'll grow up knowing their true place in the world and how they can best serve the Fatherland."

"You can't!"

"Can't?" Kruger frowned. "You're a writer, Herr Kozlowski. I'd have thought you'd have given more consideration to your choice of words when addressing a high-ranking officer of the SS."

"Please. I'll do anything."

"Anything?"

"Anything."

Kruger stared at him quizzically. "Please correct me if I'm wrong, but isn't the point of an orphanage not only to look after children who find themselves destitute but to secure those children loving homes? Instead of objecting, shouldn't you be thanking me for doing your job for you?"

"I..." In normal circumstances, Mirek was ecstatic when someone gave one of his children a home, but now? These children weren't going to be rehomed; they were going to be brainwashed into fascist, war-mongering monsters.

Kruger gestured to the house. "Even to the most untrained eye, it's clear you're struggling to care for so many strays. I don't believe you've grasped the magnitude of the favor I'm doing you."

"No, I, eh, I..." Words were his trade. He loved them, doted on them, took pride in taking out only the most appropriate ones for each occasion. Yet now, when he needed them most...

Kruger said, "Good. Then on to the next group."

"The *next* group?" Mirek's face felt cold, as if all the blood had drained.

Kruger addressed the children. "Everyone over eleven years old move over here." He gestured left.

Only a few moved. Not least because he was speaking in German, not Polish.

He groaned, then looked at Mirek. "Don't make us do this the hard way."

Mirek translated and ensured the children divided, though he held back a couple who were small for their years.

Hands on his hips, Kruger scanned the group of thirty-one older children. He pursed his lips and exhaled loudly. "It could be better, but..."

Among them, Feliks stared at the ground to avoid eye contact and angering anyone, just as Mirek had taught. Meanwhile, Pawel broke into tears, so Lena hugged him.

Mirek gulped. Dear Lord, what was happening? Eleven children had already been taken. Another thirty-one were under threat. But if he said the wrong thing, he could lose everyone.

Mirek fidgeted like a child who hadn't done his homework. "Herr Hauptsturmführer, wouldn't it better serve the Reich if its citizens were more able to fulfill the Führer's great vision?"

"Mmm." Kruger twiddled his stick. "Go on."

"We've already started teaching German and exploring the rich culture of the Fatherland."

Kruger nodded.

"So if you were to leave them with me for, say, another six months, maybe nine, they'd be much better equipped to—"

Kruger held up a hand for silence, then pointed at the children. "Some of these are Jews, yes?"

"Yes, but—"

"Then what will be next? Teaching pigs to crochet?"

Mirek frowned. "Excuse me?"

"Why teach a Jew skills he'll never need?"

"As I said, to better serve the Fatherland."

"While the sentiment is appreciated, right now, the Führer's primary goal is to increase productivity. Hence the edict for Polish children to be taught only rudimentary arithmetic skills and how to write their name. Nothing else. Please adhere to that."

That made no sense. "Isn't an educated workforce a better workforce?"

Kruger smirked. "You really are a mother hen, aren't you? So, to put your mind at ease, let me assure you that each of your wards will be given the opportunity to learn a trade and thereby live a productive life. Now, if you'll excuse me, other duties call."

He strode for the gate, waving on his men.

The soldiers herded the new group. The children shuffled out, eyes wide with fear, hands clutching their friends.

Frozen, Mirek watched. Despite everything he'd done, all the sacrifices he'd made, he'd lost forty-two children. Forty-two souls who had depended on him. Next to losing his wife, this was the worst day of his life.

He staggered into the house, praying tomorrow would be a better day. How could it not be?

28

"Busy!" shouted Mirek as someone knocked on his study door yet again.

They didn't leave but knocked louder.

Slumped in his reading chair, where he'd been all night, Mirek snapped, "Go away!"

The door creaked slowly open.

Mirek hurled a book. It clattered against the door.

But the door still opened, and Ania entered. "I'm sorry, Mirek, but you need to talk to the children."

He glared at the wall.

She crept closer. "They're all terrified."

As if he could do anything about that. He snorted with anger and frustration.

She said, "They don't know what to do. Don't know what to expect."

"And I do?" Mirek glowered at her and flung his arm in the direction of the courtyard. "Like out there, when I let that Nazi scum take forty-two children who I'd sworn to protect?"

His chin trembled. He hammered his fist onto his chair arm. Again and again.

"I should've saved them." He held the back of his neck with both hands and rocked back and forth. His voice broke. "I should've done more." Tears streamed his cheeks.

Ania rushed over and cradled him against her chest.

"I-I should've done more." He sobbed. "I sh-should've d-done more."

She hugged him tighter. "It's not your fault. If you'd tried harder to stop them, they could've shot you or taken everyone. Or both."

He wrapped his arms around her and clung to her, clawing his fingers into the thick blue cotton of her dress. He squeezed her. Like a small boy not wanting to let go of his mother after being beaten by bullies.

Ania stroked his head. "The children need you. You're what holds this place together, so if they think they've lost you, they've lost everything."

"I c-can't." He shook his head. "Th-they've seen I-I can't protect them, so they'll know any-anything I say is a l-lie."

"Maybe." Ania stroked again, calming the distraught beast within him. "But they still need to hear it."

Her soothing voice, her soothing caress, her soothing words... he felt... safe. And as she usually was, she was right. Even if everyone knew what he was telling them was a lie, there would be reassurance and security through the simple act of him joining them to share their burden, their loss.

Mirek stumbled into the dining room for lunch.

Head down, he stared into his bowl of sorrel soup. Previously, he'd loved the tart lemony flavor, but he couldn't bring himself to dip in his spoon even once. How could he eat when he couldn't stop imagining the horrors those forty-two children were suffering?

He gazed around the dining room, every empty seat the lash of a whip.

The children were eating, yet the usual banter was lost to an icy silence. And all eyes drilled into him. Waiting.

He stared into his soup again. What was he going to say?

Replaying the events of the courtyard over and over, he struggled to envisage a way he could have handled the situation differently, a way that might give him the words he needed now. Over and over and...

A hand rested on his shoulder. Torn from his thoughts, he jumped.

Ania said, "It's time."

Mirek looked up. Everyone had finished eating and was sitting quietly. Waiting.

How could he explain to children as young as five the concept of war and the horrors it was capable of inflicting upon the innocent?

His chair scraped on the floor as he stood.

"The Germans took forty-two of our brothers and sisters yesterday. And I couldn't stop them." His chin trembled, so he gazed into his soup again and gritted his teeth. He looked up. "I tried my best, but there was nothing I could do. You see, war is like a fight that no one can win. People might think they do — the Germans certainly believe they're winning — but since the start of the war, our brave fighters and the Allies must have shot tens of thousands of German soldiers, maybe hundreds of thousands. Is that winning? Because it certainly doesn't seem like winning to me."

He looked around at all the faces mesmerized by his words.

"Yesterday we lost some of our loved ones. Just like families all over Europe have lost some of theirs. One day, the world will realize that so many families have lost so many loved ones that it isn't worth fighting any longer. Unfortunately, whether that day is tomorrow, next year, or in five years, no one knows."

He drew a deep breath, catching as many of their gazes as he could.

"So today, I have two promises for you." He held up an index finger. "The day will come when all this is ended." He held up a second finger. "Until that day comes, I will never — never — stop fighting for you."

Walking away from the table, waved everyone toward the door.

"Now, to show the Germans they haven't beaten us, and to honor our family who aren't with us today, we're all going to play a game in the courtyard."

The last thing he wanted to do was to have fun, but a game seemed the easiest way to take everyone's mind off yesterday's nightmare.

The children swarmed into the courtyard, the atmosphere already brightening.

Mirek said, "Hands up if you've never played Black Man."

Hanka pointed to a rickety bench. "I'll be the umpire."

Some of the newer children raised their hands.

Black Man was a German game his father had told him about, but Mirek had since created his own version as a way for the children to have exercise and interaction.

"Okay, don't worry if you've never played because it's really simple. We call our version Run, Hero, Run. Everyone move over to that wall." Mirek pointed to the far wall, and everyone moved. He patted the wall. "When your hand is touching this wall, it means you're safe.

"Now, all you have to do is run from this safe area"— Mirek walked to the opposite wall and patted that —"to this one."

He grinned, wandering into the center. "Sounds easy, doesn't it? Except all of this space in between is the danger area where you can be caught by a catcher. To start with, there'll be only one catcher in the middle and when they shout 'Run, hero, run!' you must run from one safe area to the other, but if they catch you and lift you off the ground long enough to say 'Run, hero, run!', you have to join them in the middle as another catcher. Simple, yes?"

The children nodded, the experienced ones bobbing about with excitement.

Mirek said, "And the best part is that the last one to be caught is excused from chores for three days."

The children cheered.

Mirek held up a finger. "There's only one rule: no hitting, kicking, pushing, biting, or scratching." He clapped. "Okay, we just need a catcher. Any volunteers?"

Hands thrust into the air.

He scanned the choices, slowly running his pointing finger over them. "Let's see... how about... Agata!"

"I didn't have my hand up!"

"Which makes it even more fun, doesn't it?" This was a gamble, she being one of the tiniest here, but if it paid off, it would pay off massively.

"She can't be a catcher," said Zygmunt. "She's too tiny! She'll be useless."

Mirek grinned. "Then you won't get caught, will you, Zygmunt?" He beckoned her. "Come on, Agata. I believe in you."

Kicking her feet, she traipsed into the middle of the courtyard.

Mirek said, "Don't worry, Baba Hanka is refereeing, and Miss Ania and I will be helping to ensure there's no cheating."

He and Ania moved to either side.

"When you're ready, Agata," said Mirek.

The tiny girl stared at the fifty-five children raring to trample her. Leaning forward, she yelled, "Run, hero, run!"

The children stampeded across the courtyard. Agata flung her arms up to protect her head and crouched into a hunched ball.

Everyone safe at the other side, some of the children laughed and pointed at her as she stood.

Zygmunt grinned. "Told you!"

Agata slumped. Her face long, she gazed at Mirek.

He said, "You can do this, Agata. Don't focus on how small you are but on how clever you are. You know this isn't about catching the best player but about catching the right player. Who do you want on *your* team *right now?*"

She gazed into space for a moment, then smiled and looked at the opposition. She moved along until she spotted who she wanted to catch.

Again, she leaned forward. "Run, hero, run!"

The children stormed at her again. Instead of cowering, Agata dodged around the fastest runners and then dove on her prey: Kuba. She grabbed him and, despite his squirming, lifted him.

"Run, hero, run!" she cried.

Mirek nodded to himself. "Clever girl."

It looked like his gamble was going to work out.

Having been caught, Kuba joined Agata in the middle. She whispered to him, then they faced the next charge together, shouting, "Run, hero, run!"

By targeting the smallest children, Kuba and Agata each caught another player, and the four of them teamed up in the middle. Agata cupped her mouth and whispered, and they all nodded.

They turned and stared at Zygmunt standing proud at the front of the opposition.

Agata smiled. "Useless, eh?"

Zygmunt shuffled behind another player.

"Run, hero, run!"

While most of the children ran to the opposite safe area, Zygmunt stayed in the safety zone, shimmying this way, then that, all four catchers in front of him ready to pounce. Finally, he made a break for it.

The catchers swarmed him and within seconds lifted him into the air.

With the older children now gone, Zygmunt was one of the biggest remaining, so he was a major asset to Agata's team. Their ranks quickly swelled.

Mirek smirked. Yes, things were going exactly as he'd hoped.

But then...

Facing the enemy, Agata shouted, "Run, hero, run!"

Instead of grabbing another child, she and five catchers raced at Mirek.

He backpedaled, laughing. "I'm a referee! I'm a referee!"

Two grabbed a leg each and another two, his arms, while Zygmunt clutched him around the waist. A moment later, they hoisted him off the ground.

"But I'm a referee!"

Agata snorted. "No one's neutral today."

At the far side of the courtyard, Ania laughed.

Mirek sauntered into the middle, looking at her as he joined the catchers. "Think it's funny, do you?"

"Run, hero, run!"

Ania let Ola run in front of her, then dodged around her to try to evade capture. But Mirek was too fast. He grabbed Ania around her waist. She shrieked as he lifted her and whispered in her ear, "Run, hero, run."

He set her down.

Giggling, she playfully slapped his arm. "Crazy."

As they both wandered into the middle, he caught Hanka's gaze. She raised an eyebrow at him with a self-satisfied smirk.

As they took their position with the catchers, Mirek whispered to Ania.

The catchers' shouts initiated the next stampede. Instead of grabbing another child, Mirek and Ania darted to either end of Hanka's bench.

Hanka wagged a finger at him. "Don't you dare."

Mirek said, "After three. One, two, three."

He and Ania lifted the bench with Hanka on it. Kicking her dangling feet in the air, the old lady threw her head back and belly-laughed.

With Mirek, Ania, and Hanka having an unfair advantage because of their size, they let the children do the majority of the catching. Finally, the catchers caught the last three runners all at the same time, to an echo of cheers. Agata beamed with her accomplishment.

Mirek said, "Thank you, everybody. What a fantastic game. I bet you all thought I was crazy making Agata the first catcher and team captain, didn't you?" He ruffled Agata's hair. "But that proves one very important thing — any one of us can be a hero and achieve the impossible. You see, if we use our heads, and we work together, it doesn't matter how small we are, we will succeed." He clapped. "Well done, everybody. Well done."

Ania took his arm. "You always know exactly what to say. It's amazing."

If only he did.

He watched the children stream inside. Did they really have a chance of surviving everything the Germans were going to throw at them? Forty-eight hours ago, he'd thought so. Twenty-four hours ago, no. Today...?

29

The next morning, Mirek flung open his bedroom curtains and did a double take. He squinted at the road beyond the park, then dug out his binoculars from his dresser.

Outside the hospital, German soldiers herded patients into the back of an enclosed gray trailer being hauled by a truck. Hobbling patients, dazed patients, aged patients. It looked more like a goods vehicle than passenger transport, so what the devil could the Germans be doing with people who seemed barely able to stand? They couldn't be so desperate for free labor — such workers would surely be more of a liability than a benefit.

Mirek squinted, scouring the scene for some tiny detail that could hint at what was happening. Too far away even with his binoculars, he gave up and went to his study.

He cleared his desk and laid out the house floor plans, which detailed who slept in each room. With forty-two children gone, allowing everyone else to spread out, including the evictees, was only fair.

He scratched his head. But the Germans hadn't even let those forty-two children pack a bag, so what was he going to do with all their personal belongings? Would it be right to share everything among the remaining children, or should it be stored in the hope the owners returned?

He held his forehead. Every day brought such agonizing problems.

Someone knocked on his door.

"Come."

Ola poked her head in, chin quivering. "Papa Mirek, they're back."

"Who? Not the Germans?"

Her face screwed up and tears came.

"Oh dear Lord." He gulped. How many would he lose today?

Shaking, he staggered to the front door. However, it wasn't Kruger leering at him from the doorstep.

"Mirek Kozlowski?" asked an ordinary soldier.

He flinched. "Yes."

The soldier handed him a leather satchel, then clicked his heels and left.

Mirek frowned at the satchel. How odd. What new psychological torture was this?

He scurried to his study, then sat and stared at the satchel on his desk. This had to be some kind of trick. But what kind?

Unfastening the two steel clasps, he flipped the flap and looked inside — a hefty wedge of paper. Oh no...

He eased the papers out. The top sheet revealed the full horror of the trap he'd fallen into.

A Sea Too Far
by
Hans Josef Kruger

The manuscript!

Was Kruger serious? He honestly expected Mirek to read this piece of junk after what the monster had done?

Mirek shoved it aside. He ached to spit on it. Spit on it, then burn it.

No. That was too good for Kruger's work. He grabbed the papers and lurched up. There were hundreds of pages here, so why waste them? He'd have the children tear the thing into squares to put in the bathroom stalls.

He yanked open the study door but froze. Heaving a breath, he slunk back to his desk. Kruger had shot a family over paint daubed on a car. If the man somehow learned his cherished work had been used as toilet paper, he wouldn't punish only Mirek. In fact, Kruger probably wouldn't stop at this household — the psychopath could raze the whole town.

Mirek had no choice. His stomach churned at the thought of reading that Nazi's work, let alone giving him notes on how to improve it, but at some point, he was going to have to.

He opened a desk drawer. Another stack of papers stared up at him — *The Night Listened*, his latest unfinished work. He cringed at the thought of laying this German junk next to his new manuscript.

He slung Kruger's book in another drawer.

Again, he lurched up. He needed some air. A few moments to clear the images of that sadistic monster's sneer from his thoughts.

Grabbing his coat, he made for the front door as Hanka wandered over. "Mirek, can you—"

He waved her away. "Later."

Mirek shambled out and trudged up the sidewalk. What was he going to do about that manuscript? Kruger might be a monster, but he wasn't stupid. He'd know if Mirek hadn't read the book and was giving sweeping generalizations or if his notes were intended to make the prose worse instead of better.

What a mess he'd fallen into. And the strangest thing was that he'd thought being friendly toward the German would see the man treat his household better. Mirek snorted. Maybe Kruger had treated them better. Maybe if Mirek hadn't been so responsive, the Nazi would have taken *every* child.

A woman screamed.

Mirek jumped.

Farther along the street, a German soldier hauled a struggling young woman into the Flower of Poland.

Oh dear Lord, it couldn't have come to that. These Nazis were butchers, but surely they weren't rapists, too.

From around the corner, a second soldier appeared, yanking another young woman.

Mirek crossed the road for a better angle of the square. He didn't want to get drawn into this, but he needed to know what was happening on his own doorstep.

Around the corner, three soldiers guarded young women huddled in a truck's gloomy interior. The two soldiers came back, and the taller one beckoned the next woman in the truck. Trembling, she jumped onto the cobbles.

Woman? In full light, she looked barely old enough to have left school.

His chubby comrade said, "This is taking too long. Let's take them all at once."

The soldiers agreed and beckoned the other women. Jittery, the first few clambered out. All young. All slim. All pretty.

Mirek gasped. Forced labor in the quarry was one thing, but this...? There could be only one reason to imprison such women in a hotel, only one line of "work" the Nazis had in mind.

From the back of the truck, a woman with wild black hair leaped. "Nazi pigs!"

She hurtled into the chubby soldier, knocking him and his comrade over. All three crashed to the road in a tangled heap. In the chaos, four women bolted across the square. Two soldiers raced after them.

On the ground, the black-haired woman grabbed the chubby soldier's dropped rifle. Rolling onto her back, she aimed at the only soldier still standing. She blasted.

The soldier reeled backward and fell, blood splattering the cobbles.

The chubby soldier leapt onto the woman. He wrestled his gun back, then beat her with it. Over and over and over. When he'd finished, her face was a bloody pulp. She lay motionless.

Meanwhile, the soldiers racing across the square stopped and fired shots over the fleeing women's heads. The women froze, and the soldiers marched them back.

With everyone ordered out of the truck, twelve women whimpered, clinging to each other like startled children clinging to their mother.

Chubby marched back and forth, cursing and shooting glances at his dead comrade.

Finally, he ordered the woman to lie face down on the ground in a row.

They ignored him. Whether because they didn't speak German or were too terrified, heaven only knew.

Chubby cracked one on the head. She crumpled to the cobbles.

He yelled at a red-haired woman, jabbing at the ground next to the fallen woman. When she didn't comply, he kicked her legs from under her, and she smashed into the road.

Obviously realizing what was demanded, the others dove to the ground, forming a semicircle.

He shouted, "Hands behind your backs."

One of them must have whispered in Polish, because they all put their hands behind their backs.

Chubby said, "Close your eyes, and using your right hand, choose a number from one to five."

The women displayed a number with their fingers.

Chubby scanned the women. "This is what happens when you disobey an order or when you let someone else disobey."

The woman fourth along displayed three fingers. He blasted her in the back of the head.

The women shrieked. But no one tried to run or fight. They sobbed into the stone, probably praying that if they did nothing — said nothing — they just might survive.

Strutting before the women, Chubby blasted the eleventh woman, then strolled back and blasted the sixth. Having been passed once, the sixth woman must have believed she was safe — Chubby didn't only want to kill them; he wanted to torture them.

He shot everyone who'd picked three or four, murdering five women in cold blood.

Gibbering wrecks, the remaining seven women were bundled into the hotel.

Mirek gawked at the bodies and the blood streaming into the gutter. The impossible thing to believe was that while these women were someone's daughters, cherished and missed, those monstrous Nazis were someone's sons, equally loved. How was it possible for one person to treat another like this?

He'd wanted fresh air, but now all he wanted was to rush home, lock the doors, and never set foot outside again.

He scurried toward home. Just wait until he told Hanka and— He gasped and stopped dead. Ania? Where was Ania?

30

Mirek scuttled down a side street. He had to find Ania. Had to.

In her late twenties, Ania was older than the abducted women, but considering the behavior of those monsters, Mirek didn't think age was a deciding factor.

A young man in a red cap heaved a wooden handcart heaped with possessions. A small child sat on top, wrapped in a blanket, and a young woman trudged beside him, another child cocooned in her arms.

Poor deluded people. The town would already be deserted if salvation lay within walking distance. If his time to flee ever came, he wanted a solid plan, not a pipe dream.

He entered the bakery.

Empty wicker baskets stood before the counter, and the shelves along the left-hand wall were all bare, but plump loaves nestled on two of the four shelves opposite.

Mirek's mouth watered and his stomach growled at the smell of freshly baked bread.

In a grubby white apron, Markus held up a hand. "Sorry, Mirek, but you've had your ration."

"Is Ania home, Markus?"

"She's upstairs." He leaned inside the doorway at the rear and shouted, "Ania? It's Mirek."

When she appeared, her face was drawn. "Is everything okay?"

Mirek gestured outside. "I need to speak with you."

They exited onto the street.

Ania said, "What's happened? Is everybody okay?"

"You have to move into the orphanage."

"But I love it here. There's nothing like waking up to the smell of fresh bread."

He gripped her arm. "Pack your things. You're coming with me."

"Mirek, what's happened?"

He bit his lip. Ania was such a decent soul, he didn't want to soil her by conjuring images of what he'd witnessed, but…

He pointed back. "They're abducting young women for a…"

Peering down the street, she frowned. "For what?"

Mirek gulped. Ania was decent, but she wasn't naive. "A brothel. They're using the Flower of Poland as a brothel."

Ania snickered and touched his arm. "Thank you. It's sweet you want to protect me, but unless the Germans are now recruiting blind soldiers, I think I'm safe."

He grabbed her by the shoulders. "Listen to me. Please. Pack your things. Now."

She flinched. "Okay. Okay."

She packed, then Mirek led them along side streets to avoid the hotel. Once they were safe at home, he moved Ania into one of the rooms vacated by the female pupils the Germans had taken.

After a stiff drink, he resumed lessons but couldn't concentrate because he couldn't shake the images of innocent people having their brains blasted out. But that wasn't he only thing he couldn't shake.

What a blessing in disguise it had been that Kruger had taken his older children already. His teenage girls might suffer long days of hard labor, but anything was better than sexual abuse. Thank heaven Kruger had done what he had. His household had been so lucky. So incredibly lucky.

In bed, Mirek stared through the gloom at his ceiling, still ruminating on the situation. Was it lucky? *Really?*

The head of the local SS just happened to take his girls away barely hours before soldiers forced a bunch of women into sexual slavery. Could that really be luck?

Both in the mayor's office and in Mirek's study, the man had been a totally different person from that monster in the square. It didn't make his actions any less diabolical, but it did pose an absolutely astonishing question — was there a sliver of humanity buried inside the monster? Maybe — just maybe — if Mirek won Kruger's favor, the man would help him and his children get through this war. There was only one way to find out.

Six minutes later, Mirek plumped his pillow, turned up the gas lamp on his nightstand, and snuggled down with *A Sea Too Far*, Kruger's novel.

Mirek stared at the title page. His plan was sound, but in just a few seconds' time, all his hopes could come crashing down if the book proved to be a piece of junk and was beyond saving. He continued staring. The page ached to be turned, but he couldn't bring himself to do it. His children's future relied on a sadistic Nazi being able to pen a story that moved people.

He rubbed his head. "Oh dear Lord, what have I done?"

With no choice, he turned the page...

Chapter 1. Oftentimes, a shadow is merely a shadow. But sometimes, it's a creeping darkness, stalking all you love and aching to rip it from you. Today, a shadow is spreading across Europe. A shadow darkening the lives of farmers and priests, doctors and mothers, schoolchildren and storekeepers, and one blond thirteen-year-old girl who weeps by her bedroom window night after night, praying to see her father marching back from war.

Mirek's eyebrows raised. "Hmmm."

As openings went, that was pretty darn beguiling. He pulled the gas lamp nearer and settled back for a long night.

Kruger had witnessed, and indeed participated in, some truly nightmarish experiences. A good author thrived on their experiences, so what delights did this paradoxical Nazi have in store for him?

31

At 4:15 a.m., Mirek placed down the final page of Kruger's novel as a single tear trickled down his cheek.

He gazed into the gloom. How could Kruger be so brutal in real life and yet so sensitive on the page? Or had someone helped him? Maybe his wife had helped flesh out ideas. Or a secretary had embellished upon handwritten notes when asked to type them up.

A tragic love story set against the backdrop of the Great War, the book had a tremendous amount to commend it: the lavish descriptions allowed Mirek to picture the locations, the action scenes made his heart race, and the characters lured him into their lives. For an amateur writer, the book was remarkably good.

He placed the manuscript on his nightstand.

Unfortunately, while Kruger's raw talent was evident, the story lacked the emotional depth necessary for a reader to truly root for the protagonists.

So why had it moved him so? Mirek scratched his head.

Maybe because, appreciating its potential, he'd been rewriting it while reading, envisioning how the story could be developed to breathe real life into the characters. Yes, if its flaws were addressed, it could be proudly displayed in any bookstore.

And thank heaven for that. Now, he could tell Kruger he'd genuinely enjoyed his work and offer valuable insights on how to improve it in the hope Kruger would reciprocate by protecting Mirek's household.

At breakfast, he daydreamed about the storyline while tucking into porridge.

A woman's voice said, "Someone's in a better mood."

"Hmmm?"

Ania smiled. "You're brighter today. What's happened?"

He didn't want to speak too soon and give anyone false hope. "I'm mulling something over. Something that might help us."

She nodded. "If it's put you in such a good mood, keep mulling."

He postponed morning classes in favor of seeing if his plan held water.

At 9:20 a.m., he strode toward the town hall. The women's bodies had disappeared, and someone had sluiced the blood away, but he still shivered as he passed the spot.

A soldier stood on guard at either side of the town hall entrance. Only hours ago, Mirek would have been terrified of approaching, his heart pounding and his hands sweating, but now, armed with important information, he surprised himself at how calm he was.

As he neared, the guards turned their rifles on him. He raised his hands. "I'd like to see Hauptsturmführer Kruger, please."

The soldiers exchanged confused glances. Not surprising. Considering Kruger's reputation for slaughtering people in cold blood, why would any Pole risk angering him by expecting an unsolicited audience?

A soldier with a wispy mustache said, "And you are?"

"Mirek Kozlowski. Tell him it's about a book."

"Are you trying to be funny?"

These monsters weren't going to trample on him when he had such leverage. "Fine. Don't tell him. Give my regards to the Eastern Front." He sauntered away.

"Wait!"

Mirek stopped.

The guard dashed up the steps and into the building. Two minutes later, one of Kruger's aides ambled out. He frowned at Mirek now standing with his arms folded on the edge of the square.

The aide said, "What's this about?"

No one knew what Mirek knew, so they were rightly cautious. That gave Mirek one devil of an edge. If he was careful and didn't push too far, now would be a good time to test the extent of this newfound power.

Mirek stared at the man. "And you are?"

"Oberscharführer Steiner." The aide sneered, obviously struggling with whether he should shoot Mirek or lick his boots. "What do you want with Hauptsturmführer Kruger?"

"That's a personal matter which I don't believe the hauptsturmführer would appreciate being discussed in public."

Steiner scratched his head and glanced at the guards, who looked at him blankly. "Hauptsturmführer Kruger is due around 1:30."

Mirek reveled in his power. "And your name was...?"

The man pursed his lips. "Oberscharführer Steiner."

"Thank you, Oberscharführer Steiner. I'll be sure to tell Hauptsturmführer Kruger how helpful you've been."

The aide's attitude lightened. He clicked his heels and gave a nod in acknowledgment.

Mirek sauntered away. Remarkable. If he proved his value to Kruger, he might be able to push things further than he'd ever dreamed.

At 2:00 p.m., Mirek returned. One of the guards immediately escorted Mirek to the mayor's office.

Kruger stood silhouetted against the windows. Steiner smoked in a chair nearby while another military officer cranked a calculating machine at a desk.

Mirek's escort said, "Herr Hauptsturmführer, Mirek Kozlowski."

Without turning, Kruger waved his hand. "Leave us."

The soldier did so.

Kruger said, "Everyone."

Steiner said, "Herr Hauptsturmführer?"

Kruger shot a glance toward the door.

"Apologies, Herr Hauptsturmführer. I didn't know you meant everyone." Steiner and his colleague left.

Kruger marched behind his desk, swinging his arms from side to side. He glanced at Mirek but didn't say anything, then marched back. Was he nervous? He'd obviously want Mirek's thoughts on his work, so was it that he was scared to ask in case he heard something negative from someone whose opinion he valued?

Mirek watched. Should he put Kruger out of his misery or let him suffer?

Kruger raised his finger toward Mirek as if about to ask a question but then bit his knuckle instead.

Mirek knew the agony of revealing a work for the first time and wondering whether it would be loved or loathed. He couldn't torture another writer like that. Not even Kruger. "Don't panic, I liked it."

Kruger clapped and then slumped with a huge gasp of relief. He pointed at Mirek. "You..." He wagged his finger. "You had me worried. But you genuinely liked it?"

"For an unpublished writer, it was genuinely impressive."

Kruger squinted at him as if wanting the praise to be true but believing himself undeserving of it. Strange that someone so supremely confident in some areas could be so insecure in others.

Picking up a knife from his desk, Kruger toyed with it. "You're not just saying that because I'm a high-ranking SS officer? I take my art seriously, so I'd be deeply offended should I believe someone insincere."

Mirek cupped his chest. "Hand on heart, I enjoyed it. Did anyone help you with it?"

"Help me? What do you mean, *help me?*" The blade glinted as Kruger twirled it. Mirek wasn't sure if it was a letter opener or a service dagger the Nazi liked to have close at hand.

"Did someone help you write it?"

Kruger scowled. "You don't think *I* could write such a work without help?"

Mirek backpedaled. "My apologies, I imagined the time commitment writing demands would clash with the demands of your rank."

"Thank heaven for that. For a moment, I thought you were implying that I was incapable of writing such prose. But, yes, because of my various commitments, it's taken many years to complete. And now, of course, the publishing industry is, shall we say, somewhat in disarray." He rolled his eyes. "But there I go jumping the gun and assuming it worthy of professional consideration."

"I believe it could be."

Kruger waved him away, feigning false modesty. "Please."

"Honestly," said Mirek. "I thoroughly enjoyed it."

"Really? Be brutal. I won't accept anything else."

Mirek struggled not to balk. How did someone define "brutal" when they could shoot an innocent person in cold blood as nonchalantly as if they were deciding which hat to wear?

Mirek said, "I found it moving. The way the story weaves back and forth between past and present using locations to mark time. And that wonderful recurring motif of the reflections of clouds in puddles. That was beautiful. As for the wind symbolizing Death — such an intriguing touch. How did you develop such imagery?"

Kruger slapped his forehead. "Steiner. It's Steiner, isn't it?"

"Steiner?"

"Oberscharführer Steiner. He put you up to this, didn't he? One of his *pranks*."

"No. If you want brutal honesty, I must admit that I wasn't looking forward to reading it because I was worried about your response if it was a complete mess and I couldn't lie convincingly enough." Mirek shrugged. "Luckily, I don't have to lie. It genuinely surprised me with how much beauty there is in it."

"Surprised?" He frowned and stabbed the knife toward Mirek. "Why? Because I'm SS? So I couldn't possibly be moved by birdsong, or a waterfall, or dew on a spiderweb?"

Mirek tilted his head. "In today's world, it's almost impossible to find beauty in anything."

Kruger studied his blade, then looked up at Mirek. "I suppose that's a fair point."

Mirek said, "And the ending... it reminded me of Emily Brontë's—"

They spoke in unison: "*Wuthering Heights.*"

"Was that a conscious decision?" asked Mirek.

"I only realized the connection later. So you honestly think it's good? That it might be publishable one day?"

Mirek took a breath. If Kruger received feedback from someone knowledgeable that contradicted what he said now... "I'm not going to lie — it needs work. But it has the potential to be a very commendable piece of writing, easily deserving of publication."

"Really?"

"Really."

Kruger stroked his chin. "And you'd be prepared to offer notes on how to revise it?"

"It would be an honor." Mirek hoped he wasn't laying it on too thick, but he needed this Nazi fighting for him, not against him.

Kruger beamed and tossed the knife on the desk. "I can't tell you how much I'd appreciate that. I've slaved over this book. Lost friends, upset family, missed opportunities..."

Mirek nodded. "It's a solitary life. Often with no one to rely on but yourself."

Kruger sniggered. "People never believe what hard work it is, do they? Everyone thinks that because they can hold a pencil, they could pen a book, so a writer's life must be so easy."

"Yes, many people have a very romanticized image of the lifestyle."

Kruger stared at the bookcase. "To think that one day my work might sit in bookstores around the globe next to Kafka, Goethe, Mann..."

They were some of Germany's literary greats. Modesty was obviously not going to be a problem for Kruger moving forward.

"So what kind of revisions do you foresee?" asked Kruger. "Can you give an example?"

Mirek had a wealth of ideas. "For example, Moritz teaching Ursula to ride a bike — it's a fun interlude that gives a brief respite from the horrors of war, but ultimately, it's meaningless. Why not have him teach her to swim, then after the air raid—"

"She can jump into the river to save Heinrich herself! Genius. Why didn't I think of that?" Kruger rubbed his hands together. "Oh, this is going to be marvelous." He slumped and rolled his eyes. "But as luck would have it, it couldn't have come at a more inconvenient time — I've been ordered back to Germany to offer my expertise to mold the next generation of SS officer candidates in Bad Tölz. It's a great honor, but I'll be gone a month or more."

Was Mirek supposed to congratulate him on having the opportunity to create more monsters? "No problem. That gives me plenty of time to prepare a detailed analysis, so when you get back, you can jump straight in."

"Wonderful. And in the meantime, I must think of a way to show my gratitude."

That was what Mirek had been praying to hear. He waved his hand. "There's really no need."

Kruger slung his arm around Mirek's shoulder, turning him for the door. "No, I insist."

Mirek said, "Well, I couldn't possibly refuse a direct order from an SS officer, could I?"

Laughing, Kruger slapped him on the back. "No, it would be such a waste to see you before a firing squad."

Mirek smiled but didn't laugh. It was a risky game he was playing. Absolutely deadly. However, if he pulled it off, not only would his household be safe, he might even be able to negotiate the return of the children he'd lost.

32

The next morning, Mirek taught some basic German in the hope that if his children were ever commanded to do something but couldn't fathom what, they could at least sincerely apologize in the language.

Zygmunt knocked and entered the dining room. "Excuse me, Papa Mirek."

"Yes?"

The boy fidgeted. "The Germans are back."

Back? After all the brownnosing he'd done yesterday? It just never ended.

He trailed outside.

Three German soldiers lurked in the courtyard, and the cab of a truck was visible above the wall again.

No, no, no. They couldn't take more of his children. No.

His heart racing, he balled his fists. Not again. *Not again!* If they were taking his children, he had nothing to lose by standing up to them.

A soldier shoved a paper and pen at him. "Sign this."

Mirek pulled away. "Enough is enough." He stabbed at the gate. "Get the hell off my property!"

He'd die stopping them if he had to, but they weren't taking anyone else.

The soldier waved the paper. "You must sign this."

Mirek shrieked, "Get out!"

"Mirek, stop." Ania raced over. She pushed him back while addressing the soldiers over her shoulder. "We're so sorry. So sorry."

The soldier waved the paper again. "We just need a signature, any signature, so we can make the delivery and leave."

Wait...

Delivery?

Mirek said, "What do you mean *delivery?*"

The soldier gestured to the gate. "This way."

Mirek tramped out.

Standing on the curb, he peered into the back of the truck and at the mountain of coal inside. Propped at the base was a white envelope with his name on it. It contained a note: *Should I ever need to visit again, I trust this is what I'll smell burning.*

Mirek's mouth gaped. He'd actually reached Kruger!

The next day, another truck arrived, this time containing sides of beef, sacks of flour, assorted vegetables, rice, bread... the larder hadn't been so full since he'd received a book advance in 1938.

On the third day, nothing arrived. The fourth neither. But on the twelfth day...

Agata shot into the dining room, disrupting his class. She waved something in her hand, something paper. "Papa Mirek, Papa Mirek!"

Pointing at the doorway, he said, "Shall we try that again, Agata?"

"No, listen, it's—"

He frowned, hands on his hips. "No? Agata Karbownik, are you looking for a week's kitchen duty?"

She waved the rectangular paper. "It's Feliks!"

"What?" Mirek grabbed it — a postcard scrawled in Feliks's handwriting.

"*Dear Papa Mirek and everyone, The hours are long and the work is hard, but I'm learning something new every day and managing to take care of myself. I hope you're all safe and happy. Love, Feliks.*"

Mirek waved the postcard to the class. "Feliks. He's okay."

All the pupils cheered.

Mirek whisked Agata up and twirled around with her, laughing. "He's safe, Agata. Safe."

Hanka tramped out of the kitchen. "What's all this noise? Some of us are trying to work, you know."

Mirek waved the postcard. "Feliks is okay."

"Let me see that." She snatched it and read. Clutching her mouth, she burst into tears. "But that means..."

Mirek nodded. "If Feliks is okay, everyone should be."

Sure enough, six days later, a postcard arrived from Lena, saying she was learning seamstressing. Another three postcards came over the next few weeks. Mirek's heart glowed.

When Kruger had taken those children, Mirek had believed he'd failed them, yet here they were leading safe, productive lives. Just as Kruger had promised. How could the German be such a complete monster in some respects yet in others be perfectly reasonable? It seemed that the more Mirek learned of the man, the less he understood him.

The manuscript was the core element in their "relationship," but for someone as complex as Kruger, there had to be more. Something Mirek was missing. And if Mirek was to have any hope of manipulating the man into helping them, he had to figure out what made him tick. Luckily, there was one person who might offer some insights into this perplexing Nazi, a person Mirek had already arranged to meet that afternoon.

After lunch, Mirek headed for the square.

A truck pulled up at the hotel, and twelve German soldiers clambered out. Laughing and joking, they made the most appalling comments about what they were going to do to the women inside, comments that, should their mothers have heard, would have had every soldier hanging their head in shame and begging for forgiveness.

Giving the hotel a wide berth, Mirek glanced toward home, praying none of the children were outside to witness such behavior.

The tiniest glimpse of red hair ducked into an apartment building's doorway.

"Oh, for the love of God."

Mirek traipsed back. As he did so, Jacek peeked out, then immediately ducked back in.

On the sidewalk, Mirek glared at the boy huddled in the entranceway. "I thought we'd finished with all this silliness, Jacek."

The boy said nothing.

"What am I going to do with you? You know how dangerous the streets are, and you've seen the Germans take some of your brothers and sisters. You must follow the rules." He offered his hand. The boy took it, and Mirek led him home.

After giving Zygmunt free rein to sit on Jacek if he tried to escape again, Mirek once more set out.

He met Borys at the lower end of the square.

"Talk about adding insult to injury." Borys nodded toward the ruins of the synagogue. Behind it, a group of men dug up gravestones. He shook his head. "Having the Jewish Council send a Jewish workforce to dig up Jewish gravestones to pave a new road? That's so twisted."

Some of the workers were in tears as they wobbled the stones back and forth to loosen them. Those poor men probably knew some of the dead. Mirek cringed at the thought of visiting a loved one's grave for years, adding a pebble to a pile on the headstone as a sign of respect, only to now have to disturb that loved one's slumber.

"What have you done about the Volksliste?" asked Borys.

"Nothing. There's been another development. Something I need to ask you about."

"Okay?"

"What do you know about Kruger?"

Borys shrugged. "Nothing that means anything. Why?"

"He's asked me to help him finish a novel."

Borys picked his beard. "And you want to know if that would be seen as collaboration?"

"For a start."

"That's an odd one. If he's spending time on a book, he's not spending time on his duties, which is good."

Mirek nodded.

"However, depending on the subject matter, the book could promote Nazi ideals, which, if it receives a large enough audience, could have a far worse impact than anything a lone SS officer could ever achieve."

Mirek clicked his tongue. "I hadn't thought of that."

"Does the book explore Nazi themes?"

He winced. "In places."

Occasionally the dialogue and subtext did. He'd figured he'd be able to edit that out through carefully crafted revision suggestions, but what if he couldn't? Kruger was ultimately the one in control, so what if he used all Mirek's best ideas to create a highly marketable book only to then expand all the sections on Nazism?

But how could he now refuse to work on it?

Borys said, "There is another angle here – two in fact – but you're not going to like either."

Mirek watched a young man with tears streaming as he ripped up a headstone. "Go on."

"I take it you'll be meeting Kruger personally."

A hollow formed in Mirek's gut. An ache that clawed and clawed. Borys was right – Mirek didn't like where this conversation was heading. "Yes, we'll probably be working closely together on occasion. Literally."

"So kill the Nazi pig."

Mirek gawked at him.

"What?" said Borys. "Assassinating a high-ranking Nazi would be a major coup."

Mirek shot Borys a sideways glance. "*That's* the advice you've got for me?"

Borys shook his head. "That's an *option* I've got for you."

Mirek exhaled loudly. "You said there were two angles."

"Pass us information. Anything you hear, anything you see, no matter how seemingly insignificant."

Great. So he could either be a spy or an assassin, neither occupation usually being rewarded with long-term prospects.

Borys said, "Have you got any more articles for us?"

Mirek passed an envelope. "These are the Polish versions. If you like them, I'll create the German versions."

Borys took out three sheets of paper.

The first article described the appalling conditions on the Eastern Front and advised soldiers on the easiest ways to convincingly fake illness and so avoid the worst of the fighting there.

The second discussed a supposed rise in anti-Nazi sentiment among the regular German army, suggesting like-minded soldiers band together for moral support.

Borys chuckled when he read the third aloud. "*Avoid contracting a sexual disease after bedding a Pole by dousing your penis in cayenne pepper every morning for a week.*" He winced. "Man, that's going to sting." He read further, "*The more it burns, the more you know it's fighting the infection.*" He chuckled. "That's really good. It makes a weird kind of sense, so you just know guys are going to fall for it."

Mirek nodded. "And an unhappy soldier is in inefficient soldier."

"Your Hitler's birthday celebrations caused pockets of disruption across Germany, so keep these coming. They're great."

"So even if I help Kruger with his book, and even if I have to register for the Volksliste, the Resistance will still be there for us?"

Borys offered his hand. "You have my word."

Excellent. It looked like nothing could stop his plan from coming together.

33

Summer 1940.

Teaching in the dining room, Mirek pointed at Tadek. "What do you say if a German asks, '*Wie heißen Sie?*'"

Tadek thought for a moment. "*Ich heiße Tadek Skorupski. Wie kann ich sie helfen?*"

"Very good, Takek." Mirek pointed at Jacek. "What did he say, Jacek?"

Jacek silently stared. Mirek regularly tried to engage the boy, but thus far, it wasn't working. Maybe it never would because of the trauma the boy had experienced.

He pointed at a girl. "Ola, what did Tadek say?"

A dark-skinned girl said, "My name is Tadek Skorupski. How can I help you?"

"Very good. Excellent work today, class. Now—"

A distorted voice thundered in from outside. Mirek cringed. "Oh holy Mother of God, no."

Fearing the house walls might muffle an important instruction, Mirek dashed outside, the world basking beneath a glorious blue sky.

The black car with the rooftop megaphone rumbled down the street. "All citizens will gather in Adolf Hitler Square at noon. Attendance is mandatory."

The message repeated.

Mirek hung his head, his heart breaking for whoever was going to be punished this time.

At 11 a.m., he led his household into the square. He'd set off earlier than last time, presuming that those with children would be called to the front again and preferring to choose an advantageous spot rather than suffer what was available and thereby, risk endangering everyone.

Hundreds of people were pouring in already. Mirek positioned his group toward the top right of the square, close enough to see the town hall, but not directly outside it.

The children gripped him, Hanka, and Ania, their tiny hands clawing as if fearful of being dragged away. His household formed one terrified clinging mass.

The square filled, and as the bells chimed noon, Kruger swaggered out.

Mirek stared agog. Not only had the man returned, but he was once more going to spearhead whatever atrocity was about to befall their town.

Using a microphone, Kruger said, "It appears some of you have taken advantage of my absence to flout the regulations laid down by my office."

Whispers in Polish translated for everyone.

Kruger signaled to a truck parked just off the square. Under Steiner's supervision, soldiers hauled a group of hooded and shackled figures off the vehicle, many of them crashing to the ground as they blundered forward.

Soldiers shoved nineteen people against the cream wall running to the left of the town hall steps. The group stood, hunched, whimpering, trembling.

Two soldiers walked from either end of the group, ripping their hoods away to reveal men, women, children, and elderly. The people squinted, shrinking from both the sunlight and the limelight into which they had been thrust. In the middle of the group, a young couple cowered, each with an armband.

Like a theater actor relishing his soliloquy, Kruger pointed at a bearded man and a rosy-cheeked woman next to the Jews. "This man and woman hid undocumented Jews in their root cellar. As if that isn't heinous enough, they had the audacity to attack one of my men when he investigated."

Kruger gestured to the people on either side. "Their parents, their children, their neighbors... any of them could have chosen to do the right thing, but instead, they did nothing, condoning this diabolical act."

He nodded to Steiner. Four personnel armed with machine guns marched over and stood before the shackled group.

Against the wall, a bald man shouted, "We didn't know! We didn't—"

Kruger drew his pistol and shot him.

Many lining the wall wailed.

Addressing the crowd, Kruger said, "Ignorance is no defense and will not be tolerated."

Blubbering, the rosy-cheeked woman spluttered out a few words. "P-please, sp-spare my children. Plea-please."

The woman's hands shackled behind her, she half turned, fingers clawing to reach a grubby girl with messy brown hair.

Without a flicker of emotion, Kruger shot the girl, then the boy next to her.

The mother shrieked.

Kruger nodded to Steiner.

The machine guns thundered. And the watching crowd flinched en masse. Blood splattered the cream wall, and bodies jerked as hot metal slammed into them. In barely four seconds, nineteen living souls were reduced to a bloody heap of mangled flesh.

Kruger said, "This is what happens when you break the law or aid others in doing so. Let this be a warning. Watch your neighbors, your friends, and your family. Don't let someone else's selfish criminal act see you put against this wall."

He scanned the faces staring at him with expressions of horror and disgust.

"In the spirit of goodwill, I'm granting all of you"— he swept a pointing finger across the crowd —"a twenty-four-hour amnesty to relinquish any firearms, turn in any Jewish sympathizers, and make known the names of any conspirators against the Fatherland. Twenty-four hours, during which time there will be no repercussions for those who come forward. However, after that time"— he scowled at the crowd —"if you have anything to hide, my men will find you."

With a final sneer, he sauntered back into the building.

Mirek shuddered. This was the man he hoped would help him protect his children?

Crying, Ania said, "It's like he doesn't even see us as people."

He reached out to comfort her, but he froze at a face away in the crowd. His jaw dropped. No. It couldn't be. No!

34

Mouth still agape, Mirek stared through the crowd at a group of women guarded by soldiers and Blue Police. A couple of the women were ones who'd been forced to lie on the cobbles while the chubby soldier blasted their friends. He didn't recognize any of the others. Except for one.

One who stared at him.

One desperate and terrified.

Lena.

But that was impossible. Lena had sent that postcard saying she was at a camp and everything was fine. Why was she with that group of women? She'd barely turned fifteen. Surely even the Nazis wouldn't put a child in a place like that. Not a child. Not *his* child.

With the crowd dispersing, the Blue Police shoved the shackled group away. Lena twisted back and stared. Stared with the most pleading gaze he'd ever seen.

His children clinging to him, and with tens of people between him and the hotel women, Mirek struggled to push his way through.

He pulled one child off only for another to latch on.

"Ania, help." He stabbed a finger toward the disappearing women. "I need to get over there."

Ania gathered more children to her.

"Lena!" Mirek waded through the river of small hands clutching at him for security. "I'll get you out, Lena! Hold on."

He had to reach her. Had to.

But she was swept farther and farther away. And then, she disappeared inside the hotel.

Mirek held his head. Even if he could reach her in there, what was he going to do?

He shouted, "Hanka, get the kids home."

"Why? Where are you going?"

"Just do it, Hanka."

She guided the children away while he darted toward the town hall. He couldn't get to Lena, but maybe he didn't have to.

As he raced toward the entrance, two guards trained their machine guns on him.

He didn't stop. He couldn't stop. Hands up, he dashed on. He had to save Lena.

Nearby, Steiner directed his men what to do with the heap of bodies. He glimpsed Mirek approaching and gestured for the guards to lower their weapons. They did.

Mirek shouted, "I need to see Hauptsturmführer Kruger."

Steiner said, "Hauptsturmführer Kruger is indisposed."

Mirek pointed at the town hall. "He was standing here literally seconds ago. Tell him I need to see him. Now!"

Steiner's eyebrows raised. He rested his hand on his holstered pistol. "*Now?*"

The guards raised their machine guns once more.

Mirek couldn't save Lena if he was dead. "I'm sorry. But please, it's vitally important."

Steiner huffed, obviously in a quandary over his commanding officer's favorite Pole making unreasonable demands. Pointing at Mirek, he addressed the guards. "He comes no closer."

He entered the building.

Mirek glanced back. Under Hanka's and Ania's guidance, his children scurried toward home. They'd be safe in just minutes. But Lena?

He stared at the town hall's black doors. "Come on."

Where the devil was Steiner?

The doors didn't budge.

Mirek turned to the hotel, praying a truckful of soldiers wouldn't saunter inside.

He glowered at the town hall. "Where are you, you monster?"

An eternity later, Steiner finally returned. He swanned down the steps with a sparkle in his eye. "As I said, Hauptsturmführer Kruger is indisposed."

"But—"

"He'll send for you when he has a free moment." Steiner smirked, then sauntered away.

"But—"

The guards stepped forward, machine guns raised.

Mirek jerked back. He looked up at the building. A figure stood with his hands on his hips in the window of the mayor's office. The monster knew Mirek hadn't come with good news and thus had chosen not to deal with him.

Mirek slunk away. He had to save Lena. But how?

***

The three days it took for Borys to reply to Mirek's note felt like a lifetime. But that was nothing compared to what it must have felt like for Lena.

Mirek paced in his study. "I don't believe that, Borys. There must be something you can do. For God's sake, she's just a child."

Sitting in the armchair, Borys threw his hands up. "If you've got a workable plan, I'm all ears. And by workable, I mean one that doesn't end with everyone we know riddled with bullets."

Mirek scowled. "She's fifteen, Borys. *Fifteen!*"

Borys leaned forward. "My friend, if there was something I could do, believe me, I'd be the first one out of that door to do it."

"But we can't do nothing. I told her I'd save her." Tears welled in Mirek's eyes. "I told her."

Mirek slumped over his desk.

"Her only shot is to hold out until Kruger decides he's no longer *indisposed*."

"That sadistic piece of—" Mirek kicked his desk. "He could end it like that." He snapped his fingers. "Like that! But he won't even talk to me."

"So let's pray she can hold out."

"But it could be a day, a week, hell, even a month. Imagine what she's going through?"

Borys groaned. "Believe me, imagining that is the last thing you want to do."

"It's that bad?"

He nodded.

Mirek swallowed hard. "Tell me."

He didn't want to picture it, but if he did, maybe it would inspire him to find a solution.

"Seriously?"

"I need to know."

Borys sucked through his teeth. "Men pay three reichsmarks for fifteen minutes with a woman. And some women are chosen thirty times a day."

Mirek gawked open-mouthed. *Thirty.* Some of the women were raped *thirty times per day*. And to add insult to such horrendous injury, soldiers paid only three reichsmarks to do it. Mirek had paid more than that for a loaf of bread yesterday!

Tears streamed Mirek's face. "Please, Borys, there must be something we can do."

Borys opened his mouth to speak, but no sound came out.

Mirek gazed into space. What was he going to do? He had to save Lena, but how?

35

Borys gone, Mirek paced in his study, his mind a jumble of crazy rescue ideas and horrific images of what Lena was suffering.

Ania knocked and poked her head in. "Your two o'clock class is still waiting. They're getting pretty rowdy."

He pushed past her. "I have to go out."

He couldn't carry on as if everything was normal. Though he didn't know what he was going to do, he had to do something.

Ania called after him, "What shall I do with the class?"

He stormed outside.

His heart raced as he marched toward the hotel. This was a crazy idea, but sometimes, crazy ideas were the only ideas that could work.

Mirek stared at the two Blue Police officers guarding the hotel. After the invasion, the Germans had disbanded all forms of authority in Poland, only to later realize their mistake and reinstate many Polish police officers with vastly diminished powers. Here, the Blue Police were tasked with keeping the women inside and the town's men outside, though armed German soldiers stationed inside held the real power.

Until now, Mirek had stayed away from Blue Police. They looked the same as before with their dark blue uniforms, black brimmed caps, and knee-high boots, but for one crucial difference — the Polish national insignia had been purged from their uniforms. That one difference said everything.

Approaching a bushy-eyebrowed policeman, Mirek tried to lick his lips, but his mouth was so dry his tongue just stuck to them.

Mirek said, "How much to talk to one of the women?" If he could tell Lena help was coming soon, it would give her hope to hold on.

Bushy Eyebrows held up his palm. "Germans only."

Mirek discreetly showed some zlotys. "I only want to talk. How much?"

The policeman slapped his truncheon into Mirek's chest and shoved him back. "Are you deaf? *Germans only.*"

"How much for Volksdeutsche?" He hadn't registered, but it was worth a try.

Bushy Eyebrows looked to his fellow officer, who shrugged. They obviously hadn't been briefed on how to handle a German who wasn't military.

Bushy Eyebrows cursed under his breath. "Show me your papers and I'll go ask."

Mirek didn't have papers. "Look, I'm sure we can work something out." He offered twelve zlotys, double what a soldier would pay in reichsmarks.

"If you don't have papers, beat it."

Mirek fumbled with his money, peeling off more bills. "Twenty zlotys. Just to talk to one of the women."

Two German soldiers swaggered around the corner. One with buckteeth spied Mirek offering money. He shoved Mirek away. "Get lost. No Poles are soiling our women."

"Please, I just need to talk to someone."

Buck Teeth sneered. "Yeah, sure you do."

"Twenty zlotys just to talk." Mirek held up his cash. "Just two minutes."

Buck Teeth swung a haymaker and slammed his fist into Mirek's face.

Caught unexpectedly, Mirek crashed into the wall and sank to the ground.

The soldier reared over Mirek, whipping out his pistol. "You think you can take our women?"

Mirek cowered behind his hands, blood splattered across his face from his nose.

The second soldier yanked Buck Teeth away. "Don't, Beckmann. I've seen him talking with Kruger."

"So?"

"So I don't want to spend the winter on the Eastern Front. Do you?"

Bucktoothed Beckmann stabbed a finger at Mirek. "I see you here again, I'll kill you. I don't care who you know."

The soldiers marched inside.

Bushy Eyebrows heaved Mirek up. "He means it. Don't come back."

Mirek shuffled home, holding his nose, blood streaming through his fingers.

On seeing Mirek's bloody nose, Ania and Hanka made a great fuss, but he didn't hear most of what they said because of the question that wouldn't stop clawing at him – how was he going to save Lena?

The next day, he went back to the town hall only to be told Kruger was still unavailable.

Since the end of the twenty-four-hour amnesty, truckloads of soldiers had been conducting random house-to-house searches all over town. With soldiers having less time for "off-duty activities," Mirek hoped he wouldn't bump into Beckmann again, so he returned to the hotel.

The moment Bushy Eyebrows saw Mirek, he barred the door with his truncheon. "You're asking for a beating, pal!"

Mirek held up his hands. "I'm not looking for trouble. I'll give you twenty zlotys for getting a message to one of the women."

"Forget it. I'm not getting drawn into your mess."

Mirek pushed the money at him. "Please. Just to deliver a message."

The policeman adjusted his grip on his truncheon. "Are you going to leave, or do I have to make you?"

"Okay." Mirek backed away. "I'm going."

In his study, Mirek drew up a roster – two children would hang around in the street for an hour at a time, far enough from the hotel to be safe yet close enough to see the comings and goings. If Lena was ever allowed out under escort, they would follow her until she reached her destination, then one would fetch Mirek while the other ensured she didn't move on anywhere else.

With the schedule complete, he stared into space.

What else could he do? He didn't know any corrupt officials he might bribe, and Borys was the only Resistance he knew. He'd hit a dead end.

Mirek slumped over his desk, head in his hands.

It was over. He couldn't save Lena. Because he was nothing but a useless writer.

Wait...

That was the answer – to do what he did best.

He grabbed some paper and a pencil. The Resistance valued him because his writing could undermine the German infrastructure and morale. Maybe if he did the same for the Nazis, he could bargain for Lena.

He listed the Nazis' main goals: destroy the Polish culture, segregate the Jews, expand German territory, elevate the Fatherland, create a new world order with ethnic Germans at its center...

Tapping his pencil on his chin, Mirek let his mind fly, exploring whatever wild ideas it conjured.

What if the lineage of Copernicus, one of Poland's greatest scientists, led directly to German ancestry? That would make Poland look bad and Germany look good. But how could he twist history just enough to shake a person's beliefs without going so far it seemed preposterous?

He scrawled thoughts on potential avenues for research that might sow such seeds of doubt while yet giving such a concept an air of authenticity.

Jews? How did one make claims about an ethnic group that were simultaneously outlandish yet believable?

Hitler had managed to do it repeatedly, so what was the secret?

When the Nazis denigrated Jews, they exploited specific elements that their "audience" found either fearful or distasteful, such as greed, hygiene, disease, theft, and deceit. How could Mirek tap into those? How could he use stupidity, ignorance, and fascism for his own ends?

German propaganda often exaggerated certain features of Jewish appearance using caricatured drawings – a common one being a hook nose.

What if that bump in the nose created a cavity inside that trapped air? That air would become stale, and just like rotting fruit developed mold, a moist cavity could become a breeding ground for all manner of bacteria, viruses, and diseases. Germans should rightly be fearful of standing too close to a Jew in case they were breathed on and infected with the illnesses the Jew was carrying.

Mirek ripped the paper up and flung the pieces aside. How had he penned something so monstrous?

Lena.

"God forgive me." He took another piece of paper. Wrote it again. All the while, he cursed himself. But every ugly word, every horrendous thought, could be the one that saved the life of a girl who'd brought such joy into the world.

He spent the rest of the day drafting ideas. It was midnight before he quit, and then only because the words on the paper were blurring.

The next day, Mirek resumed teaching, though he found concentrating difficult, always straining to hear running footsteps that suggested a sighting of Lena.

Unfortunately, no news came.

But something did.

36

Standing at the front of the dining room, Mirek said, "So on November eleventh,1918, Pilsudski finally proclaimed Poland an independent—"

Running footsteps pounded down the hall. Lena. Someone must have seen Lena.

Mirek dashed to the door and ripped it open, but froze.

Tadek stared up. But Tadek wasn't on Lena lookout duty.

He pointed outside. "H-haupsu-haupstur—"

Mirek gulped. "Hauptsturmführer Kruger?"

"Yes."

Mirek darted to the window. Kruger had ignored every approach Mirek had made. Why would the man suddenly appear?

Outside, Kruger swaggered across the courtyard with seven of his men. This was *not* a literary visit.

Mirek shot outside. Before he could stop himself, he blurted the first thing that came to mind. "Where've you been? Didn't you get my messages?"

Kruger smirked. "This may seem a quaint old tradition, but in Germany, when we meet someone we haven't seen for some time, we usually greet them with some form of salutation and an inquiry as to the state of their health."

"But I've been trying to reach you for a week."

Kruger tapped the badge on his collar that featured a double stripe and three silver rank pips. "I'm a hauptsturmführer in the SS. I serve the Reich, not the whims of the director of a run-down orphanage in a nowhere town."

Mirek's heartbeat pounded in his ears. He glanced at the soldiers, each seeming to be itching to turn their rifles on him with but a nod from their commander. This wasn't the way to reach Kruger. What was Mirek thinking?

Mirek twitched a smile. "My sincerest apologies, Herr Hauptsturmführer. I had an urgent issue to discuss with you, and I was simply overexcited at the chance to finally do so. I trust you had a productive trip to the Fatherland."

Kruger turned to his men, pointing at a tall one. "You guard the door and ensure no one leaves." He pointed to three others. "You start at the top and work your way down." He gestured to the last three. "You start on this floor and work up. When you've finished, bring in the dogs to double-check."

Soldiers stampeded into Mirek's house. Screams came from shocked children.

Mirek slumped like a soccer ball with a nail in it. They couldn't be here for more of his children. Please, no. "Herr Hauptsturmführer, if you tell me what it is you need, I'll do all I can to help." And protect his children as best he could.

Kruger gestured to the house. "Shall we?"

"By all means."

In Mirek's study, Kruger took the swivel chair without asking, kicking his feet up onto the edge of Mirek's desk. Mirek stood before him, like a distraught schoolboy not knowing why he'd been summoned by the headmaster.

Kruger gestured with a limp flick to the hallway. "Bureaucratic nonsense. Because some of your retarded townsfolk look on Jews as equals and thus see fit to hide them, I now have to waste my valuable time searching the entire town. Well, not me personally, but I do have to put in the odd appearance."

"But I have nothing to hide. Has someone said I do?"

"I don't believe you have. But I can't be seen to show favoritism."

"Of course. Should I accompany your men to help?" And ensure they didn't abuse his children?

Kruger waved him toward the armchair, so Mirek sat.

Kruger picked at his left-hand fingernails. "After our last conversation, and especially after the gift I sent to show my gratitude, I'd assumed you'd be pleased to see me and that we could pass a pleasant hour while the search is conducted." With a toss of his head, he gestured outside. "Out there, my life consists of endless talk of war and victory and killing and supremacy... but there are other things in life. Finer things. I miss those. And I miss talking to others who appreciate them."

"I miss intelligent conversation too." Mirek ached to bring up Lena and ask for help, but after the reception he'd given Kruger, Mirek doubted now would be a good time to request a favor. No, this situation called for patience and tact. "Is there something in particular you miss?"

Gaze drilling into him, Kruger said, "Sincerity."

Mirek swallowed hard. After all the effort he'd put in to win over Kruger, it seemed he might have lost him by opening his big mouth before thinking. However, Mirek still had one card to play yet.

"I believe I have something that might reignite your belief in friendship." Mirek gestured to his desk. "May I?"

He hated that Kruger had appropriated *his* private sanctuary, but now was not the time to whine about that.

Kruger waved his permission.

Mirek unlocked the bottom-left drawer, retrieved two manila files, and returned to his seat. He slid the first file toward Kruger. "I think you're going to like this."

The German flicked his eyes to the file, then back to Mirek.

Mirek flipped the file open to reveal four typed sheets of paper. "This is a broad-brushstrokes outline of how I'd approach revising *A Sea Too Far*."

Kruger lowered his gaze to the pages. He read. A subtle widening of his eyes suggested his interest had been piqued. He quickly scanned the pages and nodded. Looking back at Mirek, he said, "And that file?"

Sliding the second file over, Mirek said, "This is a detailed breakdown with, amongst other things, suggestions on minor plot developments, heightening conflict at certain turning points, and strengthening each character's emotional journey to help readers connect with your hero and heroine."

Nodding, Kruger flicked through the first few sheets of the forty-three-page document.

Mirek continued, "I've also added a list of genre conventions. You've covered some but might want to consider those I've asterisked. And of course, I'll be available anytime, should you need to sound out ideas."

Kruger squinted at one section. Without looking up, he said, "Merge Anton and Uwe into one character? *Really?*"

"They both float in and out at various points, yet neither adds anything substantial, so it's hard to care about them. However, if you were to combine them, that character would become vastly more interesting than the sum of their individual parts."

Finally, Kruger looked up. And smiled with that arrogant yet endearing sparkle in his eyes.

Thank heaven! Maybe all wasn't yet lost.

Kruger patted the file. "*This* is what you wanted to speak to me so urgently about?"

Mirek shrugged. "What else?"

"I'd hoped for a few notes, but this"— he weighed the files in his hand —"is most impressive."

"You're very welcome."

Kruger snorted. "You're full of surprises, aren't you?" He patted the drawers. "You don't have anything else hiding in here, do you?"

He peeked into the top-right drawer.

Mirek gulped. In the bottom-right, beneath a file containing his almost completed *The Night Listened*, were all his anti-Nazi propaganda ideas, including rough drafts of the Hitler birthday celebration scam.

Mirek said, "Sorry, that's it."

Kruger poked about at some stationery supplies.

Mirek's knuckles whitened as he clawed the arms of his chair. If Kruger found those papers, found how he'd orchestrated the scam that had disrupted infrastructure across Germany... dear Lord, he'd be strung up outside the Reichstag in Berlin.

Kruger closed the drawer. "You know, I can see us having a very fruitful, not to mention pleasant, time working together."

"Yes, I'm looking forward to it too."

Kruger leaned back in the chair. "Of course, now I have the problem of finding an appropriate way to thank you once more."

"That's really not necessary. It's a joy to help an emerging author reach their full potential."

"Oh, please." Kruger waved his hand dismissively. "So you're telling me there's nothing you want? Nothing that might make your life that little bit easier?"

Mirek rubbed his chin. "Well, as you're determined to put me on the spot, there is one thing."

With an open palm, Kruger told him to proceed.

How could he word this so Kruger might empathize? "It's one of my girls. Lena."

Kruger said, "And?"

How could Mirek describe the problem without directly blaming Kruger – he being the one who'd carted Lena away? Mirek scratched his jaw.

Kruger said, "Out with it, man."

"Somehow, she's ended up in the hotel on the corner of the square."

Steepling his fingers, Kruger nodded. "Unfortunate."

"I was hoping there might be some way to get her out."

"Out?" Kruger wrinkled his brow. "You do know what goes on there?"

"That's not her fault." For the love of God, Kruger was a father, so why couldn't he empathize?

Sighing loudly, Kruger pursed his lips. He stared at Mirek as if debating how much gratitude was appropriate for the editorial work he'd done, and might still do.

"Oh, did I tell you?" said Mirek. "I've located the relevant documentation to prove my ethnicity, so now I can register for the Volksliste." He hadn't. But this wasn't going as well as he'd hoped.

Kruger nodded his approval but still didn't offer to help.

Mirek had hoped to keep his "secret weapon" for any later emergency that came along, but he had to do whatever it took to save Lena.

"Excuse me." Mirek took an envelope from his top-left drawer. "I want to prove my worth to the Fatherland as Volksdeutsche, so I prepared some material. I hope you like it."

Kruger withdrew a number of sheets of paper from the envelope. He read the top one and frowned. "Is this all true — your beloved Copernicus was actually German?"

"Truth is what the history-makers say it is."

Smirking, Kruger said, "I like that. I might just steal it to use myself." He read the next article, then laughed and pointed at Mirek. "Jewish noses! Some sectors of society will eat this up, while it will sow seeds of doubt in others just enough to make them uneasy around Jews. Excellent."

He read more articles.

Mirek's stomach roiled at spreading such lies. But Lena's life was worth more than a lie that only stupid people would believe. He'd struggle with the guilt later, with how to put right what he'd made so wrong. But this moment, only one thing mattered — Lena.

Kruger said, "You can produce more work like this?"

His palms clammy, Mirek gripped the chair arms. This was his last chance. He had to bargain hard enough to get what he wanted, but not so hard it upset the only person capable of helping him. "As you'll know, being a writer, it takes a lot of time and effort to create original work."

"Don't worry"— Kruger waved the papers at Mirek —"the Reich will reward such loyalty. What price did you have in mind?"

This was it. His last chance. His heart pounding, Mirek said, "Lena."

Kruger stroked his chin. He sifted through the papers once more. Finally, he said, "It might be possible if—"

A soldier with a sliver of a mustache dashed in. "Excuse me, Herr Hauptsturmführer, but we've found something."

Wide-eyed, Mirek stared in disbelief. What had they found, and how the devil had he missed it? And crucially, what was the punishment for possessing it?

37

The soldier led Mirek and Kruger toward the dining room. Mirek wiped the sweat from his brow, his legs so wobbly that staying upright was achieved purely from the power of his will.

Everyone had worked hard to Germanize the house. So whatever the Nazis had found, it wasn't something he was aware of. What could it be? Black market goods Hanka had bought? Contraband a child had innocently brought in? What?

Children clutched one another at the far end of the dining room.

Kruger and Mirek were led into the kitchen.

Weeping, Hanka and Ania stood spread-eagle against the wall, a soldier training his rifle on them.

Mirek scanned the room. This was Hanka's domain, but she was too wily to keep anything important in a room accessible day or night to the entire household.

The soldier pointed to the far left. "It's over here, Herr Hauptsturmführer."

They peered down into a concrete-lined hole, six feet long, two feet wide, and two feet deep. Crumpled blankets lay inside, and a wooden cover made of matching floorboards rested against the wall. A concrete bunker. The ideal place to hide someone.

Her voice trembling, Hanka said, "I tried to tell them, Mirek."

The soldier watching Hanka jabbed her in the back with his rifle. She shrieked.

Exhaling loudly, Kruger glowered at Mirek. "I must be losing my touch to be taken in by a few sheets of text."

Mirek swallowed hard. "It's not what you think. If you let Hanka demonstrate, you'll see it's all perfectly innocent."

As if it was a chore, Kruger waved his hand for him to continue.

Hanka scooted over and clattered an enormous brass saucepan onto the stove.

Mirek said, "Because fuel is scarce, we only partially cook food here. Then..."

Hanka connected metal claws on chains to the handle on either side of the saucepan, then, making use of a pulley system above, she hoisted the pan off the stove and guided the whole device along a metal track in the ceiling.

Mirek continued, "While the food is still boiling, we move it over and lower it into the hole."

Hanka lowered the saucepan in, unhooked the claws, then wrapped blankets around the pan so it was snug in the hole.

Mirek said, "The blankets and the concrete insulate it for the residual heat to continue cooking it. After a few hours, it's completely cooked, yet it's used only around one-third of the fuel it would've used had we cooked it completely on the stove."

Kruger glared at the soldier who had fetched them. "It's a glorified cooking crate, you imbecile. Don't you know anything?"

The soldier lowered his head. "I'm sorry, Herr Hauptsturmführer."

"Did you find anything else?"

Hesitantly, the soldier pointed to the table. "We found those in a barrel in the garden."

Kruger picked up the charred remains of one of four books.

Mirek said, "Forbidden texts. I believe I mentioned I burned them."

Pursing his lips, Kruger slammed the book down. He turned to Mirek. "I don't like to be indebted to anyone. And certainly not due to the mistake of some halfwit." He shot the soldier a sideways glance, then smiled at Mirek. "What say we put this silliness behind us by finding that young lady of yours?"

Mirek balled his fists, his fingernails digging into his palms, as joy exploded within him. He'd saved Lena. Thank the Lord, he'd saved her. It took all his strength to remain restrained when, in reality, he wanted to hug Kruger.

The sky a sullen slab of bulging gray, the world yet seemed brighter than any day Mirek could ever remember. He marched up the street beside Kruger, friends and neighbors scurrying to the opposite side of the road while staring, agog. Mirek didn't care who saw or what they thought. The only thing that mattered was that he'd saved Lena.

As they neared the hotel, Bushy Eyebrows saw him approaching side by side with Kruger. A cigarette dropped from his gaping mouth.

The man backed away as they neared.

A truck parked outside meant soldiers were inside "enjoying" the establishment's hospitality. Mirek prayed he could reach Lena before another monster abused her.

Inside, soldiers drank at two rows of tables, the air hazy with cigarette smoke. Suggestively clad women accompanied many of them, some faking interest better than others.

On Kruger entering, all the men leapt up, straightened their uniforms, and saluted. Many flashed puzzled glances at Mirek.

Kruger leaned closer to Mirek and said quietly, "What's her name?"

"Lena Jelinska."

A squat middle-aged woman waddled over from the bar area. "What can I do for you, Herr Hauptsturmführer?"

"Lena..." He looked to Mirek again.

"Jelinska."

"Where is she?" said Kruger.

"Let me check." The squat woman toddled back and ran a finger down the entries in a book on the bar. "She's with Rottenführer Beckmann, Herr Hauptsturmführer."

Oh dear Lord, no. Beckmann was the soldier who'd punched Mirek when he'd tried to get in before.

A nearby soldier said, "I thought he was with Kinga."

The squat woman said, "Oh, that's right. He couldn't decide, so he paid for both. That means he could be with both of them or be seeing one after the other."

Kruger said, "I asked where *she* was, not *who* she was with. Unless you want to serve the Reich on your back as well, I suggest you give me a straight answer."

The woman swallowed and pointed to a staircase. "Third floor, on the left, room eighteen."

Mirek tore up the stairs three steps at a time. His pulse pounding, rage coursing through his veins, he reached the top of the second flight and shot along the cream-colored hall, scanning door numbers. Moans of pleasure oozed from some rooms while screeches of pain sliced from others.

Mirek shouted, "Lena? ... Lena?"

Finally, door eighteen loomed. He barged in, ready to rip the monster off his poor child and carry her back to safety and love.

He jerked to a stop. Froze. A military uniform sat on a wooden chair, black boots nearby, but their owner was nowhere in sight. Between the chair and the metal-framed bed was Lena. Hanging from a ceiling beam by a brown leather belt. The leather creaked as it rubbed on the wood, Lena gently swaying as if she'd been kicking.

Mirek screamed, "No!"

He grabbed her and lifted, praying she was still breathing. For a teenage girl, she was so light she must have been starved. Supporting her with one arm, he reached up and eased the noose over her head.

He cradled her and laid her on the Oriental pattern rug, then leaned right down to her face. Mirek couldn't hear her breathing, couldn't feel her breath on his skin.

"Oh God, no."

He had to save her. Had to.

Mirek turned her onto her stomach and bent her arms around so her forehead rested on them. Kneeling directly in front of her head, he slapped her twice between the shoulder blades so her tongue fell forward. With her now in the resuscitation position, he prayed he could make her breathe, make her live.

Mirek placed his hands on her back in line with her armpits and leaned forward to push all the air out of her. Next, he slid his hands across to hold her upper arms, then leaned back and lifted, raising her elbows to the sides of her head, which moved her chest and drew in air.

"Breathe, Lena. Please!"

He repeated the process over and over in a rhythmical motion. But Lena didn't respond.

"Breathe!" He struggled on, manipulating her chest. He'd revived Pawel after he'd fallen in the river, so the technique worked. Why wasn't it working now?

He pushed and lifted, pushed and lifted, pushed and lifted. Nothing.

He sank back and sobbed.

A male voice said, "What the...?"

Mirek looked up.

"You!" Naked, Beckmann glowered at him, then at the noose, an SS eagle on the belt buckle. "So she'd rather hang than serve the Reich by doing the only thing she's good for?"

He spat on her.

Mirek screamed. He lunged at the soldier.

Beckmann dodged his clumsy attack, then slammed a fist into Mirek's side, followed by another into his head.

Mirek fell against the wardrobe. Beckmann hammered his fists into him.

His emotions exploding, Mirek flailed like a crazed beast. Wild swings battered the soldier backward.

Stumbling, Beckmann tripped over his own boots. He toppled back, dragging Mirek with him.

Both falling, they smashed through the window and plummeted through the air. They hit the green awning running around the outside of the building over the outdoor seating area. A mass of flailing arms and legs, they rolled across it and dropped to crunch into the sidewalk in a mangled heap.

Mirek groaned on top of the German, who'd broken his fall. Groggy, he swayed as he struggled to clamber up, while, unconscious, Beckmann lay with his left arm twisted at an odd angle and a bloody bone sticking out of his right shin.

The soldiers from the bar ran outside. They surrounded Mirek. Cocked their firearms. Aimed.

38

"Hold your fire!" Kruger marched over.

A woman's shriek burst through the smashed window. All gazes turned upward.

The squat woman leaned out. "She's dead. Dead! They hanged her."

Mirek cowered on the ground. "She hanged herself because you imprisoned her in this godforsaken place."

Kruger rolled his eyes.

Jabbing toward Mirek but not looking at him, Kruger addressed his men. "Get him up." He then pointed to Beckmann. "And get him to the infirmary."

Two soldiers hauled Mirek to his feet and restrained him while others carried Beckmann to the truck.

Mirek said, "He attacked me. I was trying to save her, and he attacked me."

Beckmann's comrade held a pistol to Mirek's head. "Would you like it here or against the wall, Herr Hauptsturmführer?"

"Lower your weapon, Rottenführer."

The man lowered his weapon. "So should I get the noose?"

Kruger stared into Mirek's eyes.

Mirek stared back. In trying to save Lena, had he just sentenced his entire household to death? He trembled.

"Herr Hauptsturmführer?" said the soldier again. "The noose?"

"The whip."

Frowning, the soldier dithered. He said, "With respect, Herr Hauptsturmführer, the usual sentence for assaulting a German soldier is death, not flogging."

Turning his head slowly, Kruger glared at the man. "I'm well aware of the law, Rottenführer. So are you questioning my authority or my competence?"

The soldier gulped and stood to attention. His face paled. "Neither, Herr Hauptsturmführer. My apologies if it appeared so. I was only trying to help serve the Reich by seeing justice done swiftly."

"Tell me, have you ever known a man to die of blood loss, or infection, or because his heart gave out through being flogged?"

Still at attention, the soldier said, "A Jew in Krakow, Herr Hauptsturmführer. He bled so much his face was white by the time we'd finished with him."

"And which would you judge the more painful — a bullet in the head or the lash on flesh?"

"The lash, Herr Hauptsturmführer."

"Which is why my decision is the most appropriate punishment in this instance. Or do you believe we should go easy on this criminal?" Kruger leaned closer and spoke in a hushed voice. "Never question me again or you'll be counting the lashes on your own back."

"Of course not, Herr Hauptsturmführer. Again, my apologies."

Kruger strutted away. "Bring him."

They dragged Mirek to a streetlight outside the town hall and bound him with his hands above his head, face squashed against the black metal post.

Kruger leaned in to Mirek's ear. "Why do you test me so? Do you derive some perverse pleasure from it?" He waited, as if expecting a legitimate answer, then heaved a breath. "I've tried my best with you, Kozlowski, so it pains me to have to do this, but you've left me no choice. Favoritism is a sign of weakness."

He marched away, saying over his shoulder, "Forty strokes. Then toss him in his courtyard to rot. You have the honors, Rottenführer."

Slitting Mirek's clothes with a knife, the soldiers ripped them away to leave him half-naked.

One of them offered the rottenführer a swagger stick, the kind many German officers carried around under their arm believing it made them look important.

Rottenführer snorted. "We're not flogging a child."

He went to the truck and returned with a bullwhip.

To Mirek, he said, "Count the strokes out loud. If you lose track, I'll start over. If anyone helps you, they'll be flogged too."

Mirek imagined excruciating pain, imagined his flesh being ripped from his bones. According to books, Indian yogis could master pain with their mind. Maybe if he put his mind somewhere else, focused on the happiest thing he could possibly imagine, maybe, just maybe, the pain wouldn't claw its way through.

Mirek pictured the most beautiful day he'd enjoyed in recent years — the day with Ania and the horse. How they'd laughed, how they'd joked, how they'd connected. His eyes closed, he lived that perfect day.

The sun glinted on the river as a kingfisher swooped, feathers iridescent in the light. Ania smiled — a childlike smile — seeing the horse and realizing it was waiting for her. Her eyes gleamed with joy and bathed him in such warmth for making her dream come—

The whip cracked.

Pain sliced into Mirek like a hot poker being laid across his back. He screamed. The perfect day vanished and hell descended.

Mirek's voice faltered. "One."

The second stroke slashed with a searing fire. Again, he screamed.

"Two."

The lashes continued. Each time, his back burned as if acid was being sprayed across it. Lash after lash after lash...

Gasping, Mirek counted, fearing he'd never survive if the flogging started over. "Twenty-seven."

The whip cracked again, biting into him. He arched backward, lacking enough energy to even cry out. Lights pulsed before his eyes, the agony warping his mind and his body.

"Twenty-eight."

Rottenführer wiped the sweat from his brow on his arm, then the whip savaged the air again to burn into Mirek like a lightning strike.

"Twenty-e—" Panting, Mirek stared at the sidewalk, his blood splashed across it. Was that twenty-eight or twenty-nine? Dear Lord, this couldn't start again. Please, no. It would kill him.

The rottenführer shouted, "Count. Or we start over."

Mirek had to gamble. No choice. His mind a panicked whirl, he said, "Twenty-nine."

He gritted his teeth, screwed his eyes shut. *Please let it be twenty-nine, please let it be twenty-nine...*

The next lash came without him being corrected. Thank the Lord.

More a noisy expulsion of air than a word, he said, "Thirty."

Again and again the whip bit at him until finally, with barely a whisper, he said, "Forty."

Someone cut him down. He crumpled, as if all the bones in his legs had dissolved. They hauled him across the square. Who saw, he didn't know and didn't care. His head dangling, all he saw were his feet being dragged across the cobbles and the smear of blood snaking out behind him.

His vision darkened, sounds dulled, movements blurred.

Down the street.

Through a gate.

Dropped.

Face crunched into flagstones.

A girl screamed.

Blackness...

39

Mirek's eyes flickered open. Groggy and lying face down, it took him a moment to realize he was in his own bed, but then searing pain engulfed him. He squealed and contorted in agony.

Ania delicately touched his arm and eased him down. "Keep still, Mirek. The doctor's here. He's going to fix you."

Mirek jerked as something gouged his wounds.

A male voice said, "I know this hurts, Mr. Kozlowski, but I have to clean these lacerations before I can stitch them."

"Hold my hand," said Ania, taking Mirek's left hand.

The doctor dug into another gash.

His back on fire, Mirek hissed through his teeth and gripped Ania's hand so tightly he thought he might break it, but she never complained, never flinched, just crouched beside him, supporting him.

The doctor cleaned the wounds and stitched what he could, then applied ointment to fight any infection and a poultice Hanka had prepared for the bruising caused by Mirek's fall from the window.

As the doctor was finishing, Mirek passed out.

When Mirek next woke, moonlight filtered through the drapes. A silhouette sat in a chair. It moved, leaning closer.

"Try not to move," said Ania. "The only way you're going to heal is by having plenty of rest." She stroked his head. "Sleep, Mirek. Sleep."

He shut his eyes and darkness stole him away.

***

A blackbird's song clawed into Mirek's consciousness, waking him. His eyes flickered open, and he instinctively tried to move but flinched, sucking through his teeth as pain wrapped him in a fiery blanket.

Ania smiled, still in the chair. "Hi."

His voice croaked. "Hi."

Crouching beside him, she lifted a glass of water and trickled some into the side of his mouth.

He barely nodded his appreciation.

She said, "How do you feel?"

"Like I won't be playing Run, Hero, Run today." He winced. "Maybe tomorrow."

"I look forward to it." She brushed the hair from his forehead. Her smile faded. "Do you want to tell me what happened?"

He cringed, picturing Lena hanging. He gave the tiniest shake of his head.

"Okay. When you're ready." Wandering to his dresser, she lifted a bowl. "Do you think you can eat a little?"

Again, he gave a tiny shake.

She sniffed it. "It'll do you good. And believe me, you wouldn't be getting something this nice if that hadn't happened."

"Special treatment, huh?"

She nodded. "So you better make the most of it."

"Later. Thank you."

He closed his eyes. Exhausted, even though he'd done nothing.

Ania caressed his head again, and once more, sleep took him.

***

He barely moved for the next few days. Occasionally, crying out with the effort and pain, he raised an inch or two to avoid developing bedsores or to pee in a chamber pot, but other than that, he did nothing but lie on his stomach. And every time he opened his eyes, Ania was there.

For the first week, the doctor visited daily to tend his wounds, infection being a major concern.

Hanka also came every few hours to update him on household events, regularly asking if he was ready to accommodate visitors. Each time, he declined. His children couldn't see him so weakened. They could know he was injured but couldn't know how bad it was because he needed to maintain his image as their protector.

By the end of the second week, Mirek could roll onto his side for a short time to change position. Moving and seeing his room from a slightly different angle became the highlight of his day.

Despite his protests, Ania stayed with him constantly. He had no idea when she slept or when she ate because every time he woke, she was there. She encouraged him when he was depressed, held his hand when he writhed in agony, chastised him when he complained about his medication, and reminded him of how his children needed him when he ached to give up. Ania was his rock in the raging river of his torment. She was his sanctuary, his hope, his everything.

On the twenty-third day, Mirek lay on his right side and reached out his left hand. Ania took it.

"Are you sure about this?" Her face lined with concern.

"I was sure yesterday, and the day before, but *someone* talked me out of it."

She tensed her muscles, tightening her grip on Mirek. "Okay, on three. One, two"— she winced —"three."

Mirek gritted his teeth, and they both heaved. Screwing up his face with the effort, he pulled with his left hand, leaving his right side limp to engage as few of his back muscles as possible.

Like a cloak of burning coals, pain smothered his shoulder. But slowly, so slowly, his body arced upward, and his legs, already dangling over the side of the bed, swung around underneath him. Finally, for the first time in over three weeks, he sat upright.

His head drooping, he gasped, his energy spent as if he'd chopped wood for hours, not merely sat on his bed.

Stepping back to give him space, Ania said, "Better?"

Around his gasps, he tried to form words but only managed to wheeze. He nodded.

Ania said, "So, Run, Hero, Run?"

Mirek shot her a sideways glance. "T-tomorrow."

She rested her hands on her hips. "You said that last time."

He smiled.

Ania said, "While you're up, how do you feel about saying hello to someone?"

He snorted, still panting.

She moseyed for the door. "He's been keeping vigil outside almost as long as I have." Her hand on the doorknob, she said, "Just a wave would mean the world to him and then — maybe — we'd have a hope of getting him to sleep in his room instead of in the hall every night."

There was only one person it could be. "Okay."

Ania opened the door and spoke to someone outside. "Someone wants to say hi."

A small boy appeared in the doorway, worry etching his face, hands fidgeting in front of his stomach.

Mirek smiled. "Hi, Jacek. I'm okay, so don't worry. Now be a good boy and do what Miss Ania asks, okay?"

The corners of the boy's lips tweaked upward. He darted away, and Ania closed the door.

"So what now?" she asked.

Without lifting his hands from his lap, he pointed up.

"Up? Up where?"

"Stand"— he panted —"stand up."

"You are joking, aren't you? Or do need a mirror to see the state you're in?"

He reached for her hand.

She huffed. "And what's going to happen if you do yourself a mischief? I'm not sitting here for another three weeks just because you have a bee in your bonnet about moving."

With his reaching hand, he grasped for her repeatedly.

"Oh, God help me." She took his hand. "Don't say I didn't warn you. After three again?"

He nodded. And felt her brace.

She said, "One, two, three."

They heaved, Mirek fighting to push only with his legs and not to move his back. Trembling, he rose off the bed inch by inch by inch. Ania clutched his left hand with both of hers, grimacing with the strain.

Mirek groaned. Through gritted teeth, he said, "Come on. Come on."

Finally, shaking with the effort, he stood. Sweat ran down his face. He swayed, so she caught him.

"Please tell me that's it," said Ania.

His head hanging, eyes drooping, he nodded.

"You're sure? You don't want to have a run in the park? Or climb Krolik Hill?"

He shook his head.

"So where do we go from here?"

He tipped his head toward the bed.

She said, "Bed?"

He nodded.

"Thank heaven for that."

Taking their time, they eased him back down.

"Happy now?" asked Ania.

"Yes."

There had been times he'd thought he'd never leave his bed again. Now, he knew he would. And not only that, with so much time to think, now he knew what he had to do.

40

Sitting the wrong way around on a wooden chair so his back wouldn't touch it, Mirek waved at Agata standing in his bedroom doorway with a bunch of children. They all beamed.

Agata handed Ania a homemade card with a drawing of a man standing in flowers and a big sun overhead. "We've really missed you, Papa Mirek."

He smiled. "I've missed all of you too."

Zygmunt said, "So you're coming downstairs soon?"

"I hope so."

Ania handed the card to Mirek. "As soon as the doctor says it's okay."

"Is the doctor coming today?" asked Agata.

Ania shook her head. "Maybe Thursday."

The little girl slumped. "Thursday!"

Mirek chuckled. "Are you really missing me so much, or is Baba Hanka keeping you busy with jobs because there are no lessons?"

"Of course we miss you, Papa Mirek, but"— Agata stamped her foot —"it's horrible. I don't think anyone has ever worked so hard in the whole of history."

Mirek chuckled again. "I bet you're right. And I bet Baba Hanka is lounging with her feet up, smoking cigarettes, all the time you're working, isn't she?"

The little girl thought for a moment. "Not *all* of the time..."

"So most of the time?"

"Not really."

"So what is she doing? She isn't working as well, is she?"

Agata frowned, then nodded. "Why do grown-ups work so much?"

"To buy food, to buy clothes, to buy fuel... everything we need to live."

"Why? Why can't the government just give it to you?"

He winked. "When the war is over, Agata, remind me to buy you *Das Kapital* by Karl Marx."

Ania shooed them away. "Okay, that's it for today. Let's not tire the patient too much." They waved, then Ania closed the door. "We can't have you overdoing things. Especially when Borys is coming later."

"Yes, Miss Ania."

"Have you done your stretching exercises today?"

"Yes, Miss Ania."

She sighed, tipping her head to one side. "You know, in your weakened state, it would be easy for me to put you over my knee."

He raised an eyebrow. "Well, aren't you the little temptress."

"Mirek Kozlowski!" She laughed and slapped his arm. "Behave. Or I'll swap with Hanka for her to nurse you."

"Oh good grief, no." Hanka would mean well, but she'd be more like a jailer than a caregiver.

"Lunch?" asked Ania.

"Please."

Ania strolled out. And Mirek watched her. Staring at the closed door even after she'd gone. If only he could tell her. They'd been close almost since the moment they'd met, but these last few weeks...

He'd probably have died if not for her nursing. Literally.

His heart clawed at him to confess his feelings. To hold her. Love her. Share everything with her. But relationships could be so messy. And with the state the world was in — *his* world was in — he couldn't handle messy. Best friends wasn't ideal, but it was stable. And that provided the greatest chance that he'd never lose her.

Mirek heaved off the chair and supported himself on his dresser. With a grimace, he twisted his torso to complete one of his stretching exercises. The more often he did them, the sooner he hoped he'd be properly mobile again.

He twisted toward the window and he stopped. Squinted. That again?

He shuffled closer, wincing with each step. Holding the window frame, he stared out over the sun-bathed greenery of the park to the hospital. That gray truck was back, soldiers loading more decrepit patients into its trailer. Why the devil would the Nazis want workers who looked half-dead?

Already tiring, he lurched to his chair.

Ania returned with lunch, and shortly after, Borys arrived. Mirek took him through the whole Lena story.

Borys clicked his tongue, sitting facing Mirek. "Wow, you were so lucky. They've strung people up for far less."

"Yes, but the problem is that I've given Kruger everything he needs to revise his book without me. Where does that leave this place?"

Borys winced. "That's a tough one."

"Unless you help."

"Me? How?"

"Get us all out."

Borys laughed. Mirek didn't.

"You're serious?" said Borys. "You want the Resistance to get *all* of you out?"

"Wherever is easiest — Switzerland, England, Sweden... as long as we're together, *where* doesn't matter."

"It's a nice idea, but"— he blew out a breath —"it's just not doable."

"Really? I understand it will take time to plan, but surely it wouldn't be such a big job with all the contacts the Resistance must have made over the years."

"You don't think it would be a big job?"

"Not that big."

Borys scratched his beard. "Do you know how many people it takes to smuggle just one person out?"

"I appreciate it's not easy."

"How many? Take a stab."

Mirek shrugged. It couldn't be that hard. "Three?"

"Ten."

Mirek raised his voice with surprise. "Ten?"

"Sometimes more. All working in secrecy. All risking their lives." Borys counted them off on his fingers. "Someone to plan it, often someone else to arrange it, and maybe a backer to finance it. Then, depending on the plan, you might have forgers, black marketeers, drivers, corrupt officials, plus people with hiding places along the route, people with access to supplies, people who can fix problems that crop up... ten. And how many children do you have?"

Mirek slumped. "Fifty-six."

"Plus you, Hanka, and Ania." Borys paced across the room.

Mirek perked up with a flash of inspiration. "But it wouldn't take ten people for each one of us because we'd be a group."

"Oh yeah, being a group would make moving fifty-nine people in secret much easier."

"So in groups of four or five. That still means we need substantially less help, so fewer people."

Borys gazed out of the window. "Groups?"

"It makes sense."

"Groups of young children. Forced into situations they don't understand, with people they don't know. Scary situations."

Mirek cupped his face. Leaving was nowhere near as easy as he'd pictured.

Borys turned from the window. "Seriously, Mirek, the practicalities are staggering. How will so many youngsters cope without an adult they trust to help them?" He sat back down. "All it would take is for one kid to get spooked at the wrong time and everyone's head is on the chopping block — not just the kids, but everyone the Nazis can trace to have helped them. Plus probably those people's families."

Mirek collapsed over the chair back, his chin on his arms.

Borys lightly touched Mirek's shoulder. "Sorry, but smuggling fifty-nine in secret or in the open with forged papers is a nonstarter."

Mirek stared at a crack in the floorboards.

"However, there is one option," said Borys.

Mirek jerked his head up.

Borys grimaced. "But you're not going to like it."

"Go on."

Rubbing his face, Borys turned away.

Mirek said, "Just say it."

Borys pursed his lips. "You, Ania, and four kids."

Mirek frowned. "What do you mean me, Ania, and four kids?"

"That's who we'll get out."

Mirek threw his arms up. "What? Not a chance!"

"We've done family escapes before, so we know how to pull

213

them off."

"So I'm supposed to turn my back on everyone else?"

"You and Ania can easily pass as a married couple, so no one would question the four kids being yours. Getting a family out, with good documentation, is a cakewalk compared to the nightmare of smuggling fifty-odd people."

Mirek shook his head. "I'm not abandoning everyone."

"Hanka can hold down the fort here, so the kids will be fine, and when all this is over, you can come back and pick up where you left off. In the meantime, the six of you will be safe."

Silent, Mirek sat shaking his head.

"We might even be able to help you establish another orphanage somewhere else. Or you could help the thousands of Polish child refugees who have already been sent abroad. You could probably do more good that way than you can ever do here."

"Not a chance in hell."

Borys held Mirek's forearm. "This way, you guarantee — *guarantee* — the safety of five people who are relying on you."

"So I'll stay and you can save Ania and five children."

"It doesn't work like that. A single woman traveling with five children is going to rouse more suspicion than an ordinary-looking family. Plus, you're the linguist. Does Ania speak fluent German to handle awkward situations?"

"So I'll find a German speaker to play her husband."

"You're not getting it." Borys sighed. "We wouldn't be doing this to save a bunch of kids, we'd be doing it to save a valuable asset — you."

"I can't leave them all."

Borys stood. "Look, you're not going to be up and about anytime soon, so I'll give you a week to think about it, okay?"

"There's nothing to think about — I'm not leaving."

"The way things are going, we could all be dead this time next year." Borys pointed at him. "This is the only viable option to save a bunch of people you care about. Make sure you have four names for me next week."

Borys was right that the outlook was getting grimmer, but he was dead wrong about that being the only "viable option." He had to be.

41

Ania drew the bedroom drapes, shutting out the night. "Should I ask?"

Mirek stared at the floor, still leaning over the back of the chair. "Huh?"

"You've barely said a word since Borys left. What happened?"

"Nothing."

She sat facing him. "You expect me to believe that?"

He couldn't discuss this with her. Couldn't give her false hope. He kept staring at that shadowy sliver between the floorboards. "Just something he said."

"Well, I guessed it wasn't because he'd sung a song you didn't like."

"He had this idea." Mirek bit his lip. "He, eh, wanted to save some of the children. To get them out of Poland."

Her eyes popped wider. "Fantastic. But wait. Why aren't you jumping up and down with glee, even with your injury? What's the catch?"

"He can only save four."

"I'm still struggling to see the problem."

Mirek looked up at her. "Even if I wanted to, how could I choose just four?"

Ania winced. "Ahhh."

"Who would I pick? And how would I face the other fifty-two knowing I could've saved them but instead left them here to rot? Any day a German could waltz in, put a bullet in someone's head, then waltz back out. And I wouldn't be able to do a damn thing about it."

"Exactly."

215

He frowned. "What?"

She took his hand. "That's why you *have* to choose four. If you've got the chance to save someone, you have to grab it. Because if the Germans do come in guns blazing, you're never going to be able to look yourself in the mirror again for wondering if you could have saved those they killed."

Dear Lord, she was right. He had to choose four children to save. But how?

Ania said, "How would they get them out?"

He ignored her. Elements of that plan needed to remain hidden or they'd prejudice any decision.

"Mirek, how would they get them out?"

"I don't know."

"Borys must've said something."

"No."

"But he does have a plan? This isn't some ridiculous idea he cooked up on the spur of the moment?"

"I guess so."

She dropped his hand. "You 'guess so?' You, the man who plans everything in the most minute detail imaginable, didn't ask him how he plans to save your children?"

Mirek purposefully held her gaze, unblinking. "I—"

She held up her palm. "Remember, you're a dreadful liar."

He wasn't. He'd managed to fool Kruger; it was just her. Something about her flustered him.

Mirek glanced away, then shot her a sideways glance. Her gaze drilled into him.

"Okay, there's a plan," he said.

"And..."

He exhaled loudly. "He wants..." Mirek looked away again, shaking his head. "It doesn't matter. It won't work. So just leave it, okay?"

She stood, rearing over him. "There's a chance to save four of our children and you won't take it? What the devil's wrong with you?"

"It's not that simple."

She leaned into his face. "You save them. Period. Simple. See?"

Cursing under her breath, she flounced away.

"You don't understand."

She spun back to him. "Then explain it, goddamnit!"

Mirek shouted, "He wants me to go with them!"

Hell, why the devil had he confessed that?

Both hands holding the back of her neck, she wandered to the window, even though the drapes were drawn. He waited for her to say something. And waited.

He said, "So now you know why it won't work."

She didn't move.

Mirek rubbed his face. "Like I'm supposed to abandon everyone."

Still she said nothing.

He twisted around to her, wincing as the movement stretched his back. "He says it's the only way, but I don't believe him. I want to get everyone out."

Nothing.

"He says that's impossible because there are so many of us, but something is only impossible until you know how to do it."

Silence.

"And I've already got some ideas." He had no ideas. But he was sure he would if given enough time.

She didn't reply.

Mirek said, "Twisting around to you like this isn't doing my back any good, you know."

Without turning from the window, she said with an impassive tone, "You have to go."

"Haven't you listened to a word I've said?"

Finally, she faced him. "Have you?"

"What are you talking about?"

"You can get four children out of this hell. And yourself."

"So I'm supposed to turn my back on everyone else?"

"Hanka and I will manage just fine. What do you think we've been doing while you been convalescing?"

He squinted at her. She was willing to sacrifice herself to save him. Tears welled. He swallowed hard to bury his feelings. "You'd be coming, too."

"What?"

"They'd forge documents for a man and wife to travel with their four children."

She twisted away again.

"Not so clear-cut now, is it?" he said.

She stood, staring at the drapes.

He gazed down at the crack in the floor again. Now that she understood the impossibility of the situation, maybe they could find an alternative solution.

Without turning, Ania said, "Hanka. You have to take Hanka. After all she's done, she deserves to live out her life away from this nightmare."

"It wouldn't work."

"So make it work."

"It's not my choice."

She spun around. Pointed at him. "Then you go. You're the important one." She gestured to the building. "The one who can set all this up again somewhere else. You don't need me. But Hanka does here."

"The plan is for a man and wife. That's what they've had success with before."

"No." Ania stomped out. Somewhere in the hallway, she shouted, "Tadek, fetch Baba Hanka, please. Quickly as you can."

A boy's voice said, "Yes, Miss Ania."

Footsteps ran down the stairs.

"Ania, no! Don't, please." Mirek knew what she wanted to do — to play dirty. "Ania! ... Ania, please don't."

Still nothing.

He had to engage her, convince her not to do what he was sure she was going to.

Mirek heaved, grimacing with the effort as the healing wounds tightened across his back. Sliding his feet across the floorboards, he shuffled to the door and leaned heavily against the doorjamb. He peered down the hallway. Empty.

"Ania!"

Still no response.

"Ania!"

He'd just walked farther than he'd walked for over two months.

No way could he make it to the staircase. And she knew that. She'd be hiding just around the corner. He was certain.

More running footsteps. "She's coming, Miss Ania."

"Thank you, Tadek."

Hanka's voice drifted up the stairwell. "I don't know what the emergency is, but you know I'm alone in that kitchen while you're administering to His Lordship."

"I'm sorry, Hanka, but this can't wait." Ania appeared from the staircase. She pointed at him. "Back in your room and off your feet."

"Ania, don't do this."

She glared at him. "Now!"

He shuffled back to his chair, wiping sweat off his face.

Ania and Hanka entered. Ania checked to make sure no one was in the hall and shut the door. An uneasy silence hung in the air as he glared at Ania and she glared back.

Hanka folded her arms. "So is someone going to tell me what the emergency is?"

Mirek said, "Borys had an outrageous i—"

Ania stepped in front of him, blocking him from Hanka. "Borys can get Mirek and four children out of Poland."

Groaning, Mirek leaned around Ania. "And Ania. She's part of the plan."

Ania turned to him. "I'm not important, so don't drag me into this."

"I'm not dragging you into anything. The plan is for a man and wife. Not that it matters, because I am not going."

Ania grabbed Hanka by the shoulders. "Tell him, Hanka. Tell him he has to save himself and the children."

Hanka sank to the edge of the bed and stared at the wall.

Mirek scowled at Ania. "This is why I didn't want to tell you. I knew there was no way you'd be reasonable about it."

"I'm the one being unreasonable?" Ania threw her hands up and turned away. "Hanka, for God's sake, tell him how ridiculous he's being."

"Ridiculous?" said Mirek. "Ridiculous is abandoning everyone here. This is *my* home, *my* orphanage, and these are *my* children. I say what happens here. No one else. *Me!*"

Ania snorted. "Then maybe it's time someone else was in charge. Someone who wouldn't make such dumb decisions."

He glowered. "I'm making dumb decisions? What the hell do you know? You couldn't even read when you came here."

Pain flashed across Ania's face. "Really? You're throwing that back at me?"

"I'll do whatever it takes to protect me and mine."

Finally, Hanka spoke. "Then do it."

"What do you think I'm trying to do?" said Mirek.

Hanka looked at him coldly. "Go with the children. Save them."

"Finally, the voice of reason," said Ania. "Thank you."

Hanka switched her gaze from Mirek to Ania. "Both of you."

Ania wagged a finger. "No, no, no. I'm needed here."

"The Germans took a third of our children and we couldn't do a darn thing about it," said Hanka. "They put one of our girls in a brothel"— her face twisted with pain —"and we couldn't do a darn thing about it." She pointed at Mirek. "They flogged you, and we couldn't do a darn thing about it. What will they do tomorrow?"

"Whatever it is, Hanka, we'll face it together," said Mirek.

Hanka shook her head. "They could come tomorrow and machine-gun whoever they like, and we wouldn't be able to do a darn thing about it." She looked at Ania, then Mirek. "You have to go. Both of you."

42

Smarting from the wounds inflicted by his two most beloved friends, Mirek sat in his bedroom, illuminated by gaslight and staring at a piece of paper. A blank piece of paper. He couldn't scrawl even a single letter, let alone an entire name.

Whether he escaped or not, he had to save four children. However, choosing four names out of fifty-six was more torturous than the flogging he'd received.

His eyelids drooping, his pencil and paper dropped to the floor, and sleep took him.

The next thing he knew, someone was saying his name. "Mirek... Mirek."

His eyelids fluttered open. He was still slumped over the chair.

Ania touched his arm. "You said you were going to get into bed. You'll never heal without proper rest."

He glared at the paper on the floor. "I can't do it."

Ania ambled to the window and opened the drapes. Gray light crept in. "Do what?"

"I can't choose only four." He rolled his shoulders, wincing after sleeping in such an awkward position.

"Well, don't be thinking of putting that on me." She poured a glass of water from the jug on the dresser and offered it. "Don't forget, I couldn't even read when I came here."

"I was upset. I didn't mean it." He caressed her hand.

She jerked away, water sloshing onto the floor. She placed the glass on a small table next to him. "It's here if you want it."

"I'm sorry."

"I'm sure you are. But do you know how much it hurts when someone you care about uses your weaknesses against you?"

"I shouldn't have said it." He reached for her again.

"But you did." She walked out.

So relationships could be messy but best friends were forever? He hung his head. Could this ever be fixed?

The opportunity to escape should have literally been the answer to so many of their prayers, but instead, it had torn their household apart.

Despite Hanka's insistence that both he and Ania leave, she would be terrified at facing the Germans alone, no matter what she said. Ania, someone who had unexpectedly come into his life and who now meant more than he'd imagined possible, disagreed with everything he wanted to do and now couldn't even bear to look at him. And on top of all that, he had to decide which fifty-two children weren't worth saving.

The Germans didn't need to punish people. The mental torture their acts inflicted was worse than anything a whip, noose, or gun could ever do.

That morning, instead of struggling to choose four names, Mirek struggled to choose the criteria upon which to choose names. His chair repositioned to face his bed, he pored over the fifty-six report cards arranged on his comforter. The obvious solution was to choose the four most academically gifted children. They'd be the ones most likely to have a positive impact on the world, so were the ones most deserving of a chance at a better future.

He sorted the cards into three piles based on mathematical ability: poor, average, and good. Good math skills meant someone was logical and analytical — ideal skills for anyone. A talent with numbers also provided an excellent path to respectable professions in accountancy, science, and economics.

Fanning the "good" pile, he read through the sixteen names to narrow the group to only four. He scratched his head, then huffed. These children might grasp math, but he couldn't imagine any of them grasping life and wringing every last drop of potential out of it.

He slung the reports down. Maybe mathematics was a poor selection device. So how about language skills? Yes, chances were that the children would have to learn a foreign language, so for someone to have a good future, they'd need good communication skills.

Again, he ranked the cards. Scanning the names in the "good" category, he smiled — three jumped out. Oh yes, this was easier. He put Tadek, Ola, and Agata to one side, then studied the other cards, looking at the finer detail of who had achieved what.

He rolled his eyes. "Of course — Bruno."

With a satisfied sigh, he laid down cards for the four lives who would be saved. And what a four they were — some of his favorite students. Excellent.

"Uh-oh." How convenient it was that the list included four of his favorite students. He slumped. Using language skills as a criterion could work, but not when used to justify favoritism, whether consciously or subconsciously.

Ania wandered in. "Any luck?"

He threw his arms up. "It's impossible."

She scanned the piles, then picked up the four cards he'd set aside. "What's wrong with these four?"

He shook his head.

She said, "Oh yes, I see now."

He frowned. What could she see that he couldn't? "Why? What's wrong with them?"

"Tadek and Agata."

"What about Tadek and Agata?"

"Are they supposed to be twins?"

He frowned. "What?"

"Aren't they in the same class?"

Mirek slapped his forehead. Tadek and Agata were only a month apart in age. "Ola's a problem too — she's only a few months older than Agata."

"Triplets! My, we *are* a fertile couple. If only they looked like each other."

"Biologically, triplets don't have to look like each other."

Ania said, "I'm sure the firing squad will find those the most informative 'last words' they've ever heard."

She was right. If they were supposed to be a family, having children that looked the same age would arouse suspicion. While everyone's papers would be forged, so in theory age didn't matter, if interrogated, a child would likely forget the birth date on their papers and give their real date. Choosing children who were at least a year apart would be better all around.

In one way, that made selection easier, though — instead of the artificial criteria he'd struggled to impose, age provided a solid basis on which to narrow the choice.

"Can't you just choose your four favorites?" asked Ania.

"That's not fair."

"Why? Don't forget, we could potentially be setting up home with the ones you pick, so it's important we like them."

"But is it? Parents don't get to pick their children, they just get stuck with the ones who come along. I can't forsake someone just because they don't laugh at my jokes."

Ania sat on the bed and flicked through the cards. "So how are we going to pick?"

He shrugged. "If I knew that, I'd already have done it."

"How about a lottery?"

"And leave it all to chance?" He snorted. He had too many promising students to risk that.

"So just go with your gut. Forget all this."

"What do you mean?"

"All this." She flicked the papers. "What does it actually tell you?"

"Who's the cleverest, so who's the most likely to have a successful career and therefore a worthwhile life."

She wrinkled her nose. "But does it?"

"Of course it does."

She picked up one of the cards and read aloud. "Bogdan Zasina — reading D−, writing D, math D+, geography C−, history D+..." She waved the card at him. "So what's this tell you? That Bogdan will never achieve anything or that he's just not good at school stuff?"

Mirek rubbed the back of his neck. She made an excellent point — potential success couldn't be measured by academic achievement alone. There were other factors that needed to be considered, such as adaptability, social skills, self-discipline, emotional stability... combining academic achievement with these other factors might be the key to identifying someone who would one day excel. The secret wasn't to find four children who deserved to live but to find four who would pursue a life worth truly living.

Mirek said, "Could you fetch the photograph taken at Hanka's birthday party, please?"

A few minutes later, they sat looking at a photograph of him, Hanka, and Ania sitting in the dining room in the middle of three rows of children.

School grades were all well and good, but he needed to look into someone's soul if he was going to give them a future of freedom, hope, and dreams over an existence of squalor, hunger, and despair.

Balancing academic prowess with social and psychological factors, they discussed each student's likelihood of not just successfully negotiating relocation but of having a positive impact to make the world a better place.

Finally, he had four students selected. "But what if I'm wrong?"

"Then you'll live with it."

"But what if I've rejected someone I shouldn't have? If I've deprived them of the future they deserved?"

"No." She took his hand. "*You* won't have deprived anyone of anything – the Germans will have. *You* will have done everything imaginable, so if anyone loses out, it isn't you to blame. You have to believe that. So no second-guessing yourself, okay?" She patted the four cards. "These are the four. The *right* four."

It certainly was four. But no matter what Ania said, was it the right four? Were these four lives worth saving over all others?

43

The next morning, Mirek started intensive one-on-one lessons in German for Ania and the four children. Each person got two sessions per day, so that by the time the escape came, they'd be capable of handling all manner of impromptu encounters with Germans. On the pretext of this being a special project, the children had also been moved to share two rooms, so if necessary, they could be roused without causing pandemonium.

The days were long and tiring, but the thought of the new life Mirek was creating for them spurred him on when he flagged. Especially as giving each student his full attention brought dramatic results.

A week after his visit, Borys reappeared while Mirek was gently exercising in his bedroom.

Borys sat on the chair, unusually cheery. "So have you picked four?"

"Yes," said Mirek. "But that doesn't mean I'm going. Once I'm fully mobile, I'll find a suitable candidate to take my place."

It didn't matter what reasons Borys conjured, Mirek would not abandon everyone here. Period.

"And that's your final word on the subject?"

"It is."

"What if I said we had another option?" It looked like Borys was struggling to stifle a smile. What did he know that Mirek didn't?

"You said there was no other option."

Borys toyed with his leather tobacco pouch. "A funny thing happened as your escape plan moved up the chain of command – the higher it reached, the more people wanted to hear about you and what you're doing here. Especially when they realized you were the Hitler's birthday celebrations guy."

"And?"

Borys grinned. "And they want to get you all out."

Mirek's eyebrows shot up. "What?"

"Everyone." Borys circled his hand in the air. "Just like you wanted."

Mirek snickered, then broke into a full laugh and clapped. It was everything he'd ever dreamed of.

Borys offered his hand. "Congratulations, my friend, you're saving your entire household."

They shook.

Unable to stop smiling, Mirek said, "But how? What's changed. You said it was impossible because there are so many children."

"That's why the higher-ups want to do it. I don't know if you're aware of what's going on out there, but—" He heaved a breath. "The stories we're hearing... some places have it far worse than here." He looked pained. "Jews starved in ghettos, children executed for not wearing armbands, mass killings."

"But why? Whether it's about ideology, territory, ancestry, or whatever, none of it makes sense."

"Since when does war make sense?" Borys's expression lightened. "Anyway, that's why getting all of you out is suddenly a priority. After we've done it and spread the story, it will be a huge morale booster for the entire country, and boy, do we need that. Plus, it will be one hell of a kick in the teeth for the Nazis — fifty-six kids escaping from under their noses. How can we resist that?"

Mirek said, "But how can you get all of us out?"

"I can't go into detail for obvious reasons, but you, Ania, and the four children will be going overland, while everyone else is going by water."

"Can't we all go together?"

"So you can continue working with us, we need easy communication channels, and unfortunately, that isn't possible where we're sending Hanka's group."

Mirek grinned and grabbed Borys's hand. He shook vigorously. "Thank you, Borys. Thank you."

Where they escaped to was incidental; all that mattered was that every single one of them would be saved.

"You're welcome, Mirek."

"How soon can we go?"

Borys snickered. "Says the man who can barely walk."

"So when?"

"We're already setting things in motion, and we're trying to organize it so both groups leave on the same date to avoid disappearances being noticed. But that's proving tricky, so the groups may be a day or so apart, but realistically..." He pursed his lips. "I figure a month, two tops."

A month? They could all be out of this nightmare in as little as four weeks?

"Please tell me you've got four names for me," said Borys, "because it will hold up the papers if you haven't."

Mirek heaved up and shuffled to his dresser. He handed Borys an envelope.

Borys stuffed it into his inside breast pocket. "In case the two groups do go separately, yours will be going first. As a precaution, we'll produce backdated death certificates for the six of you, so should anyone ask any awkward questions, Hanka has proof of what's become of you."

"And if Hanka's group goes first?"

Borys grimaced. "The numbers are too big to make believable excuses, so if they go first, it'll be a case of praying nobody comes snooping."

With how Kruger had dropped by unannounced in the past, that could be a problem; they'd have to hope everything fell into place date-wise.

On leaving, Borys sent Hanka and Ania up as Mirek had requested.

Hanka sat on the chair. "So when are you going? And you *are* going, so I don't want any arguments about that."

Mirek tipped his head toward the door. "Ania, can you double-check the hallway is clear, please?"

She did, then sat on the edge of the bed.

"Well?" asked Hanka. "Have you got a date?"

Mirek smirked. "No, we don't have a date yet."

Heaving a breath, Hanka pushed up. "I'm sorry, but I've got far too much work to do for meaningless interruptions."

"Hanka, sit back down, please."

"Mirek, with you out of action, I've barely sat down since five o'clock this morning, so forgive me if I don't want to play these games." Hanka folded her arms. "If you've got something to say, then out with it."

"We're all getting out."

Hanka frowned. "What do you mean *all?*"

"I mean, me, Ania, four children"— Mirek beamed —"and you, and everyone else."

"*All of us?*" Hanka clutched her mouth.

"Everyone."

"Oh my." Hanka collapsed onto the chair. She laughed. "Oh my!"

Ania leaned forward. "I thought it was impossible to get everyone out?"

Mirek shrugged. "It seems the Resistance's bigwigs want a big win against the Nazis, and sneaking out fifty-nine people right from under their noses is just the ticket."

"Oh, Mirek!" Hanka hugged him, but he shrank back, wary of his healing wounds being touched.

Hanka gasped. "Ooops. Sorry, that could've ruined it." She hugged Ania instead.

Ania wrapped her arms around the old woman. "I was so upset at the thought of leaving you."

"Me too, but there was no way I was going to stop you."

When Hanka and Ania separated, Mirek said, "Before we all get carried away, this isn't going to be happening for at least a month, so no one outside this room can know anything, okay?"

They agreed.

"Secondly," said Mirek, "we aren't all going together. The original group of six is going overland while you, Hanka, and the other children are escaping by water."

Hanka grinned. "All that matters is that we're getting out of this godforsaken place."

"So when will we know the date?" asked Ania.

"A few days beforehand. It will all be left till the last minute to avoid information leaking into the wrong hands. We won't be telling the children until the very last second."

Hanka wiped tears away. "I can't believe you've managed it, Mirek."

He said, "Let's not get complacent, though. We've still at least another month to get through."

Ania said, "What do they mean, 'escaping by water'?"

Mirek splayed his open palms. "I didn't want to push Borys, but I'd guess it's going up the Vistula on, say, a coal barge or a livestock vessel to the Baltic, then…" He shrugged.

Hanka said, "Sweden?"

"It's close enough," said Mirek.

"And would we all meet there?" asked Hanka.

Again, he shrugged. He didn't want to spoil the moment by saying they might be separated for some time.

Hanka took Mirek's hand. "I can't believe it's happening. I really can't."

Neither could he. It was almost too good to be true.

44

Fall 1940.

Five days after Borys's visit, having performed his exercises religiously and managing to walk the length of the upstairs hallway umpteen times per day in between giving German lessons, Mirek ventured downstairs for the first time in months. He hadn't announced his intention, not least because he didn't want any fuss — especially not any sort of "surprise" party — so he sauntered into the dining room in the middle of the evening meal. Once more, he stood to relish his children eating, chatting, bickering, laughing, joking... Children being children.

Beautiful.

Tadek spotted him and dropped his glass of water, the shatter eliciting cheers from other children. He stared open-mouthed. Others followed his gaze, and their jaws dropped too.

The whole room fell into an awed silence.

"Papa Mirek!" Zygmunt stood. Thrusting his fist into the air, he shouted, "Papa Mirek!" He punched again. "Papa Mirek!" And again.

Forsaking their meals, children joined him. In seconds, the whole room was on its feet, chanting.

Tears in his eyes, Mirek waved. He wanted to say something, to thank them for such a welcome, but he couldn't. He was a man of words, and yet none came, because none could do justice to the love filling the room. Swallowing hard, he basked in the joy of all the faces smiling at him, *for him*.

Finally, he said, "Thank you. I can't tell you how much that means to me. Now please, don't let your food go cold. Sit, eat, enjoy."

The children returned to their meals, and he stiffly ambled toward his usual table.

"Papa Mirek!" Agata waved, then patted the space beside her. "I saved your seat."

Ania appeared with a plate of food for him. "She did. Every meal."

Mirek sat and ate with his family. It was the best meal of his life.

After eating, he hugged or shook hands with almost every child there, then retired to his study.

He ran his hand over the pitiful selection of books in the bookcase and then sat at his desk. For a time, he'd thought he'd never sit at it again. He rubbed the mahogany top. It had served him well. So well, he couldn't imagine writing on anything else. Yet, no matter how much the Resistance valued him, insisting his desk go with them would probably throw a wrench in the works.

He opened his bottom-right drawer. The crisp white pages of *The Night Listened* gazed up at him. Some things would be going with him whether the Resistance liked it or not. But would he be able to take both the Polish version and the German one he'd written simultaneously? In case his group had to hide, or run, luggage had to be kept to a minimum, so maybe just the Polish.

Ania appeared in the doorway. "The children loved seeing you."

He beckoned her in. It seemed a lifetime ago that they'd had their reading lessons. "I thought it would be a nice surprise for them."

"It was a lovely surprise." She sat in the armchair. "Do you need help with anything?"

"I'm trying to decide how much of my work I can take."

"I can carry some for you. And I'm sure Hanka will."

"Thanks, but you'll have enough of your own stuff." He patted the drawer. "My next book is in both Polish and German, and though I'd like both, I can't possibly justify it."

Ania frowned. "You write your books in Polish and German at the same time?"

He nodded. "I know it sounds crazy because it means twice the work, but in struggling to express in German what I've already written in Polish, I sometimes find inspiration that would never have otherwise come to me. Over the years, it's helped improve my stories in ways that could never have happened if I hadn't developed them simultaneously in the two languages."

"You're right — it sounds crazy."

He ran his hand over his desk again and then down to the left-hand drawers. He opened the top one. "Oh, I'd forgotten about those."

"What?"

"The postcards." Mirek removed the postcards sent from the children the Germans had taken. He smiled at the message from Feliks saying he was doing well, and the one from Pawel, but then he froze. He gulped as a pit in his stomach raked all the evening's happiness into its dark void. His face twisted in pain.

Ania leaned over. "What is it?"

He put the postcards on the desk.

She picked them up and gasped at the top one — Lena's. Ania cupped her mouth. "I'd forgot about this or I'd have moved it."

Resting his elbows on the desk, he dropped his head into his hands. "I should've saved her."

Ania rested her hand on his arm, leaving the cards on the desk. "None of this is your fault, Mirek. You did everything imaginable. *Everything.*"

"But it wasn't enough, was it? It never is." Staring into the dark whirls of the grain within the wood, he wiped away a tear.

"You've found a way to get everyone out. That's all that matters now."

"Is it?" He pawed the postcards. "I'm not getting Feliks out, or Janek, or Bozena, or…" He frowned and pulled the cards closer. They'd arrived days, sometimes weeks, apart and sparked such joy he'd never looked at them side by side, but there was something dreadfully wrong.

"Read this aloud." He handed her Feliks's card.

Ania read, "*Dear Papa Mirek and everyone, The hours are long and the work is hard, but I'm learning something new every day and managing to take care of myself. I hope you're all safe and happy. Love, Feliks.*"

"Now this." He gave her Lena's.

Ania said, "*Dear Papa Mirek and everyone, I hope you're all doing well. I'm busy at the camp learning seamstressing. The work is hard and the hours are long*"— she frowned —"*but it's interesting learning something new every day, and I hope to make myself a new dress to wear for when I visit you. Love, Lena.*"

She put the cards side by side on the desk. "They don't sound right. Unless they were sitting next to each other when they wrote them."

Mirek grabbed one of the other cards. He stabbed a sentence Bozena had written. "There! *Learning something new every day.*" He picked up Janek's. "*The work is hard and the hours are long.*" He tossed it aside.

Ania said, "It's like someone told them what to write."

"Exactly. And look how impersonal they are. Why don't they ask about their best friends, or mention things they're dreaming about doing, or reminisce about good times — any of the things a child would usually care about?"

Ania nodded. "Something's not right."

He waved his hands across all the cards. "If an ordinary parent got one of these, they'd be so relieved their child was okay, they wouldn't think anything of it, but because they took so many of ours, we got more postcards, so it's right there staring us in the face."

"So what does it mean?"

"It means that all this is a lie." He flung the postcards away.

That was why Lena was learning to "sew" in a brothel. Maybe if he hadn't been so consumed by thoughts of the nightmare Lena was suffering, and then the aftermath of his failed rescue attempt, he'd have called the postcards into question earlier and put two and two together.

So where were all those other children? And although he'd been too late to save Lena, was there still time to save them?

45

Mirek beckoned Borys into his study and closed the door.

Borys said, "What's the emergency that I had to drop everything? I've no update, so don't ask."

"Sit." Mirek strode to his desk.

"It's good to see you're moving easier." Borys sat.

Mirek slid the postcards across his desk. "What do you make of these?"

Borys scanned the first, then tossed them back without looking at any others. "Lots of families get these."

Mirek pushed the top two across again. "Read these."

Borys blew out his cheeks, but read them. While scanning the second, he frowned.

"Well?" said Mirek.

"Okay, there's something a little off."

"A little?" Mirek tapped the cards. "These aren't messages from homesick children who've been ripped from their families. This is a con."

Borys stared at him.

Mirek said, "So?"

"So?"

Was Borys being awkward or merely dim?

"So what are we going to do about it?" asked Mirek.

"Nothing."

"What do you mean *nothing*? We've got to do something."

"Like you did for Lena?"

Mirek's jaw dropped.

Borys leaned forward. "Mirek, you've got one chance to save

yourself and fifty-eight people you love. Don't blow it by doing something dumb."

"Dumb?" He threw his hands up. "It's dumb to want to save innocent children from monsters, is it? Is that what you're saying?"

"I'm saying, if you don't leave well enough alone, you're going to endanger every person you care about for the sake of some wild goose chase."

"It's not some wild goose chase. My children are out there somewhere. Maybe at that camp." Mirek held an index finger and thumb a fraction of an inch apart. "I came *this close* to saving Lena. I'm not abandoning anyone if there's still a chance."

"And look what happened when you tried to save Lena — you were almost killed. If you get caught doing anything like that again, you won't be so lucky. And even if by some miracle you only got flogged again, you'd be in no state to travel, so you'd ruin the escape plans for everyone here. Is that what you want? To condemn everyone you love to this nightmare when they could escape it?" Borys leaned forward in his chair. "Listen to me, don't rock the boat when we're this close."

Mirek pointed outside. "My children are out there, facing God only knows what kind of nightmare, alone. Completely alone."

Borys stood, rearing over him. "Mirek, I'm asking you as a friend, and as the guy who's putting his life on the line to get your entire household out of the country, drop this. Now."

He stormed out, slamming the door behind him.

Mirek stared at the door. Eleven children had been taken, supposedly to be adopted by German parents. Apart from Lena, thirty other children had been taken on the pretext of teaching them a trade. Mirek had failed Lena; he would not fail the other forty-one. But alone, what could he do?

He didn't know any corrupt official or bribable military personnel. He didn't know anyone else in the Resistance. He didn't even know if the children were still in Poland.

And then there was Kruger.

Kruger could have killed him — *should* have killed him — but because of the weird relationship they'd developed, the Nazi had spared him. Kruger wouldn't do that again. No, Kruger would consider his debt to Mirek paid, and then some.

Mirek slumped over his desk. He couldn't endanger anyone here by dragging them into his investigation, so he was on his own. The obvious place to start was the camp, but if he was to avoid detection, that meant a five-mile trek cross-country. In his state?

But was he in such a state, or did he only imagine he was? He marched to the door, turned, and marched back.

He nodded. Pretty good.

He flexed his shoulders, then rolled them independently. Flinching as a mild pain bit, he fully straightened his back, then arched it to see how much mobility had returned. He nodded again. He was in better condition than he'd thought. All he'd needed was the right motivation to block the psychological trauma.

As a final test, he rounded his back. He squealed like a pig put to slaughter as agony ripped through him. Gasping, he collapsed in his chair.

A five-mile trek cross-country? No chance. Maybe in a week.

But he couldn't just sit here, even with his German lessons as a distraction. He had to do something positive, something that might help him get those children back.

Sometime later, a knock came on his door.

Doodling an idea on a scrap of paper, he said, "Come."

Ania ambled in with a cup. "I thought you might like some linden tea."

"Thank you." A flowery scent wafted up from the steaming cup. It was one of the few foraged items he truly enjoyed.

"What did Borys say about the postcards?"

"That it's not something the Resistance is interested in — especially with our impending departure so close — so we should forget about it."

She scrunched up her face.

He said, "What's wrong?"

"Nothing."

"There is. What is it?"

She bit her lip. "You're not going to, are you?"

He frowned. "Not going to what?"

"Forget about it?"

"I..." He rubbed his face. He couldn't drag Ania into this, but if he explained, maybe she'd at least understand. "If there's a chance of saving the children, don't you think I have to at least try?"

"Do you want my opinion?"

"Of course."

"Even if you won't like it?"

He pointed his pencil at her. "You agree with Borys?"

"I agree with saving everyone in this house that we can save, and not risking all of them by struggling to rescue people who can't be rescued."

"That's not what you said earlier."

She folded her arms. "I've had more time to think. And now Borys — the expert on escaping — has confirmed what I was leaning toward."

"So you expect me to turn my back on them?"

She sat, uncrossing her arms and trying to look sympathetic. "Mirek, you did everything possible to save Lena, and look how badly it went wrong. What if the same thing happens?"

He took her hand. "And what if we get out of here and later discover we could have saved them? Would you be able to start your new life with a clear conscience?"

He wouldn't. The faces of those he'd abandoned would haunt him forever.

Hanging her head, she covered her eyes and sat in silence. Finally, she said, "I can't say, so I'll support whatever decision you make."

She left, and he returned to his brainstorming.

What if instead of begging to have the children returned, he simply bartered for them to enjoy a visit? If he timed it right, they could all disappear together before the Nazis even realized they were gone.

He smiled. Now that was a plan. He just had to negotiate the biggest hurdle.

46

For the next ten days, each morning before his German classes and each evening afterward, Mirek took a walk to build up his strength, and while sitting to teach, he exercised his back. Gradually, a modicum of his former strength and stamina returned.

Mirek had hoped Borys would relent on searching for the missing children, just as he had on the number of people he would smuggle out of Poland, but the man's continued absence suggested he hadn't. And time was running out. It was clearly up to Mirek to save them.

Shortly after dawn, a freshly caught rabbit arrived, courtesy of Hanka's black market contacts. As luck would have it, Borys had left a message that he'd be by that afternoon. With everything lining up as if it were a sign, Mirek stuffed the carcass into a canvas pack and set off to answer the question that had plagued him for over a year.

Birds sang along a riverbank littered with buttercups, as if they had no idea a war was raging. The grass glistened, heavy with dew, and bejeweled spiderwebs hugged the vegetation. Mirek marched along.

Thanks to a long-ago conversation with Ludomir, he knew exactly where to head, so he followed the curve of the river, then cut across a farmer's field and strode into open countryside. Before him, a grassy incline dotted with trees rose to a dark shadow that escaped over the horizon – the forest.

His boots squelched as he negotiated a muddy patch, then he started up the incline. Halfway up, he passed an aged oak, its trunk scarred from a lightning strike.

As he neared the gloom lurking within the forest, his heart beat faster. Earlier, he could have been on a casual early-morning ramble, sharpening his appetite before breakfast, but now? Now, he was about to reach the point of no return, about to commit to a path that could change his life. Or end it.

Mirek plunged into the murky undergrowth. Twigs crunched under his feet as he wove through the trees, ducked under branches, and pushed through bushes. The old hunting trails were almost gone now, overgrown through lack of use because rifles were illegal and this area was off-limits.

Slowly, he scrambled deeper and deeper into the dark, dark forest. And the deeper he went, the faster his heart raced.

He squinted at a large holly beside a sycamore on the edge of a small clearing. Was that what he thought it was? If it was, it had grown considerably.

He approached the bush. Yes, this was it. Good grief, if he hadn't been concentrating, he'd have walked straight past, it had changed so.

Crouching and wary of the spiky leaves, he shoved branches aside and crawled deep inside. He stood and smiled. The dark green tarpaulin still hung in the hollow they'd created in the heart of the bush, but branches now speared it in various places. He moved to the front and opened one of the viewing panels. Beyond the branches, in the middle of the clearing, was the metal bathtub they'd buried in the ground, which collected rainwater to attract prey.

He smiled as he pictured Ludomir tramping over to retrieve the buck he'd shot, only to slip in the mud and splash into the bathtub. Boy, that man could curse!

Mirek pushed his way back out and resumed his path. His heart hammered.

It was close now.

He pressed on. But instead of lumbering through the undergrowth without a care, he fought to move stealthily. His eyes wide, he flicked his gaze around constantly, checking for signs of movement, while his ears strained for the tiniest of man-made sounds.

Rumors said the SS patrolled the forest to keep their secrets hidden. And while rumors were usually pure fantasy, occasionally...

Ahead, patches of light grew bigger as the trees retreated.

He swallowed hard. Dear Lord, he'd reached it.

He crept to the tree line, where bushes provided cover. An expanse of cleared land stretched one hundred feet from the trees to a ten-foot-high barbed wire fence supported on concrete posts that curved inward at the top. A second fence stood around six feet inside the first, and beyond, one-story wooden buildings stretched across a compound.

Strangely, other than a sentry in a watchtower to his left, there were no signs of life.

Mirek scanned the fence with binoculars, coming to a sign: "CAUTION! High voltage. Danger to life."

Panning further, he gasped.

Dangling by the hands, fingers still clawed around the wire, a man's body hung on the inner fence, his legs trailing across the ground behind. His face was taut, sunken, and gray. Had the man died trying to escape and been left hanging there as a deterrent?

Mirek cringed. Was there no end to the monstrous acts the Nazis would perpetrate?

Way into the compound, figures moved between the barracks-like buildings. Mirek squinted. He needed to spot one of his children — just one — to know they were here, so he still had a chance to save them.

To the far right, skeletons of beams and joists stretched out where new accommodations were under construction. Borys had said this was a small camp, suggesting he didn't know the Germans were extending it. Mirek's plan was working — he'd already uncovered valuable information with which to barter with Borys.

Yet, no matter how Mirek peered, the people were little more than blurry lumps shuffling around. He needed a better vantage point. Especially as it was possible that some of his children were on the construction crew.

A soldier and a guard dog dawdled through the gap between the fences, heading left. To stay downwind and remain hidden, Mirek stalked right, zigzagging through the vegetation.

An engine rumbled, and a truck appeared between the buildings. The truck with the gray trailer from the hospital.

Mirek gawked. "What the...?"

Gates in the fence opened, and the truck pulled onto the old access road through the forest to the abandoned mine. Another truck with four prisoners under guard in the open back followed. Both vehicles slowly bucked their way along the heavily rutted track.

Mirek scratched his head. The silver deposits were long since exhausted, so what on earth could the Germans want out there?

There was only one way to find out. Mirek cut through the forest in pursuit.

Fortunately, because of the deep ruts, the trucks crawled along, so Mirek wasn't left far behind. The Germans only covered around half a mile, then the engine noise ceased. The mine was a mile farther, so why had they stopped? Mirek raced to catch up.

Crouching behind a bush, Mirek peered into a clearing.

The four male prisoners trudged to the back of the trailer. They opened the two rear doors and climbed into the gloomy interior while a soldier leaned against the side and lit a cigarette. Two other soldiers, probably the drivers of the trucks, stood by as if to supervise proceedings.

A moment later, two of the men reappeared, carrying a lifeless body. With no more emotion than tossing away a sack of rotten vegetables, they slung the body out. It thudded to the ground.

Mirek's jaw dropped.

Another corpse was thrown out. Then another, and another, and another... they formed a monstrous, twisted heap. No blood or obvious wounds were visible, but their skin had a strange pink hue, almost red.

In the pile, one of the bodies moved — a woman was still alive!

The men threw a child on top of her.

Surely they'd see she was alive. They needed to help her.

Pinned under the child, the woman flailed her arms as if drunk or drugged, struggling to get up.

Finally, the smoking soldier noticed and ambled over.

Thank heaven, someone was finally going to free her from that nightmare.

The soldier drew his pistol and shot the woman in the head. Mirek clutched his mouth.

More bodies were hurled out, then the four men clambered from the truck. The first two picked up an old man with a gaping toothless mouth. They hefted him toward the tree line but stopped near a fresh mound of dirt and hurled him into a pit.

Mirek froze. He didn't want to see this, to have to live with these images for the rest of his life. But he couldn't look away.

The other two men picked up a young girl who had malformed limbs and tossed her into the pit. Next, they lifted an old woman so bony and angular, she looked like a starved fledgling. They tossed her in, too.

A tall man with a hunched back — into the pit.

A child with no legs — into the pit.

A woman who looked like the fish seller who sometimes worked in the town square market — into the pit.

Finally, they slung the last body in. No words were said. No prayer offered. No marking left. The prisoners shambled toward the truck without so much as a glance back.

The smoking soldier trained his pistol on them. They froze.

He said, "Back to the pit."

The men exchanged anxious glances.

The soldier shouted, "Now!"

His comrades raised their weapons too. The men edged toward the hole.

Smoking Soldier said, "Kneel."

A big man cried as he went down on his knees, facing the pit. Another prayed. The other two sank to the ground in silence.

The soldier blasted the big man in the back of the head, and he tumbled into the hole. Three more shots echoed through the forest.

47

In a daze, Mirek stumbled through the trees back the way he'd come. Branches whipped his face and roots tripped him, but he barely registered any of it.

What he'd seen couldn't have been real. It just couldn't.

But he'd seen it, so how could it not have been?

Leaning against a trunk, he mopped sweat from his brow with his handkerchief, then gathered his strength and lurched on. He had to get home. Had to tell Borys. Surely once the man knew, it would change everything.

Three hours later, he sat in his bedroom facing Borys, Ania guarding the hallway to ensure no one overheard their nightmarish conversation. Borys had come to deliver the false papers and fake death certificates in preparation for the escape, but now he stared, agog.

Mirek said, "They slung the bodies around like they were emptying a bedpan. No emotion. No respect. Nothing. As if they'd witnessed such horrors that they were desensitized to everything."

Ashen-faced, Borys said, "And you couldn't tell what killed them?"

Mirek shook his head.

"No gunshot wounds, knife wounds, bruising around the neck...?"

Again, Mirek shook his head.

"How many bodies?" asked Borys.

"Maybe forty."

"Were there any other pits or signs of digging?"

Mirek shrugged. "I ran. I couldn't stand seeing anymore." He held his head. "All those people. Children, women, the elderly, handicapped..." He looked at Borys. "How could they do that? They were people. For God's sake, *they were people.*"

"We've heard rumors, but no one wanted to believe them." Borys stared at the wall, tears in his eyes.

Mirek waited, but it was as though whatever images were in Borys's mind were too painful for him to describe.

"Rumors about what I saw?" asked Mirek.

Borys nodded. He wiped his eyes and sniffled. "This past April, a hospital orderly in Warta got trapped inside a trailer, like the one you're describing, when the Germans took psychiatric patients for"— he made quotation marks in the air like Hanka did —"*treatment* elsewhere. The orderly managed to get out but was dazed, as if he'd been drugged. In hindsight, he believes he'd been gassed."

"Gassed?"

Borys nodded again. "He says he couldn't smell anything, which suggests they're not piping in the exhaust fumes but something else. Maybe it's cylinders of carbon monoxide. What color were the bodies?"

Mirek grimaced, picturing the gruesome hue of the flesh. "A strange pinkish red."

Borys nodded. "Carbon monoxide. A doctor confirmed it will do that. It's odorless, so the victims wouldn't know until it was too late, if at all."

"So how long have the Nazis been doing this?"

"We're not sure, but it's not an isolated case. In Warta, they took around five hundred patients over three days. Every single one seemed to disappear, but with everything that's going on, people figured the hospital had simply lost track of them due to an administrative error. Then something similar happened in Poznan, and later in Lodz when over eight hundred patients were taken. And those are only the ones we know about."

Mirek's jaw dropped. "The Germans are gassing thousands of innocent people?"

"They believe the mentally ill or severely handicapped weaken society."

"So they're killing them? What are you doing about it?"

Borys sighed. "We've got no proof."

"Don't you have people you can bribe to take photographs?"

"Photography is forbidden anywhere near the camps. No one's going to risk getting shot for a few zlotys."

Mirek cupped his face. "I can't believe they're killing the most vulnerable members of society. Just when you think you've seen the worst they can do..." He grimaced, remembering the flailing woman being shot in the head.

"You know..." Borys fidgeted with his fingers. "Mateusz Dudek has a camera."

"I know. He took Hanka's birthday picture. Why? Are you thinking of taking photographs yourself?"

Borys winced. "I don't know the forest. I've only seen the camp from Krolik Hill."

Mirek massaged the back of his neck. "I suppose I could draw you a map, but if you don't know the trails, there are no landmarks that will help, so you'll probably end up going around in circles."

"Or..."

"Or...?"

Borys scratched his beard. "Do I have to spell it out?"

"Spell what out?" Mirek's eyes widened as the realization hit him. He leaned back, raising his palms. "Oh no. I am *not* going back there."

"You said yourself, if I go alone, I'll end up wandering around in circles."

Mirek held up an open palm to Borys. "I'm not seeing that again."

"So you're giving up on your children being held in the camp?"

Mirek stabbed a finger at him. "It's you who told me not to do anything dumb."

"But you did it anyway. And it paid off. Now you're going to have to do it again."

Mirek stood and lurched to the window. "Not a hope in hell, Borys."

"So you're outraged at what the Nazis are doing but won't do a darn thing to stop them?"

He spun to his accuser. "How can I? If I get caught, it isn't only me who'll hang, it's every soul under this roof."

"You know the Nazis consider Jews subhuman. What if they decide that feeding and housing people who have no place in their new world order is a waste of resources that could go to decent Germans?"

"Oh, so now the Nazis are going from murdering a few thousand people to a few million. *Seriously, Borys?*"

"Summer last year, could you have imagined the Nazis would torch a synagogue with worshippers still inside? This past spring, could you have imagined you'd be flogged for trying to stop a fifteen-year-old girl from being repeatedly raped? Just yesterday, could you have imagined the Nazis would gas innocent people in a truck?"

Mirek opened his mouth but couldn't refute anything Borys had said.

Borys lowered his voice. "We got this direct from one of our most reliable sources — in the next few weeks, all the Jews in town will be moved into a ghetto."

Mirek clutched the dresser to support himself. "*All* the Jews?"

Borys nodded.

Mirek held his chest. That would destroy his life. And the lives of so many of his children. How would that impact the escape plans?

Borys clicked his tongue. "I guess we should think ourselves lucky we've gone this long without one."

"What will happen to all my children?"

"We don't know more. We don't even know if they're going to create a ghetto here or ship everyone to one of the big ones — Lodz, Warsaw, Lublin, Zamosc... your guess is as good as mine."

Mirek staggered from the dresser. "Will you be able to get us all out before that?"

"Of course we'll try, but..." Borys shrugged.

Mirek collapsed onto his chair. This couldn't be happening. His children had been so close to escaping this hell. The plan couldn't all fall apart now. It just couldn't. He pounded his fist into the top of the dresser, then turned.

Borys eyes were filled with such sorrow. "My friend, we live in a world where if good people do nothing, the things the bad people do will only get worse and worse and worse. But if we could share this news with the world, maybe get it to Poland's friends in London and Washington, imagine the difference that could make."

Borys was right. If the Germans weren't stopped, there was no telling the nightmare world they would create.

Mirek nodded.

"You'll take me to the mass grave?" asked Borys.

"Just make sure you know how to use that camera."

48

In the kitchen two days later, Mirek stuffed another freshly caught rabbit into his pack — Borys having obtained the camera and sent word that today was the day.

While Hanka stirred a saucepan of porridge, Ania cleaned the lenses of Mirek's binoculars as he sharpened his hunting knife on a whetstone. He put the knife in his pack.

Ania said, "You're doing the right thing."

Silent, he packed his binoculars too.

Ania touched his arm. "You might not believe it, but you are."

He fastened his pack and put it on.

Ania smiled. "I'm so proud of you."

He slumped. "Don't be proud. If there was any way of getting out of this, I'd grab it."

With tears in her eyes, she kissed him on the cheek. "And that's why I'm so proud."

She dashed out of the kitchen, dabbing her eyes.

Mirek stood, his fingertips brushing where she'd kissed. If only they'd met in a different time in a different place.

Hanka toddled over and handed him a small package wrapped in brown paper. "In case you get hungry." She opened her arms. "Now give me a hug and promise me you'll be careful."

He slung his arms around her. "Hanka, I'm not going off to war. I wish people would stop treating me like I am."

She hugged him tighter. "We're all at war already, Mirek. It's easy to forget that, which means we forget the danger we're constantly in. So promise me — no heroics."

He snickered. "Like I'm going to be heroic."

She jerked him. "Promise me."

"I promise."

She ambled back to her saucepan. "Now away from under my feet. I have breakfast to prepare."

Mirek smiled. She was the most cantankerous person he'd ever met, and yet, he was blessed to have met her.

After hiking along the riverbank, Mirek crossed the field to the incline topped by the jagged shadow of the forest. Partway up, Borys sat on a rock near the oak with the lightning scars.

Mirek tramped toward him. "You found it okay?"

"Yes, but this was the easy part, wasn't it?"

"I suppose." Mirek neared but recoiled, covering his nose. "Good grief, what's that stench?"

"Huh? Oh, me. Gasoline and tobacco."

"Why the devil do you want to stink of that concoction?"

"You said there were dogs." Borys sniffed his black coat.

"So?"

"So the smell of gasoline and tobacco can throw them off a scent."

"Really?"

Borys shrugged. "That's what I've been told."

Mirek gestured to the forest. "Shall we get this over with?"

"Hang fire. I have some news."

Mirek sighed. Now what did the Resistance expect of him? Whatever it was, the answer was a definite no. After today, he was finished. He shot Borys a weary look.

Borys said, "Tomorrow."

Mirek shrugged. "Tomorrow...?"

Standing, Borys held out his right hand. "Your group goes tomorrow."

His eyes wide, Mirek froze. They were getting out *tomorrow*?

Borys said, "I know I was supposed to give you two or three days' notice, but we received word of a shipment going up the Vistula on Thursday for Hanka's group, so that changed everything."

"Wait. So I, Ania, and the four children go tomorrow, and Hanka and the others go Thursday?"

"That's the plan."

"But it hasn't been a month. Not even close."

Borys smirked. "If people know too long in advance, they get jittery, and jittery causes mistakes. A last-minute bombshell usually works best."

Mirek grabbed Borys's hand in both of his and shook it. "Thank you. Thank you from all of us."

Borys smiled. "You're welcome. From all of us."

Mirek beamed. It was possibly the greatest news he'd ever heard. One day to go and then, for them, the war was over.

Borys chuckled. "Can I get my hand back?"

Mirek realized he was still clinging onto it. "Sorry."

"Now listen, because I'm not writing this down and neither can you. Wednesday mornings, around eight o'clock, you get a delivery from your grocer, right?"

He nodded. "Julek, yes."

"The delivery will go ahead as normal, then you, Ania, and the four children will climb into the van while it's parked in your courtyard and out of sight from the street. Julek will take you approximately forty miles, then you'll transfer to another transport at 9:15. Have you got that?"

"Delivery 8:00 a.m., transfer 9:15." He nodded again. "Where is the transfer taking us?"

"You can't know that in case something goes wrong and you're picked up."

"Okay. And Hanka's group?"

"Because it's such a big group, they're going in the dark. So, Thursday, 3:00 a.m., they leave through the back of your property, go through the park, and meet a box truck that will be waiting on Brudno Street. Okay?"

"Got it. 3:00 a.m. Thursday, park, Brudno."

Borys raised a finger. "Listen, they *cannot* go early and be on the street waiting for the truck. Understand?"

"Okay."

"Neither can they be late. Everyone has to be downstairs and ready, so on the stroke of three, they can leave — quietly — through the back."

"Don't worry, when Hanka wants to, she can put the fear of God into anyone, so they'll do whatever she says."

"Good. Now—" Borys peered around Mirek, back the way he'd come.

Mirek turned. He couldn't see anything, but maybe Borys's two eyes were better than his one. "What is it?"

Borys patted Mirek's shoulder. "False alarm, sorry. Must be nerves, being so close to the camp."

"You're nervous? You're used to this cloak-and-dagger stuff. I just run an orphanage."

Borys smirked. "You've had one hundred children to control, and Hanka to contend with. Mirek, you're about the bravest man I know."

Raising an eyebrow, Mirek pointed up the incline. "Shall we?"

They trudged toward the shadowy tree line.

Mirek wafted his hand in front of his face. "How much gasoline did you use?"

"I sprinkled it all over."

"For goodness' sake, don't light a cigarette till you've washed."

Borys took a bottle from his pocket. "I brought some for you."

"Does it work?"

Borys offered the bottle. "We'll find out, won't we?"

Mirek shoved it away. "Maybe later. If I lose my sense of smell."

At the forest's entrance, Mirek peered into the gloom, his heart hammering. He wiped his palms on his pants and swallowed hard. One more day. That was all. One more day and he was out of this nightmare. He crept into the murky undergrowth.

They walked in silence, cloaked in shadows. Mirek's stomach churned so much he wanted to vomit. He was going back there. *There!*

Borys was unusually quiet, too. The stress of knowing the danger they could be walking into had no doubt affected him.

On they crept.

Mirek's nerves gnawed at him like maggots at a carcass. His hand trembled as he reached to lift a branch out of his path.

Something cracked behind Mirek. He jumped. Jerking around, he scanned for the slightest of movements while his ears strained for the tiniest of sounds.

Borys whispered, "I can't see anything. You?"

"No."

The forest was a living thing, and like all living things, it moved and breathed. That crack could have been an old branch falling, an animal stepping on a stick, or an old snare snapping... or it could have been a stalking Nazi taking aim.

Mirek said, "Do you have a gun?"

"I'm a contacts guy, not a weapons guy."

His heart racing, Mirek scoured the undergrowth.

Nothing.

He gulped. He didn't like this. Borys had thought he'd seen something before entering the forest, and now this? Something was wrong. But what?

He whispered, "I have an idea."

49

Mirek cowered in the gloom of the hunting hide. Waiting. Holding his breath.

A twig snapped nearby.

He flinched. Dear Lord, someone really was stalking them.

Sixty feet away, hidden in the undergrowth, Borys yammered on to himself, pretending he was talking to someone in order to draw the danger toward him.

Mirek's heart hammered. Hammered so hard the forest critters had to be fleeing in terror. He gulped and tightened his grip on his knife. The blade gleamed. He'd never killed anyone. In fact, other than the German in the brothel, he couldn't even recall ever having hit anyone. But now, with death lurking in the shadows and his children needing only another forty-eight hours before they were safe, whoever was out there would feel his blade. He had no choice.

The crunching of dry leaves and long-dead sticks crept closer and closer.

Mirek tensed. Knuckles white on his knife's hilt.

The footsteps sounded to be almost directly outside. Yet unless the person was a hunter, they'd pass without ever seeing the hide. He had to pray they would, because if they opened fire now, he was dead.

The noise stopped for a moment. Mirek screwed his eyes shut. For some inexplicable reason, the only thing he could think of was Ania.

And Borys had called him brave. If he were brave, he would have told her what she meant to him. Brave? He was a complete coward.

Why had the person stopped? Mirek looked at the hole through which he'd scrambled into the bush. No way could he crawl out without making a sound. As soon as he tried, whoever was outside would realize and shoot. He strained to listen. Praying the crunching would continue toward Borys.

Finally, the footsteps crept away.

Sucking in great lungfuls of air, Mirek wiped his brow. Dear Lord, and that was the easy part.

He waited until the footsteps were well past him, then carefully crawled out, disturbing as little as possible. He didn't want to take a life. Even a German life. But if he had to...

Outside the hide, he stalked toward the sound of Borys talking to himself. He strained to swallow, but his mouth was too dry. He changed hands with his knife and wiped his palm on his pants.

Stealthily, he snuck through the gloom, homing in on his prey.

A few feet ahead, beyond a bush, a stick cracked.

Mirek leaned down to see through one of the barer patches of the bush. Part of a hunched figure moved at the other side.

Oh God, this was it.

But he had to do it. Had to do it for Ania and the children.

Mirek leapt through the bush. He slammed into the figure, and they crunched into the ground, Mirek with his blade raised to plunge into the heart of the monster hunting them.

A terrified face stared up at him. A terrified face below a crop of red hair.

"Jacek!"

Mirek scrambled up and hid his knife. He heaved Jacek up. "What the devil, Jacek? I could've killed you."

The boy's face twisted as if in pain, and tears leaked out.

Crouching, Mirek hugged him. "It's okay, Jacek. I'm sorry I frightened you."

"What the hell...?" said Borys.

Still consoling the boy, Mirek pursed his lips and shook his head.

Borys said, "So now what do we do? We can't take him with us."

"Of course not." Mirek pulled back to look Jacek in the face. He caressed the boy's head. "Are you okay?"

Jacek nodded.

Pointing, Mirek said, "Borys, go straight for six or seven minutes and you'll find the track. I'll leave Jacek where I met you, then catch up to make sure you don't get lost." He checked his watch. "Give me thirty-five minutes."

Nodding, Borys turned to leave.

Mirek called after him, "Remember to stay downwind." He hoped the man understood the technique.

Borys tramped away, muttering.

"Okay, let's get you somewhere safe." Mirek offered his hand, and the boy took it. But with the first step, Jacek squealed, holding his left foot off the ground.

Mirek examined Jacek's foot. He moved it gently. "Does this hurt?"

Grimacing, the boy nodded.

"Do you want me to carry you?"

Jacek shook his head, which was a relief considering the state of Mirek's back — he wasn't even sure he could lift the boy without collapsing in agony.

"Will resting for two minutes help?"

Jacek nodded.

They sat on an old log.

After three minutes, Mirek said, "Shall we try again?"

Jacek nodded and again took Mirek's hand. Excruciatingly slowly, they started back, Jacek taking a tiny step with his good leg, then lurching forward with the injured one.

Bit by bit, they headed back. Mirek checked his watch. No way was he going to make it back in less than an hour at this rate.

But the small boy soldiered on, jaw clenched, wincing with each step. It was Mirek who'd hurt Jacek, and now the boy was doing his best to fight through the pain, so Mirek couldn't ask for more.

They passed the hide and hobbled on.

In the distance behind them, a dog barked.

Mirek gasped. He spun around. Another dog barked and a whistle blew.

Oh dear Lord, no.

He looked at Jacek and then back as shouts came in German. If he and Jacek were found, they could be shot on sight. Jacek could barely move, so Mirek did the only thing he could — he flung his arms around the boy and whisked him off his feet.

As if someone had driven nails into him, pain spread across Mirek's back. He darted around the trees and bushes, clutching the boy to his chest. They had to escape, but it was so far to the forest edge. So torturously far.

More barking and shouting came from behind them.

The Nazis were too close. He wasn't going to make it.

Mirek stumbled and they smashed against a trunk.

Shouting and barking spread across a wide area, as if a line of soldiers and their dogs was moving through the forest.

Mirek clutched Jacek. They couldn't get out in time. What was he going to do?

He gasped as an idea sprang from the depths of his mind. That might work. Or it might see them shot even sooner. But it was their only chance.

Hoisting up Jacek, Mirek turned from the way out of the forest and ran as fast as he could back into its depths, toward the danger.

German commands and baying hounds stalked closer and closer.

Panting, his back feeling like he was being whipped all over again, Mirek pushed on. It was their only hope.

Finally, he saw the holly.

Easing Jacek onto the ground near the entrance hole, he whispered, "We're going to hide. You have to promise you'll be quiet."

The boy nodded and scuttled into the hole. Mirek dove after him.

In the dark interior, Mirek crouched, hugging Jacek, while the boy clawed his coat. Mirek's gaze flashed around. Were they nice and safe in a hiding place, or ready for slaughter in a trap?

Outside, the shouts and barking grew louder and louder.

Mirek cringed. If the dogs had picked up their scents, they were as good as dead.

But what of Borys? There'd been no shots, nor any screams. Maybe the gasoline and tobacco had done its job. What an idiot Mirek had been not to have grabbed the chance to douse himself in the stuff.

Gruff German voices approached. So close it was like they were in the hide.

One voice said, "So is there anyone else out here?"

Another said, "It's impossible to tell. The dogs might be following the same scent or a different one."

The voices passed, but others approached. And all around, dogs barked and sniffed. Mirek was surrounded. He clamped his hand over Jacek's mouth, the boy's cheeks wet with tears.

Mirek screwed his eyes shut. Held his breath. Prayed and prayed and prayed. They hadn't been discovered yet, so if they were quiet, so deathly quiet, maybe, just maybe, they might escape this nightmare.

Voices moved away, and the scurrying of dogs became more distant.

Mirek dared to breathe. Just a shallow gasp. He relaxed his grip on Jacek.

Jacek's chin trembled, but he remained silent. So brave, and so silent.

Mirek gazed at the hide's exit. Was it safe yet?

If they left too soon, they might be spotted. But if they waited too long, the Germans might come back to search more thoroughly.

Should they risk it?

There was only one way to find out. Releasing Jacek, Mirek crouched to the hole. Jacek grabbed his arm and yanked him back. The boy shook his head, trembling with fear.

But they had to risk it. Had to.

Mirek leaned into Jacek's ear and whispered, "I think it's safe. We have to get home."

The boy screwed his face up.

Mirek wiped the boy's eyes. "It's okay. I've got you, Jacek." He put his arm around the boy. "Come on, we'll go together."

Shaking, the boy looked at Mirek, then the hole, then back to Mirek.

"Trust me," said Mirek.

Jacek nodded.

Together, they crouched to the hole. They crawled out and clambered up. Mirek gazed around to ensure they were safe. He gasped.

Five German soldiers stood in a semicircle twenty feet to their left. They cocked their rifles.

Standing in the middle, the rottenführer who had flogged Mirek raised his arm. "Take aim."

Mirek hunched, smothering Jacek with his body, back to the rifles.

50

Mirek stood in a large reception room at the camp's entrance, clutching Jacek. The boy stank of urine, unsurprisingly having peed himself when the soldiers had taken aim. For some inexplicable reason, they hadn't fired. But the Germans reveled in inflicting mental anguish as much as, if not more than, physical pain, so had that been a sick joke or merely a prelude to horrors yet to come?

He stroked Jacek's head. "It's okay. I'm sure we'll be allowed home soon."

He wished he believed that himself.

Two German soldiers guarding the door stared at him impassively. To one side, a couple of sofas and easy chairs sat before a log fire, on the left of which stood a large liquor cabinet with a considerable range of alcoholic beverages. In the far corner, a stuffed brown bear reared on its hind legs.

If Mirek was about to be shot, this was a strange place to hold him. Or was this part of that same sick joke?

A car engine drew his gaze to the window. A black car pulled up, tires crunching over gravel. Kruger got out of the rear. A moment later, he swaggered into the room, accompanied by more soldiers and the rottenführer.

Mirek gulped. Was this good news? Or after their last exchange, was it the worst possible?

Kruger said, "Tell me, did the Führer personally send you to try me?"

It being such a strange question, Mirek floundered. "I... what..."

Kruger rested his swagger stick on Mirek's shoulder and sighed. "Despite the compassion I've shown you, you still seem intent on testing me. Why is that? What have I ever done to deserve such perniciousness?"

Dumbfounded, Mirek gawked at him.

"After our last encounter, I neglected to rescind my orders for you not to be harmed. Which"— he smiled at the rottenführer —"seems to have provided an opportunity for a moment of levity in the grim days in which we find ourselves mired."

His top lip curling, Kruger sniffed and then jabbed at Jacek with his stick and looked at the rottenführer. "*Your* joke caused this, *you* get rid of the stench."

"Yes, Herr Hauptsturmführer." The man dashed toward Jacek.

Mirek shielded the boy.

Jabbing his stick at a chair, Kruger said, "He can either sit there or lie in the morgue. Your choice."

Mirek tried to hand him over, but Jacek clawed his coat all the more. Kruger rapped the boy's knuckles with his stick. Jacek squealed and let go. The rottenführer carried him at arm's length toward one of the chairs.

"On a paper," said Kruger. "I use this room."

The rottenführer put Jacek down, holding onto him with one hand, and opened a magazine on the chair with the other. He plonked the boy onto it. Jacek immediately grabbed the chair arms to push out.

Mirek held up his palm. "Jacek, no."

The boy hunched into a ball.

Shaking his head, Kruger stared at Mirek. "I had such high hopes for you. I could've opened doors few real Germans ever get to walk through. And this"— he snorted and gestured to the outside —"is how you repay me. Spying on my camp, no doubt for some deluded propaganda campaign that—"

"Excuse me, what?" Mirek frowned. His shirt clinging to his sweat-drenched back, he thanked the Lord that Kruger couldn't see it under his jacket. "Spying? *Me?*"

Kruger narrowed his glare at Mirek.

"I'm sorry, but I don't understand," said Mirek. "Why would you think we were spying?"

Kruger rolled his eyes.

Drawing a slow, deep breath, Mirek fought to steady his racing heart and the adrenaline shooting through his veins. If he kept his nerve, he might yet pull this out of the bag. But that demanded calmness. Supreme calmness.

Mirek said, "Is it normal for a spy to drag an eight-year-old child on a mission with them?"

Looking at the rottenführer, Kruger said, "You've got to hand it to him, he has an answer for everything."

"We were hunting." Mirek pointed to his bag on a table. "See for yourself."

Again to the rottenführer, Kruger said, "Did you search it?"

"He had a knife." The man held it up.

"A *hunting* knife," said Mirek. "You made it illegal for Poles to have firearms, so what do you expect me to have?"

Kruger heaved a breath and gestured for the rottenführer to hand him Mirek's blade. "I'm supposed to believe you went hunting with nothing but a knife? What can you kill with this?"

"Boar."

"Seriously? And how close would you have to be to hunt a boar with this little thing?" Kruger shook the knife mockingly.

Mirek reached for the blade. "May I?"

Kruger studied him a moment, then handed it over.

The guards adjusted their grips on their rifles.

Mirek hurled the blade. It spun through the air and stabbed the bear in the head.

Mirek shrugged. "Not too close."

Kruger pursed his lips, glaring at Mirek. "I shot the beast myself. I should make you pay for the taxidermy repairs."

He marched to Mirek's pack, then pulled out the rabbit, so fresh the body was still limp, followed by a coil of wire.

He looked at Mirek. "You snared this?"

"How else would I have it? Or are you suggesting that Polish spies take not only a small child on secret missions but dead game?" The rabbit had been costly from Hanka's black marketeer, but it might just have saved both their lives.

Kruger glared at the rottenführer. "Was he with the other man?"

"I'm sorry, Herr Hauptsturmführer, but it was impossible to tell."

"You had trackers and dogs."

"The way the undergrowth had been disturbed suggested the other man had approached the camp alone, but I couldn't say for sure."

Kruger flexed his stick in both hands. "You found them close by?"

"About ten minutes later. Hiding in a tarpaulin tent in a bush."

Mirek said, "Not a tent, a hunter's hide."

Kruger rubbed his brow. "Rottenführer, is it possible they were hunting?"

"I... maybe, Herr Hauptsturmführer."

Pinching the bridge of his nose, Kruger closed his eyes, muttering under his breath. Finally, he looked at Mirek. "Hunting? I'm supposed to believe you were hunting?"

"What else would we be doing?"

"Hunting in a restricted area?"

Mirek frowned. "It's restricted?"

Kruger huffed. "Rottenführer, there are signs posted all around the perimeter of the forest, are there not?"

"There are some, yes, Herr Hauptsturmführer."

"Some?" Kruger rubbed the back of his neck, then nodded to one of the soldiers with whom he'd entered. The man clicked his heels together and left. Kruger bent forward right into Mirek's chest and sniffed.

Mirek leaned back.

Still close, Kruger said, "You don't smell of gasoline."

Mirek sniffed Kruger. "Neither do you. Is that a problem?"

"Some Resistance fighters use it as a means to throw dogs off their scent."

"They do?"

This was looking good. Very good. All Mirek needed to do was create just enough credibility to sway Kruger. The rabbit, the hide, the child, and now the lack of gasoline... it all sounded extremely plausible. But was it enough?

"You know," said Kruger, "I'm almost inclined to believe you."

Mirek smiled. "Thank you."

Kruger wagged his finger. "I said *almost*."

Mirek's heart raced. His hands clammy, he ached to wipe them on his pants but dared not because of the signal that would send. He gulped. "If I intended to spy on a secure German installation, why would I put myself at risk by taking a bumbling child?"

"Maybe as cover. Should you be apprehended."

"I'm the director of an orphanage. My job is to protect children, not to endanger them."

Sucking through his teeth, Kruger gestured outside. "So if you weren't spying, you won't know this man?"

Two soldiers, including the one who'd been instructed to leave moments earlier, stood at either side of Borys, who knelt on the ground, face bloody, wrists and ankles tied.

Mirek winced. "No, of course I know him. That's Borys. He undertakes carpentry work for me."

Kruger frowned. "You admit you know him? So you must also know he's Polish Resistance?"

Mirek popped his eyes wide. "What? No!" He threw his hands up. "How could I possibly know that?"

"You're sure?"

"Of course I'm sure. Why? Has he said I do know?"

"No."

"Then there you go."

Kruger snorted again, then tipped his head toward Borys. "Your friend seemed to believe gasoline would save him. Shall we see if he's right?"

He waved to the soldiers. One lit a match and tossed it on Borys. The gasoline caught, and Borys's coat burst into flame.

Borys screamed and lurched forward but, being bound, he crunched into the ground face-first. Wailing, he rolled from side to side as the flames devoured him.

Mirek bit his lip, his chin trembling.

With an air of satisfaction, Kruger said, "It seems Borys was wrong."

"Please. For God's sake, do something," said Mirek as Borys writhed.

"The man brought it on himself." Kruger wagged a finger at Mirek. "Don't expect me to waste a bullet on someone like that."

In tears, Mirek stared at Borys, at the death throes of his friend.

"Now, where were we?" said Kruger. "Ah, yes — what to do about you." He put his fist to his mouth.

From outside, screams sliced through the air. Jacek sat with his hands over his ears, eyes screwed shut.

Kruger shouted, "Will someone stop that noise so I can think?"

One of the soldiers kicked Borys in the head. Borys slumped to the gravel, the only thing moving being the fire savaging his body.

Kruger shook his head. "I'd hoped the flogging would see you become a little less problematic, but it's obvious that taking action against you personally is never going to work. So, you leave me little option."

That could only mean one thing. Mirek's legs almost fell from under him. He struggled to catch his breath as the icy hand of dread raked down his spine. Around him, the room seemed to darken as his vision tunneled, until the only two things that existed in the universe were him and Kruger.

Mirek's hands trembling, voice shaking, he said, "Please, no. Not them. You can't punish them for something I've done."

Kruger lifted a finger. "Here's what's going to happen..."

51

On the sidewalk outside their courtyard, Mirek crouched and held Jacek's shoulders. "This is important, Jacek, so you must listen. You *cannot* say anything about what you've seen today. Understand?"

The boy stared, eyes puffy and red.

"Jacek, you need to tell me you understand." Mirek couldn't risk Jacek jeopardizing tomorrow's escape and what Mirek now had to do.

Nothing.

"Jacek!" Mirek jerked him.

The boy nodded vigorously.

"Thank you. Now let's get that foot looked at."

As they entered, Ania peered from the dining room window. A moment later, she raced outside. "Where've you been? We've been worried sick."

Mirek waved. "Don't panic, everything's okay. In fact, I have some wonderful news, but I have to run an errand first."

She touched Mirek's arm. "Thank heaven you're okay. I've been picturing all kinds of horrible things."

"No, we're fine. Well, one of us is." He tousled Jacek's hair. "Someone's been in the wars, hasn't he?"

Ania crouched to the boy. "Awww, what's happened?"

Mirek said, "The little rascal went over on his left ankle in the forest. Can you apply some liniment and bandage it, please?"

"Of course."

"I'll be back soon." Mirek tramped away, his legs shaking and back aching after having carried Jacek much of the way home. Kruger had let them return via the road, which snaked around Krolik Hill, but the last mile had been like wading through a river. All Mirek wanted was a lie-down, but such luxuries would have to wait.

Borys had been the only member of the resistance he knew. However, it appeared his grocer was also involved with the underground movement. Mirek prayed Julek was actively involved and thus had the contacts to be able to resolve the problem Kruger had created. If he couldn't... boy, were they in trouble.

In the grocery store, Mirek waved his ration cards. "Julek, I have a special order that I need to pay for in advance. Can we speak in private, please?"

Instead of smiling at the prospect of extra money, Julek's face lined with anxiety. He showed Mirek into a storeroom littered with crates and wooden tubs, most empty.

Julek shut the door and whispered, "You shouldn't be here."

There was no easy way to say what needed saying. Mirek said, "Borys is dead."

Julek sank onto a stack of crates, wide eyes staring into space.

"Long story short," said Mirek, "the Nazis are gassing innocent people and burying them in the forest. Borys wanted evidence that the Resistance could pass to the Allies but was caught spying on the proceedings."

Terror flashed over Julek's face. "He didn't talk, did he?" He relaxed. "No, of course not, or it wouldn't be you here but them."

"I need to contact someone else in his group."

Shrugging, Julek said, "He was my contact. I don't know anyone else."

"No one?"

Julek shook his head. "Maybe the person I'm transferring you to will know someone."

The transfer was at 9:15 a.m. tomorrow. "That's too late."

"So is tomorrow off?"

Mirek grabbed Julek by the arms. "No. You have to come at eight o'clock as arranged. Understand?"

"Okay, okay."

"When you meet the transfer, tell them I need to speak to someone about what's happening the next day. Promise me you won't forget."

"I promise."

With nothing more Julek could do, Mirek left.

Head down, he shuffled along the street. He was so close to getting everyone out, everything couldn't fall apart now. But what else could he do?

Groaning, he slumped. There was one thing he couldn't put off doing any longer.

A few minutes later, he sat facing Ania and Hanka in the dining room.

"As usual, I have some good news and some bad news." He stared at a glass of water, then forced a smile. "First, the good news — my group is leaving tomorrow and Hanka's is leaving the day after."

Beaming, Hanka and Ania hugged. When they separated, Hanka wiped her eyes, and Ania reached over and held his hand.

"I always knew you'd do it," said Ania.

His smile faded, his face aching with the effort, even though he'd only held it a few seconds. Ania always knew when he was lying, so overcompensating would only make it worse.

She squeezed his hand. "What's wrong? This is wonderful news."

Hanka dabbed her eyes with a pale blue handkerchief. "So is that the bad news? That we can't go on the same day?"

He winced. "Borys couldn't swing it."

Hanka snorted. "Bad news, my eye. You had me worried for a second." She squeezed Ania's arm. "I can't believe we're going."

Ania's smile faded too. "No, neither can I." Her gaze drilled into him.

Mirek swallowed hard. "There is one other bit of bad news. Two, actually."

"Does it matter now?" Hanka grinned.

"I—" Mirek cleared his throat, then avoided Ania's eyes. "I'll be going with you, Hanka."

"But that's good, isn't it?" said Hanka. "It'll make managing the children easier."

Unblinking, Ania glared at him. "But that's not the bad news, is it, Mirek?"

How did she do that? Good Lord, if she worked for Kruger, he'd be dangling at the end of a noose right now.

Mirek bit his lip, staring down. Finally, he met Ania's gaze.

"I might not..." How could he tell them when he didn't know himself? "There's been a problem. Something big that Borys can't fix and, eh..." There was nothing to be gained by sharing the whole truth. Nothing except pain, upset, and anxiousness.

This time, Hanka touched his hand. "Mirek, you're starting to worry me. What's going on? Because no matter how bad you believe it is, it's meaningless when we're all getting out of here."

Mirek rubbed his mouth and shot a glance at Ania.

That unblinking stare still nailed him.

Mirek rubbed his face. "Ania and the children leave tomorrow at 8:00 a.m. At noon, there'll be another event in the square that we all have to attend. The whole household."

"Do you mean us and the children or everyone living here, including the families?" asked Hanka.

Mirek said, "Everyone. Families included."

"Why?" said Hanka.

"I don't know."

"So what kind of event?"

"I don't know."

Ania said, "So what do you know?"

He reached for her hand. "If I went with you, my absence would be noticed. Within minutes, there'd be roadblocks, railway networks would be notified, and neighboring towns would be put on alert. And when they caught us, which they undoubtedly would, how many of the children would they machine-gun as an example for others?"

Hanka frowned. "All that for you? Why are you so important?"

"Because me escaping will make a fool of Kruger, and you've seen what a sadistic megalomaniac he is."

"So you can't go tomorrow?" said Ania.

Mirek shook his head.

"But you *can* go the day after?"

"If everything goes as planned. I might even be able to catch up with you."

Ania folded her arms. "And what are the chances that everything *won't* go as planned?"

"I don't know. I honestly have no idea what Kruger intends to do." He didn't. Short of them all having to report to the square. But whatever it was, it wasn't going to be good.

Ania said, "Is it to do with your and Borys's spying trip?"

"Possibly." Mirek sipped water, trying to hide behind his glass.

"So is it or isn't it?"

Mirek gestured to the doorway. "Do you see Germans bursting in, guns blazing?"

"So everything should go okay?" she asked.

"That's what I'm trying to tell you. Unless there's some nasty surprise in the square tomorrow, everything is going ahead as planned."

Finally, Ania nodded. "Okay."

Hanka frowned. "You keep saying it's going ahead as planned, but what exactly is the plan?"

He shared all the details of the escape with Julek the next day and the second one for Hanka's group the following morning. In both cases, the children would be told nothing until one hour before, with the disappearance of Ania and her four children being explained as an emergency trip to the hospital due to food poisoning.

With everything said that could be said, Mirek informed the families of the impending event, then fought to take his mind off the horrors he'd witnessed by running some last-minute German classes.

After dinner, he retired to his study, where he collected the few items he would be taking, *if* there were no surprises in the square. Standing at his bookcase, he scanned what remained of his library. If he did escape, having a book to read while traveling would be wonderful. He reached for one but pulled back.

Someone knocked on the study door.

"Come."

Ania peeped in. "I don't want to disturb you."

He beckoned. "No, please."

She ambled over. "Are you packing books?"

"I was thinking about it, but a Polish book will immediately give away my nationality to anyone who sees it."

She rolled her eyes. "Of course. We're going to have to be so careful, aren't we?"

Heaving a breath, he nodded.

Ania gazed at the floor, twisting her right foot. "Listen, in case I don't get the chance tomorrow, I wanted to say how much I've loved working here."

She flicked her big hazel eyes up, eyes he wanted to drown in. "And I've loved you working here."

"You know, neither of us knows where we're going to end up, so we might never meet again unless we do something crazy like, say"— she meandered over to gaze up at his painting of the Eiffel Tower —"arrange to meet on the top of your tower at midday on June first, the first full year after the war ends."

He smiled. "It's a date."

"A date? Not an appointment? That's a little presumptuous, Mr. Kozlowski." She smirked.

He chuckled. How he longed to hold her. To bask in the joy she brought to this dark, dark world.

"I stand corrected."

She squinted at him, maybe picking up on his strange mood despite their impending escape being only hours away. "There's nothing else Hanka and I need to know, is there?"

Was there anything Ania *needed* to know? No, nothing that wouldn't devastate her. He couldn't tell her about Borys, about the meeting with Kruger, about the Nazi's suspicions being the basis of the "event" in the square tomorrow. Nothing could interfere with *her* escape. The slightest hint that he or the household might be at risk, and she'd refuse to leave, stubbornly staying to help. He couldn't risk that.

"Of course not," said Mirek. "It's wonderful that we're all escaping, but this place has so many memories, it's going to be a real wrench to leave it all behind."

She frowned. "You're sure that's all it is?"

"What else could it be? In little more than a day, we'll all be miles away, heading for new adventures goodness knows where."

She touched his arm. "Let's hope we don't all end up too far apart."

A tingle ran through him. He nodded.

"Do you need any help packing?"

"No, thank you. You go get some rest. Heaven knows when you'll next have a comfortable bed to sleep in."

"You're sure I can't do anything?"

He waved his hand.

"Okay. Good night." She strode toward the door.

He ached to rush after her, spin her around, and take her in his arms. Feel her warmth, her frailty, her unbelievable strength. But most of all, he wanted to kiss her. Long, lingering, loving. And when their lips finally parted, he wanted to whisper, *I love you.*

He said, "Ania?"

She turned. "Hmmm?"

"I..." He gritted his teeth. "Sleep well, Anna-Maria Kisiell with two *L*'s."

She grinned. Held his gaze for another second, then disappeared.

How could he tell her how he felt? Give her hope that they might have a chance together? Give her a reason to put her life on hold while she waited and waited and waited for him? Give her years of disappointment and misery?

A fleeting moment of pleasure now would be the most selfish thing he'd ever done.

But maybe he was worrying over nothing. Maybe tomorrow would come and go, and he could leave with Hanka, then in a few weeks or maybe months, he might find Ania again.

It was a nice thought, but he couldn't help but feel that Kruger had one last sadistic joke up his sleeve.

52

After a sleepless night worrying over what the day would bring, Mirek rose at dawn. He dressed, then slumped onto his chair, struggling to formulate contingency plans for whatever scenario befell his household later. Unfortunately, someone knocked on his door, interrupting him.

"Come."

Agata entered, still in her nightgown. "Morning, Papa Mirek. Baba Hanka asks if she could see you, please."

"Morning, Agata. Tell her I'll come to the kitchen in thirty minutes."

"She says to go to her room. Now. She was very, *very* sure about that."

Odd. Why was Hanka not preparing breakfast as normal? What could be so important?

Two minutes later, he stood in her room, looking at her back while she stared out of the window. "What can I help with, Hanka?"

No reply.

"Hanka, we're pressed for time this morning. Is something wrong?"

Hanka turned. Scowling, she arched an eyebrow.

Mirek swallowed. What did she know? And how could she know it? He shrugged. "What?"

"Don't 'what' me, Mirek Kozlowski. You know very well what."

"Hanka, I'm sorry, but—"

"Roadblocks, my eye. You could be a hundred miles away by the time anyone discovers you're missing. You might be able to pull the wool over Ania's eyes, but don't think you can play that game with me. Now get your things because you're going. And that's the end of it."

"How can I put the well-being of four children ahead of that of the fifty-two I'd be leaving behind?"

"You do it because you have to do it. Because it might be your one chance to get away."

Mirek slumped. "I can't, Hanka. I'm positive Kruger will be there. He'll instantly spot if I'm not. And then all of you will pay the price. Do you honestly believe I could live with that?"

Her glare softened.

Mirek touched her shoulder. "I can't put all of you in danger. And if it turns out to be a false alarm, we'll all be getting away together tomorrow anyway."

"And what if it all goes wrong? If this really is your only chance to escape this hell? You and Ania deserve a shot at—" Hanka's eyes welled up. She covered her mouth and turned away.

Mirek hugged her. He ached to say something reassuring, but what if she was right? What if this was his only chance to live a life worth living with the woman he loved?

Should he risk escaping? Risk everyone here being safe without him?

Maybe Hanka was correct. Maybe he—

The photograph on Hanka's dresser caught his eye. The photograph from her birthday, featuring tens of children who had been ripped from their home and tens of others who could disappear in an instant if no one stood to protect them.

Could he risk it? *Could he?*

He gulped. Hard. Swallowing the pain. He drew a wavering breath and prayed his voice would be steady. "It will be okay, Hanka. You'll see. This time tomorrow, we'll all be far, far away from this nightmare."

She wept against his shoulder. "I pray you're right, Mirek. I pray you are."

***

Julek parked his blue delivery van in the courtyard at an angle to obscure its rear from most windows. With the goods emptied to maintain the ruse, Mirek held Zygmunt's brown suitcase as the boy clambered into the back. Taking the case, Zygmunt offered his right hand.

"Be careful, Zygmunt." Mirek shook it, fighting back tears.

Hunched over, the chubby boy toddled to the far end near the driver's cab, where he sat, clutching his case.

Rafal grabbed Mirek around the waist and squeezed.

Mirek hugged him. "Okay, in you go." He would've loved to spend hours saying proper goodbyes, but they had barely minutes to spare.

A girl with long black hair beckoned him down to her level, then kissed him on the cheek. "Thank you, Papa Mirek. I'll never forget you."

Tears blurring his vision, he stroked the back of her head. "And I'll never forget you, Baska."

He turned away for a moment and drew a deep breath to clear his head, the worst goodbye yet to come. But when he turned back, she'd disappeared.

Ania shuffled outside, wiping her eyes.

Mirek said, "Where's Agata?"

"I left her with you."

He looked at Julek, who tapped his wristwatch.

Mirek dashed toward the house. "Stay with them. Make sure no one else goes AWOL."

He had a few ideas where she might be, but no time to check them all. He raced into the dining room, gaze flying around. "Kuba?"

Munching, Kuba looked up at the far end.

"Where's Agata?"

Kuba shook his head.

Mirek darted out and stormed up the staircase, two steps at a time. On the girls' floor, he darted into the first room. "Agata?"

No answer.

"Agata?" He opened the large closet. Nothing. He ducked to look under the nearest bunk beds. Nothing.

Scrambling across the floor, he peered under the other beds.

In the dusty gloom, a little girl huddled. She sniffled.

"Agata, it's time to go, princess."

She shook her head.

Mirek said, "I'm sorry, but you have to. Everyone is waiting for you."

Her voice breaking, she said, "I don't want to leave you and Kuba."

"And I don't want you to either, which is why we'll find each other as soon as we can."

"You promise?"

He reached toward her. "I promise we'll try our best."

She took his hand and shuffled out, clutching a small blue bag.

He picked her up, raced down the stairs, and hurried outside.

Ania was sitting in the back of the van with her three children. When she saw Mirek dashing over, she opened her arms. "Agata, we were worried you'd gone without us."

Ania made a space between her and Zygmunt.

Mirek lifted Agata into the van. He cupped her face and sniffled. "You're going to live a wonderful life, Agata. Make sure every moment of it is unforgettable."

She hugged him.

He cradled her, then patted her on the back. "Time to go, princess."

He pulled away, pain in his heart as if he'd been stabbed.

Ania took the little girl's hand and guided her to sit.

Mirek gazed at Ania. Words were his love, his strength, his reason for living. Or so he'd thought. He stared at her, but not a single syllable came to his mind.

"We have to go." Julek slammed one of the two rear doors.

Still Mirek gazed. If only he could find the words.

Ania lunged at him. She flung her arms around him and kissed him. For a few seconds, there was no war, no hatred, no fight for survival; there was only one man and one woman. And a universe cocooning them with love.

Ania pulled away, eyes big with guilt. "Sorry, I didn't know if I'd ever get another chance."

Mirek opened his mouth to say something, but Julek slammed the door.

A moment later, the van was gone, and he was alone.

In a daze, Mirek tramped into the dining room, Hanka having been instructed to keep everyone there after eating.

Mirek sank onto a chair.

Whatever was going to happen today, no way could it be more heart-wrenching than what he'd just suffered. And it was the children he had to consider now, not himself.

But he couldn't. All he could picture was a small blue van growing smaller and smaller as it meandered along a country lane.

Elbows on his knees, head in his hands, he stared at the floor. Just stared and stared and stared.

Something prodded his shoulder. "Mirek."

He didn't move.

It prodded again. "Mirek."

Finally, he raised his head.

Hanka said, "It's time."

Mirek scanned all the faces staring at him. How long had he been oblivious? This wasn't the way to care for all those depending on him. He drew a long slow breath and stood.

He could do this. He *had* to do this.

Mirek recalled Hanka's birthday party and the joy that had filled the room. Smiling, he clapped three times. "Thank you for waiting, everybody. Now, I have some good news — we're all going on a grand adventure this morning."

Many children gasped, their eyes lighting up as they chatted excitedly.

"When I say so, you have forty minutes to use the bathroom and put on your favorite clothes. And as a treat, you can each bring your favorite toy."

A doll, a car, a book... Mirek hoped his children wouldn't need consolation from their most treasured possession, but...

He scanned the faces all eager to be off, then held his hands wide. "Okay, run, run, run!"

The children scooted away.

He shouted after them, "When you hear the gong, it's time to go, so form a line in the courtyard."

As the children streamed out, he smiled at the joy on their faces, but then his chin trembled at the thought of what might be awaiting them. When he turned, Hanka stood with her arms folded.

As the last child darted away, Mirek ambled over.

She arched an eyebrow. He wished he could get away with using so few words and yet be understood perfectly.

"I'm sorry, Hanka. I couldn't tell you everything when Ania was still here because I couldn't risk her wanting to stay and the five of them losing their chance to escape."

Her face softened. "So do I want to know what's really happening this morning?"

"I honestly don't know, but I worry it could be bad. We all have to report to the square at ten thirty-five, with our papers, but after that..." He shrugged.

"So not noon?"

He shook his head.

Hanka frowned. "Ten thirty-five is an odd time."

It was. Which made it all the more worrying.

"I'll fetch my coat." She toddled away. Over her shoulder, she said, "Wrap up, there's a nip in the air."

53

With Hanka counting the children in the courtyard and ensuring none drifted onto the street, Mirek struck the gong again. Tadek and Bogdan hurtled down the steps and outside.

Poking her head in the door, Hanka said, "That's the lot of them. The families, too."

Mirek hung the mallet up and turned for the door but stopped. The hallway walls were now bare of children's artworks, paper for the bathrooms being far more important than decoration. The carpetless staircase climbed silently up into the gloom, yet the echoes of tens of thousands of footfalls still sounded. And the dining room — a source of endless clatter and endless chatter — now sat as forlorn as a toy a child had discarded in a darkened closet.

Home.

He sank to the bottom step and sobbed. He'd sworn to protect his children, whatever the cost. How had it all gone so wrong?

Hanka shuffled over. "It's seen some good times, this old place, hasn't it?"

Mirek sniffled. Too choked to get words out.

Hanka touched his shoulder. "I'm sure the old place will be bursting with laughter and squabbles all too soon again."

Drawing a faltering breath, he wiped his eyes. He had to be strong for his children.

He stood. "Let's go."

Hanka patted his arm. "Take a moment. You deserve it."

Mirek shook his head. Being late would only anger Kruger all the more.

He crooked his arm. "Time to face the music."

She hooked her arm through his, and they strode for the door. "I'm sure we're fretting over nothing, and this will all be over by lunchtime."

But in the doorway, Mirek froze.

Sunlight filtered through the apple tree to dapple the courtyard in golden pools, while high in the tree's branches, amid leaves hinting at turning gold or red, a bird sang, its melody teasing the day.

How was the sun shining? The birds singing? The world simply going on as if none of this was happening? Was Hanka right — was he fretting over nothing?

"What would happen if we just didn't go?" asked Hanka.

Dear Lord, he dreaded to imagine. The SS would probably lock the children inside and set the place ablaze.

Hiding wasn't an option. Just as running wasn't. There was nowhere left to run to, nowhere left to hide. The only way they'd survive was to comply with the order and pray Kruger was in a generous mood.

In the courtyard, children laughed and joked and smiled and played. All in their favorite clothes, holding their favorite possessions. Any other day, it would've been the most beautiful sight he'd ever seen.

Mirek closed his eyes and drew three slow breaths. Today was for them. Quieting his mind about the horrors that might lie in wait, he opened his eyes.

"Ready?" he asked.

Hanka said, "You lead, I'll follow."

Mirek stepped outside. He clapped three times to gain everyone's attention. "Okay, are we all ready for our grand adventure?"

Children shouted, "Yes!"

He smiled. "Then what are we waiting for?" He headed for the gate, watching all the children swarming after him but stopped short.

In the middle of the crowd, a red-haired boy hobbled as everyone streamed past him.

Mirek held up his hand and everyone stopped.

"Jacek." He beckoned.

The boy lurched over.

Turning away from the boy, Mirek crouched and patted his back. "Hop on."

Jacek beamed and climbed on Mirek's back, Mirek catching under the boy's knees. "Everyone else, find a partner and hold hands."

The children grabbed for their nearest friend.

"And off we go." Mirek led them onto the street, Hanka bringing up the rear to make sure they stayed together as they walked two by two. The families Mirek had taken in followed behind.

Walking backward, Mirek said, "Who knows a good song?"

Children shouted various suggestions, Ola saying, "'The Bears Are Going Out.'"

"Oh, I like that one," said Mirek. "Let's start with that."

Marching up the street, the children sang,

The bears are going out today,
Tra-la-la-la-la!
They laugh and sing and run and play,
Cha-cha-cha-cha-cha!
In woods so green and fresh in May.
Ha-ha-ha-ha-ha!
With lots of friends along the way.
Fa-fa-fa-fa-fa!

Passersby smiled and waved, the children waving back. A woman and her small daughter stopped and clapped in time to the song as the children strolled by. An old man with a cane did a little jig, then tipped his hat as the children glided on. The street glowed with the joy that the children spread.

But approaching the square, Mirek wiped his palms on his jacket.

A group of soldiers stood in the middle of the square.

Mirek's pulse raced as he led the children toward them. What were these monsters going to do? Was there any way he could yet protect everyone?

The soldiers swarmed around Mirek's group. One with a bushy mustache appeared to be in charge and pointed toward the bottom of the square.

Mirek stumbled as his legs gave way, almost dropping Jacek. Oh Lord, no. Please, no. The Nazis could flog him, burn him, hang him... anything. But not this. Not when they were so close to all getting away.

At the far end of the square, more soldiers stood outside the railway station. Waiting.

Borys had said Jews were soon to be shipped to a ghetto. And Kruger had insisted on Mirek's whole household attending, including the Jewish families he'd homed. It all made sense now. Mirek wasn't going to be physically punished like before. No, this time his punishment was going to be far worse. This time, he'd suffer having half his children ripped from him and crammed into some filthy, overcrowded slum.

Kruger could simply have visited the house and snatched the children. But no. That wasn't Kruger's way. That monster needed to put on a show. Needed Mirek to be there, to witness his loved ones being imprisoned in hell.

The ghetto.

It was so obvious now. Why else would the families be forced to attend? Why else would he have to take everyone's papers if not to prove who was Jewish and who wasn't? And why else would the time be so oddly precise if not to accommodate a train schedule?

Mirek gritted his teeth. He couldn't let the children know what was coming. For as long as possible, they had to believe everything was okay. That this was another grand adventure with Papa Mirek.

The soldiers at the railway station funneled Mirek's group inside.

Mirek marched in, waving at the soldiers, the children behind him smiling and waving too. In the ticket booths, a balding man and a bespectacled woman stared agog.

A train stood on the platform. Four soldiers waited beside three cattle wagons, a tall one gesturing to the open sliding door of the first. Beyond the cattle wagons, open wagons stretched away, each piled high with building materials.

Mirek marched to the wagon. As he climbed the grimy ramp, he shouted back, "Don't forget to thank the nice gentlemen for lending us their train."

Children clambered up behind him, one after another saying, "Thank you, sir."

Mirek had no idea into what hell they were heading, but he was going to make darn sure that those responsible saw the innocence they were ruining.

The wooden cattle wagon stank like a public bathroom that hadn't been cleaned for years. What — or who — had the Nazis transported in this thing? The wagon was empty other than a bucket in one corner, the handle of a ladle sticking out of it.

Setting Jacek down, Mirek beckoned everyone in. "Come on in. There's plenty of room."

Marta stopped at the top of the ramp and peered inside. "Ewww, it's stinky!"

Mirek grinned. "I know. Isn't it fun!"

She sniffed again, then smiled and nodded.

"The Germans don't let just anyone go on these adventures, you know?" He waved her in. "Come on, before they change their minds."

She scurried in, others following.

Shooing the last few children in, Hanka climbed the ramp. "My, we are lucky to get a wagon all to ourselves, aren't we?"

For a moment, she turned back to the opening and wiped her cheeks, obviously hoping no one would see.

On the platform, the families were directed to board the next wagon.

With everyone in, a soldier appeared in the doorway and glared at Mirek. "There are supposed to be fifty-six children and three adults."

Mirek handed him the death certificates Borys had provided for Ania and the four children.

The soldier scanned them, then nodded. With children waving at him, he dragged the rumbling door shut.

Light struggled in from narrow barred windows in two opposite corners. Suddenly immersed in gloom, some children glanced around the filthy interior with anxious faces.

Mirek didn't know what horrors they would be facing, but until that moment came, his children were going to enjoy their childhood.

He clapped three times. "Okay, who wants to pick the next song?"

Hands flew into the air.

He panned a pointing finger over them. "Let's see, who shall we have?" Back and forth his finger swept, children bouncing, fighting to push higher than anyone else. "Tadek!"

Tadek grinned. "'Boating on the River'!"

"Oh, excellent choice, Tadek."

The children sang again, cheerfulness and camaraderie fighting off any despair that attempted to claw from the shadows.

A whistle sounded, couplings clanged, and their wagon jolted into movement.

And the singing continued. Song after song.

Face drawn, Hanka passed him a folded sheet of paper. "I didn't know if I should give you this yet."

"What is it? Don't tell me it's your letter of resignation."

She chuckled. "That would be about thirteen years too late, wouldn't it?"

He smiled. She'd been his most loyal friend for the majority of his adult life. He'd never have been able to help so many hundreds of children if not for her. And this predicament was how he'd repaid her.

He took her hand, tears in his eyes. "I'm sorry, Hanka. I truly am."

She patted his arm. "Don't be silly. There's nowhere else in the world I'd rather be than here with you and our children."

They hugged.

Marta pulled his sleeve. "You're not singing, Papa Mirek."

"Sorry, Marta. I forgot the words for a moment."

Hanka took the girl's hand. "I'll sing with you, Marta, while Papa Mirek remembers the words."

She turned the little girl away, glancing back at Mirek and tipping her head toward the paper.

Curious. Why would Hanka write him a note when she was standing right beside him? He faced the corner to read in private and unfolded the paper.

He gasped.

"*My dear Mirek,*

Though I've ached to be wrapped in your arms, I knew it could never be, so I was content to remain by your side. Your life is your children, and I would never come between you and your purpose. Love isn't clinging onto someone at the expense of all else, it's letting them go to be all they can be. Doing that ripped my soul apart, but I'm sure that one day there'll be a time for us. Until then, I'll be waiting, in this world or the next.

Always yours,

Anna-Maria Kisiell with two L's"

Mirek slumped, his head banging against the wooden wall. Tears rolled as he slipped the note into his breast pocket. Why hadn't he said something? Why hadn't he held her? Why hadn't he done what he'd always preached — lived a life worth living? He sobbed, his shoulders shuddering.

Something tugged the back of his jacket.

Mopping his face with his handkerchief, he turned.

Marta lifted a ladle of water to him. "Whenever I was sick traveling, Mama made me sip water."

Tears streamed, but this time it was through a smile. Lived a life worth living? There wasn't a man alive or dead with whom he'd change places.

"Thank you, Marta, that's very thoughtful." He took a sip.

She pulled his arm downward. "Sit on the floor. That will help too."

He sat. "Thank you. I'm feeling better already."

Beaming, she picked up where the song had reached and turned back to everyone else.

Sunlight broke the clouds and shafted into their wagon, lighting up the joy in the all the faces going on their grand adventure with Papa Mirek.

He snickered. He was so lucky. Few people would ever get to experience the wonders that he did every day thanks to his children. Kruger be damned — if Mirek lived to be one hundred, he'd never have another day like today.

He checked the time: 10:52. In the second transport, Ania and the children would be a hundred miles or more from this nightmare. Finally, they were on their way to a new life, a good life. Tomorrow, they could be as far away as Switzerland. The days following? France? Maybe even England?

He smiled, picturing Ania lounging in the sunshine in a leafy London park with the children. Gradually, she'd build a life. Maybe she'd even go to the Eiffel Tower the year after the war ended — and maybe he'd be there. And if not...

She'd meet a man who'd give her the love she deserved. She'd build a successful career, start a family, follow fashion, read books in English, listen to jazz, and never again have to suffer stinging nettle goulash.

The train clanged, jolting Mirek from his daydream. The children were still singing as the brakes squealed.

Oh Lord, were they there? But they'd barely traveled any distance, so they were miles from any major ghetto. Where was *there*?

54

The train stationary, the door of the families' wagon rattled open. German voices bawled orders.

In Mirek's wagon, the singing stopped in the middle of a line. Children glanced around anxiously. Before Mirek could say anything reassuring, dogs barked close by.

The children nearest the door jerked back, and others clung to each other, faces twisting with fear.

Mirek wove his way to the door. "This might seem scary, but whatever happens, remember that Baba Hanka and I are with you. And together, we're far stronger than the Germans imagine."

He had no idea into what hell they were about to be thrown, but he was determined to make it as painless for his children as possible.

The heavy metal clasp locking their door clanked over, and the door rattled open.

Standing in the doorway, Mirek gawked.

The camp.

Kruger had brought them to the camp.

Soldiers glared, shouting, "Out! Out!"

The children pulled against the far wall, so the soldiers shouted all the more and dogs barked.

The noise snapped Mirek back to the nightmarish reality. His hands up passively, he said, "We're coming!"

With no ramp, Mirek leapt the three-foot drop to the ground.

To his side, the families clambered out of their wagon. Faces stared. Bewildered. Shocked. Horrified.

Mirek offered his hand. "Hanka."

If the two of them were outside, it would give the children more courage to get out.

Hunched, eyes darting, Hanka shuffled to the opening. She took his hand, sat on the edge of the floor, then dropped to the ground.

He pointed to a space. "Watch the children as I get them off."

Some of the children had moved closer now, with both their surrogate father and grandmother off the train.

Standing near him, a German soldier yelled, "Faster! Out! Out!"

Without looking, Mirek said quietly, "That's not helping, you imbecile."

But it wasn't quiet enough.

The soldier jabbed Mirek in the back with his rifle. Mirek crumpled against the doorway. Children screamed. And all of them scrambled to the far side of the wagon.

Wincing, Mirek pushed up and beckoned them. "Quickly, please. Quickly."

Whether fearing for themselves or for him, he didn't know, but Marta and Tadek scrambled over. He lifted them down, and they ran to Hanka. That started the flow, children now rushing to get out, possibly terrified at the thought of being left alone. Finally, they were all gathered around Hanka, desperately clawing at each other, expressions warped into shapes children's faces should never know.

Mirek scuttled over, the nearest children turning and grabbing him. Ahead, a wall of soldiers faced them, a handful sitting at desks, while behind him, an army of scrawny men in ragged clothing swarmed over the open wagons, unloading the building materials.

Was that to be Kruger's punishment — for Mirek to witness his children turned into slave laborers?

A soldier with a scar on his cheek shouted, "Form a column. Five wide. Families at the front."

Soldiers with rifles shoved people this way and that. All around, dogs barked and snarled.

Hanka's face collapsed into despair, and all the hands clawing at Mirek clutched even tighter.

The scar-faced soldier shouted, "Have your papers ready."

The families and their children clung to one another as they maneuvered into a column while Hanka and Mirek's children huddled in a large ball of sobbing.

Scar Face yelled, bringing his gun up. "Five wide! Five wide!"

Screams erupted as Mirek and Hanka struggled to ease children into a column.

Mirek begged with them, dying inside at how he was pushing away those who loved him in their darkest hour. "Please, everyone, it's only for a short time. Please."

Gradually, a bulging, wonky column formed.

From the group of soldiers ahead, one with bushy sideburns strutted forward. "There's no cause for alarm. This is a labor camp, and you're only being processed. Once completed, instead of living the worthless lives you have, you'll have the honor of helping to create a magnificent new world order that will last a thousand years. Be proud that your lives will now mean something."

Mirek shot Hanka a glance. The announcement was typically overblown but thankfully reassuring. Work in a camp would be grueling, but conditions had to be better than in a ghetto. Plus, they'd all get to stay together.

Sideburns jabbed his swagger stick toward someone at the front of the column and swiped toward the desks. "You."

The young couple Ania had persuaded Mirek to take in gripped each other, not moving an inch.

A guard gave his dog a little slack. The beast reared at the pair, gnashing.

The woman shrieked and jerked back. Cowering, the man shuffled forward.

Scar Face jabbed his rifle at Mirek. "Kozlowski?"

Mirek cringed. All the children clutching him shrieked.

He nodded. "I'm Kozlowski."

The soldier pointed to the front. "Take your party's papers for inspection."

Tiny hands clutched Mirek tighter, clawing his clothing, his arms, his hands.

"Please, children, you have to let me go." He pushed them away. "I'll be right back. I promise. And Baba Hanka is still with you."

The children clung to one another, many wailing. All except one black-haired girl who clung to him as she would to a life raft in a stormy sea. He fought to pry her fingers off his coat without hurting her.

"Please, Kasia, you have to let me go."

She shook her head, face buried in his torso.

Marching closer, Scar Face shouted, "Move, you Polish scum!"

"Please, give me a second," said Mirek.

The soldier lifted his rifle butt. Except he didn't aim at Mirek but at Kasia. As the weapon crashed down, Mirek spun the girl out of the way. The wooden stock slammed him in the side. He sprawled on the ground, feeling like he'd been kicked by a horse.

Kasia screamed and flung herself at her nearest friend.

Mirek clambered up and hobbled to the front. He presented a satchel containing everyone's papers to a soldier with red hair sitting at one of the desks, Sideburns standing alongside.

Ginger studied a file.

Mirek gulped. What information did they have?

At the next desk, a soldier in glasses spoke to the young man, "And you completed a full apprenticeship?"

"Yes."

The soldier stamped a paper APPROVED.

Maybe this was legitimate and, while brutal, the Nazis *were* simply looking for labor.

Ginger looked up. "Your party is only two adults and fifty-two children. Where are the others — four children and one adult?"

Mirek said, "I gave one of your men five death certificates at the railway station."

"We have those." He patted his file. "Do you have any other evidence that these people are dead?"

"What do you mean *other evidence*? They're official death certificates. What other evidence could there be?"

"These people all died within weeks of each other. That isn't normal."

"It's normal when you're starving and living in unsanitary conditions. Death is a part of everyday life in our town."

Sideburns stared at Mirek. Hard. As if ripping the flesh from Mirek's face, drilling through his skull, and peering into his mind.

Mirek balled his fists, fighting to stop from trembling. Sweat trickled from his brow.

Finally, Sideburns slapped his stick onto Mirek's satchel. "Process them."

Mirek almost collapsed as relief flooded his body. They were in. All of them. And more importantly, Ania and her four children had escaped and no one would ever look for them.

He dared to turn to give Hanka a reassuring look but froze. His eyes widened at the horror of what he saw.

A tiny hand reached between the people at the front of the column. A tiny boy's hand. Jacek's hand.

Jacek reached toward Mirek, fingers clawing repeatedly.

Under his breath, Mirek said, "For God's sake, not now, Jacek. Please." He gently shook his head.

But still the boy clawed at the air between them. Tears running down his cheeks, Jacek took a teetering step toward Mirek, leaving the column.

Mirek's heart hurt as if Kruger had ripped open his chest and was pounding the cavity with a hammer. He shook his head more vigorously, mouthing, "No."

But the boy staggered on.

Scar Face spotted Jacek and marched over. "Back in line!"

It was as if Jacek never heard it. Oblivious, he took another doddering step.

Scar Face kicked Jacek in the stomach. The boy cried out and crumpled, his face smashing into the ground.

Mirek shouted, "No!"

Nose gushing blood, Jacek gazed at Mirek with terror in his eyes. His hand reached once more. "Papa Mirek!"

The soldier lifted his rifle to smash it down.

Mirek bolted back. He slammed his shoulder into Scar Face. The soldier crashed into the dirt.

Mirek grabbed Jacek, cradling him against his chest.

Two other soldiers leveled their rifles at Mirek while a third let his dog rear. It gnashed its fangs, spittle showering Mirek's face.

"Hold your fire!" shouted Sideburns. All eyes turned to him, but he looked away to a building nearby. The door opened, and a man swaggered through...

Kruger.

Sideburns scurried over, then nodded while Kruger gave instructions far too quietly for anyone else to hear. He then scurried back and gestured to the soldiers threatening Mirek. "Bring the whole group."

"Yes, Herr Unterscharführer."

Mirek gawked. He'd thought Kruger would have washed his hands of him by now. The man was a sadistic, manipulative monster and yet, every so often, a shred of humanity surfaced. Instead of being flogged or even shot, were Mirek and his household to be allowed to stay together?

He nodded to Hanka. "I think it's going to be okay."

The lines of fear in the old woman's face eased but didn't disappear.

Herding the group at gunpoint, the soldiers moved Mirek, Hanka, and the children forward.

Mirek carried Jacek with one arm so he could also hold Marta's hand as he led everyone. Guards guided them past the first building and toward an alley on the left. Mirek turned the corner. And froze.

His face grew cold, as if all the blood had drained from it.

"Owww!" Marta yanked her hand that he was holding. "You're squeezing, Papa Mirek."

He heard but didn't say anything, didn't do anything. He couldn't take his gaze off the sight before him.

In the shadows of the alley, a truck was parked. A truck with a gray trailer that he'd seen in his nightmares. A trailer with its back doors open. Welcoming.

Like rats were gnawing away his insides, Mirek felt hollow. So unbelievably empty.

He gulped. His children couldn't know. Whatever was about to happen, he had to hide it until the last possible moment.

"Look—" His voice broke, so he cleared his throat as he glanced back. "Look, everybody, we have another special transport."

He marched into the alley. "Let's get in quick so we can leave this horrible place and enjoy ourselves."

The children scuttled behind him.

But a side door in the adjacent building opened. Kruger strolled into the middle of the alleyway, blocking their path.

Mirek wanted to express so many thoughts, but without

spooking the children, there was little he could say. He stared at Kruger.

Oozing hatred would have been easy, but Mirek needed this monster to know that, while he'd won this battle, in the grand scheme of things, he was nothing — a man who believed he had great power, and yet, in the cosmic blink of an eye, he would be dust and meaningless. Just like everybody else.

With indifference, Mirek gazed at the man who had signed all their death sentences. "Hello, Hans."

Kruger's eyes widened at someone having the audacity to use his first name instead of his SS rank.

Mirek said, "May I help you with something?"

"With your talent for propaganda, the Reich could still find a place for you."

His articles on Copernicus and what have you must have delivered impressive results.

Mirek sniggered. "And all I have to do is betray my countrymen?"

"What?" Kruger looked wounded. "How is saving lives a betrayal? Thanks to your forces and the Allies, we have plenty of orphans in Germany. You could do great work there. Work that actually *means something* because you'll be working with children who mean something."

So was everything today merely more of Kruger's psychological torture and there was yet a chance to save his children? The price was steep. So incredibly steep. But in exchange for their lives, he'd sell his soul a thousand times.

Mirek said, "And my children?"

Kruger shrugged. "Every war has its casualties."

He stared at Kruger. What did the man see when he looked in a mirror? A monster? Or a good man fighting to make the world a better place?

Mirek sidestepped to walk around Kruger. "Excuse me, we have a busy day planned."

Kruger rested his stick on Mirek's chest to stop him. "You know, your story didn't have to end this way."

"No, it was *always* going to end this way." He pushed past Kruger.

His head up, Mirek strode to the trailer. He could live in a world in which he betrayed his countrymen, but he couldn't live in a world in which he betrayed his children.

He called over his shoulder, "Come on, children, it's time to get away from this horrible place."

At the rear of the trailer, he set Jacek inside and then held Marta's hand while she climbed the three wooden steps placed there. He pointed to the far end. "Wait up there, please."

He entered.

A single low-wattage bulb protected by a grille illuminated a sealed metal interior — a giant windowless box. Standing in the entrance, Mirek helped in child after child. "Go all the way in, please, so there's room for everyone."

Once the children were inside, he offered his hand to Hanka. She took it and clambered up. There were no words. And no need for them. She cupped his face. And smiled.

Scar Face removed the wooden steps and shut the doors, sealing them in gloom, but for the bulb and a small porthole in one door.

Smiling, Mirek said, "Okay, it's a long way to where we're going, so everybody sit down and get comfortable, then we'll choose our next song."

While Hanka sat at one side, he wove his way to the front and sat, resting against the wall, Jacek and Marta next to him. A shaft of light sliced through the gloom from the porthole. As he'd intended, the beam landed on him so everyone could see him.

The truck's engine rumbled to life and their compartment shuddered.

"Let's see, Amelia chose the last song, so"— Mirek's pointing finger roamed across the children with their arms thrust up —"Natalia."

A girl with brown pigtails grinned. "'The Skylark Song.'"

"Oh, another excellent choice."

The vehicle moved off. And the children sang.

But halfway through the second verse, Ola said, "The air tastes funny."

Mirek sniffed. He couldn't smell gas. But his breathing did feel odd. Borys must have been right – odorless carbon monoxide.

Tadek croaked, "Papa Mirek, my throat is scratchy."

Hands clutched at him and bodies snuggled against him for hope, for reassurance, for him to be their beacon in the darkness.

Dizzy, he cleared his throat, the inside irritated. "I... eh... I want everybody to... eh... lie down and hold hands."

Shuffling, everyone squashed together to lie in a huddle, the odd child coughing.

"That's good. Now"— Mirek took a moment, feeling as woozy as if he'd downed a gallon of ale —"it's going to be a long day when, eh, when we get there, so maybe..." Another moment. "Maybe we should have a nap." Another moment. "So close your eyes and, eh, I'll tell you about the adventure we're going to have together."

Some of the hands clutching him didn't clutch so tightly anymore, and the fidgeting and the shuffling died down.

"First, we're going to paddle in the sea. I know many of you have, eh, only seen photographs of the sea, but boy, you aren't going to believe how breathtaking it is in real life."

His eyelids drooping, he fought to keep them up. He would not abandon his children. Never.

"Then we'll play some games on the beach while Baba Hanka works her magic with dinner — beef goulash and chocolate cake for dessert." He strained to breathe, gulping air but it never seeming to fill his lungs. "And tonight, we'll camp around a fire and sing songs."

He stroked Marta's head, but it was so much effort, his hand flopped down and he couldn't lift it again. "You're all such g-good children. I-I'm so proud of every single one of you."

The light shafting from the porthole illuminated him lying on the floor with children spread around him like petals of the most beautiful flower.

"Such good children."

His eyes closed.

And a dream took him — a sunny day, a horse, a woman.

Mirek smiled.

The End

Almost. Mirek wasn't the only person with a story to tell...

Ania

Having traveled far more than the five hundred miles she'd dreamed of, Ania settled in London with Agata, the two of them having been separated from the other escapees in France. Initially, Ania undertook low-paid menial jobs, but as she slowly mastered English, so her options improved. Having lived such a frugal life in Poland, she squirreled away as much as she could, a plan forming in her mind.

At 9:00 a.m. on June 1, 1946, she climbed the Eiffel Tower. Gazing out at Paris, she breakfasted on a ham and cheese baguette. And waited. Midday came and went. As did sunset. But still she waited. Darkness blanketing her hopes as much as the night blanketed the city, a tear trickled down Ania's cheek when a guard instructed her to leave because the tower was closing.

Ania returned to London and picked up where she'd left off.

Later, with Agata studying at university on a scholarship, Ania put her plan into action.

Living life as much for Mirek as for herself, she traveled the world. She trekked the Inca Trail to Machu Picchu, scuba dived on the Great Barrier Reef, marveled at the Taj Mahal... *she lived to live.*

Her only regular companion on these expeditions was her camera, a parting gift from Agata on the day she'd set off. In the hope Mirek had somehow survived the war, yet knowing deep down that was impossible, Ania photographed everywhere she went. Once her savings ran out, she took any job offered in whatever locale – waiting tables, washing dishes, herding animals, cleaning toilets... no job was too lowly if it meant she could continue her exploration of the globe.

After twelve years of traveling, she returned home, a heart condition making her adventures too arduous to continue. At a party, a friend of a friend introduced her to a London publisher who found her stories fascinating. The following year, her first and only book was released — *One: One Woman, One Camera, One World*. Lavish photographs revealed the hidden parts of the planet that ordinary people rarely saw, even in such magazines as *National Geographic*, thanks to a color television still being a luxury item and most movies being filmed on sets instead of at exotic locations.

Her work receiving rave reviews, her publisher asked if she would tell the story of her time in Poland and her breathtaking escape from the Nazis. She declined, saying she'd share her photographs because the world belonged to everyone, but her story was hers and hers alone.

One spring morning in 1978, a Tuesday, Ania lounged in a garden chair on her lawn, grinning at the antics of Agata's three-year-old son as he chased a butterfly — one of the rare visits when Agata's family was in the country.

Ania closed her eyes for a moment, basking in the warm sun and even warmer laughter of the small child. She'd been all over the world, and yet, this instant felt the closest thing to heaven she'd ever known. She smiled, picturing how Mirek would have enjoyed the moment.

When Agata returned from the kitchen with a tray of drinks, ice cubes dancing in the glasses, Ania had peacefully passed away.

Two weeks later, 1,500 feet over central Poland in a hot-air balloon, Agata clicked the play button on a portable cassette player and Louis Armstrong sang "What a Wonderful World." Leaning over the side of the basket, Agata tipped Ania's ashes into the wind to honor her last wish — that she be reunited with Mirek "*in this world or the next.*"

The End.

(You can read about the lives of some of the other characters in the free ebook, *A Song of Silence: The Story Behind the Story*. See below for details.)

The Girl Under the Ghetto

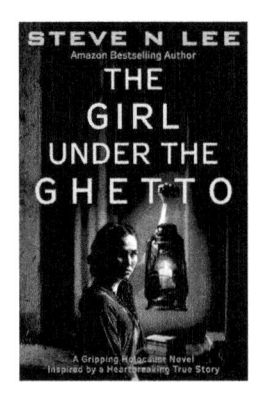

Inspired by a true story.

Following the Nazi invasion of Poland, 14-year-old Halina is imprisoned in the Warsaw ghetto, a squalid hellhole rife with disease and starvation. And her world crumbles. Yet, although the Nazis have destroyed her home, her life, and her future, they haven't destroyed the only thing that truly matters — her family.

Halina might be just a child, but she's a fighter, and she'll do whatever it takes to protect her loved ones. Against all the odds, Halina's struggles pay off. Until the Nazis unleash new horrors upon the ghetto.

Deportation, slave labor, random killings... Every single day becomes a fight for survival. Halina bravely battles on, making sacrifices no child should ever have to make, seeing horrors no child should ever have to see. But just when she believes that the worst of the nightmare is behind her, she makes a terrifying discovery — there's a fate worse than deportation. Far, far worse. And she's caught in its clutches...

Inspired by a heartbreaking true story of unbelievable courage, resilience, and the strength of the human spirit, *The Girl Under the Ghetto* reveals that, even in the darkest of times, one person can make a difference through the greatest power of all — love.

www.stevenleebooks.com/girl

Behind the Scenes with Steve

You're known for your heartwarming dog stories and pulse-pounding thrillers, so what draws you to tales about the Holocaust?

When we read fiction, we do it for escapism. To journey to places we've never been and to experience things we've never encountered. But above all, we want to meet heroes – characters who show incredible courage and fortitude in the face of overwhelming odds. This period of our history shows both the worst of humanity and the best, so its stories can be utterly captivating for both their extreme ugliness and their intense beauty. It's that contrast that makes them so unique and that draws me to them.

Who or what inspired A Song of Silence?

It was inspired by the events surrounding a Polish man called Janusz Korczak. He was a doctor, author, and advocate for children's rights who ran an orphanage in Warsaw when the Germans invaded Poland in 1939. I was inspired by the underlying story – a man running an orphanage when the Nazis invade – and by the heartwrenching ending – everyone being gassed.

So everyone in the real-life orphanage really was gassed? Children too?

Yes. They were all deported by train to Treblinka extermination camp and gassed on August 7, 1942.

In the book, the Nazis offer Mirek a way out, which he declines because he won't abandon his children. In real life, Korczak was offered a similar reprieve but refused it for the same reason.

If many of the main elements are true, what was fictionalized?

I took that essence of the true story and then set it in a fictional location with fictional characters, but with everything based on extensive research so it's an accurate portrayal of small town life during the occupation.

Why fictionalize it?

Three reasons.

Firstly, I wanted to give readers something they hadn't encountered before, such as the gas vans.

Secondly, I didn't want to write a biography. My first Holocaust novel, *To Dream of Shadows*, features real-life characters about which hardly anything was known (through my research, I created the most detailed biography available). The story at the root of *A Song of Silence* is very different because there's a huge amount of information available about Korczak as he was very well-known during his lifetime. I didn't want to simply add to that collection of information about him, creating something of little value because it had all been said before.

Thirdly, I wanted to explore things that wouldn't have been possible if I'd written his story because they never happened to him. For example, the gas vans weren't used in Warsaw.

So the gas vans were real? They weren't something you invented?

Oh, no, they were real and were used long before the gas chambers that everyone has heard about. Everything stated in the book about them is completely true – the number of patients that were taken, the way they were gassed with bottled carbon monoxide, the secret burials in the forest... All true. (I go into detail about these in the free book. See below on how to download it.)

Were there any other major deviations to the true story?

Yes, the hero. One big difference character-wise is age – Korczak was in his sixties at the time of the invasion, whereas Mirek is thirty-seven. I wanted someone young so I could have some action sequences. And a love story.

Another difference is that Korczak was Jewish but Mirek isn't. This was partly to give me more storytelling options. For example, I didn't want Mirek's story to be set in a ghetto because that would have imposed far more restrictions on how I could develop the plot.

Plus, everyone knows that the Nazis targeted Jews purely for the "crime" of being Jewish, but the Nazis also targeted Poles who had committed no "crime" other than to simply appear more Slavic than Nordic. And that leads to a truly horrifying statistic that few people appreciate.

Of the six million Jews that the Nazis murdered, around 2.8 million were Polish. However, what most people don't know is that the Nazis also murdered 2.7 million non-Jewish Polish people. So, in Poland, almost as many non-Jews were murdered as Jews.

When so many millions suffered such unspeakable horrors, I didn't want to focus on one ethnicity/religion at the expense of another, to make one life seem more important than another life, so instead of writing a story featuring a Jewish hero fighting for Jewish children, I decided to make my hero a-religious and to have him fight for both Jewish and non-Jewish children.

Your dialogue is very realistic. How do you date your vocabulary to know it's appropriate for the period?

I use a collection of specialist reference books and a number of websites. It took days to double-check anything that was even remotely suspect. The strange thing was that some expressions I'd have put money on as being too new, were actually old, but others I thought were old, were too modern.

Do you have a few examples?

The strangest one is "air quotes." Many people use these when they talk, but they were actually in use back then too, even appearing in some Hollywood movies of 1930s. However, they hadn't been named "air quotes" then, which is why instead of using that term, I describe the character's actions.

Other than that, things like "doable," "baby steps," "toddler," "rock the boat," "poker face," "brownnosing," and "face the music" all predate 1939, some of which surprised me. Ones that were in my first draft but which had to be removed because they were coined after the war include, "no holds barred," "hang in there," "writer's block," "people person," "deal-breaker," and "crash course."

Some people mistakenly think that because the war was eighty years ago, people must have spoken in an almost olde worlde way. No. People in the 1940s ate ice cream, drove cars, chatted on the phone, slaved in offices, followed fashion, complained about taxes, danced to music… they were modern people living in a modern world. Of course some vocabulary and slang was different, but in general, the people weren't that different from you and me. (I know because my parents grew up during the war and it was they who taught me to talk!)

Your partner is called Ania and Mirek's love interest is called Ania. Is there a reason?

Yes, Anna-Maria Kisiell — with two *L*'s — is my Ania's full name. Being Polish, Ania couldn't work when she first came to live with me in England because Poland hadn't yet joined the European Union, which left me supporting both of us on an income so tiny that you wouldn't believe it was possible. (Seriously! I kept all my paychecks so I'd never forget that we were living below the official poverty line.) Anyway, one of Ania's dreams was to write a book, so I fought to convince her to try as a way for her to make money. She refused, saying it would be too difficult. I couldn't help wondering how difficult it was to write a novel and before I knew it, all these ideas started forming, so I wrote my first book — a 140,000-word *Lord of the Rings*-style fantasy. So, you see, even though I've always been creative, if not for her, I might never have become an author. Naming a character after her is a thank-you for her setting me on this path.

Also, as Ania and I chose not to have children, it's nice to think that while I'll be remembered through my books, Ania won't be forgotten either but will live on through her namesake character.

There's one last benefit too. The biggest and best...

Giving a character this name has finally resolved a decades-long argument Ania and I have had. For years, Ania has foolishly believed that she is the romantic one in our relationship. I think immortalizing her in print pretty much seals the deal. "In your face, Kisiell!!!" (And cynics say romance diminishes as a relationship ages!)

Is anyone else real?
Baba Hanka.
Ania's maternal grandmother was an active member of the Resistance during the war. Amongst other things, she published an underground newspaper in Warsaw, kept a secret cache of weapons in her home, and spied on a provincial Gestapo headquarters. After her spying mission, she tried to return to Warsaw to fight in the famous 1944 Uprising, but the Germans had closed all roads into the city, so she couldn't get in. Ania's name for her was Baba Hanka — Granny Hanka. After all Hanka did to fight for freedom against the Nazis, I figured she deserved to be remembered.

Is anything else about Ania or her family real?
One thing. And this is mind-blowing!

In the story, Mirek buries his books, including Wladyslaw Reymont's *The Peasants*. Reymont really was awarded the Nobel Prize in Literature in 1924 for that work, making him one of Poland's most celebrated and loved writers. And here's the mind-blowing part — Reymont is Ania's maternal great-great-great-uncle! (He had no children to have direct descendents.) Yep, she's the great-great-great-niece of a Nobel laureate who is one of Poland's most beloved writers. And he is beloved — I've been to his grave and it is massive!

What's next? Another Holocaust story?

There might — might — be some movie interest in my action thriller series, *Angel of Darkness*, so I may finish book #11.

There'll also be *The Girl Under the Ghetto* (working title), a Holocaust novel set in Warsaw, about a teenage girl. Her story is unbelievably unique and yet is utterly unknown — I've scoured the Internet, yet only found mention of her on one obscure website. What she went through is mind-blowing. So, in the same way I gave Inge's moving story the audience it deserved with *To Dream of Shadows*, I want to do the same for this young girl.

Use this link for *The Girl Under the Ghetto*:
www.stevenleebooks.com/girl

I Need You!

My Holocaust books get one-star reviews from "readers" who have *not* read them. (Seriously. *A Song of Silence* started getting one-star ratings while I was still writing it and it was only on pre-order. No one can "review" a book that hasn't been written!)

Please don't let such trolls win!

If you enjoyed Mirek's story, please post a short spoiler-free review. It only needs to be a handful of words.

Thank you!

Amazon review link: **www.stevenleebooks.com/mirek**

To Dream of Shadows

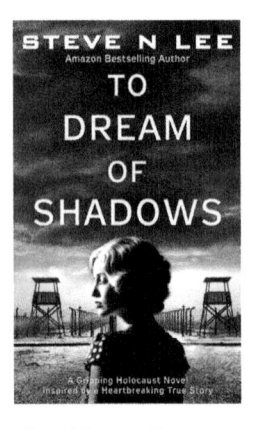

She'll save hundreds of lives. But can she save her own?

Inspired by a previously untold true story.

18-year-old Czech, Inge is torn from her family and imprisoned in some godforsaken hellhole. There, she suffers month after month of torturous labor while praying for liberation by the Allies. But rescue never comes. And her dream of surviving the war dies.

Heinz, an SS Sergeant, has been force-fed the Reich's poison since childhood, but nowadays, he covertly helps prisoners.

So when a random act of kindness thrusts Inge and Heinz together, an unlikely friendship develops. A friendship which sends waves of compassion rippling through the entire camp, saving lives, giving hope, easing suffering. For a fleeting moment, there is beauty in a world drenched in ugliness.

But their relationship does not go unnoticed. And Inge and Heinz must pay a terrible price for foolishly believing they could make a difference, have a future.

Yet it's in this blackest of nights that the tiniest spark can cast the brightest light...

Read *To Dream of Shadows*. Use this link:
www.stevenleebooks.com/dream

As The Stars Fall

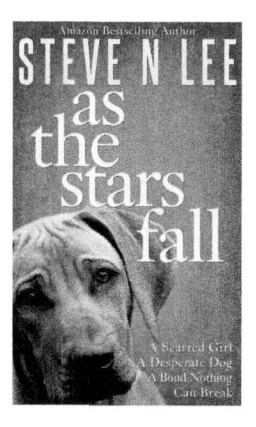

A Desperate Dog.
A Scarred Girl.
A Bond Nothing Can Break.

An injured, young dog trudges the city streets, trembling from cold, from fear, from lack of food. Battered by the howling wind, he searches desperately for his lost family, yet day after day, week after week, all he ever finds is heartbreaking loneliness. But then, one magical spring morning...

Across town, a little girl sobs into her pillow in the dead of night. Her life devastated by a family tragedy, she can't understand how the world can just carry on. Her days once overflowed with childhood joys, yet now, despair, darkness, and emptiness smother her like a shroud. But then, one magical spring morning...

... the dog and the girl meet.

Read *As The Stars Fall*. Use this link:
www.stevenleebooks.com/stars

Free Gift

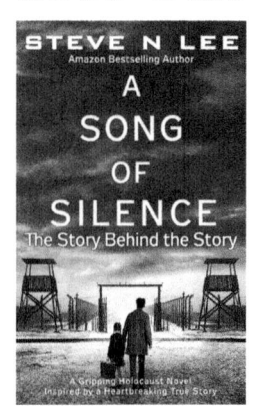

Get a free ebook — *A Song of Silence: The Story Behind the Story.*

Written especially for readers who want to go behind the scenes, this book dives into various aspects of the story for readers to:

> uncover what happened to some of the other characters who survived the war

> enjoy a secret chapter that wasn't in the final edition of the book

> read a deleted scene

> see photos from Steve's personal collection

> find out how Steve discovered this story and how the book evolved

> learn about the real-life gas vans

> and more...

Use this link to get your free ebook:

www.stevenleebooks.com/ASOS

Book Club Questions

1. Early in the book, Mirek witnesses the sacking of his town and is frozen with horror. Should he have tried to help people?

2. Should Mirek have risked telling Ania how he felt about her, knowing that if their relationship failed, it would negatively impact the entire household? Was he brave or stupid?

3. Did you know that foraging for common plants is a viable means of feeding yourself? Would you ever do it?

4. Borys repeatedly asks Mirek for help. Should Mirek have risked doing more for the Resistance? Explain your answer.

5. How many acts of courage can you identify in the story? Which were the most important ones?

6. Explain why you believe Mirek was right or wrong to aid the Nazis with their propaganda efforts.

7. The story includes flashes of humor, particularly between Mirek and Hanka, which shows their love for each other. How important is love in facing such an ordeal? And how important is humor?

8. Has A Song of Silence revealed aspects of the Holocaust that you were unaware of, and if so, which ones?

9. If you had lived under Nazi occupation, would you have joined the Resistance or would you have done whatever necessary to protect your loved ones, even collaborated?

10. Kruger was essentially a twisted fanboy and a user. Was Mirek right to kowtow to him to try to save everyone, or could he have handled the situation differently?

11. How common do you believe it was for Nazis to abuse their positions to further their personal agendas?

12. Do you have a favorite quote, passage, or theme?

13. If this book becomes a movie, who should play Mirek, Ania, Hanka, and Kruger?

14. What lasting impression has the book left you with? Is it positive or negative, hopeful or despairing, uplifted or saddened?